CITY OF BETRAYAL

CITY OF BETRAYAL: An Isandor Novel
Copyright © 2017 Claudie Arseneault.

Published by The Kraken Collective
krakencollectivebooks.com

Edited by Jess Sutton.
Cover by Gabrielle Arseneault.
Interior Design by Key of Heart Designs.

claudiearseneault.com

ISBN: 978-1-9746-9990-2

Published in the
City of Spires Series

Book One
City of Strife

Book Two
City of Betrayal

Book Three
City of Deceit

Book Four
City of Exile

CITY OF BETRAYAL

AN ISANDOR NOVEL

CLAUDIE ARSENEAULT

À MARIANNE ET AUDREY,
Sans qui ces histoires dormiraient encore dans un tiroir.

PREVIOUSLY

IN THE CITY OF SPIRES SERIES

THE SCENE:

Isandor, the City of Spires. A nexus of eccentric towers in which bickering merchant families vie for power through overbearing shows of wealth and endless trade wars. At its edge is an enclave from the Myrian Empire, a conquering mageocracy of dubious ethics and an economic powerhouse meddling in local politics.

A FEW KEY PLAYERS:

Diel Dathirii, Head of Isandor's only elven noble house, an eternal idealist.

Master Avenazar, Leader of the Myrian Enclave, ruthless and powerful mage.

Nevian Ollu, young Myrian apprentice, stubbornly trying to learn magic despite Avenazar's abuse.

Varden Daramond, High Priest of Keroth. Talented artist, loving soul, powerful fire-wielder.

Branwen Dathirii, Dathirii spymaster, master of disguise and owner of the greatest wardrobe.

Our story begins on a cold late autumn day, on a plaza surrounded by a great many shops. **Avenazar** has caught his apprentice, **Nevian**, there, and he intends to show his discontent in the traditional means: by shooting pain through his forearm until it overwhelms his mind. For **Diel Dathirii**, a witness to the event, this is one-too-many horrible acts from the Myrian. He interrupts, and tells Master Avenazar know that the Myrian Enclave will no longer be tolerated, and he will do all in his power to eradicate them from Isandor's politics.

Thus begins the hostilities that underpin our tale. Diel Dathirii returns home and musters his forces: cousins, nieces and nephews, lover and steward. The plan is two-pronged: to protect his network of local merchants, and to convince other Houses of Isandor to rally against the Myrian Enclave. Master Avenazar is, however, much more direct: he instructs the enclave's High Priest to walk into a Dathirii-affiliated shop and burn it to the ground.

Varden Daramond knows better than to refuse. His position is ever-precarious; in Myria, his people are more frequently slaves than titled priests. When he finds **Branwen Dathirii** inside, he knows he is expected to kill her. Instead, he whisks her away to his quarters, hiding her until she can escape. Winter solstice is coming, and most of the Enclave will be attending an all-night ritual to mark it, providing a perfect opportunity. In the meantime, their rocky start turns into mutual respect, then quiet friendship.

Little do they know, Varden will not make it through winter solstice unscathed. You see, all this time Nevian has been sneaking out of the enclave to meet with a mentor, and Varden, feeling kinship with another rebellious soul, has known and helped this. But when Nevian is spotted leaving—in the distance, unidentified—it is Varden, the outsider and easy scapegoat, who is accused.

Master Avenazar is all too happy to confirm the accusations by invading Varden's mind—and in the process, he learns of Branwen's ongoing escape and Nevian's outing in Isandor. He ditches the High Priest and teleports to his apprentice. While Master Avenazar carefully and painfully erases all of Nevian's knowledge of magic, Branwen interrupts him with a well-placed dagger throw then makes a narrow escape afterwards. Helpful, but not quite enough to save Nevian, who falls of the bridge.

And here we must interrupt, for there is another story unfolding in Isandor, one far from the high towers of nobles and the troubles of the Myrian Enclave. This second tale started in a Shelter, little more than a hovel squeezed between two towers, where those of meagre fortunes can find a roof and a meal for free. We should, perhaps, introduce **<u>some new key players.</u>**

Arathiel Brasten, drifter from the past, returned after 130 years in a magical trap, all senses drained.

Calleran Masset (Cal), servant of Ren, luckiest and most generous soul.

Hasryan Fel'ethier, secret assassin for the Crescent Moon Mercenary, open sass master.

Larryn, owner and cook of the Shelter, a bubbling stew of anger and spite.

Drake Allastam, firstborn son of House Allastam, uses the power and privilege to harass those less lucky.

Sora Sharpe, investigator for Isandor's Sapphire Guards. Quick of wits and pigheaded.

Lady Camilla Dathirii, centuries-old elven lady, dispenser of tea, cookies, and wisdom.

Now that we have that settled, let's rewind a moment, to **Arathiel**'s arrival in the docks of Isandor, wet and out of luck, a stranger in his own city, a ghost uncertain of his future. He finds his way to the Shelter, where through luck and **Cal**'s insistence, he integrates three friends'—Larryn, Hasryan, and Cal—regular card games. In particular, he bonds with **Hasryan,** with whom he shares an easy understanding; two outsiders struggling to let others in.

It is during one of these card games, up in a fancier tavern of the Middle City, that the group is interrupted by **Drake Allastam,** who has an antagonistic history with **Larryn.** It takes less than a minute for it to devolve into a fight, and while Hasryan gets a solid headbutt in, the fight lasts long enough for guards to walk in, and Hasryan is arrested.

Nothing would've come out of it if not for **Sora Sharpe**'s eagle eye. She ties Hasryan's dagger—an unique weapon with a jagged blade and the ability to produce electricity—to several unsolved murders, and pins him down for them, prolonging his stay in prison. One of these, the death of Lady Allastam, remains the highest profile assassination of Isandor's history. No big deal, Hasryan tells himself. He didn't do it. A bribe and a lie, and his boss will get him out of there.

Except she doesn't. The head of the Crescent Moon organization leaves him out to hang, confirming the dagger is his—a dagger she gave him, shortly *after* Lady Allastam's death. After a decade of working together, the person Hasryan trusted most, the woman who'd picked him off the streets and taught him to survive has scapegoated him through a ploy she had set up over a decade ago.

That knowledge shatters Hasryan as surely as his trust and, dejected, he is ready to give up and wait for his execution—but his friends certainly aren't. Unaware of their friend's real job and angered that he is being scapegoated, Larryn and Cal plan to use the winter solstice as cover to sneak into the prisons, pretending to be two priests.

And this brings us back to winter solstice, and to poor Nevian falling off a bridge—only to crash right in front of Cal. Cal, with his very limited healing skills and big heart, with his absolute faith in the randomness of life and his own, ridiculous luck. Cal, who is awaited for a prison infiltration but stops, knowing this teenager's life is in his hands. He can only interpret this happenstance as the will of his deity.

He patches what he can, and is running back to the Shelter to gather help bringing Nevian back when he finds Arathiel. Flustered, desperate to save Nevian, filled with guilt over his absence from the prison heist, Cal unburdens all of his worries on calm, patient Arathiel.

It is worth noting that Arathiel, who was alive in the city a hundred and thirty years ago, held a noble title at the time. He has been recognized by **Lady Camilla Dathirii**, with whom he has shared tea multiple times since, and to whose door he runs that night. She had offered help—any help he wished—and it is direly needed now. To send healers to Nevian, certainly, but that is not all he intends to ask. Arathiel has no intention of letting Hasryan's execution go through, but he'll need help to stop it and to hide afterwards.

Larryn is not one to be deterred by Cal's absence (although he is certainly one to be angered by it). He makes his way to Hasryan's cell and prepares to free him—until Hasryan, desperate for someone, *anyone*, to accept him without any lies left, tells him about his true job. Shocked, already primed for anger, Larryn tells him off, and is forced to flee before he can get over himself and fix his initial reaction.

When he reaches his Shelter once again, all of his anger is bottled tied and ready to blow at the one friend who should have been there. Cal's attempts to defend himself only infuriates him further, and in the heat of the yelling match, his fist flies faster than his brain, knocking Cal to the ground with a solid punch.

And thus the winter solstice night comes to an end. Branwen has returned to the Dathirii Tower and into her family's loving arms, but few others have had such luck. Varden is imprisoned in the Enclave, at Avenazar's mercy, and Nevian clings to life only through sheer stubbornness, his memory of magic erased. The long-standing friendship between Cal, Larryn, and Hasryan has shattered, existing fissures finally cracking.

But not all is lost, as they say, and in the following days, as Branwen and Lord Dathirii struggle to convince Isandor nobles to ally against the Myrian Enclave, Arathiel's plans solidify and come to fruition. On the morning of Hasryan's execution, he is ready.

So we come to our last scene, a park commemorating one of the city's founders with the delightful habit of hanging criminals above it. On bridges above, the high-born have gathered to celebrate the capture and execution of Isandor's most infamous criminal. Below, Lower City residents fume at one of their own once more sacrificed on the altar of politics.

Moving through the crowd towards the investigator responsible for it all is Camilla Dathirii, an old elven lady—perfectly innocent and respectable, here only for congratulations, of course. And when, in the process of doing so, she drops her purse and provokes a small commotion of guards trying to help pick it up before everything rolls off the bridges, it is also without malice, and not at all the distraction Arathiel has been waiting for. *Of course.* (It is.)

Nevertheless, Arathiel uses the opportunity to drop into their midst, blades drawn, and sprints for Hasryan. He is outnumbered, but he possesses one advantage no other has: he does not feel pain any more than he does cold or touch. Wounds that would stagger other fighters leave him unfazed, and so despite his profuse bleeding, he pushes through the Sapphire Guard surrounding Hasryan and they escape by leaping into the park below.

The landing is hard—impossible for one who does not feel the pressure of ground under his feet. Arathiel's ankle snaps when they hit the park, destroying any chance he has of walking away from his spectacular rescue and the chaos that will ensue. Only Hasryan slips away, clinging to the written address offered by Arathiel and the certainty he still has at least one friend in Isandor willing to risk it all for him.

He does not expect the safehouse to be Lady Camilla's quarters, nor does he anticipate the delicious butterscotch cookies awaiting him and the crash of emotions they will bring. He sits in the living room, cookies in hand, unexpected acceptance washing over him while on a balcony nearby—a few stories above, really—Diel Dathirii considers his few remaining options.

The nobles of Isandor refuse to help him, the Myrian threat is growing, and they hold a man to whom his niece owes her life. But today he saw a man who does not know pain—a man he knew, over a century ago, as caring and courageous. Arathiel's aid would destroy the political goodwill he has left, but what good is that, when all of his allies rebuked him? The choice is simple and dangerous, and he is ready to make it.

Here ends *City of Strife*, but certainly not their adventure.

CHAPTER ONE

DEAD man had freed her assassin.

Lieutenant Sora Sharpe stared at the body sprawled in front of her on the hard bed of the Sapphire Guard's headquarters, his ankle cuffed to a railing. He didn't look like much. A bit strange, yes, but white cornrows and threadbare outfits from another era didn't mean a dangerous opponent. Yet this man, Lord Arathiel Brasten, had lived in Isandor a hundred thirty years ago. She'd asked Aren, their old agender healer, if they had an explanation. According to them, Arathiel should be dead.

"Only magic keeps his body together," they had said, "a spell worthy of Ezven, Lord of the Dead and Reborn."

Magic wouldn't heal Arathiel either, not completely. Aren had described the healing as a cold pull, numbing their senses until they couldn't feel the room around them. They had been forced to stop, then, but at least Arathiel had recovered enough not to die. Sora had let him rest, chafing at the unexpected wait. Nothing she could do about it, however.

She turned over the events in her mind again, reflexively doodling on her notepad. She wished she could pace, but if Lord Arathiel woke up and caught her in the act, she would start his interrogation from a position of weakness. It had started a dozen days ago with a routine arrest. A tavern brawl involving a noble—which meant whoever had invoked the noble's wrath had found themselves dragged into a cell and taught a lesson. Only this time, the chosen dark elf had a unique dagger on him. One which fit the description of several unresolved cases they'd gathered through the years. Sora would know: she'd pored over those every few months in the hope fresh eyes would let her pick out new leads.

She had investigated, reviewing old notes on these cases, digging out every occasion on which she or her colleagues had run into wounds corresponding to Hasryan's dagger. After a full night of work cross-referencing old information with this new weapon, she could connect half a dozen murders to it. These included the most noteworthy assassination of the last decade, which had sparked a bloody feud between two Houses unlike any Isandor had seen: Lady Allastam's death.

From the very start, Hasryan had sworn he hadn't committed that particular murder. Sora clenched her pencil at the memory of their interrogations—all infuriating sparring matches. He'd been smug, taunting her, certain his boss would get him out of trouble. And why wouldn't he? Sooner or later, Brune would come, and no one refused the leader of the biggest mercenary organization in Isandor. The Crescent Moon had its hands in every pocket. Half the city owed them, and they could get almost anyone out of prison if they wanted. It didn't matter if Sora dragged the necessary tidbits of information from Hasryan—even building a grudging but solid respect between them as her investigation progressed—their corrupted system would protect him.

Sora stared at her doodle, its shape strangely reminiscent of the arches above Carrington's Square from which they hanged criminals sentenced to death. Brune had had other plans for her assassin. She had let Hasryan take the fall for Lady Allastam's murder, framing him with the very dagger that had first caught Sora's attention. Hasryan's shocked betrayal had shattered Sora's determination to bring him to justice. He should hang for his crimes, but from the moment Brune had blamed him for the city's most heinous assassination, Sora had understood he'd had nothing to do with it.

Innocence in one case didn't erase how Hasryan had killed several others, however. When Hasryan was sentenced to death, she told herself it was good news for his real victims. She schooled herself to think of him as an assassin, to ignore the vulnerable, broken half-elf sulking in a cell. He wasn't a poor soul betrayed by the one he trusted most. He was a murderer, and he deserved to die.

"I wished you hadn't killed anyone," she'd told him. And when Arathiel had saved him the following day, snatching Hasryan from right under the noses of two dozen guards and all of Isandor's most noteworthy nobles, she had been relieved. Sora tapped the center of her doodle, groaning at herself. *Relieved*. Despite all of her previous efforts, despite the destruction of her promotion, despite the complicated days to come, and despite the relentless pursuit she intended to give now, Sora Sharpe was glad Hasryan had survived.

Somewhere along the line, she had allowed herself to grow attached to him. To see the man behind the crimes—the broken, vulnerable elf who'd carved a space for himself in a world that wanted to eat him alive. She and Hasryan had little in common, but she recognized that fight. She'd had her own, claiming her rightful place as the next Sharpe investigator, the last in a long line of women—and, she knew with absolute certainty, not the first trans woman in it. Except that unlike hers, Hasryan's confidence and sense of self were projected. She'd watched the illusion shatter and hoped she could support and befriend the man laying behind it.

She still wanted him caught.

Sora tore away the page with her drawing, brushing aside her conflicting desires. She had enough mysteries to unravel without dealing with the tangled mess of her heart. Not to mention it was a lot easier to focus on other people and mine their secrets than to face her own.

Arathiel stirred, and she straightened, attentive. He might not wake, but he'd mumbled many words over the last few days. About a Well, and a girl named Lindi—his sister, for whom he had left Isandor all those decades ago. She had interviewed the head of Arathiel's noble family, but Lady Brasten didn't have a lot of information to give on Lindi. Her sickness was a family disease, one that had grown more frequent and taken several members of House

Brasten over the last century, including her father. She spoke of it with a tight voice and a dark gaze. Sora hadn't pushed the matter. While it might help her interrogations to understand Arathiel, she could feel the grief below the surface. Exposing it wasn't worth it.

Except Arathiel didn't mumble anything this time. He groaned, opened unfocused eyes, and raised a hand. He stared at his fingers with wonder for a moment, then tried to sit up. The cuff at his ankle slid along the railing with the movement, and he froze, perhaps hearing the sound. He hadn't felt it around his skin, Sora knew. The healer had been adamant Lord Arathiel didn't perceive hot, cold, pressure, or pain. She wondered what he did sense.

Arathiel finished straightening, and Sora allowed him time to take in the room. His gaze rested on her first, sitting nearby, and he frowned at the crumbled page in her hand before moving on. She followed his eyes as they passed the eleven empty beds separated by large potted plants, then the double doors leading to the rest of the headquarters. The Sapphire Guard's symbol had been engraved over them, a half-circle with four spire-like lines jutting out. The barren room didn't hold much else, and his attention reluctantly returned to her.

"You must have questions," he said.

Three days without speaking turned his voice raw, and he cleared his throat. Sora withheld a bitter laugh. Questions? She had so many—about him, his reasons, his past, his relationship to Hasryan—she didn't know where to start. Only one mattered, however.

"Welcome back," she said. "You have been out for three days.

Three days in which Hasryan gets farther away from me."

"Good."

"Where is he?"

Arathiel smiled. Not a mocking smile, not even a self-satisfied smile. She'd grown so used to Hasryan's quips and smirks that Arathiel's soft, almost sad expression caught her off guard. He tilted his head, staring at the chain on his ankle. "I have no intention of telling."

"Did anyone help you?"

He shrugged. Silence stretched between them. Sora tried to size him up. She'd always been a good judge of character, and though Arathiel was in many ways a mystery to her, she could draw some early conclusions. He didn't strike her as outgoing, yet she suspected he formed quick and solid friendships. He'd risked a lot and almost perished for Hasryan. Yet Arathiel had stayed calm when she had put him under arrest, despite knowing he'd lost a lot of blood and was dying. Either he was ready for that sacrifice, or death didn't scare him. Perhaps he'd experienced it before, she mused, or close enough.

"Anyone from the Well, perhaps?" It was a wild guess, one not meant to hit home but to break his composure. From the way he stiffened, it worked. He kept staring ahead.

"What does it have to do with anything?"

"I'm just trying to understand." And she was, though the ultimate goal was to find Hasryan. "Lord Arathiel Brasten, a noble born a hundred fifty-seven years ago, dead at an unknown date, has just—"

"I'm not dead."

"—just freed an assassin of dark elven descent accused of a half a dozen murders, including Lady Allastam's."

She'd knocked him off balance. His dark brown skin might hide his flush, but she caught the uncertain lick of his lips, and his voice fell to a whisper. "I'm not dead. I never died."

"My healer thinks otherwise," she replied, and when Arathiel cringed, she pushed on. She needed to break his calm. "A spell worthy of Evzen himself, they said. Congratulations, I guess?"

Arathiel drew his legs back to himself, sitting tucked together in the way scared children do. Sora tapped her notepad with her pencil, shoving her guilt deep down. Arathiel closed his eyes. "So I'm … half-alive, is that it?" A bitter laugh escaped him. "I've been feeling like a ghost ever since I returned. You're not helping."

"I'm not here to make you feel better about yourself." She tapped her notepad, not bothering to take up a quill. She doubted this would lead them anywhere, or that Arathiel would share anything worth investigating this early on. "Several members of House Dathirii have confirmed your identity, and Lady Brasten found proof of your existence in their records. You might be a ghost, but all this tells me is that ghosts are real, and they can destroy my career as easily as anyone else. What is the Well?"

"I don't know!" Arathiel clenched his hands. "A trap, perhaps, but not one that provides an explanation while it sucks senses out of you. I'm afraid you'll have to live with the mystery, as I do."

Sora gritted her teeth. If she enjoyed mysteries unsolved, she wouldn't be a Sapphire Guard investigator. Understanding the Well was not her job, however. "Where is Hasryan?"

"Long gone."

Determination filled his voice. Sora hoped he was wrong, but with three days of delay? Their search hadn't yielded any results, and without Arathiel's knowledge, she might never find his trail again.

"Why did you free him?"

More than the Well, that was the true mystery behind Arathiel's very public rescue. Everyone she'd talked to had shared the same story: Arathiel and Hasryan had only played games of cards together, and Arathiel hadn't even been in town for a full month. How did a bond so strong grow over such an insignificant activity, in so short a time?

Arathiel's expression softened. He studied her in silence, and his intense gaze made her squirm. As if he could see behind her professional mask and unravel the very contradictions she'd been unwilling to examine herself. Arathiel's survey was thorough, yet heavy with kindness, as if it couldn't contain an ounce of aggression. He did not mean it as an attack, but still Sora disliked the scrutiny. She forced herself to endure. Perhaps he'd be more forthcoming with answers after.

"You already know," he said. She didn't bother to deny it, and Arathiel continued. "Sometimes you meet someone who immediately understands you thoroughly, and whom you understand, too. Hasryan is that to me. We knew each other, even from the start. We didn't need years. It ... isn't friendship, not quite." Arathiel gestured at the air, as if the vague movement could explain. "It's something different altogether, a unique deep link. I know him. I know his struggles. He doesn't deserve to die."

"He killed for money."

"There's more to it than that."

She knew that. Sora gritted her teeth. Her relief at Hasryan's freedom was a crack in her armour, and Arathiel hammered at it. She reached for her extra protection, which lay on the table next to her. Six scrolls, each detailing an assassination she could attribute to Hasryan without a sliver of doubt. "Not to me, and not to the law," she said, dumping them on Arathiel. "These are the cases he is responsible for. I don't care if they framed him for Lady Allastam. I can prove he killed these six. Merchants, travellers, other mercenaries. People who had families and saw their lives cut short in the Crescent Moon's rise. But their deaths didn't provoke a feud, so no one cares. Maybe you should open them and look at the names."

Arathiel didn't. He played with the string keeping the scrolls rolled, a frown marring his otherwise calm face. "Hasryan is not the source of their death. You know this, too. He was a tool for her, the middle man. But he is not … evil."

Sora lifted her chin and met his gaze. She'd stared down monstrous criminals who had taken glee in their horrendous acts and held the prideful glares of nobles convinced of their superiority, but faced with the tranquil certainty of Arathiel's eyes, she found herself looking away, her throat tightening. Sora snatched the scrolls out of his lap, more uneasy than she'd been in years.

"I cannot afford to care about that," she snapped, then stood.

"Rest. We are far from done here."

Interrogating Hasryan had tried Sora's patience to its limits. Until Brune's brutal betrayal, every question had been answered with smirks, laughs, and candid jokes. She'd brought years of experience with insufferable criminals to the table to deal with this assassin, who was so convinced his boss would snatch him out of the boiling water that he could mess around and play with her. Sora had thought of it as one of the greatest challenges of her career. And yet, here she was, storming out of the infirmary with as much dignity as she could muster, thrown off by Arathiel's calm faith in his friend and the way he could, with a few choice words, bring her own doubts to the surface.

This, she knew, would be harder than Hasryan's games. She would arrive better prepared next time, but Sora had to accept a simple, obvious fact: every moment sparring with Arathiel would chip away at her desire to capture Hasryan, until it vanished. She could not let it happen. The entire city watched her now and, more importantly, six victims and their families counted on her. They would be her shield, her anchor to this duty. She refused to let them down.

Chapter Two

HEAVY blankets were pressing down on Hasryan when he woke. Panic shot through him at the throbbing in his leg—a wound!—but the comforting scent of lavender soothed him. Nothing to worry about, not here in Lady Camilla Dathirii's quarters. He was no longer in a prison cell.

He'd tried to leave yesterday. The safety had been too much. Never before had Hasryan relaxed so thoroughly. Surrounded by delicious cookies and soft tea, Hasryan had let his guard down, dropped the constant alertness that had seen him through the difficult years of his existence, and allowed himself to feel completely, utterly safe.

It terrified him. It wouldn't last, he knew that. Nothing peaceful endured in his life. What was he thinking? He couldn't count on this, and so he'd slipped out in the middle of the night. He would gather what little he still had, hidden in the Crescent Moon

Headquarters, and leave.

He never made it past the guards. Brune had doubled the men lurking in the shadows around her base. They spotted him, chased him, wounded him, but he got away.

Fleeing Isandor had still been an option. He could have climbed down the web of stairs to ground level, then struck out of the city with nothing but the clothes on his back and the baked goods stolen from Camilla. For a long time, Hasryan had considered it. He had stood at Carrington's Square, where they had tried to hang him, where an unexpected friend had saved him, and he'd thought to flee. The cold night wind buffeted him. Blood ran down his leg. He should leave, he knew. It would be safer.

It would be lonely.

And staring at the small hole through which the Sapphire Guard had sought to push him, reflecting on the life he'd built in Isandor, he realized he was trapped. Locked in the city, as surely as if they had him in a cell. It didn't matter if his partnership with Brune lay shattered in a thousand pieces, if Larryn resented his profession and his secrets, or if Cal hadn't even tried to save him from death. He couldn't leave. He didn't have the strength to start from scratch, not anymore, especially not without Arathiel. Isandor was his home now, and Lady Camilla's quarters were the only place safe for him. He would stay there for however long this lull of peace lasted.

Hasryan pushed the blankets off himself. His memory of the previous night became fuzzy after that. He'd returned to Camilla's, his limp growing as more blood trickled out of his cut. Brune's men hadn't inflicted a deep wound—nothing he wouldn't overcome within two days—but in the lightheadedness that had followed, the weight of his decision had hit him hard. By the time he'd reached the Dathirii's tree-shaped Tower and Camilla's private door, he had turned into a shaky mess. He flushed at the memory, from shame and more than a bit of gratitude. She'd opened the door for him, and he'd fallen into her arms, weeping.

He had lost control. It unnerved him, how easily Camilla could reach past defences set up through the years, how comfortable he felt around her. Not many could do that. Arathiel had shared his struggles, prompting a natural understanding, but Camilla and Hasryan had nothing in common. He couldn't explain this casual proximity, and it made him wary of his own reactions. He would have to be more careful and establish clear boundaries.

A good first step would be to find his pants. Camilla had removed them to treat his wound, leaving him in nothing but tight red underwear. They used to be his favourites—the lucky ones, he would call them, before teasing Cal for a blessing—but that didn't mean he wanted to parade in them in front of an aging elven lady. All he found after a quick scan of his surroundings was his shirt. Lady Camilla was humming a melody from the nearby living room. At times, he heard the delicate *clink* of a teacup being put down. Hasryan couldn't help but smile. Of course she had tea. Perhaps she had his pants, too.

Carefully, he slid down the bed and set his weight on his wounded leg. He winced at the pain and sat, steadying his heart as much as his body. Hasryan hated to rely on anyone. He had left in a fit of panic, convincing himself he would rather strike out alone than depend on Camilla. He knew better now—not that it made his situation any easier. But, well, Hasryan had seen his share of hardships. He could deal. He always did. His resolve hardening, Hasryan limped his way across the room, still wearing nothing but underwear.

Lady Camilla sat in a comfy chair, a kit of strings and needles on the small table in front of her. She held his pants and was sewing the bloodied rip with obvious practice. Hasryan stared, allowing the sight to sink in. She was repairing his pants. First she had tended to his wounds, and now she was stitching his pants. Why did she put so much effort into helping him? A grazed leg wouldn't have killed him. She should have let it go. Hasryan cleared his throat to draw her attention, but he didn't know what to say. This was too weird. She smiled.

"I knew you were there, dear," she said without looking up from her work. "Are you certain you should stand on your leg so soon?"

"It's nothing. I've had worse."

"I noticed."

This time her gaze did leave his pants to trail over the many scars crisscrossing his skin—chest, arms, and face alike. The intense sadness in her eyes scared him. He wanted to go over and shake her, to tell her he'd gotten most of these trying to kill people—and succeeding. Not all, of course. Some came from beatings triggered by his dark elven heritage; others had been earned during his years surviving the wild as a kid. Most important of all, however, was the slim scar that ran across his throat, stopping under his chin. Given by his mother. Sometimes he wondered what she regretted the most upon dying: trying to kill him, or failing?

"They're nothing," he told Camilla. "A series of misadventures."

That's what he would call people's attempts to murder him from now on. Misadventures.

"They started early."

"You have no idea." His fingers reached for his neck, but he stopped himself. He didn't want her to notice if she hadn't yet. She already worried too much. "I can repair the pants myself."

Camilla laughed and shook her head. "I'm almost done, it's fine. Do you need a cane? I take care of Isandor's elderly and have gathered many spares through the years."

Hasryan tried to picture himself leaning on a cane, and a slight smile curved his lips. Maybe he could make it work—find black and white outfits, build a classy style. Larryn would never let him hear the end of it. Or … well, he would need to know about it, first. Hasryan's mirth vanished. Larryn wanted nothing to do with him. He had abandoned Hasryan in prison, fleeing when he'd learned about the assassinations. Another lost friend. It cut deep, that betrayal, more than Hasryan cared to reflect upon. He had always thought he could count on Larryn, even if only as one of the Shelter's flock. It seemed he had been wrong.

"I'll manage." His voice rough, he made his way across the room and threw himself into the sofa. He ought to thank Camilla, but the words flitted out of his grasp. How could he? Since Arathiel had removed the rope from his neck, Hasryan had stepped into this strange, inexplicable universe where he could safely lounge on an old lady's couch with nothing on but his tight underwear. Not for the first time, he wished his saviour could see him. When the thought had first occurred to him two days ago, he had voiced it with a smirk.

"Will Arathiel not come to enjoy my illustrious presence?" he'd said.

"He can't." Camilla's calm and pleasant tone had given him no warning of what followed. "They arrested him."

The words had smashed Hasryan's breath away. He had straightened up, horrified. Even now, thinking of it, Hasryan's heart sped and twisted. "We need to get him out."

In an instant, his mind had revised everything he knew about the Sapphire Guard's headquarters. How to enter, where they kept the keys, how frequently they changed shifts. There had to be something he could do. Camilla had rested kind eyes on him and shaken her head.

"If you get caught, we will be back at the beginning, except he'll share your rope."

Hasryan had wondered if that would kill him. Did Arathiel need to breathe? How much of him was still human? No, that was wrong. Hasryan wrenched his thoughts away from that pattern—from thinking of Arathiel and his body as separate entities. They were the same, and Arathiel was a kind soul, with hopes and fears and compassion that exceeded any Hasryan had met. Arathiel had saved him, carving himself a special space in his heart. And wasn't he also Camilla's friend? They couldn't let him rot in a cell.

"Then you do something!" he'd exclaimed. "You're a noble! The Dathirii have influence. What's the point of a fancy title if you can't make this right?"

Camilla had started shaking her head before he finished. "Officially, my relationship with Arathiel was limited to the sharing of infrequent afternoon tea and a promise of help should he choose to return to House Brasten. If I push to free him, I imply there is more. I already caused a distraction among the guards to facilitate his approach on the day of your execution. I do not dare get involved further. Sora would connect the coincidences."

She would. Hasryan had learned how acute Sora's instincts and logic were. She would understand the pattern if given the chance. And no matter how often she'd told him she would rather not hang him, she had still put him at the end of that rope.

One from which Arathiel had saved him, risking his life and getting captured in the process. One thing Camilla had said still bothered Hasryan, even two days later.

"So he's a noble? He has family here—House Brasten?" Arathiel had never talked about it.

"By the divines, he didn't explain anything to you, did he?"

Hasryan bristled. She made it sound like a lack of trust. "We don't ask. We take people as they are. Arathiel was himself, and we didn't need titles to appreciate him."

"But it is a part of who he is," Camilla said. "He may not share, but the grief he carries from that time impacts him." She inspected her handiwork, then snapped the sewing thread with a satisfied smile and threw the pants at Hasryan. "His full name is Lord Arathiel Brasten. He was their weapon master, a little over a century ago."

Hasryan almost choked. "A century?"

His family would be dead, then. No wonder he avoided the topic.

"Yes," Camilla said. "For a hundred thirty years, he was gone. His sister was very sick, so he left in search of the Well, a magical place reputed to cure everything. Back then, wild tales about it flew all around Isandor. Most agreed one should travel north, though no one truly knew what to look for. I never dared prompt Arathiel for what he'd found, in the end."

Hasryan craved more details, but it would be unfair to Arathiel. They did not ask, he'd said a moment earlier. He didn't need to know.

Larryn would have wanted to, though. A bitter snicker escaped Hasryan. "He's a noble. Larryn will tear him to pieces when he learns."

Hasryan slipped his pants on, careful not to worsen his wound. As he tied the belt around his waist, he noticed the worried frown on Camilla's thin features. "Nothing angers Larryn more than a noble abusing a resource not meant for him. The Shelter, where Arathiel was staying, is a haven for homeless folks. It doesn't cater to oblivious jerks who feast every night and just want to try out the cooking."

"I hardly think that is a proper way to describe Arathiel."

Hasryan raised his hand and shrugged. "I know. He saved my ass, I'm not about to forget." He'd done that, and so much more. "Larryn's another matter, though."

He didn't handle shades of grey very well. He had run away as soon as Hasryan had admitted to the assassinations. One moment, they were best friends; the next, Larryn was terrified of him. Hasryan couldn't even blame him—it had happened too often before. Camilla would be the same if she learned how many he'd killed. She could offer him all the cookies in the world, or brew the best tea, or fix every piece of clothing he'd ever owned. It wouldn't change anything. If she knew, she would return him to the city guards faster than he could put his pants on.

"So … what now?" he asked.

"What do you mean?"

"I can't stay here forever!"

"Forever?" Camilla laughed and shook her head. "Must it always be absolutes with you? You can stay here as long as you like."

"I don't like it." A lie. He loved it, and the more he did, the stronger his fear of losing it became. He would rather leave on his own terms. But not now, not if it meant starting over.

"As long as you must, then."

"Look, lady, you're nice, but this is just another prison. A sweet-ass deluxe prison, but a prison anyway. I'm stuck here. Everybody out there hates me. I need some sort of plan! I can't spend my life trapped, eating your cookies and drinking your tea."

"Wouldn't that be fantastic, though?" She winked at him, chuckled at his horrified expression. "I jest. Of course you cannot stay here forever. Arathiel and I had hoped to dig through Brune's activities and unearth what we could, with your help and input, but I am afraid such plans must be delayed. House Dathirii has an entire enclave of Myrians to fight, and Arathiel is detained. I understand you want an answer, Hasryan, but I know very little of what should come next. The truth is, I would love to speak with my nephew—Lord Dathirii—about this. About you. I trust him. My life is not the one on the line, however, and we will not approach anyone you don't trust."

Fear squeezed Hasryan's heart at the mention of Lord Dathirii. His muscles went taut, ready to spring on her, as if he needed to stop her from reaching to the elf immediately. Despite her reassurances he would always have the final word on whom they spoke with, Hasryan's swirling panic didn't lessen. *She will betray you*, a voice inside repeated, again and again. A reliable advisor, that instinct.

"I don't even trust you," he said.

Camilla tilted her head to the side with a saddened expression. She pressed her lips together and leaned forward over the centre table between their respective seats. The moment she set her wrinkled fingers on his hand, he snatched it away. She held his knee instead.

"It doesn't matter. I trust you."

She stood, picked up her sewing kit, and headed back into her room. Hasryan looked out the window and stared at the city, shadowed by the Dathirii Tower. Outside, people went on their daily business. They had friends and families, and their lives rolled by without his string of betrayals and fights. They were free—of crimes and prejudice alike. Would he ever be one of them? Hasryan brought one leg back to his torso, leaving the wounded one stretched out. He'd tried so hard to build a normal life, only to be pushed back to the edges again.

He missed Larryn and the Shelter. They welcomed everyone, and for a while Hasryan had found his place there. A home, with lively music, amazing food, and friends. And despite his previous resolution to stop thinking about Larryn, his mind drifted back to the tiny refuge nestled at the bottom of Isandor, in the deepest layer of the Lower City, where the best people hid under the city's filth.

Chapter Three

W HEN Vellien stepped into the Shelter for the second time, everyone was awake. Patrons lifted their heads to glare at them, dirty fingers curled around bowls of warm soup, their clothes ragged, thin, and full of holes. Without the fire, those inside would freeze, and their lack of proper winter garments made Vellien self-conscious about the thick fur cloak on their back. Larryn had scolded them about it on their first visit, and the young owner of the Shelter would no doubt do it again today. Vellien swallowed hard, their cheeks flushing red with guilt and shame—a sure-fire way to make their freckles stand out even more than usual. They wished everyone would go back to their conversations, but instead the patrons stared at Vellien as they picked their way through the tables. This much attention made them want to recoil and run, but Nevian still needed a healer's help for his mind, and they wouldn't abandon the grumpy teen because of a few hard looks.

Being in the Shelter was always a little difficult. Few places made them feel like they didn't belong and were not welcome. At first it had been profoundly disturbing, but although Vellien struggled to accept it, they understood. Few establishments dared to outright shun nobles, to so clearly expose they were unwanted. Larryn didn't care about the risks involved. His place had been built by homeless folks, for homeless folks. When Vellien stepped inside, they disturbed the Shelter's status as a haven for Lower City residents where those without means could always grab a meal and find a warm corner to sleep. The first time, Vellien had been unaware of how their arrival would be perceived. It was the middle of the night, a teenager was dying, and their Aunt Camilla had asked them to help however they could. They'd strode in without considering the impact of their presence and quickly slammed into the wall of bitter indignation that was Larryn.

Now Vellien knew what awaited them. Anxiety built in their stomach as they approached the door on the other side of the common room. The Shelter lay nestled between two towers, at the very bottom of the Lower City and Larryn had somehow gathered the funds to buy one of their ground floors. He kept his kitchens there, along with several private rooms for paying customers or disabled residents in need. Nevian had been granted one of them, which meant Vellien had to stride past the kitchen door to get to their patient. They doubted the Shelter's owner would've missed the sudden silence in his common room, or that he wouldn't come out to investigate. Vellien struggled to control their rising stress, but by the time they pushed through the door, their hands shook.

As expected, Larryn waited for them, arms crossed and scowling, blocking the corridor.

"You returned."

Vellien's courage shrivelled inside. Larryn's strangely calm tone didn't mask the anger in his eyes. They didn't want any trouble, or an argument. They just wanted to heal Nevian's mind, help him recover his memories, and finally talk to the teenager they had saved.

"I-I … yes. I'm sorry." Vellien cleared their throat. They couldn't even meet Larryn's gaze. Vellien fumbled with the clasp of their cloak and removed it. With a glance up, they extended it forward, like a peace offering. "Here. It-it's for you. For everyone."

Silence stretched, and to Vellien it seemed to last forever. They almost dropped the cloak, as they had on their first night in the Shelter, but Larryn snatched it away with a laugh. A laugh! Excited relief surged through Vellien and they smiled.

"Does he need you?" Larryn asked.

"Nevian? I wish he didn't. N-not because I hate coming here or anything like that! I didn't mean to imply that, I swear. I am scared at how damaged his memories are. It's a lot of work. But I don't mind! It's just sad—"

"Stop." Larryn raised a hand. "I get it. You're selfless and worried about his well-being or whatever. I don't care. All I want to know is how often I should expect your prissy noble ass to grace us with its presence."

"I-I have no idea." Vellien hated how Larryn put them on edge.

Not that it was all that hard: Vellien didn't deal well with aggressive people. But this was different because they knew part of his anger was justified. Misdirected, perhaps, but not baseless. Vellien needed to hold their end, however. Hopefully, if Larryn had accepted the cloak, it meant he was in a better mood than the other night. "As often as Nevian needs it."

Larryn snorted. "Then we need rules. Follow me."

He opened the doors to his kitchens and motioned for Vellien to come. They stood rooted to their spot, hesitant to obey. Did they want to enter Larryn's untouchable space? It felt like overstepping. But Larryn had invited them, no? Shouldn't that mean it would be okay, even if only for this one time? Vellien might never have another chance to establish boundaries with the Shelter's owner. Refusing might even anger him further, so Vellien gathered their courage and hurried after Larryn.

A strong cinnamon odour greeted them as they slipped through the door, and it overpowered the other sweeter scents. Vellien's eyes widened as they took in the enormous pot, the cutting boards, the pans, and dozens of tools they couldn't name, let alone guess at the uses for. A huge bag of apples rested on the counter next to a pile of potatoes and carrots, and Vellien focused on those familiar elements, desperate not to appear too wildly impressed with their surroundings. Larryn was not fooled.

"Don't tell me you've never been in kitchens before."

"Well, I—" Vellien sighed, then shook their head. House Dathirii had cooks. "There was never a point."

Larryn stared at them, his mouth a thin line, anger boiling right under the surface. Vellien dropped their gaze to their feet, sheepish.

"This is why I hate you people," Larryn said, and though the words were harsh, his tone managed to stay contained. "My patrons don't even have a home, but you can bet your ass they can cook for themselves, and would if they had a chance."

"I-I know. Larryn, sir, I understand. I mean, I understand that I can't really know, and I realize that when I step in your Shelter, I take this space away from them."

Larryn leaned on his counter and studied them, looking straight at Vellien instead of tilting his head to the side to hear better. Was that newfound respect in his expression? Perhaps Vellien shouldn't get their hopes up. Larryn clacked his tongue. "You're less oblivious than your peers. Or you have a little someone telling you what to say."

Perhaps it was the "little" in Larryn's words, but Vellien immediately thought of Cal. They raised their hands and shook them. "Cal didn't say anything! He only admitted to me you didn't like us, but he wouldn't explain why or—"

"Let's not talk about Cal," Larryn snapped. "In fact, that will be rule number one. Don't mention Cal to me."

"Is he barred from coming? He was supposed to help me."

"You're already breaking rule number one."

Larryn crossed his arms and glared at them. Vellien didn't recoil, despite very much wanting to. Instead, they met his gaze without flinching. "If he is not talking with Nevian, it may take longer for him to heal. I need to know."

It earned them a little huff. "Cal comes and goes," Larryn said with a dismissive wave, before moving on. "Rule number two: in my Shelter, you're a nobody. There's no 'milord' and 'sir,' and no one owes you shit. Keep making yourself small or you won't be tolerated."

This time, Vellien smiled. "That's good. I don't like being gendered." Not that it would stop the crowd from using masculine pronouns. Vellien would rather not, but they didn't intend to spend their days correcting the Shelter's patrons. Larryn didn't miss the implications of their answer.

"Do you use neutral pronouns, then?"

"Yes!" Excitement coursed through them briefly. They didn't often get asked for their pronouns, even though many non-binary folks walked Isandor's bridges or lived in their legends. It inevitably brought a grin to their lips. "It's 'they.' Please."

"Yeah, sure." Larryn's expression softened. "Don't worry about it. I'll tell others if you want. Rule number three? Keep giving us cloaks. We love those peace offerings."

"Each time? One for every new visit?" Vellien didn't have enough spares for that, and all their money went straight to fighting the Myrian Enclave. How would they comply?

"You heard me. I'm sure you're resourceful enough to find what you need. You sure can't be too poor."

Vellien swallowed hard. They would have to ask Camilla and Branwen for extras. Who would have guessed it would cost them so much to help one teenager? "All right. A cloak."

"The last rule is the hardest. For both of us."

That didn't bode well. Vellien gritted their teeth, reminding themself this Shelter was Larryn's home and creation, and that every time they came, they trespassed into a space not meant for them. Vellien hated confrontations, and none of the rules so far justified one. "Go on."

"I want you to stay." Every word obviously cost Larryn.

"Stay?"

"Not long! I'm not patient enough. But … it's not fair for Nevian to have all the treatment because of some connections with you people. The others are sick, too. They got colds and rotting teeth and disgusting mouldy shit crawling up their feet. Heal a few. None of them can afford a healer, and Cal's no good at it."

It could have been a plea if Larryn hadn't been glaring at them, daring Vellien to mock or pity his people. Hard to believe he'd even asked when he had called their very existence—as a noble and as a Dathirii, but still—a problem. When Vellien thought about it, they were being asked to pay through cloaks to work here and help these people. Yet they couldn't refuse.

"I'll do what I can until I'm too tired. Nevian's first, however. It's a complicated task and I could cause irreparable damage if I tried exhausted."

Silence slipped in the conversation. Larryn studied Vellien for a moment, and his expression flicked between a scowl and something altogether softer, almost curious and relieved. Vellien withstood his scrutiny. Considering their first encounter with the boiling half-elf, this calm chat seemed a miracle. They didn't want to break the frail balance achieved today, and with Larryn, any wrong word might. With a weary sigh, the Shelter's cook returned to his work.

"Nevian's waiting for you."

He didn't thank Vellien, but they knew it was hidden in his

permission to stay. Hoping this truce would last, they left without another word. They had a young wizard's mind to heal.

DINNER time had flown by. It always did, in a way—who watched time when they ran around trying to get everyone fed at once? But on most days, Larryn didn't endure the rush-hour sprint alone. Several of the Shelter's patrons had learned to balance plates and lent the occasional helping hand, but none as frequently as Cal. His friend used to show up almost every evening, compensating for his short legs with boundless enthusiasm and endurance. They would chat as they worked, either exchanging a few quick sentences each time their paths crossed or yelling across the common room in a desperate attempt to cover the buzz of conversations. Hasryan occasionally joined the routine, and when patrons became rowdy and impatient, he quickly taught them to keep their peace.

Without their help, dinner time became gruesome and exhausting. When the rush diminished, Larryn dragged his feet, shoulders hunched, fatigue setting deep into his bones. He hid in his kitchens, slumping against the counter and closing his eyes. Larryn clung to the many smiles and thanks he had once more received. Cooking, serving, and cleaning for the Shelter was endless work, but it was worth it. His folks were worth it, just as they were worth inviting a Dathirii within his walls.

His stomach churned at the thought, a low nausea settling in. The Shelter was his space, his only refuge. How could he trust any of these elves in it? His mother had paid for their lies with her life, and they had stranded him alone in Isandor's cold streets before he turned seven. When Vellien stepped into the Shelter draped in cozy fur-lined clothes, Larryn remembered the nights curled in a corner, the stabs of pain from an empty stomach. His fingers tingled from the countless times guards and merchants had snapped them as punishment for stealing, and when cold crept up his toes, he glanced at his feet to ensure he did, in fact, still have good boots to ward him against the cold. It had been hell, and no Shelter could truly protect him from the consequences. The memories would follow him as surely as his left ear would remain deafened by an untreated infection.

It didn't matter if Vellien hadn't done any of this. They were a Dathirii, and to Larryn's body and mind, the distinction quickly vanished. He should be more careful to lay the blame where it belonged, but that involved staying calm. Not his strong suit. Larryn brought his knees closer and leaned his forehead against them. Vellien had stayed so calm earlier, accepting Larryn's every request without a word of complaint. Perhaps there had been no need for the brutality with which he'd set boundaries, but Larryn had never met a noble with whom gently asking worked. None of the usual rules seemed to apply, leaving Larryn stranded in new and scary territory. Anger he was familiar with, but even that had betrayed him too often recently. He wished he could talk with Hasryan about some of this—any of this, really—but had no idea where to find his friend. No one but Arathiel knew now.

Larryn shoved the thoughts away. Hasryan would turn up

eventually. Why not? No shackles or prison bars held him now. It might be difficult and dangerous, but when had that stopped his friend? Larryn could hold on tight until then. Somehow, the ground always felt more stable when Hasryan was there.

He pushed himself to his feet once more and studied the mess in his kitchens. He cleaned as much as possible while he cooked—the limited space wouldn't allow otherwise—yet piles of knives, pots, and cutting boards still clamoured for attention. And there would be everyone's plate, soon. No way he would let his tomato-based sauce stick overnight. Not now, though. Dishes would have to wait: he needed a break, and one patron had yet to eat.

Larryn prepared a final plate and slunk out of the kitchens, down the corridor toward Nevian's room. He stopped upon hearing a tiny snort-laugh that could only come from Vellien and gritted his teeth. He had hoped Nevian would be alone now, but no such luck. Larryn knocked anyway, steeling himself for another brief encounter with the Dathirii. He might as well get used to it.

When Cal invited him to enter, his voice muffled by the door, Larryn almost didn't. Could he deal with both at once? Larryn resolved to keep it short and professional, then pushed the door open.

The three of them overcrowded Nevian's tiny room. Cal occupied the desk, his small fat legs dangling from the chair, a sheet of parchment in his hands. He focused on it, clearly avoiding Larryn's gaze. Nevian and Vellien sat cross-legged on the bed, facing each other. Nevian's fingers dug into the thin blankets, twisting them, and bullets of sweat covered his forehead. Healing, it seemed, would not be painless.

"I, um …" All three of them stared at him now. Larryn was not used to being treated as an outsider in his own Shelter. He gritted his teeth and stayed in the doorway. Short and professional. "I brought a plate for Nevian. I noticed he hadn't come to dinner."

"Not hungry," Nevian replied, his words slow and stilted, as if pushed out only through great effort.

Cal's eyes widened. "Refusing Larryn's food is not permitted." He tried to keep the familiar teasing out of his voice, as if pretending he hadn't essentially lived in the Shelter for the last two years could ease the tension between them.

Silence stretched, until Larryn cleared his throat. "Should I bring more?" He didn't want to, not really. Vellien and Cal could afford to feed themselves, but if they meant to stay and help …

"It's all right. We're done for the night." Vellien unfurled their legs and slid down the bed. Nevian's head snapped up, a protest clear on his lips despite his sorry state, but Vellien didn't let him utter it. "I cannot do more tonight, Nevian, and neither can you. Rest and food will help you. We'll continue tomorrow.

"So you're leaving," Larryn concluded, his grip tightening on the plate in his hands. Did Vellien want to hurry out because he had scared them? Or was the young healer already skirting on their promised duties to the other patrons?

"Yes. I'm tired." Vellien straightened their shoulders before adding, "Your patrons may have to wait two or three days, depending on our progress here. This is … draining."

"Whenever you can," Larryn replied, and the softness in his

voice surprised him. The voice in him screaming that this noble only wanted to escape work had gone silent in the face of Vellien's and Nevian's obvious exhaustion. It coiled below the surface, ready to yell again. Better to leave now before it returned in force.

Larryn handed the plate to Cal, and as his friend's small hands clasped around it, their eyes met. Anxious hope shone bright in his friend's gaze. Larryn's stomach churned. He inhaled, as if about to speak—and part of him desperately wanted to! Cal deserved better than the anger and violence he'd received. But his throat tightened, and his body refused to cooperate. A part of him might desire an apology, but too much of him clung to the fury of winter solstice. He tightened his lips and turned away, addressing Nevian instead.

"Just don't waste it."

Nevian cast a doubtful glare at the plate. "No promises. I have work."

Larryn scowled. Others could use the food if he didn't want it! Something in Nevian's tone kept him from snapping back—a hollowness Larryn recognized from his own experience. Hunger had gnawed at his stomach for so much of his life, yet in the weeks following Jim's death, Larryn had gone without touching any food for days. He hadn't wanted to. He had neither cooked nor eaten, busying himself with the challenges of building a new Shelter, until Cal picked up on his growing thinness and forced the barest meal into him. If Nevian grieved, even a bite would be a victory, the rest of the plate notwithstanding.

"Eat what you can, then. I promise you won't regret it."

The tension in Nevian's shoulders eased. He closed his eyes and flopped down on the bed, arms spread, fatigue and frustration mixing in his expression. "Understood."

Larryn hoped the meal's quality would help, but Nevian might not even notice. He promised himself he would keep trying and get what food he could into the teenager, then excused himself. Every minute spent in a room with Cal and Vellien tested his reserve, and he didn't want to ruin an otherwise calm interaction. Besides, a mountain of dishes awaited him, and he needed to consider breakfast for the following day. He couldn't afford to stop when exhausted: the Shelter's people wouldn't wait on him.

Chapter Four

THREE thick lines of pain spread across his back. Three burns, three days. So many more to endure. Varden curled on the ground, despair filling his mind so fully that not even sleep could find room.

Avenazar had continued to come. Varden had tried to keep him out, but he'd smashed his defences, cracked them like a nut, and now he was peeling him apart one layer at a time. Tearing pieces of his self away, brutal and gleeful, until Varden lost track of who he was. Never of where, though.

This was the Myrian Enclave, which would surely see him dead. Once its leader left—uncontested, all-powerful—Varden stayed sprawled on the ground, cold stone against his cheeks, bits of himself scattered through his jumbled mind. And he rebuilt it. Every time, knowing Avenazar would return and mock him, knowing it could never last. What else could he do? He had to resist somehow.

Whatever the end, Varden would meet it as himself.

He was Varden Daramond, Isbari, leader of his community. He had fought and prayed and cried for them, and himself.

He was Varden Daramond, High Priest of Keroth. He thrived within the flames, had survived the fire burning his childhood home, and climbed the ranks of priesthood.

He was Varden Daramond, and he loved men. He loved to talk with them, touch them, draw them, kiss them. He had been with one, too, for a decade.

Varden continued to hammer his own name, to cling to its sound, attaching parcels of self to it. Varden, the charcoal artist, who found peace in detailed portraits and sketched flames. Varden, who had defied every Myrian's expectation of him and channelled Keroth better than priests twice his age. Varden, who had helped young Nevian slip out of the enclave in secret, and who had saved Branwen and hidden her from Avenazar.

Pointless acts, in the end. Avenazar had found and killed them both. Nevian with his head cracked on a bridge, and Branwen in a much slower, much more horrible manner. Nausea pushed up Varden's throat as he recalled the detailed memories Avenazar had shared with him—steady fire crawling up her legs, acid splattering her arms and face. He wondered which was worse: her painful death or his pathetic life?

No, no. Varden struggled against those thoughts. They would drag him down, defeat him. He was Varden Daramond, and he was proud to have helped them. He refused to regret it, even now. As long as he remembered who he was—loved who he was—Varden had won.

A key turned in the lock, jolting Varden further awake. So soon? He'd thought only a few hours had passed since Avenazar's last visit. But what was time in this cursed, sunless cell? He lost track, flitting in and out of consciousness, too weak to feel the sun rise and set through the walls by the grace of the Firelord's power. Varden missed Their presence, wild and comforting at the bottom of his soul, always with him. Not anymore, not so clearly. Avenazar had blocked Keroth with iced manacles, horrible cold devices that crawled up his wrist and forearm, and stalled his access to Them. This battle was Varden's alone to fight. He struggled into a sitting position, schooling his mind into an empty calm, preparing the litany of himself as a defence against Avenazar.

Bright torchlight invaded his cell, and he squinted against it. A figure stepped in the doorway. Too tall for Avenazar, whose malevolence was packed in a short stature. Relief flooded through Varden, an intense moment of release, of struggles delayed. Then he recognized Master Jilssan, and wariness doused his fleeting enthusiasm.

Second in command at the Myrian Enclave and a master of transmutations, Jilssan was one of the rare members of the enclave who had chosen this position, so far from the Myrian Empire. Avenazar had been sent to the farthest location the Circle of Mages could think of—a consequence of his erratic and destructive behaviour—and Varden had been deliberately kept apart from the steadfast Isbari community forming around him and his exclusive service. Jilssan, on the other hand, had seen opportunity in the faraway appointment, not punishment. Isandor stood at the intersection of key trading routes, and bringing it into the Empire would lead to rapid and massive expansion eastward. The prestige of such an accomplishment would earn her a place of choice among her peers, and Jilssan's ambitious designs didn't balk when faced with years far from Myria's capital. Two had passed already—two painful years during which they'd discovered the extent of Avenazar's violence, and through which he'd watched Jilssan walk a fine line between obeying the wizard's orders, providing advice to him, and never landing either herself or her apprentice on his wrong side. They had had Nevian to draw most of Avenazar's rage, and now they had Varden. He knew better than to hope for help from her.

"I would never have guessed a beard would look so good on you," she declared.

She flicked her fingers and a soft ball of light appeared above them, its glow gentle and unobtrusive. Varden reached for his face, but stopped halfway there. Either she mocked him, or she still flirted, undeterred by his previous rebuttals or the iced shackles climbing up his wrists. Varden grunted. "Leave me alone."

Jilssan, of course, ignored him. She crouched in front of him, cupping his chin and running her thumb over his thick stubble. Varden jerked out of her grasp, deeply unsettled.

"Don't touch me."

The words escaped as a croaked whisper. Varden hadn't meant to beg but to demand. As if he had any authority left for the latter. Jilssan leaned back, however, giving him room to breathe. She inspected him—the dirt, the hollow cheeks, the haunted look. Varden could only imagine what she saw under the beard but a weight settled over her shoulders and her voice grew softer, losing its usual playfulness.

"I will have to. I came to tend to your wounds. Avenazar asked your acolytes if someone wanted to, and they all froze in terror. No one wants to anger him by agreeing. He counted on that, so I said I would."

Varden brought his legs closer, curling in on himself. The acolytes at Keroth's temple had followed his lead because they had no choice, not out of love. Some might have developed a grudging respect for his power, but now that Avenazar had thrown him into a cell, no one would volunteer for his sake. No one, it seemed, except Jilssan.

"Why would you?"

She shrugged. "Believe it or not, I figured you'd need it. Avenazar wasn't serious, but he only laughed when I stepped forward. I took that as permission." She slid a bag off her shoulder and retrieved a healing kit from it. Varden recognized the tools: bandages, alcohol, needles, the unguent against burns … she had come equipped. She meant this. Warmth stirred inside him, and a solid lump formed in his throat. Varden struggled to contain it. Jilssan was not an ally. She never would be. He looked away and let her talk. "He thinks it's amusing that I like you. As long as that holds, he'll allow me to come and mock me. I'll have to stop if he starts to believe this is more than a passing fancy, however. He'd mark me as dangerous—another potential traitor. I can't have that."

Her passing fancy had involved undesired commentary on his appearance, hands flitting to his back when he'd rather be left alone, and a continuous half-hidden flirt he'd been careful never to encourage.

"It's not, though," he said. "It's nothing more."

"Well, for you, obviously, it can't even be that much. I saw the sketches. You have talent." Of course. They'd found his art, stored in the bottom drawer of his desk. Four sketch pads, most containing Isbari portraits or fires. But the last … the second half was filled with naked men, imagined or real. Varden thought of his private drawings of Miles, who had been so shy about his rolls of fat, yet so gentle and beautiful. Even in the dim light, Varden's flush must be visible under his olive skin, and he gritted his teeth. These images had been meant for them and no one else. He glared at Jilssan, yet her eyes held something strange—not mockery or disgust, but a genuine interest, with a touch of disappointment. "Such a shame for me."

Varden snorted. The invasion still burned. "Your gender is the least of all problems in this absurd scenario. You're …" He trailed off, surprised by his acrid bitterness. So unlike him—or rather, so unlike the him he wanted to preserve. Varden sucked a deep breath in and stilled his anger.

Jilssan laughed at his sudden silence. "Go on. I'm sure you meant to complete that sentence with kind words such as 'pragmatic' or 'witty.' Certainly nothing the likes of 'morally corrupt' or 'power hungry.'" Varden froze. He searched for an edge in her laughter, the dangerous tell-tale sign of falseness and thin ice.

Finding none unsettled him more than he cared to admit. Jilssan shook her head. "I'm all four, depending on how you measure morality, and I see no reason to change."

"Perhaps that's the biggest problem of all," Varden countered, too fast to think over his words and withhold them. Jilssan grinned, unfazed. Avenazar would have made him pay every insult, no matter how slim or implied.

"And thus we once more conclude that we are an impossibility, my interest notwithstanding. My heart breaks from such a surprising rebuke."

She brought a hand to her forehead, faking a faint, and Varden smiled. The corners of his mouth turned only a little, too exhausted for more, but he smiled without bitterness, out of real amusement, and felt lighter for it.

"You'll have to give me instructions." Jilssan pointed to the healing kit, bringing them back to the matter at hand. "What did he do?"

"Destroyed my mind. Left it scattered. You know how he works."

"Not truly. I've never made the mistake of drawing his ire." She sighed, pointlessly rummaging through the kit. "He said you might not like fire as much as you used to."

Varden's mouth dried. He had loved sitting cross-legged in the temple's great brazier, warmth seeping into him without causing harm, wrapping him in a cocoon of serenity. Avenazar had tried to ruin it, pressing a white-hot iron poker against his back to mark the days. Fire had never affected Varden before, and the throbbing pain served as a reminder of the new distance between himself and Keroth. Because of the iced shackles, he told himself. He had not lost faith, and They had not abandoned him. He couldn't allow himself to believe that.

"On my back," he said. He still did not trust Jilssan, and letting her see his burns felt wrong—an admission of weakness. As if he had any strength to hold onto in his current position. As she straightened and walked around, he gritted his teeth. Her low whistle made him wince.

"Must have hurt."

"Still does." In addition to the constant throb, the tatters of his High Priest ceremonial outfit had stuck into the wound and pulled at it sharply when he moved. She would need to cut the fabric around the burns, leaving what was caught in the blisters. Nothing she could do about that with her meagre means. And no matter how pleasant her earlier tone, Varden didn't relish the thought of Jilssan removing his clothes. No way around it, however. "You'll have to cut it," he said, gesturing vaguely at himself. "Leave what is caught in the burned flesh."

Jilssan let out a disgusted huff and tapped her feet to the ground, before returning to the kit. She rummaged through it, handing him the bandages when she found them, and eventually drew a sharp knife out. "Here we go."

To his surprise, she worked in silence. Varden shivered every time the cold metal touched his skin, clutching the bandages in his hand harder. She sliced through entire section, exposing his back to the chill air, making him feel more vulnerable with every passing second. Soon he had nothing but his sleeves and underwear, and he wished he could disappear into the ground. Jilssan stepped away, inspecting his back. He waited, expecting a disagreeable comment of some sort, until she asked him what came next.

So he explained, his voice steady and neutral, masking his increasing surprise as Jilssan followed his instructions to the letter without wasting time or teasing. She listened to him more now, as he sat curled on a cold cell floor, half-naked and weary to the bone, than she ever had while he had any standing in the Enclave. Did she only feel comfortable with him beaten or broken? He hated her for it, and yet was relieved to finally be treated as more than an object. The conflicting emotions swirled inside, threatening to burst out in laughter and sobs alike. Varden no longer trusted the intense swings in his mood. He didn't have the energy to keep himself under control.

He closed his eyes as she finished applying the healing salve—a cool paste that had awakened the searing pain at first, then numbed it down to a distant prickling. It would stave off infections, allowing him to heal faster. If Avenazar didn't destroy everything. Jilssan bandaged over the cool paste, wrapping the fabric around his chest in a solid hold. She pinned it, then her fingers trailed on his bare shoulder. He froze, panic surging in an instant.

"You should beg, Varden." The softness in her voice surprised him. Not a demand, not even advice. It was almost a plea in itself. He caught Jilssan's gaze, troubled by how affected she seemed. She tried to disguise it, to hide her concern. Maybe she had even convinced herself she didn't care that much. Yet she'd come, taking the very real risk of angering Avenazar. Asking him to bend and beg.

"I won't."

"It worked for Nevian. You could buy yourself time and have it a little easier."

Varden's eyebrows shot up. "Nevian's dead. He endured for years only to smash on a bridge. Don't tell me it works."

She straightened up, slinging the bag back on her shoulder. "Your pride will be your death. You could protect yourself better without it."

"No. Pride's all I have left." His voice cracked, but he met her gaze without hesitation. "It's keeping me together. I won't give it away."

She smiled, then, and shook her head. "You really are something else, aren't you? I wish people like you didn't die so fast. Maybe my life wouldn't be so filled with … pragmatism." She chuckled, but there was no mirth in the sound. With a flick of her hand, Jilssan's light vanished. "I'll be back with new clothes."

Then she exited the cell, leaving a trail of peppery perfume and a whirlwind of exhausting, conflicting thoughts in Varden. She was not an ally, he reminded himself. Yet he felt so much like himself now. A confused and drained self, certainly, but his brief interaction with Jilssan grounded him. In what others saw, in who he was, and in who he wanted to be. When Avenazar came again, he would remember more than pieces of himself to love; he would know how they fit with one another, and the world around.

CHAPTER FIVE

NEVIAN spent every minute he could sit without nausea studying, ignoring advice to rest and eat. How could he, when so much work awaited him? He had forgotten everything. No matter how hard he stared at the clear and concise words on the page before him, Nevian's knowledge remained locked away. *Taken.*

That had been the point, of course. Avenazar had left no doubts about his goals when he'd caught him sneaking through Isandor, out of the enclave. *You will die without the spells you worked so hard for*, the wizard had warned. *When I'm done, the most basic knowledge of magic will have been wiped from your mind.*

Nevian had survived. A miraculous strike of luck, brought about by a priest of Ren, Master of Luck, whose gender flipped like the two sides of a coin. He had still crashed on a bridge, cracking his skull so hard he'd forgotten more than his spells. Upon waking up, he could barely remember who he was, let alone where.

Vellien had helped. Their visits always turned out awkward and painful, but they helped. A great deal, even. Nevian didn't understand what had prompted a Dathirii to come all the way to the deepest stinking pit of the Lower City in order to help a Myrian, especially in the middle of the winter solstice, but he was—inwardly, secretly—thankful. Despite the discipline and hurt involved in healing the broken threads of his mind, he always looked forward to Vellien's arrival.

On their first visit after Nevian regained consciousness, Vellien had crouched near him. Neither had talked much: the young elf's clumsy introduction had been met by a doubtful grunt from Nevian, still bedridden, still more shaken than he'd cared to admit.

"I came to work," Vellien had said. "This is your life and your memories. If you don't want them back, I'll go. It's your decision."

Of course he wanted them back. Even if it seemed pointless to rebuild what he could before Avenazar returned, Nevian's stubbornness wouldn't allow him to stop trying. So he'd given permission—and regretted it shortly after.

Vellien had been nothing but gentle. They had taken Nevian's hand, and a soft glow had enveloped their fingers. It had spread up Nevian's forearm, to his shoulder and head. Then Vellien's mind had slipped into his, and anguish had crashed into him.

There was no way around it. Vellien needed to enter in order to study and repair the damage—they had to step on Avenazar's well-worn paths. And no matter how soft, how benevolent their intervention, Nevian recoiled at the invasion. He had panicked and snatched his hand back, memories flooding in, assaulting him. The details of Avenazar's abuse had come first, before any real healing, and they left Nevian breathless and shaking. He had wept, then snapped at Vellien when the young elf had offered reassurance, his head hot with bitter shame. Vellien had waited, impassive and patient, and a minute later, Nevian had ordered them to try again. He needed his magic back.

Acquiring it had required all the discipline in the world, and if Nevian had to use every ounce of his rigid, unrelenting self-control to recover his knowledge, he would.

And he had. Twice, Vellien had come to the Shelter. Twice, Nevian had let them inside his mind and allowed them to roam and repair freely as he fought his crawling memories of Avenazar's attacks. Twice, he'd ended up a trembling and exhausted mess. Vellien would watch in silence, their presence more reassuring and respectful than any physical hug. Once Nevian had rested, he had noticed the progress.

He remembered studying now. First as a kid, sneaking into libraries late at night to learn the very basics of magic from books, then as a young teenager, pooling all his money to buy more advanced copies, and bending over them until the sun rose. Finally as an apprentice, after he'd passed the tests, alongside Master Sauria. Those had been the good days. She had been supportive and kind, and in six months he had learned more than in the previous years combined.

Master Avenazar had shattered that little oasis of peace and progress. He had killed Sauria over an insignificant dispute, claimed

Nevian as his own apprentice, and been sent to Isandor, far from Myria. Instead of learning new spells, Nevian taught himself how to dodge notice, pay respectful obedience, and work through exhaustion. He still recalled the sleepless nights bent over magic tomes trying to figure out rune components, or how protective spells functioned, or anything really. Countless hours of headache-inducing work, candles flickering as he scratched notes for himself and deconstructed complex concepts.

Nevian remembered the pain and frustration, but the knowledge earned through them had vanished.

Nevian sighed and forced his attention back to the page. Back to the beginning, to the very basics of magic and the countless hours of studying. He could do it again. Maybe it would be easier this time. His other memories had returned in bursts, sparked by random questions, and Cal had believed the same could happen here. Nevian tried to convince himself of it and focused on the duality of Creation and Destruction.

All power stemmed from the gods. Once, there had been only one, Sellan, who could bring forth mounds of rock with one hand, then sculpt them down into mountains with the other. But They were never satisfied with Their work, building and destroying endlessly, never finishing. Eventually, They brought forth four helpers to control Them—the elemental deities. Sellan's state continued to deteriorate. They would be struck by a large creative frenzy, filling the world to the brim, using every little space available. Their creations choked, unable to sustain themselves, too tightly packed. But then Sellan's destructive nature took over, and

They annihilated all They had done. They snuffed out all life forms, razed mountains and dried oceans. With time, Their crises became even more violent, shorter and more dangerous. Sellan's duality did not allow for a stable self, or a stable world.

The four elemental deities joined their strength, creating the Halkaar—the ever-shifting blade—and splitting Sellan into two discrete beings: Seldare, of Creation, and Lanne, of Destruction. Although the fight between these two opposites didn't vanish, it became more easily contained, and a viable world had come to pass, on which mortals could live. Some became priests, calling directly upon the six original deities. Others, Thanh of the Phong Peninsula first among them, studied the power coursing around them and the means to harness it.

A knock interrupted his studies, and Nevian's head shot up. He glared at the door as though it would make the intruder vanish.

"Go away, I'm busy."

But of course, the door creaked open instead. A young girl stepped inside, no older than ten, with rich brown skin and a crown of curly hair. She held a plate in one hand, her smile so bright it stalled Nevian's urge to send her away. Not for long, though. He hated being bothered.

"Has no one taught you the meaning of 'go away'?"

"Larryn warned me you'd say that. He also said to ignore it." She strode across the room to his minuscule desk and set the plate down. His mouth watered at the sight of chicken chunks drowned under a golden sauce and a mountain of vegetables, and his stomach growled at the slightly sweet aroma. Nevian glanced at the girl, and she grinned, obviously quite aware of the quality meal she'd brought in. "I'm Efua, and this is your dinner. Larryn said I'm not to leave until you're done, because you'll forget about it if I do."

Nevian snorted. Larryn had made sure to bring or send a plate every day since his arrival. After the first remained almost untouched despite its tastiness, the Shelter's owner had diminished portions. Nevian had yet to finish even the smallest plates, and it seemed Larryn had decided today would be the day.

"Oh, so now he sends minions to make sure I'm fed. Great. I hope you're not as annoying as the halfling." Cal visited often, interrupting his desperate study to chat. He asked one question after the other and no longer pretended they were from a list given by Vellien. The first ones might have been, but curiosity drove him now, and Nevian didn't care about satisfying it. He needed to focus, and Cal's well-meaning visits disrupted his time.

"Cal is not annoying," Efua answered. "He is nice and funny." She crossed her arms and stared at him. "Unlike you."

"I have no time to waste being nice and funny."

He ignored the plate and tried to finish the section of text he'd been reading. Too bad for her if she wanted to stick around until he ate. If he interrupted his work now, he'd never remember any of it. As the girl *humphed* next to him, Nevian returned to the book. Magic, like everything else, was a mix of Creation and Destruction. It had emerged when Sellan had been split into two divine forces. The energy from that still permeated the world, and with the right runes or prayers, it could be drawn upon to create or destroy.

Nevian had little faith in anything but his logic and

determination, and his rare prayers went to Thanh, who had first studied the mechanics of magic and eventually become a demigod. He would relearn the runes and words of power and master the tools to call upon the magic of this world.

"What are you reading?"

Efua's question disrupted his concentration, and he groaned. He picked up the tome and showed her the cover. She clacked her tongue.

"That's not helpful, Mister Nevian, sir. I don't know my letters."

"You're ten." What kind of child hadn't learned to read at ten? He frowned and put the book down. "It's called *The Basics of Spellcasting*. Cal brought it to me. How come you can't read?"

"Should I? Why?"

"Everyone knows."

Confusion twisted Efua's round face. She climbed on his bed, removing her shoes with her feet before crossing her legs. "You're weird. You say these things like they're true."

"They are."

"Are not." She giggled, sinking what little patience Nevian had for her. Was she mocking him? Yet when her shining brown eyes settled back on him, they held no derision. "I have my job because I can't read. People give me their letters and I deliver them. They know they'll stay private, and I have the location of every house in the city stored in here."

She touched her forehead. Nevian rubbed his temples, confused by her words and attitude. First, the idea she could remember every address was preposterous. And she sounded like she enjoyed being unable to read? What a weird kid.

"Good for you," he said. "I am appalled to observe you prefer things this way, but it's your life, not mine. Now hush, I want to study."

"It's better than starving."

Apparently, 'hush' was just as hard to understand as 'go away.' Nevian sighed and pushed his book away. He might as well eat if she meant to force a conversation on him.

"Larryn can feed you."

"Today, yes. And before him there was Jim. But Jim didn't have enough to feed everyone like Larryn, so I fed myself when I could. Larryn might run out too, one day. Everybody does, sooner or later, down here. You have to stay prepared."

"Wouldn't learning to read be a form of preparation? You could do more than deliver letters. Why don't you use this chance, while it lasts?"

She lowered her head, her tiny shoulders shaking in a dismissive shrug. "There's just no one to teach me. And I like the delivery job. It makes me feel safer and useful."

Finally, words he could agree with. The strict discipline Nevian had submitted himself to throughout his life had always been a source of pride. Even now, his self-control allowed him to endure the brutal healing sessions and study. But he had been striving for a goal, not repeating the same routine each day. This struck a chord within him, dragging to the surface the disagreeable memories of the slow, lonely grind of his studying, of being forced to fend for himself. Nothing had changed, even today. Avenazar had flung him back to the start. Nevian shoved a mouthful of sweet carrots down his throat and examined Efua. She stared at her feet, and Nevian's stomach twisted. He would never wish his life on anyone.

"Being useful is a lie," he said. "I was useful to Avenazar. I did all the dirty, painful tasks he asked because he would hurt me if I didn't. I learned that if I wanted something, I had to grab it myself. You don't look like you want to be the mailman all your life."

Efua raised her chin, met his gaze, then shook her head. Determination shone in her eyes. Nevian took another bite of Larryn's excellent dish, savouring it as he had every meal before. Nevian hated the constant stink of Isandor's ignorant and unwashed populace, but the delicious food doused his desire to move out. As if he had anywhere else to go. At least he had helped by breathing some ambition into the girl charged with watching him eat. Proud of himself, he shoved another chunk of chicken in his mouth.

"Teach me," Efua blurted out, and he almost choked.

"What?" That wasn't what he'd meant. Someone else should teach her the letters. Nevian needed to relearn magic all over again first. He was barely making any progress; he couldn't devote any time to some random kid! "No way."

"But you said—"

"Ask Cal. Ask anyone but me. There's no point."

She jumped to her feet, crossed her arms, and stared down at him. "You spend your days doing nothing but reading and sleeping. Larryn told me. You said yourself I should learn. I want to, and you're going to teach me."

"I don't have time to waste on—"

"It won't be a waste." She grinned as if she'd won by simply contradicting him. "You'll see. I'll learn faster than you can say 'magic'! I have a great memory."

Nevian rolled his eyes and ran a hand through his tuft of blond hair. How had he wound up arguing with a child?

"Magic," he said.

"What?"

"I said magic. Do you know how to read now?"

"No, but—"

"Then you are *not* faster than I can say 'magic,' as evidenced by my recent test."

"That's unfair!"

"It is, and I don't care." Nevian pointed at the door with his fork. "Now get out. I'm not teaching you how to read."

"I'm not leaving. You aren't done with your plate." Her big brown eyes met his, and he recognized the expression within. She wouldn't let it go, no matter how solid his rejection. "Teach me whenever you eat."

"No."

He lifted his fork for another bite, but she grabbed it. "You have to."

"I really don't."

His tone had lost some of its edge. Her refusal to back down amused him—she wouldn't even let him eat!—and it touched him, too. He stared at her again, all stubborn pride, and remembered how adamant he'd been about learning magic. He had given everything to become a powerful wizard, finding a way past every obstacle, starting over several times. But he hadn't always been alone. Master Sauria had helped, and Brune. High Priest Varden, too, though Nevian preferred not to think about the price he'd paid. Even now, Nevian was still trying to learn magic despite losing all his knowledge to Master Avenazar's spell. And he could count on Vellien's healing during the struggle. He never gave up, and he knew that neither would Efua. But like him, she would need help.

"Okay. But only when I'm eating, and you are forbidden from slowing the speed at which I do so for your personal gain."

Efua clapped her hands, then sprang on him to wrap her arms around Nevian. He froze, fork in hand, as the chair under him tilted dangerously to the side before landing back on its four legs. Nevian's heart threatened to burst out of his chest, and he stared at a wrinkle in his blankets, waiting for the sudden nausea to pass.

"N-never do that again." She was too close, way too close. He swallowed hard, hot and sweaty, struggling to remain in control. His speech became halted. "Your enthusiasm and gratitude are noted, but get off me."

She squeezed before climbing down, frowning. Nevian forced himself to inhale deeply. As she watched him, she seemed to recognize the reaction. She put a hand on his knee. "I'm sorry. I didn't know."

Nevian wiped his forehead, then took his book on magic and threw it on the bed. "It's fine," he said—a transparent lie. "Sit against the wall. I'll be there in a few seconds with my plate."

Efua climbed back on the nearby bed without a word. Nevian

wouldn't be fine, not for several hours, but he couldn't do much about it. Even without the girl so close, an uneasy itch clawed at his throat. He had never liked being touched, but Master Avenazar's habit of grabbing his forearm to inflict atrocious pain had multiplied the sickening feeling. Nevian handed Efua his tome on magic, then sat next to her, light-headed. He waited for the worst to pass, his plate on his knees until he could eat and think again. Then he slowly began to demonstrate what sounds each letter made. She repeated after him with a determined frown, garbling words more often than not, but Nevian was too busy sorting out his panicked thoughts to correct her. He hated these irrational reactions and losing control over himself, but he had no idea how to cope with the sudden panic.

By the time his anxiety had abated, his plate had gone cold and Efua could voice most of the letters without fail.

CHAPTER SIX

INSPECTOR Sora Sharpe sat down on the archway above Carrington's Square, her legs dangling down the very hole through which criminals were hanged. She wasn't sure why she'd chosen to meet Kellian Dathirii here instead of in the park below, where benches offered a somewhat comfortable sitting option. She preferred the hard marble, its cold seeping through her tights and skirt. It kept her awake, and cooled some of her anger. Sora tapped her flask of alcohol with the tip of her finger, took a long swig, then stored it back in her bag. Kellian would arrive soon, and she knew he preferred to see as little liquor as possible.

Her gaze moved downward to the impressive jump one would have to make to land into the park below. No one had dared before, not in her lifetime at least. Hasryan had nothing to lose, however, and Arathiel's resistance to pain made it less risky. With the hanging rope to help … She groaned, angry at herself. It shouldn't have happened. There had been so many guards. Every noble of note had been there, watching, eager to congratulate her and Lord Allastam. And the city's most wanted assassin had escaped right before their eyes, to her secret—but undeniable—relief.

Sora rubbed her temples with two fingers before running them through her hair.

"I am the most pathetic investigator this city has ever known."

"Don't be so hard on yourself." Kellian stood at the outer circle. He smiled as she turned to him, and walked toward her. The small elf had a warrior's grace in his steps, and anyone with fighting experience could recognize the formidable opponent in him despite his size. "It took over a decade before someone found him. You did, and you tied six murders to his name in just two nights. That's impressive work."

He settled down next to her, his presence a reassuring balm on her doubts. They had first met five years ago. Sora had watched him fight, captivated by his swift and deadly grace, knowing he could best even the most skilled warriors in the Sapphire Guard. She had challenged him immediately, striding into an obvious defeat with determination. Kellian had her beaten in a handful of seconds, so she'd struggled to her feet and asked for a rematch. He had taught her more in an hour of exhausting battle than she'd learned in a year and even today, after she'd grown experienced and confident, she found herself turning to Kellian for support. She had missed his steadfast faith.

"I bet you're sad I couldn't arrest your house thief that fast."

He laughed, but the sound lacked mirth. His shoulders slumped, and hair fell from his usually tidy half-ponytail. Sora had seen so little of Kellian, she hadn't realized how draining their conflict with the Myrians had been.

"You look like you sleep even less than I do," she said.

"It's about to get worse." He pulled his fur-lined winter cloak tighter. "How is Lord Arathiel?"

"Recovering." She had yet to transfer him from the infirmary. They had talked twice since that first encounter, and Arathiel hadn't provided any new information. All she knew for certain was that he hid something from her. She would find out what. Kellian's question surprised her, though, and Sora shot him a sharp glance. Either he didn't want to talk about how their conflict would worsen and had changed the subject, or Arathiel was connected to it. Judging from the hint of guilt in his hard mouth, she would guess the latter. "Might I ask why you're inquiring?"

A small *heh* escaped Kellian's lips, and he tilted his head back. His gaze had gone straight to the Allastam Tower. At night, the magical gardens at its top glowed a soft blue. "Diel intends to visit your headquarters tomorrow, first thing in the morning."

A sense of foreboding grew in Sora at Kellian's measured tone. He was hiding his disapproval, out of respect for Lord Dathirii. "I have a feeling I won't like this," she said.

"He will ask to free Lord Arathiel on a … probation of sorts."

"You can't do that." She needed Arathiel in her jail, close at hand so she could question him every day—every hour, even. Sooner or later, he'd give her the right lead to find Hasryan. How would she ever track down her assassin if her last source of information walked out with Lord Dathirii? Isandor's nobles all watched her now, and six families relied on her to bring Hasryan to justice. Sora turned towards Kellian. At least he had the decency to meet her gaze and frown apologetically. "Why? Why would Lord Dathirii risk this? You have no allies against the Myrian Enclave, your resources are spread as thin as can be, and he seeks to anger Lord Allastam? This won't end well. You cannot free Arathiel."

"Why is a secret, at least for the moment." Kellian tucked strands of hair behind his long ears with a weary sigh. "I'm sorry. I wanted to give you a heads-up. You'll want to use all the time you have left."

"I don't understand." Sora pushed herself up. She had always perceived House Dathirii as her ally, and coming from Kellian, the news felt like a betrayal. "Hasryan killed more than Lady Allastam. Without Arathiel, I'll never catch him. Shouldn't you care about that? Shouldn't you help me instead of destroying my one chance at progress?"

Kellian straightened up after her, unwinding in a single graceful movement, to end a full head shorter than Sora. "I wish it was this simple. This concerns the Myrian Enclave, and Master Avenazar is our priority. Hasryan's criminal actions do not outweigh the dangers this wizard embodies, for us and the city. Branwen's report left us no doubts about that."

Sora forced a calming breath in, then out. He was right. Hasryan was *her* priority, but he shouldn't be everyone's. She had seen the ruins of the tailor's shop, scorched to cinders by the enclave's High Priest. If that was only a taste of what they could do … Then she should be glad if Arathiel could assist them, despite the consequences for her.

"Of course, yes. I let my personal struggles get to me and lost sight of the larger context." Everything seemed to conspire to stop her from reaching Hasryan. Only House Allastam and the Crescent Moon helped her with enthusiasm, and their respective goals didn't please Sora. Everyone else who knew Hasryan clamped down about him, even if they had barely talked to him before. The Lower City protected their own, no matter the crimes they were accused of. Or perhaps thanks to it. She doubted the homeless folks living at the Shelter had any love for House Allastam.

House Dathirii's desire to free Arathiel was another obstacle, yet now that the initial shock had passed, her anger vanished. She believed in them, in their goals and moral compass. This, in truth, provided the first excuse for slowing the investigation both her heart and mind could get behind. Not unless she used her best interrogation skills before Arathiel was out of her reach, of course.

"Lord Arathiel barely knew Hasryan, yet he threw everything he had down the shitslide to save him. There has to be more to this than a few card games." Sora rubbed the back of her neck and stretched her muscles. She'd spent too long sitting these last days, either at her desk or Arathiel's bedside.

"Thanks for the warning, Kellian. I'm glad I can always count on you."

He clasped her shoulder and nodded. "You're not alone. I'm busy, but call on me if you need help. I'll figure out a way."

Sora smiled, knowing he would. She'd yet to find anyone else more reliable in Isandor. "Only if I can return the favour. If you need help …" She waited for his nod of agreement. "Good. Now I must go. This could be my last night with Lord Arathiel, and I have a lot of unanswered questions."

Would it lead anywhere? Arathiel's answers so far had been steadfast, cool, and coherent. She lost temper more often than he did. But Sora had a duty to try—for herself, and for those six families. Her repressed attachment to Hasryan's easy wit couldn't stain her diligent work. She would have Arathiel explain every single detail a dozen times if she needed to. Something was bound to come up.

THE questions had dragged on for hours. Arathiel hadn't even been awake for such a long time since his arrest, but Sora Sharpe was relentless. She had hauled him out of the infirmary, sat him in an interrogation room, and battered him with questions. Where was Hasryan? How had they met? When had they first talked? About what? Did they have any common friends? Who else at the Shelter might want to help? He couldn't mean 'no one'—think harder! And when she let the subject of Hasryan go for a few minutes, she dragged his past to the front of the conversations. When had he left? Who had he known back then? Did he know the Dathirii very well? How often had he trained with Kellian? Talked with Camilla? What had he shared with Diel?

Arathiel did his best, but the answers blurred in his mind. He didn't even need to lie; he couldn't keep track of what he had said and what he had kept silent, of the dates and details of his own life. He needed rest. His ankle might not throb with pain, and his wounds had been closed, but Arathiel knew he hadn't healed yet. Rescuing Hasryan had required an enormous amount of energy, and he could sleep for weeks without recovering.

Not that Sora would allow it. He supposed he should have expected this. Hasryan had probably lived through it several times. Exhaustion and stress could lead to a slip, and she would jump onto any information she could use. If she was in any state to notice it. He stared at Sora during a brief lull in their back-and-forth, noting the bags under her eyes, her agitated tapping on the table, and her growing frustration. Arathiel straightened in his chair. He'd had enough of this ridiculous charade.

"What's going on?" he asked.

"An interrogation. What does it look like?"

"A desperate attempt to drag information out of me through verbal bludgeoning? You're tiring yourself, hitting so hard." A hint of mockery had slipped into his voice, and fury flashed across Sora's face. Good. "Why now, however? Pressure from the lords and ladies of Isandor?"

"Not the kind you're thinking of," she said. "Why are you surprised? You're a criminal withholding essential information from Isandor's Sapphire Guard. You're lucky an all-night interrogation is the hardest we go on you."

Arathiel laughed, but his heart twisted inside. Was she threatening him? What would even be the point? "With all due respect, Miss Sharpe, I don't think torture would lead you anywhere with me."

She paled, and Arathiel suspected she hadn't realized what her words implied. Sharpe used brutal determination as a mask for her doubts. The more he insisted on Hasryan's humanity, the more aggressive she became about the crimes committed. He already knew better than to believe her tough front. She had let Larryn point a bow at her without retribution and had allowed Cal to partially heal him on the very day he'd freed Hasryan. She might sling threats his way, but Arathiel doubted she'd resort to physical violence—with him, or anyone else under her watch.

Sora squared her shoulders, letting her temporary horror wash over her. "Nothing leads me anywhere with you, does it? You're bound to crack at some point."

"I spent a hundred thirty years in stasis. I've grown very patient." Ironic, that his first blatant lie to Sora wouldn't even concern Camilla or Hasryan. The years trapped into the Well had snapped by, time passing beyond his consciousness. Arathiel remembered going down the stairs, determined to find a cure for Lindi's fast-degrading health. His memory grew confused as he travelled farther down. The Well had sapped his energy and awareness, and only with an immense effort of willpower had he pulled out of the magical torpor and crawled out. Boots and clothes had fallen to pieces as he stumbled up one step at a time, unable to feel the stone under his hands, confused and increasingly terrified. Half-alive, paper-thin, and hungry. Arathiel chased the memory away and found himself staring at a very concerned Sora.

"Are you back with me?" she asked.

"I never left." His voice was rough. Black spots obscured the edge of his vision and receded as he focused. What had happened there?

"You've been unresponsive for a handful of minutes. I was about to get a healer."

"I …" Arathiel trailed off. Thinking about the Well did not usually make him lose track of his surroundings, and his heart raced at potential explanations. What if he'd never escaped? Would he forever be connected to it? Could the Well continue to leech his senses, even now, so far from it? Arathiel curled his fingers around the chains of his shackles, tightening his grip until he could feel the cold metal digging in. A month ago, he would have greeted the perspective with reluctant fatalism—proof that he was never meant to escape and should have died in the Well. Not anymore. He'd come to Isandor searching for a goal, a sense of self, and a home. Meeting Hasryan had given him the first, and helped him toward the second. And while Arathiel had no idea what to call home yet, he knew it was nearby, and he would fight for it. "No need. I'll be fine. I'm here to stay."

"True enough. Neither of us is going anywhere any time soon." Her voice had softened, and Arathiel wondered how disturbed he'd looked. He'd rather not give Sora too much insight into what troubled him—he didn't trust her not to use it against him—but she must have realized his mind had gone elsewhere for a moment.

"This is pointless. Exhausted or not, I won't betray Hasryan. He's my friend, and you're dangerous to him."

"Who isn't?" Sora countered, and an instant later, her expression shifted. She leaned forward, linking her hands. "Who, in your tiny circle of acquaintances and friends, would not be a danger to Isandor's most famous assassin? You keep repeating Larryn had nothing to do with it, yet everything brings it back to the Shelter."

"Then investigate. What stops you?"

Sora huffed, refusing to answer. Either she didn't believe Larryn was involved or she'd already searched the Shelter and questioned its patrons, to no avail. Arathiel had known not to speak of his rescue to any of them, not even Cal. They were the obvious scapegoats, the first ones any good investigator would think about. Unlike Camilla Dathirii, the peaceful old elf known for her tea chats and her dedication to Isandor's elderly. Asking her had been a terrible risk, but Arathiel trusted her heart. She would see this through.

"Run me through your winter solstice night again," Sora said. "Slowly, with ample details."

Arathiel heaved a sigh, leaned against his seat, and started at the beginning. Slowly, as requested, which pleased him. More time to recover from his strange fade-out earlier, and more time to cover the tiny lie protecting Larryn's attempt to break Hasryan out of prison. This was a story he'd practised before, and Arathiel told it with the careful ease of someone who knew each word counted.

Chapter Seven

T HE brutal stench of his new cell surprised Arathiel and sent a jolt of joy coursing through him. He clapped his hands, striding inside with childlike enthusiasm.

"This stinks!"

The pungent smell of urine filled his nostrils and scorched his throat. Even the Lower City hadn't fazed him, yet in this cramped space, the disgusting odour of human refuse pierced through his numbed senses, and he felt more awake than he had since his arrest. After the night of unrelenting questions, Arathiel welcomed this change.

Two steps behind him, Sora Sharpe met his outburst with a groan. Fatigue hunched her shoulders, and she had grown too distracted to ask coherent questions over the last hour, leading her to admit defeat and call a stop to their interrogation. Arathiel had caught sight of sunlight through a window, but none of it reached this cell. His new home, though not for long, he suspected.

"You're so strange," she said, then dropped to a whisper. "But loyal. How did Hasryan earn this dedication?"

Arathiel didn't turn around. He doubted she had meant to voice that question, but exhaustion took its toll on self-control. He walked to his cell's opposite wall and ran a hand over the stones, wondering if they were cold or rough.

"He accepted me." Wasn't that what had mattered most, in the end? Hasryan had seen him bleed without flinching, had sensed Arathiel's secrets and difference, and he had taken it in stride without prying further. Better, he had sought to protect and help him. "I'm not strange to him. Hasryan knows what it's like to be the odd one out." This explanation didn't cut it, but words could never cover the depth of comprehension that had passed between them. Arathiel didn't even quite understand it himself. The bond they had formed was unique, similar to what he had experienced through romance before, yet with a different love at its core.

"What a huge mess." She sounded like she wanted an escape. Arathiel wished he had one to offer. "Rest. You have a visitor tomorrow, and you might find it taxing."

"I'm allowed visitors?" No one had had permission to see Hasryan, and he had expected the same rules would apply to him.

Sora grimaced. "Some people go as they please. If a lord of this city demands to speak with you …"

Arathiel's stomach twisted at the mention. A lord? Had Lord Allastam come to put a different kind of pressure on Arathiel? He hoped not. Although Camilla had shared some insight into Isandor's current politics, his grasp remained tenuous, and he might blunder in a face-off with a hostile noble. He had no idea how his actions impacted House Brasten. Did Isandor link them by mere virtue of his name? Sora had said they'd confirmed his existence in their records, but Arathiel doubted they had endorsed him. Did he still count as a Brasten, then?

"May I ask which lord?"

Sora's eyes glinted with amusement. "Perhaps we should trade information. You tell me where to find Hasryan …"

Arathiel laughed. She expected nothing from the proposal. "As if."

"It's Lord Dathirii," she said, then closed the door without another word, as if angry at herself for sharing.

Arathiel sat down, removing the weight from his recovering ankle. He might not feel the pain, but that didn't mean he should needlessly slow his healing. Once his initial shock passed, a wave of relief washed over him. He knew Diel, even if only through brief and now long-gone contacts. Arathiel would much rather speak with him than face Lord Allastam's anger or, worse, meet with Lady Brasten. Camilla had only good words for the young leader of his family, but thoughts of this encounter left him anxious and restless. What would Lady Brasten say to Arathiel once they met? She could deny his bloodline, treat him as the outsider he now was, really. The odd one out. Would she cast him out? Titles had been removed from nobles in the face of unforgivable crimes before. Perhaps it would be best this way—a clear cut from his previous life. Yet it terrified him. Few threads connected him to Lindi still, and House

Brasten was the biggest one.

The Dathirii might well be the second, though Arathiel suspected Diel hadn't requested an interview to discuss the past. The elf had a trade war to win and no time for remembrance. This mystery led Arathiel to waste his precious hours of rest lying on the ground, wondering how he and Hasryan's escape fit into Diel's fight with the Myrians, and why Lord Dathirii would approach him now. He hoped no one had noticed the new resident in Camilla's quarters—if Hasryan had made it.

The wasted night only made Arathiel more exhausted, yet his fatigue washed away as he entered the interrogation room and found Diel Dathirii sitting in a chair, fidgeting with a loose strand of hair. He recognized the habit from over a century ago, and as guards chained him to the table, he searched the lord's face for more of the familiar, idealist elf he'd known.

A hundred thirty years had aged Lord Dathirii, giving his youthful features a more mature appearance, and the smallest wrinkles now decorated the corner of his eyes. He had the same lush hair, presumably golden, braided back to keep it from his face. Their gazes met, and for a moment, Arathiel was caught in Diel Dathirii's eyes. He remembered their intense green, but like everything else, the Well had washed it into a dull grey, with just a hint of emerald left. Arathiel cleared his throat, heat rushing to his head. He hadn't expected the elven lord to grow even more handsome with time.

"The last century has been good to you, milord," he said.

"I wish I could return the compliment." A quick silence

followed Diel's answer, heavy with the implied meaning. The Well had turned his hair white, his face gaunt, and his limbs bony. His time at the Shelter must have helped, but Arathiel doubted he carried a peaceful and healthy aura about himself. Diel frowned and shook his head. "I'm sorry, I didn't mean to say … You look great, if exhausted. I heard it hasn't been easy."

"It hasn't."

The lord's clumsiness amused Arathiel more than it insulted him. He remembered Diel as a smooth talker, prone to jump into idealist rants which always, somehow, pierced through the prevalent cynicism and convinced others. He had a way with words—except, it seemed, when it came to greeting long-gone acquaintances. Arathiel let the mishap slide, waiting to see what Diel wanted to say.

"When you sprang into the fray during the execution, I thought I had imagined the resemblance. I asked Jaeger if that was you, and even with his confirmation, I could hardly believe it." Diel settled back into his chair, a thoughtful smile lighting his face. "It's good to see you again, despite the circumstances."

Arathiel's eyebrows shot up. Had they been on friendly terms? They rarely spoke, and he had seen Kellian a lot more than he had Diel. At the time, the young lord had been too busy feasting with friends in various establishments or striking off on unannounced expeditions down the Reonne River or one of its tributaries. It had been somewhat of a joke, how Diel Dathirii skipped on ceremonies and events he ought to attend, yet turned up unexpected at others. Charming and irresponsible all at once. The former had endured through time, but from what Camilla had said, he'd grown into a reliable leader. Perhaps Arathiel had disregarded him too quickly back then, and had never noticed any interest Diel might have given him. Arathiel raised a hand and shook the shackles. The rattling sound echoed in the small room. "These circumstances?"

"Yes, and everything tied to them. How are they treating you?"

Arathiel shrugged. "Well enough. They healed my wounds and transferred me into a scented cell. I am the unwilling subject of all-night interrogations, however."

Diel leaned forward, setting his elbows on the table and resting his chin on his hands. He studied Arathiel in silence, his deep gaze searching him as he asked his question. "Why save him? Investigator Sharpe had me sit through a list of his crimes before I could enter. Protecting assassins is unlike what I would've expected of you, long ago."

"Hasryan is my friend, and no more a monster than I am. We understand each other." How many different people would need to hear this explanation? Would any of them even believe it? Arathiel gritted his teeth, a wave of defiance surging. "Would you rather defend his boss? Siding with corrupt schemers rather than the tools they casually betray is unlike what I would've expected of *you*, long ago."

Their eyes locked, Arathiel daring him in silence to deny it. Diel instead threw his head back and burst into laughter. "I knew I could come to you." He ran a hand through his hair, pushing back the strands that had managed to escape his tired half-ponytail, and the simple, casual gesture immediately made him more approachable to Arathiel. It had always been easy to like Diel Dathirii. With the flash of a smile and a quick laugh, he could melt barriers and make himself welcome. "I need your help. In exchange, I can arrange accommodations for you. Several of Isandor's Towers have individual cells in them, comfortable quarters meant to imprison nobles who have committed crimes. It's not freedom, not yet, but it'd be better than this place."

Arathiel's heart leaped, and he tried to rein in his enthusiasm. The Diel he knew promised a lot but rarely followed up on his word. He trusted Lord Dathirii more—responsibilities and power seemed to have had a positive effect on him—but he didn't want to become too hopeful. This imprisonment had been more difficult than he'd anticipated. Immobility reminded Arathiel of the Well, and sometimes he imagined magic sapping more of his senses away, as if he were dying still. His short blackout during the interrogation last night hadn't helped.

"Why would you?" Arathiel leaned forward, fingers wrapping around the chain of his shackles. "I've been gone for a long time, but I'm not completely out of the loop. You have this enclave on your back, and allying with me would turn the city against you. Lord Allastam will make you regret it."

"I am aware, but I cannot accept the alternative. Brune is dangerous, more so than I thought, but she has too many friends within Isandor's guards and nobles. I can't go after her at the moment. I know that, and so does Miss Sharpe. Once I'm ... cleared of the Myrians, however, I'll look into it. For now, I need your help." Still an idealist, Arathiel thought with a smile, but he had lost a veneer of naivety. At least enough not to pick more battles while the Myrian Enclave threatened him. Yet Arathiel didn't understand how angering Lord Allastam would make things better. Diel pushed his hair back, then caught his gaze again. The distance between them vanished, and Arathiel's throat dried. "Whatever happened to you … I'm sorry. I am. But if you would use it to save another man, I would be grateful."

Of course. The warmth in Arathiel's belly disappeared, replaced by acrid bitterness. Why else would he catch anyone's interest? His abilities made him a unique asset, an incredible tool to use when at war. Arathiel looked down at his manacled hands, a sharp refusal on the tip of his tongue. Elven fingers settled on his, squeezing just enough for him to feel the pressure and forcing his gaze back up. The lump in his throat tightened at Diel's apologetic expression.

"Please hear me out," he said. "I wouldn't be here if I didn't trust your judgment."

"Go ahead," Arathiel whispered.

He owed it to Camilla. She had given him so much since his arrival, and never asked anything in return. If her nephew had a special request, the least he could do was listen. Besides, Arathiel couldn't deny that Diel's very presence sent his heart rushing, and he wanted to help. He just hated *why* he was being asked to. Diel hesitated for a moment, perhaps trying to decide how to start.

"My niece vanished ten days ago."

"Oh, yes … Lady Camilla told me." They'd been at the tea house again, and she had kept forgetting what she wanted to order. Branwen had been missing for a few days, and although Camilla had tried to maintain a dynamic and pleasant conversation, she had often lapsed into worried silence. "I thought she'd escaped."

"She did. Someone kept her safe while over there. He hid her from Master Avenazar and the rest of the enclave, but they discovered it the night she fled. He's the one who needs help." Diel Dathirii grew more agitated. He stood from his chair and begun pacing alongside the table. "I glimpsed what Master Avenazar is capable of. I couldn't even watch him abuse that teenager for more than a few seconds. I stopped him then, and I want to do so again. Too many days have already slipped by."

"He might be dead."

Diel shook his head in emphatic denial. "No."

He didn't offer a reason for his conviction. Arathiel hesitated. Avenazar had a formidable reputation and was not to be trifled with, and rescuing Hasryan had almost cost Arathiel his life. "How am I supposed to do this? I am not invincible, Diel. I'm only half-dead, and a solid wound can destroy the other half as easily as with anyone else."

"Half …"

"It's a manner of speaking." Arathiel waved his head dismissively. He wished he hadn't used the expression, but Sora's words still burned hard in him. Half-alive. "Forget it."

Diel clearly didn't want to, but after an insistent stare from Arathiel, he let it go. "You would have help. Branwen would forever resent me if I suggested she should stay home while her friend suffered, and Kellian can provide extra fighting power. Anyone else you'd want to invite would be more than welcome. I'd love to give you more men, but we can barely protect our allies as it is, and I fear it might get worse once Lord Allastam catches wind of this. He wouldn't dare touch us, but I wouldn't put it past him to harass local merchants loyal to me. I wouldn't ask this of you if I weren't so short-handed."

Meaning he needed a new pawn in his war. One with peculiar abilities for tasks he couldn't otherwise accomplish. The magic dead man. Arathiel scoffed, shaking his head. He despised this, and despised that he wouldn't have the heart to refuse. The moment he had stepped forward and revealed himself, people sought to use him, and he would fall for it. Diel noticed the bitter shift in his mood.

"Arathiel …" Diel's intimate tone caught his attention. The lord set his hands on the table. "I know I'm asking you to risk everything for a stranger's life. I am aware of how offensive it is of me to show up here and do this, only because you can withstand hits without flinching. I … I can see it pains you."

"Why do it, then?"

"A man is being tortured. I've learned to make sacrifices."

A bitter laugh escaped Arathiel's lips. He pulled his hands back and crossed his arms, rattling the small chains. "You know how to lay a trap. Now if I don't accept, I'm the jerk who can't sacrifice his feelings to save someone from a horrible fate."

Diel's eyes widened in genuine horror. "That's not—no! I'm not the one who'd put my life on the line. I'm not the one who endured whatever happened to you. This decision is yours. I'm not trying to tell you what to do with your abilities." He let himself fall back into the chair with a heavy sigh. His shoulders slumped, and he seemed a lot less confident all of a sudden.

"But you are telling me."

"I'm sorry. I just want him freed. I promised Branwen I would try everything." Diel rubbed the bridge of his nose, his voice soft. "But I understand. Thank you for your time, Arathiel. Hopefully we will talk again when I have the resources to deal with Brune."

As he pushed himself back up, Arathiel lunged forward and grabbed his wrist. "I'll do it." For Camilla, and for this mysterious stranger who had risked everything for Diel's niece. "I can't let this man suffer because you're insensitive, and I think you knew all along."

The smile returned to Diel Dathirii's lips—an admission that he was right—and Arathiel struggled to hold onto his anger. "I did say I knew I could come to you. I trust your judgment. I always have."

Always. Had Diel Dathirii looked up to him all those decades ago? How strange, to learn he had been appreciated without ever noticing, and that despite the time lost in between, this still counted for something. It offered him an opportunity to save another life. Perhaps that was why he'd managed to pull himself out of the Well—what he was meant to do. Arathiel had failed to save his sister, but he'd rescued Hasryan, and now there could be this stranger. How many lives could he buy with his own, before his luck ran out? Would they be worth it?

"What's his name?" he asked.

"Varden Daramond."

Arathiel repeated the name as if tasting it. Diel thanked him again and reiterated his promises for a better cell and potential help against Brune. The lord left the dull interrogation room with renewed confidence, the weight vanished from his shoulders. Arathiel tilted his head to the side, wondering if his assurance would last once the city caught wind of their deal. Perhaps Diel didn't mind if it meant he was doing the right thing. Camilla had been right about him: although the idealism hadn't left him, Diel Dathirii was no longer the carefree youth Arathiel had known.

Chapter Eight

I SRA crept down the damp corridor, her heart in a wild frenzy. Her fingers trailed along the cold stone as she moved past empty cells. She shouldn't be near the prisons. Master Avenazar would be angry if he learned, and she never wanted to endure that. Not after last time, when he'd come to her room and promised horrible punishments if she ever fed him false information again. Her wrist still throbbed from the brief discharge of energy he'd shot into it before Jilssan had stopped him. Isra didn't want to think about what he would have done if her Master hadn't been there. Memories of it brought tears to her eyes.

She should have listened to Nevian. He had known she was wrong. Isra wished he had told her. She wouldn't have said anything! But Nevian had never liked her, or anyone else. He had let her believe the Isbari priest betrayed them by sneaking out of the enclave at night, heading into Isandor, until Master Avenazar had found the truth.

They were both traitors. Now Varden rotted in a cell, and Nevian was dead.

How could Nevian sell information on them like that? He always rambled about rules and obedience and respecting Avenazar's wishes, no matter how ridiculous. Was that all an elaborate cover? His obsession with precision and laws had seemed genuine, if bizarre. Perhaps because of his constant seriousness, like he had forgotten how to have fun. But eventually, Isra had understood: work must have been the point of his betrayal. Avenazar ruined his studies, forcing Nevian to sneak into the library late at night for a few hours of peace. He must have traded insider knowledge for outside help. Nevian was stubborn, and he had wanted to learn magic. Nothing would have stopped him.

Which meant everything wrong was Avenazar's fault. If he had taught Nevian anything, the apprentice would have stayed at the enclave, Isra would not have seen him sneak out, and he would be alive. Not that she would ever share that belief with Avenazar. Once, she'd thought being Master Enezi's daughter would keep her out of trouble. Her father's influence meant most people worked hard not to anger him. But High Priest Daramond had an entire church behind him, and it hadn't made Avenazar hesitate at all.

He was Isbari, though. Everyone knew he was Isbari, unlike her. She had kept the secret hidden all her life, following her father's advice. Isra reached for the amber amulet around her neck, crafted by him when she was still in the cradle, his best attempt to shield her from Myrian hatred. It never left her. Not when she slept, not when she bathed, and especially not when she kissed other girls. The spell shifted her form and maintained it without requiring any energy from her—a perfect object, created by Myria's most powerful master of transmutation. Her father often said love kept it working—both his, and her Isbari mother's.

To everyone around, she was a full-blooded Myrian with a small nose, peachy skin, and pale blond hair. It had been so long since Isra had removed the necklace, she had no idea what else she looked like. She didn't want to know. She had the luxury of choosing her appearance and wouldn't waste it. Some days it hurt to think her successes were built on lies, but Isra had become excellent at avoiding such thoughts. Everything was easier for Myrians, simpler and safer. Why wouldn't she use that if she could?

Being perceived as Myrian might not stave all questions if someone caught her down here, however. What would they think if they saw her with Varden? They might peg her as an ally, become wary of her. She shouldn't have come. Isra couldn't help it, though. Not since she'd heard of the sketchbooks hidden in Varden's desk.

She stopped in front of Varden's cell and shoved a trembling hand in her satchel. Varden was not a friend, not even an ally, but who else could she talk to? In Myria, girls were meant for boys, never for one another. Varden had defied that, too, and she needed to know how—how he'd found the courage, how he'd kept it secret, how he'd staved the loneliness that haunted her. No one ever talked about these things. Isra was so tired of hiding, of stringing lies together, of avoiding other girls to stay out of trouble, and of projecting the perfect girl she was not. Varden could help. He'd kept his own secret for a really long time, no? Isra touched the amulet at her neck. It always calmed her to sense her father's power so close. She retrieved a chunk of wood from her bag and readied herself. Even if she brought bread and water, Varden would not welcome her.

Her palms sweaty, Isra placed the wood over the keyhole of Varden's door. She whispered the words to her spell, reaching for the magic around her and in the material. It swirled, hard to grasp and redirect and control. Isra gritted her teeth—why was this always so difficult?—and she pushed forward. Bending wood shouldn't pose a problem, and yet she struggled. Isra focused, and energy coursed through the organic structure as she reshaped it, fitting it into the hole one little bit at a time. The wood adopted the form of every nook and cranny until it became a perfect key. She released the slippery magic, unlocked the door, and opened it.

Light slipped inside the cell through the crack, falling upon the Isbari priest. He leaned against the wall, tucked into a tight ball, one arm thrown over his head to protect himself. Grease weighed down his curls, and large bags hung under his eyes. Isra's throat clenched, and she cast her gaze down. A few days had turned the healthy, confident priest into a skeletal mess. She conjured a little brown glow and let it hover above her head. Its glare would be softer, easier on Varden, allowing her to close the door and block the torchlight.

"High Priest?" she asked.

"Not anymore." His voice cracked, but he lifted his chin and met her gaze. "Since when do you use my titles anyway?"

"I always have," she protested, knowing full well she hadn't.

He mocked her answer with a grunt, and anger spiked through Isra. When Varden wrapped his arms around his legs, however, tightening his small ball, guilt overrode her irritation. She had done this by talking to Avenazar. Isra focused on his strange shackles—ice crawled over his wrists and forearms and melded at the centre, forming a bridge between his arms. They glistened in her brown light, a reminder that while he looked like a famished and broken man, Varden wielded powerful flames and probably hated her. Good thing she'd brought an offering.

"I have water." She reached inside her bag and lifted out a skin, along with a loaf of bread. "Water and something to eat."

Varden stared at her. Had his eyes sunk deeper? Isra didn't remember this scary look on him. Perhaps she ought to leave. He seemed about to attack her.

"Why?" he asked.

An excellent question, that. Avenazar wouldn't be pleased if he found her feeding his favourite prisoner or talking to him at all. She had needed to come, however, and doing so empty-handed had seemed inhuman. It was kind of her fault he had wound up here.

"I don't know. I just did."

"I'll tell you why." Anger threaded his tired voice, discreet, almost impossible to hear. "You needed to assuage your guilt. You know I don't deserve this. You already did, when you watched Avenazar walk down the temple aisle to interrupt the Long Night's Watch. In your head, this gift makes you a decent person."

"No!" She clenched the waterskin tighter, frightened by the flat, empty cadence of his words. "I did what I had to. You betrayed us."

"I was never a part of 'us.'"

He settled back against the wall and closed his eyes, his frown easing into an exhausted expression. Isra could find nothing to counter that. Isbari didn't mix with Myrians. They weren't meant to be together—not in a room, and certainly not in a single person. Varden had always been a bothersome exception, an outsider. He didn't belong in the upper spheres of Myrian society, and he must have felt it keenly, as she so often did.

"Do you want it or not?" Isra stepped forward, offering the waterskin, her head high.

Varden hesitated, scratched his beard, then nodded. "I'll take it. Did Jilssan send you?"

"Master Jilssan doesn't know I'm here." She wouldn't approve. Too risky, and what for? Jilssan had urged her not draw Avenazar's attention again, to obey and stay safe.

Isra crouched next to Varden and offered him the waterskin first, withholding comments on the shake of his hands as he drank. Every sign of his weakness squeezed her insides, reminding her of the pain she had inflicted. Isra tore a bit of bread as he downed the water in large swallows and offered it. He snatched it with such speed, she wondered if Avenazar fed him at all. She avoided staring at him. This cell was about to become even more awkward than it already was.

"I—um … I came for a reason, actually. It's kind of hard to explain."

Varden froze mid-bite, his eyebrows shooting up. Hard to

explain or not, he waited for her to do so.

"I just … I heard you were really into men."

She had whispered, unable to say it any louder. The priest crunched down on his bread, taking his time to swallow it. When he spoke, his voice dripped with bitterness. "What of it? Need advice?"

"Of course not!" Isra lifted her chin. "I don't need your tips. I don't even care about—about dating!"

Her head spun a little. She'd been half a second away from saying "about men." Varden's amused smile told her he wasn't duped by her cover up.

"I'm sorry, this is …" He laughed, ran a hand over his face. "Is the obnoxious teenager who put me into this cell paying a visit to ask about same-sex relationships, or has Avenazar pushed me over the deep end?"

Isra jumped to her feet. "I'm not obnoxious!"

"I can't believe it. You came all the way down here with food, water, and some fake guilty look on your pretty Myrian face, but it's all about you."

"No! I did feel bad. I still do." She shoved the rest of the bread on him. The lump in her throat almost stopped another word from coming, but instead they spilled out all at once. "If I hadn't said anything, you wouldn't be here, and Nevian would be alive! Now everything is terrible, and I miss his grumpy face."

There was a long stretch of silence during which Varden ate his meagre meal, washing it down with water, his gaze lost somewhere ahead. Isra shuffled, wishing she had kept her emotions in check.

Varden snapped back to the present, his expression unreadable.

"Then I apologize for the wrong conclusion."

He didn't quite sound like he meant it. Isra pouted. "You should apologize for calling me obnoxious."

"No." He laughed, drank again from the water. "Not until you prove you're not."

"I'm not!"

"Just ask your questions."

The brittle playfulness of his tone vanished, turning his words into an attack. Isra stepped back, surprised at the sudden virulence. No more patience, no more calm. Isra swallowed hard. Avenazar tortured him every day. Of course he wasn't in a mood for games. She forced herself to settle next to him despite the small needles of fear in her heart.

"How did you keep it a secret for so long? How do you hide something like that?"

"Not by telling the prisoner who has an evil wizard in his mind every single day."

Isra's eyes widened, her mouth drying. Her stomach felt like it had taken a plunge to the deepest abyss, only to fling itself back up her throat. She put a hand over her lips. Varden offered the waterskin.

"I'll do what I can to keep it from him," he said.

The softness had returned, and Isra found herself wiping tears from her eyes. Avenazar was awful, and she didn't want him anywhere near her head. It contained too many secrets. If he started to unravel any of them, she would end like Nevian. Or Varden. She didn't know which would be worse.

"O-okay." She had given Varden a chance to avenge himself on a silver platter, and he promised to protect her instead. Isra didn't quite believe it. She drank slowly from the water, then passed it back to him. "You're nice. Nicer than you should be. Did you have a boyfriend?"

Varden smiled, and it brightened his face, smoothing out the exhausted lines and masking his gauntness. She wondered if he often looked so approachable, and why she'd never noticed, then remembered the sharp exchanges they'd always had. Varden had treated her as an enemy, and she'd replied in kind. Or perhaps she had started it—he seemed willing to open up now.

"I did," he said, "for several years. His father became suspicious of it, and they moved far from the capital. We risked one last farewell, then never spoke again. That's how you hide it. You either don't act on it, or you stop the moment it turns dangerous."

Isra knew how the distance and absence felt. Her girl was tall, with long dark hair tied in a ponytail, perfect blue eyes, and a tiny round nose Isra liked to poke. She had a fairy's laugh and kissed like a goddess. They used to walk through her father's gardens every day, and Isra would pick the most beautiful flowers to slip into her hair. Sometimes she shaped one from whatever she found. Her father had warned her such behaviour could get them killed. They had stopped.

"It's not fair."

"No, it's not." He shrugged, then finished the last of his bread. "That's all there is to it, though, at least in Myria. You keep it under wraps all your life, like it's some horrible disease, but it's not. Never forget that, or you'll start to hate yourself—to think you're worthless, that it's better hidden away. Never let others decide which parts of you are deserving of love."

The priest leaned back against the wall and spread out his fingers. His olive skin seemed even darker in Isra's brown light. She reached for her necklace, fighting against her tears. Could he read minds? Varden meant more than his sexuality here, unknowingly speaking to Isra's camouflaged Isbari heritage. Did she really think that half of her was worthless? Some days she envied Varden, unafraid to live his truth and love himself. Hiding was easier, and she didn't draw any pride from it the way Varden did. He would never wear an amulet like hers, but that didn't make it wrong! Didn't she have the right to choose how she wanted the world to perceive her? It's not like she'd ever had access to Isbari spaces before. She didn't even know her mother. With a deep breath, Isra stood up.

"Must be hard."

None of her turmoil showed through her words. Her voice remained solid, confident. One lie after another. She had trained well, and would always manage to bury it.

"You never get used to people bringing you down for what you are." Varden drank more water before handing her the skin. "You learn to endure."

She wondered if he was speaking about Avenazar again. It sounded like him, to strike at Varden's core. "I have to go. I'm … I'm sorry for everything. Thank you."

Isra turned away and hurried out of the cell. She thought she heard whispered thanks from him as she locked the door once more and retrieved her key, but she didn't linger to find out. The priest's words of resistance stayed with her all the way back to her room.

CHAPTER NINE

BRANWEN leaned against her chair, booted feet thrown over the table, her large hat concealing both hair and elven ears. She tipped it lower, casting shadows over her features and hoping they would mask the failings in her male contouring. The tavern's smoky atmosphere helped, as did its reputation. Although they imposed no restrictions on actual gender, *The Jostle* had always entertained masculine crowds. As long as she didn't stand out as too feminine, no one would look twice at her—and all she needed was not to be identified as Branwen Dathirii. She drained her ale, scanning the patrons until she spotted her informant worming his way through the crowd. Alton had shaved his head since their last meeting, leaving only short and curly black hair that highlighted his long elven ears, but Branwen could pick him out in any group. They had known each other for decades now, even before his transition, and she would always recognize the sway of his wide girth and his half-amused smirk.

Branwen raised two fingers as a greeting, then pushed a still-full tankard his way. Alton made a point of glaring at her feet on the table and mumbling, "Must you always forget basic courtesy?" before sitting into a chair. He wore an ugly pale blue shirt criss-crossed with green lines, bright against his dark skin, and as much as she approved of his new haircut, she couldn't say the same of his outfit choice.

"Perhaps when you develop a sense of fashion," she countered, but she did bring her feet down. "What is this monstrosity on your back?"

"I picked it out just for you. I knew it would make an impression."

She laughed, yet even she could hear the frayed exhaustion in her voice. Most of her informants had a great sense of humour and banter to match her own, and she hadn't realized how much she had missed it. Since returning to the enclave, she had only contacted a few of them—the strict minimum to stay alert to Myrian movements. She didn't have time to properly revive her network while she dedicated days and nights to designing a Myrian acolyte disguise.

Alton's mirth vanished, and he tilted his head to the side. "I have been worried about you."

"Others have it harder. You wanted to see me. Anything happening at the Enclave?" She had dragged herself out of the Dathirii Tower for the exclusive opportunity to learn key information about Avenazar's activities. It shouldn't have taken such energy out of her, but Branwen had barely slept over the last days. Picking an outfit, applying make-up, and slipping out unseen used to excite her; tonight, it had drained her already-limited pool of energy. She hoped it would be worth it.

"My Isbari contacts confirm they have been torturing your friend," Alton answered.

Branwen clenched her mug, and she leaned forward, her jaw tight. She knew that, but hearing it still sickened her. "What else?"

Alton spread his arms with an apologetic shrug. "Nothing—not from the Myrians anyway."

"So you called me over information I already had," she said. "I don't have time for games, Alton. As you *just* said, they are torturing him. If this is a ploy because you were worried—"

"I called you because House Allastam is in an uproar, and I think it concerns you." He set his thick arms on the table and leaned closer to Branwen. "We don't have a lot of information, but hours after Lord Dathirii left the Sapphire Guard's Headquarters, they started sending out several letters. Our sources inside said they were addressed to other nobles."

"When are they *not* in an uproar? Lord Allastam thrives on resentment and unjustified attacks on others. Tracking his movements is not why I paid you. It's the Myrians we're at war with, and it's the Myrians who are torturing Varden."

"At the moment, you're not paying me at all," Alton pointed out. "We both know there's little left to your coffers. I know my work, Branwen. You're losing sight of the larger picture."

She didn't want to hear about Allastam's crusty face—not before

Varden was safe, at any rate. How could she keep track of the larger picture when her mind always whirled back to Varden's torture? She imagined his screams at night, and creative torture ideas plagued her during the day. Even concentrating on her disguises demanded a lot out of her, and she couldn't bounce ideas off Garith, Vellien, or Camilla as she usually did in such situations—they all had their own problems to deal with.

"I don't care. Varden needs me. The rest of House Dathirii can take care of the larger picture." She pushed her chair back, purposefully rattling it on the floor boards. "I'll make sure Garith keeps *some* funds for you."

"Branwen, that wasn't—"

"I know." She forced herself to smile at him. Alton was trying his best, and doing it for her sake. She didn't want to be unfair. "Thank you for the information. I just … I can barely focus on one thing at the moment. That thing needs to be Varden, because I'm the only one who will. Keep doing your job, though. I'll be in touch."

She left Alton at their table, her own tankard still half full. Alcohol wouldn't do her any good at the moment either way. Branwen pushed through the increasingly thick crowd, eager to return to her quarters and her work. She wondered briefly what her uncle had wanted with Lord Arathiel Brasten but pushed the idea aside. One thing at a time. For now, she had a rescue to plan and execute.

DIEL'S happy humming always lightened Jaeger's heart. It didn't follow any known song, but simply filled their morning routine with joy, hovering in the air as they dressed. Listening to him, Jaeger could almost forget that their position in the city's politics had worsened, not improved. But Arathiel had agreed to rescue High Priest Varden Daramond, and Isandor's Sapphire Guards had allowed his release into House Dathirii's custody. Diel's thin plan to save Branwen's friend would see the light, come what may.

This, however, did not completely explain why Diel seemed to float. Jaeger smiled and slipped behind his love as the other elf buttoned his doublet. He ran his fingers along the collar and folded it expertly, looking at the other through the mirror. A hundred thirty years ago, Diel had developed strong feelings for Arathiel, who had been House Brasten's weapons master. Nothing had come out of it—Arathiel had barely noticed Diel, instead spending his time with Kellian—but it didn't surprise Jaeger that this attraction had carried through decades.

Jaeger couldn't resist this chance to tease. Diel's crush on Arathiel had led to their first in-depth discussion of polyamory, and Jaeger knew the morning's joy came from more than finally having a viable chance to rescue Varden. "I can't remember the last time I made you sing like this."

For a brief instant, Diel froze, then he threw his head back and laughed. "You're not jealous. I know you better than that, and you know me better, too."

"I do." Jaeger ran his hand over Diel's shoulder, leaning in closer. How often had Diel fallen in love with another through the decades? His heart shifted that way, expanding to greet the latest amazing person he'd met but never letting go of Jaeger. They had no secrets from one another, and when Diel wished for something more serious, he was the first to know. Jaeger often pushed him to act on it—faced with his love's unaltered felicity, Jaeger could find no jealousy in himself. The occasional third angle to their relationship enriched his life, too. Even though Jaeger didn't fall for most of them, he enjoyed the shifts in their dynamic and the special intimacy he often developed with them. Jaeger pulled the golden hair back a little to land a short kiss behind Diel's ear. "I assume you'll want to tell Branwen the good news."

"Absolutely. I thought we might share breakfast."

Diel examined himself once more in the glass, squaring his shoulders and taking a deep breath. The last few days had been hard on him, but the bags under his eyes had shrunk overnight. He glanced at the window, where the first sunlight filtered through white curtains. "It's a bit early, but Aunt Camilla taught me all I need to know about strong teas. If you could go get Branwen? I'll call someone to help me set the table."

The request surprised Jaeger. Diel usually invited his niece and nephew himself while his steward readied everything. Could Diel manage the preparations? Jaeger bit his lip and withheld the question. An informal breakfast with Branwen didn't require elaborate protocols, and while Diel might not know all the household servants by name, he didn't need Jaeger to interact with them or get their help. Still, it bothered him that Diel had decided to reverse the roles, until he realized that at this hour, Branwen would be sound asleep and unwilling to wake.

"I see you are once again leaving me with the arduous task. Should I find armour? Alert Kellian we might have an incident on our hands?"

Diel pressed his lips together, trying his hardest not to laugh. After a playful shove to Jaeger's shoulder, he schooled his expression and conjured some poor defence for his niece. "She's not so terrible. Use the promise of good news as your shield and you'll be fine."

Jaeger grinned and saluted. "There are causes worth dying for," he said before taking his leave.

Diel's laugh followed him through the office and into the corridor, and Jaeger marvelled at how relaxed he was. He missed their brief banter—it vanished when Diel became anxious, and the Myrians spread his patience thin. Perhaps it was selfish of him, but the obvious impact this war had on Jaeger's domestic life pushed him even more to stop Avenazar quickly and put an end to the stress and loss affecting the family. Jaeger wasn't sure how they would see this through without the help of other Houses, but he trusted Diel to find a solution, even if it led them down less desirable pathways.

By the time he reached Branwen's door, Jaeger's grin had given way to a more neutral expression. He knocked loudly, ensuring that he'd wake her, and prepared himself for the messy-haired, slightly more aggressive version of their otherwise cheerful spymaster. For all of Jaeger's gross exaggeration earlier, Diel was right: she wasn't that terrible. Just a little grumpy at being seen before any of her morning routine was complete. Branwen never came out of her room without a carefully picked dress and matching makeup. The ritual mattered to her, and without it, she didn't feel ready to face the day.

To his surprise, she opened almost right after his knock. Even stranger was the perfect bun holding her brown hair, the alertness in her wide eyes, and the fact that she was dressed—a flowing garment with a simple cut but a detailed pattern along the corset.

"Milady, you're … awake."

Branwen's clear laugh startled him. She leaned against the frame, one hand still holding the door. "Good morning to you too, Jaeger. To what do I owe the visit?"

"Did you sleep at all?" Jaeger regretted his question right away. How unprofessional. After the initial shock, he'd picked up on a few more details—how the makeup didn't quite hide the bags under her eyes, and the small yawn she'd stifled before answering him—and it seemed the most logical conclusion. It still wasn't his place to ask. "I apologize. It's none of my business, and I didn't mean to pry. Lord Dathirii sent me."

Her smile vanished, and her eyes darkened. She resented Diel's lack of immediate action to save Varden, and Jaeger's stomach squeezed at the change in her expression. He missed Branwen's incessant and demonstrative love for her uncle. He missed so much of the Dathirii before they had provoked the Myrians. Branwen's lifeless shrug just added to the pile.

"You shouldn't apologize for asking, Jaeger. You're not a steward to us, you're family. You know that. And no, I haven't slept. I can't, even after so many days." She opened the door a little wider and motioned for him to enter. "I've been working on something."

Jaeger followed her inside, and the sewing area drew his gaze. Branwen's quarters were outfitted with three mannequins, including one carved to her measurements. Sketches and paintings of clothes covered the wall behind them—most were of elaborate dresses, but not all. Disguises and men's outfits also featured prominently. A round wooden stand flanked them, poles jutting out in all direction. Hundreds of fabrics of all colour and texture buried it under their weight. At the moment, Branwen's usual image wall was hidden behind drawings of Myrian outfits. Most looked like robes for Keroth's acolytes, but others were more akin to what Master Avenazar or his apprentice wore. Jaeger studied them a little before shifting his attention to the red—or so he suspected, anyway—orange, cream, and black fabrics she'd laid out near her sewing table. Branwen specialized in disguises, and it wasn't hard to guess what she had in mind.

"I'm not sure—"

"Someone has to do something." She strode to the piles of fabrics and ran her fingers over one. "My back's feeling great now, and I'm tired of waiting for Uncle's miracle. Don't even try to stop me."

"I wouldn't." Some fights were lost ahead of time, and one look at Branwen's grim determination told Jaeger this counted as one of them. "You could, however, say that Diel's miracle is underway, although the use of 'miracle' in this instance may prove hyperbolic. There is a solution, risky as it may be, and your uncle would love to discuss it over breakfast."

Branwen's delighted squeal was another one of those sounds that always put Jaeger in a good mood. How fast her attitude had changed! Branwen might have prepared her own plan, but she clearly had never given up hope Diel would come through. She clapped her hands, then grabbed Jaeger's wrist. "Let's go. I want to hear it now!"

And just like that, she was pulling him through the Dathirii Tower, running toward her uncle's quarters. Relief untwisted Jaeger's stomach. He hated when Diel fought with the closest members of his family, and Branwen's enthusiasm washed his worry away. She'd never really lost her faith in him, even faced with the limits of his power. He stayed a few steps back as she burst through the office door. Diel was placing the forks near three full plates and barely had time to lift his head before she sprang into his arms and buried her face in his neck. Diel squeezed her tight, his gaze meeting Jaeger's over her shoulder.

"I'm sorry it took so long," he told his niece.

She nodded without pulling back, then whispered broken thanks. Jaeger didn't need to see to understand she was crying. Lord Arathiel Brasten hadn't stepped into the Dathirii tower yet, but as he watched Diel and Branwen's embrace, Jaeger already knew freeing him would be worth every subsequent problem.

CHAPTER TEN

OVER the course of the last two weeks, Yultes Dathirii had spent almost as much time in the Allastam Tower as in his own. People used to greet him with a smile, some even stopping to ask for news or trade tidings. As House Dathirii primary liaison with Lord Allastam and his family, Yultes had become a regular fixture. He knew everyone who mattered by name, maintained agreeable relationships with them, and facilitated dealings between members of their respective Houses. It was an art—a delicate balance between personal interactions, business opportunities, and the constant tempering of Diel's incessant flares of ethical conundrums.

It had gotten more difficult recently. The smiles had stiffened, then turned into outright scowls. Instead of greeting him, Allastam nobles huffed and avoided his gaze. The tension between the head of their House and Diel had trickled into the rest of the family, but today it achieved a new height. News of Lord Dathirii's visit with Arathiel and its purpose had reached Lord Allastam. Yultes waited for his audience, his stomach in knots, when Lord Allastam rushed out of his lush gardens and brutally moved their meeting forward. His stormy eyes found Yultes, and he pointed behind himself with his cane. "Get your bony elven ass in there, and pray you have enough honey on that tongue of yours to keep you safe."

Safe. Yultes rose with diligence, trying not to scramble. His mind had scattered at the threat. He had known without a doubt what had provoked Lord Allastam, and he'd yet to find convincing arguments to weather the hurricane Diel had stirred. Lord Allastam might have aged quickly—his gnarly hands clutched a cane, his shoulders hunched, and his hair greyed past his temples despite being in his early fifties—but he hadn't lost an ounce of wit, arrogance, or ambition. When he'd taken the mantle of Head of the House, the Allastams had trailed far in second place, well behind House Lorn in influence. Now, both families tied for first place, and Lord Allastam had crushed several houses on his climb to the top. Dread filled Yultes as he followed the powerful noble down the cobblestone pathway, under overgrown trees with dark blue leaves. How often had he pleaded for Diel not to provoke Lord Allastam and make their family a target? But why would Diel listen to Yultes' advice when he could champion a criminal and set the entire city against them?

"Milord, I will not defend his actions," he said.

"No?" Lord Allastam snorted and spun around to face Yultes. "Isn't that your only use? To grovel and plead forgiveness for your stepbrother's ill-advised decisions? Better get to work, Lord Yultes."

Yultes stiffened. His only use? Lord Allastam was taunting him, but the words stung nonetheless. Was that how everyone saw it? He'd done much more than placate Lord Allastam through the years. Surely Diel realized that. "Ill-advised or not, his decision was predictable."

"Trust Lord Dathirii to make mistakes? Or trust him to try and humiliate me?"

Mockery didn't surprise Yultes, but when Lord Allastam dropped his voice and continued, a chill ran up his spine. Prideful men didn't react well to perceived slights. Preventing Lord Allastam's ire at Arathiel's release was an impossible task, but if Yultes could convince him not to see it as a personal offence, he might avert a disaster.

"Trust him to go to extensive lengths to protect allies."

"Are the Brastens allies now? Have they not turned down your pathetic Coalition, same as every sensible noble in this city? Lady Brasten may have a softness in her heart, but she has more political sense than to side with your failing House."

Yultes gritted his teeth. By ally, he meant the High Priest Diel wanted to save, but he couldn't slip a word of it. It was a family secret—one Yultes doubted Diel had planned to tell him. He had badgered his stepbrother with questions until it spilled out. A team would soon set out under the cover of the night, led by Branwen, to save her imprisoned friend. With Arathiel in the group, Diel believed they could succeed. It wouldn't be worth the sacrifice in Yultes's opinion, but when had anyone ever listened to him besides

Hellion? Hellion and Brune, although Yultes wished the latter was false. She only cared for the secrets he was willing to trade to keep his own silent. She already knew about Arathiel. Yultes refused to betray Diel's trust twice and share the plan here, however, which meant he would never convince Lord Allastam this had nothing to do with the assassin's escape.

"House Brasten may have acknowledged Arathiel as their ancestor, but they didn't condone his actions. Arathiel himself, on the other hand, lived more than a century ago. Several of us had met him, and some called him a friend, Lord Dathirii among them."

Lord Allastam scoffed. In a quick movement, he threw his cane upward, grabbed it at the centre, then prodded Yultes' shoulder with the golden tip. They rarely stood so close to one another. "Tell your Lord Dathirii he should care more about whom he calls a friend. I'll summon him in forty-eight hours, and I expect this foolish behaviour to have stopped by then. Now get out!"

"You're wasting your time, milord. He won't—"

"Get. Out." Lord Allastam shoved him with his pommel, then turned on his heel and started down the pathway. "Your very presence angers me. Leave, and send my next audience in."

A dismissal as brutal as his demand to follow into the hall. Their meeting had lasted a handful of minutes, but it shook Yultes to the core. Had Allastam asked him to call someone else after? Like a servant? Yultes stared as the aged noble walked away, too shocked to move. He was a lord of this city, had been for over half his life now. He deserved to be treated better, even by those higher in power. Yet Yultes knew it would help no one if he argued, and that no amount of brandishing his Dathirii sigil brooch could erase the simple truth of his lowly bloodline. He had been proving his worth for almost a hundred fifty years now, but he had learned long ago it would never end. A single mistake would expose him—it had already landed him in Brune's unrelenting clutches, and it would get him kicked out of House Dathirii if he wasn't careful.

Yultes straightened with a huff, squared his shoulders, and strode out with as much pride as he could muster. Diel would never change his mind, but at least next time, he would have to face Lord Allastam and defend his decision.

WHENEVER Yultes stepped into Lord Hellion Dathirii's quarters, he simultaneously became more tense and more relaxed. Here, he didn't need to withhold his opinions on the often self-destructive behaviour of the rest of the family, and he could receive counsel from one who understood Isandor's politics. Over a century had passed since Hellion had forged a friendship with Yultes, guiding him as he wrestled with his new responsibilities as a Dathirii noble, and Yultes still turned to him for advice.

He had no one else, really. Others of his generation—Diel, Kellian, even Jaeger—went to Aunt Camilla, and the younger Dathirii either talked with her or Diel. Yultes couldn't, not anymore. They used to be close, he and Camilla, two elves poring over theoretical physics late into the night, until Diel inherited the mantle of Lord Dathirii … and named Jaeger as his right hand. So much had changed in that moment. Yultes had lost his future position, and his nascent relationships with most Dathirii had shattered through one fight or another. At least Hellion had seen his talents and encouraged him to persevere. He had understood his bitter disappointment at Jaeger's arrival and agreed Yultes should have inherited the position. He had always perceived his worth, even when doubts surged forward once more. Even when no one else did.

"Yultes!"

Hellion's smooth voice greeted him as he entered the expensively decorated living room, and in a swift motion, Hellion placed a full glass of wine between his hands. He moved with a grace that surpassed most elves', his silky golden hair flowing freely behind him, its colour richer than Yultes' dull, straw-coloured hair. As with everything between them, really. Where Hellion had deep green eyes, Yultes' were a pale blue, and instead of the other elf's delicate and angular traits, Yultes had hard prominent cheekbones that granted him a constant scowl. You could tell at a glance who was a full-bloodied Dathirii, and who had entered the family through marriage, a washed-out shadow of the other elves.

Yultes brought the wine to his lips and downed a large gulp of it as his friend guided him toward the thick sofa. The last two days had turned into an exhausting marathon of audiences and dinners, all in an attempt to calm Lord Allastam. No Allastam family member was willing to reach out to their leader, however. They either agreed with him or dared not confront him.

His only break from them had been the mandatory meeting

with Brune, and that had turned out more exhausting than any audience with Lord Allastam. He hated their dynamic. One month after Yultes had found Larryn and started funding the Shelter, she'd intercepted him on a Middle City bridge, striking up a casual conversation about the variety of origins of Lower City inhabitants and how amazingly resourceful some were when it came to *sheltering* others. He had frozen, his head buzzing, and she had set a hand on his back.

"You and I should talk," she had said. "I own a teahouse not far from here."

She had made two things very clear during that conversation. First, she knew every relevant detail of Larryn's origin, from his parentage to his mother's fate. Second, she would not hesitate to either reveal these secrets or wipe Larryn out of existence if he refused to answer her questions. From now on, she required him to inform her of every development in House Dathirii, failing which his son's life was forfeit.

Yultes would have endured the first consequence to protect Larryn, but if selling their secrets could save him from both threats … he hadn't hesitated. Every time they met, Brune badgered him with questions, dragging out details he'd meant to omit, mocking his attempts at subtlety until his last shred of dignity and energy had vanished. In comparison, Allastam's angry rants rolled off his back.

Yultes crumpled into the sofa as Hellion filled his own glass, humming a soft song, more cheerful than he had a right to be. Not the way everything was going. "Have you finally been kicked out of the Allastam Tower, or did you tire of catching the brunt of the abuse that should by all means be directed at our dear Lord Dathirii?"

"Both." Yultes sank further into his seat with a weary sigh. "They hinted I should disappear, and I no longer had the strength to hold on. I let go and left. Tomorrow marks the last day of Allastam's ultimatum, and our alliance with them."

"You should rest. Drink and stop working." Hellion motioned toward the wine with a steady smile, as if his suggestion wasn't utterly absurd. Yultes could not take a day off. He rarely did, and his presence in the Allastam Tower had become a necessity. If he could salvage even the tiniest part of this wreck … Hellion sensed his doubts, perceptive as ever. "You worry too much. Stop trying to save Diel from the consequence of his mistakes. He doesn't deserve your loyalty."

Yultes flushed and hid his unease by drinking more wine. He knew he should have abandoned his attempts to knock sense into his stepbrother a long time ago, but Diel remained Lord Dathirii, and his leader. House Dathirii had accepted him as a noble, and he already betrayed them to Brune. He refused to go even further. "This family does. I don't want it to sink."

"It won't." Hellion's tone brimmed with confidence and mirth, as if the very thought of House Dathirii failing amused him. "I'll say it again, Yultes: you worry too much. Take my friendly advice and forget about it. I guarantee House Dathirii won't collapse over this matter. We are old and resourceful beyond what humans imagine. Lord Allastam is nothing but a brief speck in our long existence."

Yultes did not think of himself as old, even though he was of an age with Hellion, and neither did he feel resourceful. Not tonight. If he had been, wouldn't he have found a way to placate Lord Allastam? To dodge Brune's clear blackmail about Larryn's paternity and safety? How he wished he had Hellion's easy trust in the future! But to him, living longer than humans only meant he had more time to make mistakes, and centuries to carry his burden.

He washed down his bitterness with more wine, emptying his glass. Perhaps Hellion had it right. He needed a break, no matter how small. Relentless pessimism was unlike him. Yultes extended his hand, asking in silence for a refill.

"As usual, I find myself agreeing with your counsel. I'm glad you're here to take care of me, my friend."

Hellion poured the wine with a grin. "Someone has to. You certainly don't."

And neither did anyone else in the family. Only a select few had made it into Diel's inner circle, and Yultes' spot had been taken by Jaeger. Sure, Diel reached out to the twenty or so Dathirii elves living within the Tower, but they all understood whom he actually listened to. And neither Diel, his close guards, nor the rest of the family truly cared for him. As if they could sense he wasn't worthy of them. Hellion must have realized that, too, but he had never let it drive him away. Without him, Yultes would be alone.

CHAPTER ELEVEN

HASRYAN flung another book aside with an exasperated sigh. How many of these had he tried to read? Ten? Twenty? Camilla brought one novel after another from the Dathirii library, but none of them caught his attention. Why would he care about powerful tales of love? They seemed so distant, so fake. These stories were reserved for others, for people unlike him, who knew trust and romance. Sure, his life had been an adventure of sorts, riddled with murder and betrayals, but what good had really come out of it? He was stuck in these tiny quarters with an old lady convinced he was a wild wounded animal that could be tamed with butterscotch cookies.

Hasryan sighed and pulled the nearby curtains apart to look out the window. A thick snow fell outside, covering the bridges and obscuring his sight. A handful of Isandor's lawful citizens went about their business despite the wintry weather, free to do as they pleased while he was trapped. His leg was getting better, but even once healed, Hasryan had no idea where else he would head. Taking tea with Camilla would always remain preferable to freezing to death or being captured. If Hasryan left, he would be alone again.

"Would you like to go out?"

He shivered at Camilla's question. Sometimes, he wondered if she could read his mind. He *had* been staring at the falling snow, so perhaps you only needed a little perceptiveness to follow his train of thought. Hasryan released the curtains and turned. She stood in the doorway, her pale winter cloak already thrown over her shoulders.

"Life's never about what I want," he said.

"It could be, for once." She smiled at him, and Hasryan waited for her miraculous explanation. "I drop by Esmera's place today. She's an old girlfriend of mine, and she'd love the company while I clean her house."

Camilla regularly spent a few hours with Isandor's aging humans. One half social calls, one half cleaning services, her visits helped them care for their pets, homes, lives—whatever they required. But while Camilla often referred to them as good acquaintances or even friends, she'd never mentioned a romantic involvement before. Hasryan perked up, unable to imagine the dignified old lady in the middle of passionate kissing, and confused about the nature of Camilla's proposition. It was almost cruel for her to offer. She knew he couldn't stand lying low and hidden, but neither could he risk showing up at a random lady's house.

"I don't think the local assassin is the best company for her."

Camilla laughed, and not a hint of doubt sipped through her

mirth. "You'd be surprised. Esmera does not deal in tea and butterscotch, though she has a knack for brewing."

"Brewing," he repeated. Her tone indicated something darker and deadlier than beer.

"Indeed." Camilla's eyes shone with an intensity that confounded Hasryan and made him wonder about what lay in her past. He'd been so caught up in the flowery curtains, the tea, and her kindness that he'd never considered what it took to welcome an assassin into your quarters without flinching. He'd always assumed she believed he hadn't committed any crimes, but now …

"I still can't trust her," he said.

"Can you trust anyone, really?"

Hasryan froze. No, he thought. He couldn't. They could all turn on him and sell him out to Brune or Isandor's guards. So many had betrayed and abandoned him already! But not everyone, not quite. "I can trust Arathiel," he said, and with wariness creeping in his voice, he added, "I want to trust you."

"You can." She stepped forward, her expression softening back into the kind old lady's. Hasryan couldn't forget the glimpse into a wilder past, however, nor did he have any desire to. "Don't stay here. Esmera knows what confinement and pursuit are like. The two of you have common enemies, and you know what they say about the enemies of your enemies …"

"I know it's a shit saying that's never applied to me," Hasryan countered with a scoff, but he lumbered to his feet nonetheless, ignoring the painful pull in his leg. He had needed to leave the quarters, and he doubted another similar opportunity would present itself. Hasryan buried his worry under a smirk. "I'm coming, though. What's the worst that could happen, after all? It's not like the entire city wants to put a noose around my neck!"

"Wonderful!" Camilla clapped her hands, and warmth spread through Hasryan at her genuine pleasure.

"Do promise me one thing." He tried to keep his tone level and serious despite his mood shifting back into something more playful. "Don't turn this into the motive for a dramatic break up or something."

Camilla's laugh echoed through the living room, clear and melodious. Hasryan loved it more than the home-baked cookies or calming tea. He'd missed being the source of real amusement. Brune always stayed serious, and Sora had found his humour inappropriate at best.

"We haven't been together for years, Hasryan. I think we're well past 'dramatic break up.'" She opened a small closet near the outside exit. "I just fixed one of my grandson's winter outfits, and he's just a tad taller than you. Take it. With the heavy snow, you should be able to conceal yourself."

Camilla pulled out a fashionable coat, double-lined with fur inside. The outfit was a dark red with black stripes, and two lines of large silver buttons ran down the front. Hasryan pressed his lips together, uncertain he wanted to wear someone's else clothes, never mind ones so expensive. Camilla didn't give him a choice. The moment he extended a hesitant hand, she slipped the sleeve up his forearm, then walked around and lifted his second arm to put on the rest of the coat. Hasryan froze, too surprised to protest. He stared ahead in stunned silence as she buttoned the front, folded the collar down, then smoothed the jacket over his chest. Her proud smile when she stepped back frightened him.

"You look fantastic," she said.

"That's great!" He didn't even try to hide his bitterness. The way she had casually dressed him up had shaken Hasryan, and he needed her to back off. "Maybe once everyone sees how handsome the dark elven assassin is, they won't want to hang him!"

Camilla set her hand on his arm and squeezed it. "No one will hang you. Not while I'm here."

Nice words, but what could she do? She already hid him from the city guards, and had treated his wounded leg. If he was caught, not even her title would save him. Yet her willingness to try triggered a warmth at the bottom of his stomach. Hasryan attempted to quell the feeling before he allowed himself to become too fond of Camilla, but it persisted.

"Let's go."

He forced the words past the lump in his throat and moved to the door leading outside, stopping only to grab a hooded cloak from the wardrobe. He'd spent so much of the last days in sullen silence, doing his best to avoid communication with the elven lady. Any form of relationship was too risky. He didn't think he could endure another let down, like Cal's absence or Larryn's turnabout. Better to be a little rude and keep his distance. Yet the desire to explain himself and please her grew with every passing day, and Hasryan wondered if it didn't scare him even more than a rope around his neck.

⁂

FREEZING rain had fallen during the night, icing over Isandor's bridges. Hasryan kept his cowl down and his knees bent for balance as he followed Camilla into the city. He was glad for the curtain of heavy snow, obscuring sight and muffling his footsteps. Hasryan knew himself too remarkable to melt into a crowd—obsidian skin and thick white hair contrasted even with the various shades of brown common in Allorian folks. When he needed to go unnoticed, he tended to dash around the smaller bridges, sometimes leaping from one to another or climbing down the towers' walls. Everything was far too slippery today, however, forcing him to stick close to Camilla and hope for the best.

The elven lady maintained a brisk pace despite the conditions. A stylized beige hat kept the snow out of her hair, curled on one side with violet flowers spilling from the cup, and she carried a matching bag. She hummed a soft melody as they progressed through the city, and despite knowing it changed nothing none of the ridiculous risks of this escapade, it appeased Hasryan's nerves—which in turn made him angry at himself. It was just a song from an old lady! He couldn't allow these things to lower his guard.

When Camilla stopped in front of a door in the Middle City, Hasryan eased out a sigh. He might have enjoyed the muffling weather if his life hadn't been on the line. An aged voice called for them to enter, and Lady Camilla pushed the door open. Hasryan slipped in after her, tiny knots tying his stomach as he realized it might not be safer inside at all.

Esmera sat in a swinging chair in the middle of her living room, knitting needles on her lap. An almost complete scarf flowed down along her small legs and to the ground. Her sinewy body couldn't measure more than five feet, and the massive chair made her seem minuscule. Pale clumps of frizzy hair framed a sharp, wrinkled face, and moles spread across her brown skin. Most remarkable were her eyes, however. Or rather, the deep grey stone covering them, emerging from Esmera's temples as if fused with them and making her effectively blind.

Hasryan's mouth turned to ashes, although only in part because of the shocking sight. Its familiarity freaked him out more than anything. The first time he'd met Brune, almost a dozen years ago in Nal-Gresh, she had used this very tactic on a rival mercenary.

Common enemies, Camilla had said.

"You're late," Esmera declared, her voice a rattling of bones.

Camilla smiled at the reproach. "I brought company."

Hasryan wanted to vanish through the floor. The longer he stared at Esmera, the more he recognized her. His instincts flared in alarm—they had met before, he knew, in less than friendly circumstances. His mind scrambled to guess when and how, and he stepped back, ready to bolt.

"Oh yes, I heard the sneaky boots. Can he talk? Did no one ever teach him basic courtesy?"

Camilla laughed, but a glance at Hasryan killed her mirth. His panic must have shown. He swallowed hard, and although he feared she'd recognize his voice, he blurted out, "I can speak just fine!"

"Then it's about time you did, young man." Esmera's fingers

wrapped around her needles with a frown. "Why don't you introduce yourself like a proper guest?"

"Sorry. I'm …" He stopped. He couldn't give his real name! Not with so much of Isandor after his head, and even less to someone he might have antagonized in the past. He needed a replacement, and fast. Something credible, something natural. "Larryn."

Great. Esmera probably hadn't heard of Larryn's Shelter, but Hasryan couldn't have picked a more painful reminder of the friends he'd lost. He closed his eyes with an internal swear—not that he could do anything about it now.

"Well, welcome to my tiny home, Larryn. Come on in and keep me entertained while my servant cleans."

This drew another sharp laugh from Camilla. She gathered a bucket, some clothes, soap, and something weird with an acrid smell. Hasryan watched Camilla redo her hair, and only now noticed her robes were made of thick linen rather than silk. She pumped water into her bucket, and Hasryan looked away. It felt too strange. She was Lady Camilla Dathirii, matriarch of the noble elven house, probably the oldest citizen in Isandor … and she was preparing to clean someone else's home. Ex-girlfriend or not, the complete contradiction with expected roles set him even further on edge. He wished he had something *normal* to help him get his bearings, yet Camilla always managed to both surprise him and reassure him. He reminded himself he'd never seen a servant in Camilla's quarters except to bring the hot water for baths. Perhaps she enjoyed tidying up her place and others'.

"What are you waiting for?" Esmera asked, snapping him out of his contemplation. "I don't have all day."

"Yeah, you do, actually." Hasryan dragged a chair closer and sat down, fighting his wary nerves every step of the way. Esmera's constant scolding might have intimidated others, but Hasryan was too used to disparaging comments to let it get to him. He could deal with that as long as she didn't recognize him. "I'm afraid your wits form a dangerous weapon. You're grounded here for the day."

She laughed, a rich cackle that emerged from the deepest part of her stomach. Hasryan loved the sound immediately, and it washed away a chunk of his stress. It had something honest and vicious that contrasted with Lady Camilla's soft and enveloping chuckles. One of these ladies gave you tea and cookies while the other insulted you for acts of standard politeness. Dealing with both of them together would become an experience in constant destabilization.

"So apart from reminding me what a useless sack of bones I am, what are you skilled at?"

Thoughts of his past crimes flitted through Hasryan's mind, and he almost blurted out, 'sneaking and killing.' The words stuck in his throat, and he tried to chase them and focus on innocuous conversation. Camilla couldn't fill the silence while he raked his brain for an answer. She'd vanished into a nearby room, leaving him to his own devices. What else was he good at, though? Losing friends? His presence often bothered others, and Hasryan enjoyed playing with their unwarranted fear. Which almost always led to the same dangerous conclusion.

"I'm good at getting in trouble," he said.

"Are you?" She leaned forward, tilting her head so she could hear him better, as Larryn so often did. The familiarity sent spikes of longing through Hasryan. Her tone lacked any surprise, and worry needled at him. "Sounds like you'll have a lot of stories to tell today, then."

Hasryan hesitated. He wished she would talk instead, so he could place her. He'd worked with Brune in Isandor for a decade but hadn't often dealt with older folks. Brewing, Camilla had said. And it hit him like a thunderclap. She'd had deep-set, rich brown eyes, nimble fingers manipulating vials and herbs with ease. Only a few stragglers had resisted the Crescent Moon's swift rise through Isandor's lower life anymore. *The Blue Lips*, everyone had called her shop, and if Esmera had still worn the makeup that had earned her the name, Hasryan would have known instantly. Brune had sent him to threaten her, hoping to scare the old poison maker into submission. She'd cackled at him back then, too. If the stones in her eye sockets were any indication, Brune hadn't taken kindly to her refusal.

Hasryan let out a slow breath. He had pressed a blade—the very magical dagger over which Brune had him arrested and framed for Lady Allastam's murder—to Esmera's throat. She must not have fond memories of him. Now that he knew, however, he felt calmer, more in control. A lot of his adventures might involve screwing up early assassinations or the subsequent escape, but Hasryan found one more innocuous.

"I guess there were those pies I stole as a kid." He'd been starving and desperate to eat. Anything could have done the trick, but he'd rarely smelled something so delicious. "I think I was nine?"

"Don't ask me. You're the one who knows."

"Let's say nine." Time had grown fuzzy in those years, and Hasryan hadn't cared to count. Old enough to have killed, old enough not to bother. He'd traced back the years in his life only later, after he'd caught Brune's attention. "There was this cook—I think they were in training? Because they put three to four pies to cool on the windowsill every day. So I stole them. My stomach hurt, and I figured no one ate that many. They wouldn't be missed. How naive."

Deadly mistakes had riddled his first years alone, and it was a miracle Hasryan had survived. He'd stopped counting the narrow escapes and last-minute bids for freedom. Inexperience and gullibility had almost killed his child self several times, but his age had also saved him. People had constantly underestimated him. No one expected a kid to stab them, dark elven ancestry or not.

"Pie thievery is a horrible crime," Esmera said, with a touch of sarcasm. "I assume you were punished."

"The cook poisoned the next batch. I became so nauseous I couldn't stand. Then the first hallucinations came. I didn't understand, had no concepts of figments of imagination. Shadow monsters crawled into my vision, and I tried to outrun them, only to fall and vomit and roll over. I clung to the pie and hid and ate more, stuffing myself. My mother laughed in the background, and I kept eating. I was so hungry! And maybe if I ate enough I would feel better, and the deep chants ringing in my ears would vanish." He still heard them, loud and clear, from so many tall figures around him, towering, blocking out the sun and any hope of love. His mother no longer laughed. Hasryan fell silent—or had he been silent for a while now? Esmera stared at him, and Camilla hovered at the edge of the room. Reflexively, he reached for his neck and the thin scar running across it. Hasryan's history of pressing daggers at others' throats had started with one at his own. He coughed. "Anyway. They weren't fun hallucinations."

"Clever cook, though."

Hasryan forced himself to chuckle, as if mirth could evaporate the cold sweat on his back. He should've picked another story, but he had half-forgotten the consequences of his poisoning until he'd reached them. At least Esmera didn't press the issue, latching instead on the excellent administration of poison.

"I learned a valuable lesson on the dangers of routine."

"Seems like you've been getting into trouble for a long time," Esmera said.

"Yeah. Lots of misadventures."

His gaze met Camilla's—that's how he had called the scars, a few days ago, standing in underwear in her living room. She offered a sad smile, but no comment. None now, anyway. The piercing blue eyes held all the worry and determination in the world, and he wouldn't escape her. He wasn't sure he even wanted to.

"Then by all means," Esmera said, "tell me more."

Hasryan launched into another tale, choosing a far less personal one. Esmera stopped him every now and then, most often to pinpoint the exact moment he'd messed up. It amused her, how his urge to sling witty retorts frequently screwed him over. The way she laughed, however, he could guess she'd had her own share of problems due to talking back. Encouraged, Hasryan revealed some of his worst mistakes, and before long, he'd told a dozen short anecdotes, his voice punctuated by the tapping of knitting needles. When Camilla finished her work, she sat with them and listened with intent. Esmera noticed she no longer moved about the house and frowned.

"Over already? I can go and spill something if I must."

"Please don't," Camilla said with a laugh. "We can stay."

Esmera dismissed her with a gesture then put her hand on Hasryan's. He raised his head, surprised at the precision of her movement.

"There's still a story I'd like to hear." Before she even continued, Hasryan detected a new sharpness in her tone, a hard edge that doomed him. "The one about intimidating old alchemists for a less-than-loyal boss."

"You say that like it worked." His answer sprang out, shattering any caution, any chance at denial. His own daring stunned him. Hasryan froze, his ears ringing, until Esmera's laughter broke his trance. "That's how you reacted back then, too. You laughed."

"What else should I have done? You walked in there like the very sight of you should make me quake and piss myself." She snorted. "Should've seen yourself, kid."

Most people *did* freak out when he strode into a room. She hadn't—not back then, and not today. When had she recognized him? Hasryan reviewed most of the afternoon, trying to pinpoint a shift in her attitude, but he found nothing. Had she known from the very start and waited to trap him? His mouth dried. He could outrun them, escape. The steady click of her needles together kept him rooted to his chair, and his voice hushed to meet their softness.

"I killed people," he said. "I would have killed you if that had been my order. You should have been scared."

The needles stopped. Esmera turned his way, lowering her work. "Perhaps, but it's not in my nature. I have an underdeveloped flight reflex, much like you. I prefer to stay and fight, even if it's just through words. Even when the price is high."

At first, Hasryan didn't understand why she would say "like you." He bailed out all the time, unable to summon the courage to approach others. And yet he'd come here, hadn't he? He had stayed even after recognizing Esmera, despite risking her anger. And he refused to flee Isandor itself and start his life over, alone once more, with no guarantee he'd fare any better.

"Brune made you pay, didn't she? I know that technique."

Esmera nodded. "She won. I could have kept going, learning to brew without my eyes, serving customers in secret or even with my shop still open. A part of me wanted to fight, out of pride and stubbornness, to the bitter end if need be. I restrained myself. Too old for such things, perhaps." She scoffed, and Hasryan knew she didn't believe her own words. "Mostly, I didn't think it was worth it. Let Brune rule as a queen over the Lower City. I'd had my good years, and I wanted to escape it—to do something new! So I called my favourite servant girl, got settled up here, and learned to knit. It's fun, you should try it."

"I don't plan on retiring," Hasryan replied with half a laugh. Perhaps he should. Wouldn't it be simpler? Let Brune win and leave the city. But he couldn't give up the life he'd had here yet.

"Your choice," she said, and she obviously agreed with it. "That's the thing, isn't it? You decide what you do, just as I chose to retire and learn different skills. I hope you kick her ass."

Hasryan smirked. He couldn't—Brune wielded magic with terrifying ease, and she could always sense him behind her—but he basked in the heart-warming dream. "Pay me in scarves and mitts, and I just might."

Esmera cackled, wrinkles lightening as a grin broke her face. She finished a row, and as she started the next, she began casting off her work. "Half before and half after, isn't it? Your payment is incoming."

Hasryan stared at the moving needles, slipping in and out of the thread, and with every new stitch off the long wooden stick, his chest tightened a little more. It had been a joke. Did Esmera ...? He turned to Camilla, and her soft smile was as unrevealing as Brune's grimaces.

"I didn't mean it seriously," he said.

"Take the scarf anyway." Her job finished, she reached for the scissors behind them and snapped the last thread off. "I've got tons of them, and I don't go out that much."

Esmera flung it at Hasryan without waiting for his answer. He ran his fingers over the thick wool, in awe at the neat rows and the rich red colour. He'd never owned anything so comfy. Hasryan twisted it around his fingers with a happy sigh.

"Thank you." He shouldn't trust her. Experience had taught him not to rely on his instincts. Brune had betrayed him; Larryn had abandoned him. Clearly, he was a bad judge of character. Why wouldn't this old enemy sell him out? Yet Hasryan refused to give up, to assume the worst and leave Isandor. That, too, would be letting Brune win. Hasryan stood, his throat thick with emotion. "We have to go, but I'll return. Someday, I'll be back with more stories."

"They all say that, my boy."

"I will." A smirk split his face. "Whether or not you're still alive by then is up to you, though."

She laughed, and Hasryan allowed the cackle to warm his heart one last time. He and Camilla headed for the door, and as they stepped out, Esmera called out to him.

"You'd better get in plenty of trouble!"

Hasryan chuckled. A cold wind had risen, and it blew through the opening, snowflakes spinning around him and into the room. "Don't worry. There will always be more where that came from."

Unless, of course, one of the several folks intent on killing him finally succeeded. That prospect didn't scare him as much anymore. He still would've chosen this. Chosen to trust Camilla and Esmera, chosen to stay in his city—his home—and believe he could find his place in Isandor again.

HASRYAN shed the classy winter cloak as soon as he stepped inside, flinging it on a nearby chair before removing his boots. Camilla had tried to initiate several conversations on their way back, but he had cut all of them short. His mind reeled from what he had admitted in front of her. She'd taken him in because Arathiel believed in his innocence, and no one would now. Not to mention everything he'd let slip about his mother and his past …

He had chosen to stay and trust these old ladies, but would Camilla even allow him? He wanted to believe in her, but where had that led him in the past? Brune, Larryn, and Cal had all let him down, each in their own way. Hasryan tried to reason with himself—to cling to Camilla's calm, to the concern in her voice when she had uttered his name on their way back—but panic swirled inside despite his best attempts. Everyone had always left. She would too. He just knew she would.

Hasryan ran a hand through his hair to shake away the snow while Camilla removed her gloves, hat, and coat. He knew what to expect from old ladies whose days were filled with hot baths, delicious food, and stories about the power of love. They never had the perspective to accept sometimes you couldn't save everyone— that some lives managed to continue only by cutting others short. Camilla might have had comfort and family, but he'd always been surrounded by death and betrayal. This respite in Camilla's warm quarters had lasted longer than it should have. He was only glad he'd had it.

"I'll get what little I have and go."

Camilla's bony fingers grabbed his shoulders before he could move. She forced him to turn, and her blue eyes pierced him, nailing him to the floor.

"Don't be ridiculous, Hasryan."

His heart clenched. Was he ridiculous? He wanted to believe in her gentle grip and tone, in the hope blossoming in his chest. He shouldn't. Hasryan stared at his feet. "It's okay," he lied. "I understand."

"I don't think you do," she said, and kindness filled her voice. She lifted his chin to stop him from looking down, and he found himself unable to glance away from the intense sadness in her eyes. The undeniable care for him. Hasryan's insides melted; his composure and drive to leave vanished. She did not want him to go at all.

"You're a fine young man, Hasryan. Plenty of people out there are ready to judge and condemn you, and I won't be one of them. You deserve someone to help you—someone who will listen, no matter what. Especially if you need to talk about your mother's laugh, the strange chants, or the line at your neck."

Her finger trailed his thin scar, and his head spun. Hasryan choked down a sudden sob and stumbled backward. Away from her, and away from the gentle affection.

"I ... I can't."

The throaty hymns of his mother's cult filled his mind. His breath turned into a long wheeze, and black spots crawled into his vision. The ground shifted under him, and he reached for his neck with a whimper. He shouldn't have talked about the pies and brought these memories back to life. Now they clung, closer and realer than ever before. Hasryan struggled to clear his mind, to see past the circle of adults intent on sacrificing him. He hated the panic paralyzing him, keeping his lungs shut and stabbing at his heart.

A cool hand picked up his own, removing it from his scar and squeezing it. Camilla's soft voice whispered his name and wrinkled fingers brushed away his tears. He sobbed, and she pulled him close, running a hand through his hair.

"It's over," she said. "You're with me now."

Over. No more betrayals, no more attacks, no more solitude. Camilla's frail arms would keep it all away. Or so she promised. The memories still hovered at the back of his mind, threatening to surge forward, but he clung to her robe and the scent of lilac and acrid soap. Those chants were in the past, and his future could be different. He had to believe that. Hasryan rested his forehead against her shoulder, shaking.

"It won't go away. I … I tried to lock it all away, but it always comes back." He wished he could control himself—wished he'd outgrown this. Maybe he never would. Maybe the nausea and flashbacks would always lie in wait.

"If you want to talk about it …"

"No." Even trying to put words to the events squeezed his chest with pain. He couldn't talk about it. Not now, and perhaps never. "You don't happen to have any of those cookies left, do you?"

Camilla laughed, then caressed his cheek. He flushed at the touch, torn between his natural urge to flee and his desire for more. He was so desperate to nestle in her arms and believe in this. It might kill him—lead straight to his death—but he couldn't help himself.

"I'm afraid not," she said, "but we can make more together."

Hasryan nodded and followed her to the kitchen. His

movements were dazed and uncertain. Were the last minutes real? His cheek still tingled from her touch, a reminder of her inexplicable care. Like … motherly love. A completely foreign feeling. Hasryan wiped more tears away, cursing himself. Why was he crying again? He needed to stop. But Camilla knew about the assassinations, she knew he'd killed others, and she'd still held him in her arms. He dried his eyes, clinging to that thought, and flipped through her notebook for the recipe she no doubt knew by heart. They were going to make the best cookies ever.

CHAPTER TWELVE

NEVIAN had believed he would regret giving in to Efua's demands, but the young girl proved as fast a learner as she'd promised. Every meal, he spent a little less than an hour on her letters, after which she stayed and sat on his bed with a small book, reading aloud and struggling with the sounds on her own. She became better with each passing day—enough to make Nevian a little jealous of her progress. At least he'd managed some, too. He had found the simplest spell in his tome and tried it out in front of Efua. Just a tiny ball of light—the kind Isra conjured all the time to show off—but the girl had clapped her hands and laughed.

"Please, Mister Nevian, promise you'll teach me magic!"

His fingers tingled as power coursed through them, the light floating above them, and his chest had threatened to burst from hope. His magic hadn't vanished. It was forgotten, hard to reach, but still within him—accessible. Light-headed, excited, he'd almost agreed to Efua's request. How much time would he have to dedicate to her then, though? And what if Avenazar found him again? Anyone close to Nevian risked retribution. He shouldn't make promises.

"If you learn to read and write fast enough, we might still have meals left together," he had said.

Since then, the number of hours she spent in his room had doubled. Nevian no longer minded. She didn't make a lot of noise, and only bothered him when he ate.

Unlike a certain halfling, who brought a complete questionnaire every time he visited. Once, Nevian had suggested to Vellien they should order Cal to give him some peace, but the young healer had laughed and waved the idea off. "It's still good for you. Endure and you'll progress faster, I promise."

Nevian would have scoffed at the advice if it had come from anyone else, but Vellien had yet to let him down. Their visit boosted Nevian's energy, calmed his throbbing headaches, and left him with the growing hope he would make it through this ordeal intact.

Accepting Cal's help was harder. The halfling had saved him, however, so in order to express his gratitude, Nevian endured the endless enquiries without a word … literally. He sat through them, studying rather than answering, sometimes grunting vaguely. Efua had told him it was impolite once, and he had shrugged. He didn't care, or rather, he didn't want to. Deep inside, despite his progress with Vellien, he believed Master Avenazar would return to finish what he'd started. The less attached Nevian grew to the Shelter's inhabitants, the better.

Efua made it difficult. Nevian had never encountered such a perfect study partner. Cal had been easier to ignore until he had come into his room with a brand new proposition. He had climbed into the bed next to Nevian's desk with a proud grin.

"Nevian, I have found a paradise for you, and today we're paying it a visit. It's full of books! Tons and tons piled together and threatening to fall down on everyone. There's so many it's almost impossible to walk around the shop, and they have an entire section on magic. A tiny section, but a section!"

Nevian's breath had caught in his throat, and his head had turned slowly toward Cal. He craved new books, but a cold sweat ran down his spine at the very thought of leaving his room. What if Avenazar was right outside the Shelter? Or a Myrian spy? He touched his forearm, imagining the pain waiting to ambush him beyond the crumbling planks of the walls.

"I can't pay for books," Nevian said.

"I can. Let me."

"No."

Cal crossed his arms and raised his chin in defiance. "You can't live forever cloistered in the Shelter. It's not far, I promise, and I won't leave without you."

"Okay. Fine."

A glimmer of hope flashed across Cal's face until Nevian returned his attention to the tome before him. He owed him too much already, and an escapade into a bookstore would only make matters worse. It might make Nevian like him. He didn't need new friends; he needed to restore his magical skills. He had a plan, and it didn't involve getting tied down. With solid spells, he might be able to land small casting contracts, save enough coin and leave Isandor for somewhere safer.

"You're being stubborn," Cal said.

"I am."

Was that supposed to insult him? Without persistence, he would never have progressed through life. He would be nothing, even more so than his almost-magicless self.

"And you're being ridiculous," Cal continued.

"I am not."

"Yes, you are!" Cal put his chubby hand on Nevian's page to stop him from reading. "I'm offering you free books. They'll help with your magic stuff."

"I don't want free books. I want to be left alone."

"What if you could have both?"

A mischievous smile spread across Cal's features, warning Nevian not to ask. Peace was too tempting a prize to dodge the obvious trap, however. How much could he learn if he didn't have to endure Cal for a while? He should at least consider the opportunity.

"Go on."

"Come to the bookstore with me, and I'll leave you alone for a whole week."

A whole week. Cal said it like seven days were a huge break. Nevian's mouth quirked. Judging by how desperate to string him along Cal sounded, he could negotiate better than that. "Two."

"Two what?"

"Two weeks."

Cal pouted. "You're no fun."

Nevian shrugged. Indeed, he was no fun. As with stubbornness, he considered it a primary reason for his survival. He'd rarely had the luxury of fun. The same was true of this little outing to the store: if it didn't help him along, then he couldn't afford it. Nor could he muster the courage for it. Silence stretched between them until Cal threw his arms upward. "Fine! Two weeks."

A thin smile curved Nevian's lips. He set his bookmark down, closed the tome in front of him, and straightened. Nevian towered over Cal, who intensified the height difference by jumping off the bed. Most halflings managed to grow past three feet, but Cal never had, and he seemed minuscule compared to Nevian's tall and lanky frame. Size meant little, however. Avenazar's meagre five feet contained more power than Nevian would ever wield, and Cal had amply proven his overbearing generosity and kindness with his endless questions.

"Let's get it over with," Nevian muttered.

Despite the obvious lack of enthusiasm, Cal grinned. "It'll be great, you'll see!"

Nevian withheld his deep doubts as he slipped on an ill-suited coat and raised the hood over his head. He'd snorted when Larryn had brought it, asking him if he'd found the bare threaded rag at the bottom of Isandor's shitslides. Larryn's dead serious affirmative answer worried him, but Nevian had figured those slides should only carry human refuse to the Reonne River, not clothes. Larryn must have been mocking him. Surely he wouldn't give Nevian a coat once covered in piss! Yet as he sniffed it, Nevian couldn't help but wonder.

Cal led the way out, an obvious skip in his step. Nevian followed, confused about why his companion was so pleased to spend his day with the grumpiest person in the neighbourhood. Didn't he have any better friends? Efua had mentioned a fight with Larryn, so perhaps that was it. Or perhaps he just enjoyed rubbing Nevian the wrong way. Whatever the reason, Nevian had bought himself two whole weeks of peace. With a smile, he stepped out into the snowy weather.

"BOOKSTORE" wasn't how Nevian would have described the minuscule structure Cal brought him to. "Book dumping ground" would be more accurate. They rose in swinging piles all the way to the ceiling, the shambling towers leaning into each other and threatening to collapse upon any poor soul who nudged them. Two narrow alleys snaked through the stacks, meeting at a counter in the back. Dust filled the air, along with the musty scent of old pages and ink. Nevian breathed in deeply as he stepped inside, closing his eyes to enjoy the familiar and comforting smell. Cal chuckled at his reaction, then walked off, but Nevian lingered at the entrance. Although he had been a ball of tightly-wound nerves outside, here his mind turned to the knowledge surrounding him, leaving Avenazar behind. He exhaled, slowly letting out some of his stress before ignoring the knots remaining in his stomach and starting his way through the columns of books.

These climbed so high that Nevian had to crane his neck to see the titles despite his considerable height. He tried to get a sense of the organization around, but would such a mess have one? The deeper he progressed into the store, the more he doubted anything but chance had put these books where they waited. How could he ever find something interesting in this chaos? Some of these books didn't even have a cover! He walked farther into the shop, frustrated, until his eyes caught a cute illustration resting at the top of a distant pile. Nevian approached, his smile widening as he confirmed his initial impression: a kids' story.

He leaned over the tomes with enthusiasm, bracing his left hand on a fairly low pyramid as he reached for the small book. Nevian had to stretch his long arm to its very limit before the tip of his fingers touched the spine and he pulled it back. Victorious warmth displaced the cold fear in his stomach as he flipped through the drawings of a cat living among Isandor's spires. This might be above Efua's reading level still, but he knew she would manage it anyway. He slammed the book shut with more than a little pride.

Nevian hurried along, eager to show Cal, but he found the magic section long before he spotted his halfling companion. Easy to notice it: all the strangest tomes had been thrown into a pile. One leather cover glowed softly, another had arcane runes on top, and a third seemed made of solidified fog. Not to mention the one oozing a suspicious substance, which he had no desire to touch. Nevian dug into the tomes, scanning their forewords and a few random pages to get a sense of tone and content. He created two piles of his own, separating the simpler theories within his reach and leaving the difficult treaties for later. He'd be back for advanced lessons and essays. One day, he would become a mage powerful enough to cast every spell in these pages.

"All right, magic tomes!"

The jovial voice interrupted his search for the perfect book—a voice he knew too well and dreaded almost as much as Avenazar's. Nevian stopped breathing. Isra's exclamations had come from right behind him, and she must have spotted the eclectic tomes from a distance. Panic drowned his thoughts, and the edges of his vision darkened as he stared at his fingers, hoping, praying he'd imagined it. It couldn't be her. Why would she be in this store, of all places? But Isra loved to brave the Lower City and shop in obscure locations. The thrill of discovery and danger, or some other nonsense explanation. And if she stood close enough to notice the books, she was bound to recognize him—there would be no mistaking him for Varden this time.

"Nevian?" she asked.

Nevian jerked up at his name, whirling around to face her. She repeated it, her expression lightening with surprise and … joy? The fear returned to Nevian's stomach in a heavy lump. He needed to run. Now. He couldn't defend himself; all he'd learned again was one inoffensive spell! He stretched backwards and cringed as his fingers sank into the oozy tome, but he flung it at Isra. She cried out and scrambled out of the way, falling into the mountains of books. Dizzy, terror stealing his breath, Nevian sprinted past her. She reached out, and he slapped her hand with the kids' story.

Cal skidded into his path not long before Nevian arrived at the exit. Was he trying to block passage? Why would he—a trap! It explained Isra's presence. He should have known. Why would Cal insist on this outing? Why stay so nice despite the wall of silence Nevian had erected since the first day? A lump clogged his throat and a thousand insults rushed through his mind, some for Cal, but most at his own naivety.

"Nevian, are you—"

Nevian didn't give Cal a chance to finish. He barrelled into a nearby tower of books, pushing them down on the halfling. Cal exclaimed in confusion as heavy tomes buried him, and Nevian leaped past him, his long legs compensating for his crappy athletic skills. Then he was out. Outrunning Cal now would be easy; he had the tiniest legs. Isra was another matter.

A light snow covered the ground outside, and he almost slipped as he dashed down a flight of stairs. A powerful squawk warned him of Isra's close pursuit, her bird form unhindered by the recent weather. Nevian swore and ran faster, but the hawk swooshed over his shoulder. He skidded to a stop as Isra landed in front of him, her claws lengthening into legs and feet, her wings retracting into a rapidly-enlarging body. For a split second, there was a mass of brown hair through the feathers, but it vanished as her human form became more distinct: a thin blonde girl with bright blue eyes. Isra stood with her hands on her hips, lips pinched into a disapproving frown.

"Stop running, I'm not going to attack!" Blonde strands blocked her sight, and she flicked them away. "I'm glad you're alive, Nev Nev. Master Avenazar told everyone he'd killed you. Horribly."

"He did?" Relief crashed through his body, turning his legs into wool. Nevian bent, hands on his knees, trying to recover his breath. His lungs burned from the run, and his mind spun with the potential meaning of Avenazar's story. If Avenazar thought Nevian dead, he wouldn't hunt him.

"Yeah!" Isra said. "You have to tell me how you faked death!"

"I didn't." Did she believe he'd built an elaborate escape plan? "I threw myself off the bridge."

Isra stared at him, blinking, her mouth a perfect little circle. Then she laughed. "You look fine for someone who plunged. Come on, Nevian, won't you tell me the truth?"

His relief drained out of him, leaving a hollow disbelief. Isra never listened. No matter what he said, she'd only believe the version she liked. And she would repeat it. How long before she told the enclave he'd survived? His respite from Avenazar was over. Small footsteps behind him warned Nevian that Cal had caught up to them. Trapped again. He focused on Isra.

"I threw myself off the bridge."

Isra crossed her arms with a pout. "Fine, if you want to be like that! Your famous fall didn't change you one bit. You always keep everything to yourself!"

Nevian gritted his teeth. "Why wouldn't I? You keep nothing to yourself!"

"That's a lie! I don't repeat secrets." She raised her chin, trying to stare down Nevian despite being shorter than him. He withheld a snort. "If you'd told me about your nightly excursions, I would never have gone to Master Avenazar. I could have helped you."

As if, Nevian thought. She might have been useful for a while, but the moment it bored her, Isra would have moved on and become a danger to him. "Nobody could know," he protested. "A word out and I was dead."

"Oh yeah? Then why tell your Isbari priest? Why was *he* worthy of your trust?"

"I didn't tell him anything. He figured it out himself." Nevian mimicked her prideful sneer. That was why she was angry at him. She had wanted to know, and she had wanted the exclusivity. "You can't accept that Varden outsmarted you."

Her frustrated huff was the most satisfying sound he'd heard in a long time. He shouldn't enrage her, not when she could tell on him, but her attitude grated on his nerves. Her retort justified every insult so far.

"Not sure he feels so smart right now," she said.

Nevian crossed the distance between them in one long stride and grabbed the front of her dress. She yelped as he pushed her against the wall, surprised and confused. Nevian didn't understand himself either. His head spun, and blood throbbed against his temples, but the words flowed out on their own.

"High Priest Varden didn't deserve this. Your obsession with him is disgusting. He's not an out-of-control pyromaniac, he's the only soul in the enclave who helped me. He cared."

Nevian's voice turned rough, and he let go of Isra. He had done everything he could to avoid thinking about Varden since awakening at the Shelter. When he dwelt on what Avenazar would inflict on the poor priest … a shudder ran down his spine. This was his fault, too. He should have warned Varden, should have tried something.

Isra batted his hand away, then smoothed her robe. "I can't be blamed because he hid that woman for a week. Act high and mighty all you want, but I was right about him. He betrayed us, protected a Dathirii elf, and paid for it."

Nevian recalled the girly giggle he'd heard when he had returned Varden's rekhemal. Why take such a risk for a stranger? But perhaps she wasn't one. They had been partially undressed, after all, and while Nevian had never grasped attraction, he'd seen how it could govern others' behaviour. Varden's actions might follow a logic that felt foreign to him. He'd always had too much heart for his own good. "What happened to her?"

Isra shrugged. She didn't know, and clearly she didn't care either.

"She escaped," Cal answered from behind, moving closer to Nevian and throwing him an apologetic look. "The news is all over the city. That's Branwen Dathirii, and she returned to her family. People say she was pretty beat up, though."

"She's lucky if that's all she got from Avenazar." Nevian reached for his forearm. He wanted to curl up in his bed, inside the Shelter, and hide for the rest of his life. Why had he risked going out? Now he'd been discovered, and he still held the kids' book. A fugitive and a thief. What a horrible day. "Isra. You need to keep this a secret."

"If you define 'this' and ask nicely, I might."

Nevian glared at her, and his jaw worked as he stomped on his pride. Ask nicely. As if she had any right! But he couldn't afford her betraying him. "Please. If you tell anyone I'm alive, I won't be for long. Avenazar …"

"I know." Her voice hitched, and the sudden emotion surprised Nevian. Her haunted gaze shared a story he'd experienced often. "He … he attacked me too. Jilssan stopped him." She touched her amulet once more, just as he reached for his forearm. Isra met his eyes. "I told you, I'm glad you're alive. I miss having you around, but I won't say a word. I swear I'm a pretty good liar."

"Okay." He stepped back and swallowed hard, struggling to accept this. If he stopped her from returning to the enclave, it would arouse suspicion. As much as he hated putting his fate in the hands of another—let alone in the hands of a spoiled brat who never thought of anyone but herself—he had no choice. "Thank you, Isra."

"No problem. See you around someday, I hope!"

She morphed into a hawk again, wings stretching out from her arms, her blonde hair turning into a mass of brown feathers. Her final caw as she flew away made Nevian's heart sink. He wondered how long he had before she let it slip.

A tiny hand touched his forearm, and he glanced down. The contact triggered slight dizziness, so he pulled away and stared in the opposite direction. Cal must be happy to have so many of his incessant questions answered. Perhaps Nevian really would get his two weeks of peace, but he doubted it. Something would interrupt. Something always did.

"I thought you'd trapped me," he said as an apology for the

bookslide.

"Don't worry about it." Cal tapped the book and added, "Nice choice. I'll go back and pay for it once you're at the Shelter, okay? Let's get you to safety."

Nevian gave a tiny nod, and they started off. He was glad he didn't have to return to the shop, and that Cal would make sure he hadn't become a criminal on top of everything else. Not that it would change anything. Sooner or later, Isra would say one word too many, and Avenazar would start looking for him. Nevian stared at the children's story in his hand, and something hardened inside him. Being with him was dangerous. The next time he saw Efua, he needed to tell her to keep her distance until it was over. He'd miss her small voice reading in the background, but he couldn't allow Avenazar to touch a single hair on her head.

Chapter Thirteen

JILSSAN avoided Avenazar's office as a general rule. She hated the decor inside. A massive black sculpture of Master Rannar dominated the room, dwarfing Avenazar yet reminding his visitors of the man who deserved his adoration. Although astute observers might question the expenses of transporting this ridiculously huge piece of art from their homeland, Myrians and Isbari had Rannar's name carved into their collective memories—as a glorious conqueror to the former, and as a mass murderer to the latter. He might not have drained the Bielal Sea himself, but he had led Myria's army across Isbari land, and stories of his devastating influence now travelled through time. They said he could stand outside a city and cause siblings to turn on each other, or soldiers to kill themselves from terror before an assault. Perhaps Rannar's mastery of others' minds had first seduced Avenazar, but every fraction of his legend suited their enclave leader's style.

Jilssan's gaze slid from the black statue to Avenazar, who glared at her.

"I didn't call for you," he said.

"Didn't you? I must have dreamed it!" As if her nights weren't filled with much more agreeable things. Jilssan rolled her eyes and raised the object of her visit: a thick missive from Myria. "I figured you'd want to read the important news first."

Avenazar set his quill down. She risked a glance at his scribbles and spotted a few runes. Magic, then, not threatening letters to Isandor's merchants. "Unless it's from the Protection of Citizenship Department, the pile is over there."

He pointed to a dozen other parchments on the ground, all bearing the Circle's seal, all ignored and gathering dust. How long had they been there? The Circle stood at the very top of Myria's hierarchy, way above Citizenship. Why would Avenazar even care about the latter? Especially more than he cared about the Circle? Jilssan's heart dropped at the realization. Varden. Almost every resource of Citizenship went to regulating and issuing ownership papers for slaves.

"What did you request from them? We have more than enough slaves to cook and clean for the entire enclave." She knew what. She knew *who*, and found it hard to remain calm. Jilssan cursed herself for the strong reaction—nothing good would come out of rooting for Varden. "If you require manual help, you should ask for another apprentice instead."

"Why waste a Myrian's time?" He brushed the idea aside with a dismissive gesture. "Keroth's clergy already threw him out. All I need is a final confirmation."

"And everything else is meaningless until you get it?" Jilssan shook the letter. She would much rather discuss the lapse in his duties than Varden's future. "What even is the point? He won't make a great slave if he can't stand, and he'll never obey an order from you."

"Truly?" A dangerous light brightened Avenazar's gaze. "I've always wanted to find permanent ways to subjugate individual willpower. Continuous magic is tricky, but imagine how much we could accomplish! This is a great opportunity to test the limit of my skills."

Jilssan's throat dried. This conversation had taken a turn for the worse, and she regretted bringing the Circle's letter. She flung it on the pile, unable to hide her fear entirely. "We have more pressing concerns. Must I remind you we have a war unfolding? We're crushing House Dathirii, but a distraction could cost us our advantage. This is the time to finish it cleanly and avoid an escalation, not to tamper with Varden's mind."

"Don't forget yourself, Jilssan. You might convince me our priest friend has truly turned your head."

Avenazar didn't have to spell out the underlying threat. She'd survived in the Myrian Empire long enough to know she'd stepped too far and needed to tread carefully. "He's just a pretty face," she said. "My head's right where it should be, I promise." And yet she couldn't stop thinking of his rough voice, his stubborn *pride is all I have left*, his unyielding determination to fight. His resistance had impressed her, overcoming her usual disdain for idealism. If Jilssan was honest with herself—and she was the only person with whom she always was—Varden *had* turned her head, and she loathed every plan Avenazar made for him.

"Then perhaps you ought to stop complaining and start contributing to our success," the wizard said. "Read the Circle's letters and spare me their quivering. I must prepare for a meeting with our next decisive ally and have no time for bureaucratic drivel."

Jilssan choked down her protest. The last time someone slighted Avenazar, he'd razed several houses to avenge himself before claiming her apprentice for two years of free labour. He had no shame, no inhibitions about massive and violent reactions. By comparison, the Circle's calculated decisions looked like pointless handwringing. Besides, she'd love to get a peek at the correspondence they sent and—even better—become their main contact with Isandor's enclave. What a great opportunity, and all because—wait … a decisive ally?

"Who are you meeting?"

Avenazar snorted. "You take care of Myria, and I'll crush Isandor under our foot, all right?"

The level of condescension in Avenazar's tone stunned Jilssan. She schooled her expression into impassiveness, too used to men relegating her to the role of secretary to snap back at the most volatile of them. "Of course!" she chirped with the brightest false smile she could manage. "Let me get that drab business right out of your hands."

Too bad for him if he didn't understand the importance of this communication. No one offered meaningful positions to complete strangers if they'd befriended a good candidate before. Jilssan's sheer magical power might never equal Avenazar's, but climbing the Circle's ranks relied on more than spellcasting. By the time he established their dominance over Isandor and Jilssan could return home, she would have a network of strong allies waiting to help her along. Master Enezi could even vouch for her steadfastness in training Isra should anyone ask about her potential.

Jilssan gathered the letters and flipped through them, letting the papers flap noisily against each other to distract Avenazar. A petty revenge, but his glare was worth it. Jilssan trotted out of his office, and as her gaze passed over Rannar's statue, her heart twinged. No Myrian contact would ever listen to a petition for Varden. He'd have to fend for himself, and his best chance relied on Avenazar growing distracted with this new ally. Doubtful. He'd been scribbling spells when she entered, and she had framed controlling Varden as a challenge. Avenazar didn't care about Isandor, or even Myria's politics. He loved his magic and the power it brought him over others. Here, far from the Circle's immediate sphere of influence, he could exercise both at will. Varden was the most recent victim, but he wouldn't be the last.

JILSSAN found her apprentice sitting in the inner garden, on the low stone wall around the central willow. The ancient tree was the only one they hadn't cut down upon building the enclave. Jilssan had suggested a small resting area might benefit everyone's mood—one of the rare occasions Varden had agreed with her. She'd caught him with a large sketch pad and charcoal a few times the first summer. He had been more relaxed back then. They had only spent a few months together at the time, and none of them had known Avenazar's true nature.

They had all discovered with time, of course. One by one, at their own expense, they had triggered his wrath. Even Isra had crossed enough lines that he'd given her Nevian's treatment. It had lasted only a brief moment—one strong burst of magic—but her apprentice hadn't been the same since. Isra's cheerful carelessness had vanished. Instead, she sulked about, avoiding Jilssan and her routine exercises. Today, she was staring at a white flower, spinning it between her fingers, deep in thought.

Jilssan traversed the gardens, ignoring the tightness in her lungs as the cold air hit them in full force. She disliked this about Isandor's winters—when days turned dry and freezing, even breathing became a struggle. She'd never caught herself wheezing in Myria before, and she hoped no one heard her here. Signs of weaknesses were too often used against you in her cutthroat world. She smiled as she settled next to Isra. Seeking out the gardens to walk around them or play with the flowers had been a habit of hers in Myria, too, whenever she felt down.

"You always choose the white ones," Jilssan said.

Isra lifted her head, then shrugged. "They're prettier."

Jilssan disagreed, but she had no wish to debate flower colours. These last two days, Isra's already sullen mood had grown even worse, and Jilssan had resolved to investigate. "Was the shopping trip any help?"

"Help with what?"

Bright blue eyes met Jilssan's gaze, as if challenging her to voice her concerns. It was kind of cute, how Isra seemed to think her master hadn't noticed. They'd spent the last three years together, and since coming to Isandor, Jilssan was the only adult in charge of Isra. Of course she kept an eye on her to make sure everything was okay. She wasn't Avenazar.

"Isra, I said you could talk to me when something's wrong. You're still thinking about Nevian and Varden, I can tell, and you shouldn't keep it all in. So my initial question was: did the shopping trip distract you a little, at least?"

Isra gripped her knees. She wouldn't look at Jilssan anymore. "Yeah, it was distracting all right. Now I just feel worse."

Isra heaved a sigh, then shook from a deep shudder. She dropped the flower and closed her fingers into fists. For the first time, Jilssan noticed she had neither gloves nor a cloak of fur. No one should be outside without proper clothing at this time of year.

"Let's go inside." Jilssan slid down the small stone wall and grabbed one of Isra's freezing hands. "We'll get a fire roaring, and I know a spell that turns milk into hot cocoa. You'll be all set for a long girl-to-girl talk. All right?"

Isra resisted the pull, staring ahead. "I don't think—"

"Consider it a magic demonstration, and a required part of your training."

This time, Isra jumped down the wall and followed Jilssan,

doubts plain across her face. Her shoulders remained slumped as they headed back into the wizards' quarters, almost as if she were hugging herself.

JILSSAN needed a while to get everything ready. Temple acolytes had been in charge of keeping steady flames in all of the enclave's fireplaces, but their diligence had taken a hit since Varden's imprisonment. Dying embers had been all that remained in Isra's room, leaving Jilssan to start the fire anew. She'd sent her apprentice to fetch them milk while she struggled with it, and eventually managed hot and stable flames.

The extended pause worked out for the best. Isra came back long before Jilssan succeeded. She wrapped herself in her blankets, sitting cross-legged on her bed, and stayed silent. It seemed she was preparing what she wanted to say, and how—so she had at least decided to voice some of her worries. Excellent progress, as far as Jilssan was concerned. Isra talked a lot, but never about things that mattered. More than once, it had felt like she was holding something back, covering her deeper thoughts with mindless chatter.

Once she was finished, Jilssan straightened up and motioned for the milk. She had barely taken the cup out of Isra's hands when the teenager started spilling it all out.

"I don't believe what Master Avenazar is doing to Varden is fair." Her voice dropped as she named Avenazar, as if she were afraid the wizard would hear her through the walls. "And it's my fault, isn't it?"

Jilssan lowered the two cups of milk. It wasn't fair, not in a million years, but what could they do about it? Varden had sealed his own fate, and opposing Avenazar would get them killed. "High Priest Varden hid a member of the enemy family in his quarters for days. You cannot be blamed for that."

"I know. You said that before, but—"

"Stop." Jilssan set the two cups on the ground. Hot cocoa could wait; this discussion couldn't. "You are not responsible for others' safety. You thought Varden was selling us out, and you did what you had to. No one here can reasonably ask you to risk your life for him—not when the source of punishment is Master Avenazar. Varden's fate is horrible, but if you'd hidden what you knew from Avenazar, it might have become yours. Don't blame yourself."

Isra pulled the blankets tighter around her until she could hold them with one hand. Jilssan suspected the other had gone to the amber amulet at her neck. "So you think I should always tell these things."

"At least to me. You can always tell me."

Informing Avenazar directly would be risky. Too unpredictable, and she didn't want Isra ever facing him alone. Silence stretched between them. Isra stared past Jilssan at the flames, her lips moving. While she let the last exchange sink in, Jilssan returned her attention to the cups of milk. She whispered a few words, dipped her fingers in, and smiled as white turned to brown and a soothing chocolate smell wafted out. She grabbed both and scooted closer to her apprentice, staying on the ground but leaning her back against the bed.

"I saw him," Isra said. "Varden, I mean. I went down to his cell with bread and water."

Her tone made it sound like it was a big secret. Jilssan handed Isra her hot cocoa and smiled. "I hope he appreciated it."

"He called me obnoxious."

No need to turn around to see the offended pout on Isra's thin face: it was all over her tone. Jilssan used every ounce of willpower not to snort in laughter. Since his imprisonment, Varden shared his opinions more willingly. She actually liked this side of him, but she knew voicing them before would have sped his downfall.

"He said a lot worse to me, Isra, and I've been treating his burns. Don't pay it any heed." He had several reasons to despise them and lash out. Jilssan let it slide, aware she deserved most of the scathing comments he dared to make. She didn't mind—she knew and loved herself as she was. "Why did you go? Guilt?"

"I like girls."

Isra's answer sprang out on its own, and Jilssan turned around to get a good look at her expression. Her skin grew several shades of red deeper, and she brought the hot cocoa to her lips to hide part of her face. Relief flooded briefly through Jilssan—the fewer secrets there were between them, the better she could protect her apprentice—but when she worked out the link between Varden and Isra's answer, however, her heart squeezed.

"You told him?"

Isra lowered the mug and stared into it. "No, but I think he guessed. I wasn't … I didn't know how to ask him anything without saying too much."

"Ask him what?"

"How to hide it."

Asking anyone amounted to taking an enormous risk, but this went double for a man under constant assault by a mind reader. Now her secret was well within Avenazar's reach. Jilssan hoped Varden didn't have a vengeful fibre in him. Letting even a sliver of information slip might earn him respite from Avenazar by redirecting his energy to Isra, and the possibility sent a shudder down Jilssan's spine. She doubted it. Varden would do his best to hide it, but that might not be enough.

She sipped at her hot cocoa, trying to decide what to tell her apprentice now. Nothing they could do about Varden. The safest way to get Isra to trust her involved sharing her own secret—a risk she rarely took. But if she couldn't rely on Isra's discretion, how could she ask for her trust?

"Isra, the next time you need advice about this, come to me. I have years of experience, and it's not the same for women and men."

"You have …" She trailed off, staring at Jilssan with wide eyes, her lips parted. Jilssan almost snapped her fingers in front of Isra's face, uncomfortable with her surprise, but she remembered how miserable it was to believe you were alone. She drank down her mug instead, waiting for her apprentice to get over the shock. Isra tried to clear her throat, yet only managed a squeak. "So you like girls too?"

"Not just girls. I have a wide array of tastes." Including Varden, despite her most pragmatic inclinations. Nothing would come out of it, and Jilssan considered her sporadic help with the burns acknowledgment enough of that crush. "Once we're back in Myria, I'll show you how it's done—where you can meet others, how to recognize them, what you have to be careful about. Everything. Until then, you need to keep very quiet about this, and don't get attached to others. It's not like we're staying forever."

She hoped not, anyway. There had been no formal duration for their mission here. Jilssan assumed that once they'd established a dominating presence in Isandor and taken control of their political caste through trades, she'd be allowed to return with Isra. Avenazar's increasingly violent and erratic behaviour worried her, however. The Circle had demanded an aggressive but mostly peaceful takeover, and Jilssan doubted Avenazar would meet the Dathirii's continued resistance with bloodless tactics. The longer they lasted, the more crushing he'd make their defeat to prove the cost of defying him. Jilssan would stand by and watch, ready to contact Isra's father should the danger become too immediate. Master Enezi's political pull would get them back safely to Myria if need be, but her reputation would take a hit.

Isra downed the rest of her chocolate, then untangled herself from the blankets and laid flat on her bed. Her grin had returned, and her legs swung above her in unrestrained excitement. She'd buried her guilt and fear once again, eager to hear more.

"I won't say another word about it! Except tonight." She grabbed a pillow and put it under her chin, wrapping her arms around it. "This is girl-to-girl talk, isn't it? You need to tell me everything!"

"You got it."

Jilssan's smile came more naturally now. This wasn't a safe conversation to have, but it was obviously one Isra needed. She made a quick trip to the door, put her palms flat against it, and transformed it into a stone wall. Guards, acolytes, or servants passing in the corridor wouldn't hear them, and without magic, no one could enter. They could kill their conversation long before such a visitor arrived. Her precautions taken, Jilssan climbed on the bed with her apprentice, her back against the wall.

"So what do you want to hear? My first girl crush or my first kiss?"

Judging from Isra's unhelpful but very enthusiastic "yes!", they would still be there late into the evening. Jilssan glanced at the roaring fire, snatched a pillow to settle against comfortably, then launched into her story. It didn't matter how long it took, or that neither of them would be doing any work. Some things were more important than magic.

CHAPTER FOURTEEN

NEVER before had stress prevented Nevian from concentrating on his work. Exhaustion might overtake him, but looming deadlines or dangers pushed him to better heights, his fear sustaining him through long nights of learning. Yet the words in his tome now turned into confused scribbles, and he jumped at every loud noise from the common room. It had started after meeting Isra, and it wouldn't stop. Nevian wished he still had Varden's rekhemal. The holy bandana had heightened his senses, sharpening his concentration and clearing the fog of exhaustion. Perhaps it would have countered his stress, too, kept him present and aware.

Guilt snuck through the haze of fear at thoughts of Varden. Would a simple warning have saved him? Shouldn't Nevian have tried? But no, there had been no point. They would have fled together, and they would have been caught by Avenazar. No one escaped the vengeful wizard. And now that Isra knew Nevian was alive … He closed his eyes, inhaling deeply. Sooner or later, the news would spread, and he would share Varden's fate.

Nevian didn't have a lot left to protect, but his gaze went to the children's book immediately. He picked it up again, staring at the cover. Efua was smart, discreet, stubborn—the perfect study companion. He'd grown accustomed to her small form on his nearby bed, mouthing out words, and her absence saddened him.

He had a problem.

When Avenazar came, Nevian wanted the girl to be as far from his mind as possible. Avenazar's initial interest in Nevian had emerged because of his position as Master Sauria's apprentice. She had slighted him, and after a violent and deadly retort, he'd carried his vengeance over to Nevian. He would take Nevian's betrayal and attempts to flee as insults, and if Avenazar discovered how attached he'd grown to Efua … Why wouldn't he repeat the cycle? Nevian should not have allowed anyone close. Too late now. The best he could do was to impress on her how important it was that she carried on without him.

She would arrive with dinner any time now. Nevian pressed his shaking hands to the desk and made one last attempt to learn from his magic book. He needed to focus and understand as much as he could before Avenazar found him again. Yet no matter how hard he tried, his concentration slipped away. His eyes slid over words without a hint of comprehension, and his mind returned to Efua without permission. When she finally arrived, he hadn't flipped a single page, and panic wound his stomach tight once more.

Her characteristic knock grounded him and slowed his frantic heart. Calm and perseverance would see him through. They always had before. Nevian called for her to enter as he picked up the book and sat on the bed, hiding his gift behind his back. Efua walked in with his plate—flatbread wrapped around beef, lettuce, and other vegetables Nevian couldn't quite identify, including a bright fuchsia one. Before tasting Larryn's delicious food, he had never paid attention to what he ate. Now he waited for meals with as much eagerness as he did Efua's arrival.

"You're on the bed," she said.

"Astute observation. You can leave the plate on the desk."

Efua frowned but did as she was told before climbing next to Nevian. Her small legs dangled over the side. "What does 'astute' mean?"

"It's when you're very perceptive." She lit up at perceptive, but still seemed uncertain. "Like when you notice a lot of things and draw the right conclusions from them."

"But … you were sitting on the bed. It was obvious."

"I was being sarcastic."

"Oh, I know that word!" She laughed and clapped her hands. "Larryn and Hasryan are sarcastic all the time!"

Nevian didn't doubt that. His rare interactions with Larryn led him to believe he was fuelled by indignation and coated his anger under thick layers of sarcasm. "It's a good word to know," he said. "I have a gift. Cal dragged me outside earlier, and I found something for you."

Efua's back straightened immediately, and she stared at him with wide eyes. "You did?" She leaned forward, opening her arms for a hug. Nevian recoiled, and her smile stiffened, her last attempt fresh in their minds. Instead, she touched his hand with her smaller fingers, very lightly. "Larryn and Cal are the only ones who ever offer me gifts."

The soft awe in Efua's voice slammed into Nevian's guts. Master Sauria had given him the occasional notebook or quill—another thread in this cycle he was repeating, and another proof of the danger it put Efua in. Yet she clearly thought his attention was marvellous, and how was he supposed to push her away now? She wouldn't want him to, and neither did he.

"It's nothing. I just saw it, and well …" He withdrew the little book from behind his back, and Efua squealed in delighted surprise. "You might lack the skills for it now, but I know that won't last."

Her dark brown eyes had become even wider and brighter. She wrapped her hands around the gift and stared at it, slowly deciphering the title. Nevian's insides tightened as she opened the cover and looked through the pages. "So I am learning fast!"

He laughed—a short, throaty sound. "Again, very astute observation. Yes, you are."

Efua radiated pride. He slid a finger under her upraised chin, then snatched his hand back, surprised at his own movement. Nevian cleared his throat. Now came the delicate part.

"There's something else we need to talk about," he said. Her shoulders slumped as she picked up the change in his mood. Nevian rubbed his sweaty palms on his pants, fixing his gaze on the door. "A promise must accompany this book. No, two. One from me, and one from you." What was he saying? He shouldn't make promises he couldn't hold, especially not when he had to burn bridges. Yet after a glance at Efua, who stared at him with fascination, the words flowed out. "Being around me isn't safe, and I don't want you to get hurt. There's a bad man after me, and I can't fight him. No one can. So you need to promise me you will … hide. Visit less, if ever. And when he comes, run." He closed his eyes, struggling against visions of Avenazar appearing in this room and destroying everything. He had almost stopped reliving the assaults with Vellien's help, but one unlucky meeting with Isra had brought it all back. "That's your promise. And in exchange, I swear that once all of this is over, I'll teach you magic."

"Magic."

Her voice fell to a whisper, as if she feared saying the word too loud would make it disappear. Nevian forced himself to meet her gaze, fighting against his guilt. He'd never live to fulfill that vow. In a way, he was baiting her to make sure she didn't die alongside him.

"I'm serious, Efua, you can't—"

"I know." Her determined pout had grown familiar by now. "You're always serious. I understand, and I promise. I'll stop coming." Her voice faltered. "Even if you're not there, I'll keep going. And I'll learn magic one day. For you instead of from you, if I must."

A sudden surge of warmth made Nevian dizzy. His fingers curled into the bed's blanket as he fought the tears flooding up. If only Avenazar could stay away, just this once! He wanted time to regain his skills and rebuild his life. He might never return to Myria to sharpen his magic, but he liked it here. Everyone cared about him, one way or another. Cal had saved him and dragged him out for some fresh air, Larryn made sure he didn't skip any meals, Vellien worked with him to repair his mind, and now Efua was vowing her life to magic on his account.

"I hope I'll be there. You'll become better than I could ever be." He wiped his eyes, then put a hand on her bony shoulder. "I think I could use a hug. Just … slowly."

With a slight nod, Efua wrapped one arm around his back, then another across his chest. He inhaled deeply as her small hands squeezed his skinny body. The contact had sent a shiver up his spine, but he focused on the feeling of her head against him and returned the embrace for a brief second before clearing his throat. Efua backed away at his signal, and smiled.

"You should eat," she said. "I'll start reading this."

Nevian glanced at the dinner, uncertain any of it could make it past the lump in his throat, but he reached for the plate anyway. He'd said everything he needed to, and more. Now they waited, studied, and hoped for the best.

LARRYN had always been a light sleeper, but he didn't need more than a handful of minutes grabbed here and there to function. Since Hasryan had escaped execution and vanished, however, even so little became hard to find. What if he missed Hasryan's knocks on the window because of it? Larryn hesitated to light the fire in his kitchens, afraid his friend would need to crawl down the chimney. Irrational or not, guilt needled at his heart every time he fed the flames. What if? He had already betrayed Hasryan once. He couldn't bear the idea of doing it again. But the Shelter's patrons depended on him for food. That much never changed.

Larryn set one of his countless wooden plates to the side, satisfied by its cleanliness. He barely paid attention to his movements, nodding off where he stood. Maybe he should talk to Vellien about this. Find a way to sleep, or to sharpen his senses. He didn't trust himself around the young healer, however. The two of them had reached a delicate balance, acknowledging each other's presence without engaging in conversation, and Larryn feared breaking it. Once, Vellien had asked if Larryn needed help with any ailment, and it had taken every ounce of willpower to keep his response calm. One day, perhaps … Larryn wondered if Vellien could heal old wounds, too, but discarded the idea. Poverty had taken its toll on his body, leaving him with crooked fingers and partial deafness, but he had adapted to both. They were his battle scars, and the idea of asking a noble to remove them left a bitter taste in his mouth.

A single knock broke through his daze, and he wondered briefly how long he'd been staring at the wall. He had a new plate in hand, one he'd picked up and cleaned without realizing. Larryn set it down with a groan. Efua ran in, brandishing a book, words spilling out of her at astonishing speed. Nevian had finally ventured outside the Shelter, and he'd brought back reading material. Larryn smiled at Efua's pride despite his exhaustion. She said that Nevian had admitted she learned fast and could tackle this more advanced story. And that he had promised to teach her magic one day. Efua wrapped her arms around his waist as she told him about Nevian's bad man. She leaned on his right, knowing it helped him hear, and he rubbed her back, waiting for the torrent to end.

"Listen to Nevian," Larryn said. "It's always best not to challenge people with too much power."

Disbelief spread across her face. "But Larryn, you don't—"

"I know." He provoked them regardless of what was best. What had that gotten him, though? Defying Drake Allastam had led to Jim's death. He and Efua had both lost a father that day, and his unwillingness to back down and swallow his pride had brought that upon them. "I'm careless, and not a good example to follow. Please."

"He made me promise," she answered, as if nothing else needed to be said.

Larryn forced himself to smile. He'd yet to unravel his mixed feelings about Nevian teaching Efua. Rude and stubborn teenagers didn't make for great role models, but really, had Efua ever known anything else? She wanted to learn, and Larryn couldn't even read simple sentences. He stomped down his protective instincts and kissed Efua's forehead. "Then this is fantastic news. You never told me magic interested you."

"I didn't know, but now I do."

Then she continued chatting as he cleaned the remainder of the dishes, listing all the cool spells she wanted to learn. Larryn wondered how many of them existed, and how many Nevian could really cast. Hadn't his magic been erased? But from the moment he could sit without getting sick, Nevian had studied relentlessly. Perhaps his situation had improved. Larryn ought to ask Vellien. They could give him a complete overview of Nevian's progress.

Then Efua spoke dreamily of magic to see the future, and Larryn froze, forgetting all about Nevian's health. Casters cost a lot to hire, even for simple spells. Divinations were so out of his world, Larryn had never considered them to track down Hasryan. Except he had a mage, here in the Shelter, and Nevian owed him.

Efua poked him. "Is something wrong, Larryn?"

"No. No, I think something is finally right." He smiled at her, and put down the large pot he'd just cleaned. "I need to talk to your new teacher, though."

Ten minutes later, Larryn knocked on Nevian's door. Once he knew where Hasryan was hiding, he'd be able to sleep. He hated this mystery. Hasryan would have sent news, despite the way they'd parted. And if not, then Larryn only need to speak with him even more—to fix his mess. Time chipped at his fragile trust in Arathiel. Sure, he'd jumped in and saved Hasryan, but at what cost? He had hidden everything from them, and now Larryn had to wait in the dark, as if his best friend's life wasn't still on the line. No matter how many card games they had played together, Arathiel would always remain a noble, which meant he had a flimsy grasp of the power dynamic they lived with every day in the Lower City. Arathiel's quick release by Lord Dathirii only proved his status. Nobles protected each other. But Hasryan had no title, no safeguard. Whatever Arathiel's plan, Larryn refused to rely on it.

Nevian still hadn't answered, so Larryn knocked again. This

time, an exasperated voice called, "Just enter!"

Larryn scowled as he grabbed the doorknob. Couldn't Nevian be bothered to stand and come open himself? Did he think he stayed at a deluxe inn for his Lordship? Larryn huffed, a familiar outrage swirling at the bottom of his stomach, and he stepped in.

Nevian sat a tiny desk Larryn could not remember bringing in the room. He didn't glance up from his book, his shoulders hunched over what seemed a fascinating read. Larryn cleared his throat, his irritation spiking. Nevian sighed, rubbed his temples, and finally looked his way.

"Yes?" he asked with a slight frown. "Did I do something?"

"You're a wizard, aren't you? You can do magic."

"After a fashion, yes." Nevian broke eye contact, fingers nervously tapping his desk. "Why?"

"I need your help to find Hasryan. My friend."

Nevian's brow furrowed. He sat in silence, the rhythm of his tapping changing with his thoughts. Calculating, hesitating. Then he shook his head. "I don't work for free."

Larryn's lips parted, but only a strangled sound made it through. What had he just heard? Nevian didn't work for free. Never mind how Cal had dragged his unconscious body all the way to the Shelter, or that Nevian had received healing, a safe room, and regular meals at no cost whatsoever. Never mind how he would be dead several times over without them. None of it mattered! Nevian couldn't help Larryn with magic, because *he didn't work for free.*

It took every bit of willpower for Larryn to contain his anger and keep his tone cool. He didn't want to yell at Nevian. "You owe us this spell. Any decent person would be offering it, out of gratitude."

Nevian's jaw tightened. "It's not so simple. I can't … I can barely cast anything. Whatever you ask of me will require time to learn, and I don't even know if I can make it."

"How are you supposed to teach Efua if you can't do it yourself?"

Nevian's hand slammed the small desk with surprising strength. "I'll figure it out. Magic is all I have. If I'm ever to make it out of here, I need to put it to good use. That means taking contracts, not flinging away my time and energy. Efua is the exception, because, well—she is! But every minute I spend working on this spell for you would be subtracted from the rare hours I can study. Everyone tells me to look forward and plan as if Master Avenazar won't ruin my life again, and I am. I cannot build a reputation as someone who gives without pay."

Larryn couldn't believe Nevian had just suggested that one free spell for those who had saved his sorry ass would end his non-existent career. Had Nevian never heard of favours or cooperation? Larryn didn't have time for this shit. He shoved a hand in his pocket, withdrew a copper piece, and threw it on the desk.

"Here's your pay," he said with a level of scorn normally reserved for nobles. "I hope it's worth Hasryan's life."

Nevian slapped his palm on the coin before it rolled off the surface. A tight smile curled his lips. "That's all I wanted."

"What?" If Nevian played games with him … "Really?"

"Of course." Nevian pocketed the coin. "I don't lie. Now I can still say I never cast custom spells for free, but it would be indecent to ask for more. I'll … I'll do my best."

Larryn stared at him. He didn't understand. The coin was a joke, not a real payment. He'd meant to provoke Nevian, not give in to his weird demands. Yet Larryn had now officially hired a wizard. He would have his divination spell. "Huh … thanks," he said. "The sooner, the better."

"Then I should get back to it."

Nevian put a hand on the large tome opened before him, then threw a significant look at the door. Wow. Dismissed in his own home by some scrawny teenager. Larryn shook his head and left before something more ridiculous happened. What an odd bird. How did Efua ever get anything out of him? Dealing with Nevian's absurd and unbending rules might be a hassle, but it would be worth it. Larryn dragged his feet to his room, and this time he slept without a hitch. Even if he missed Hasryan's knock at his window, he would find his friend again.

Chapter Fifteen

Diel combed his fingers through Jaeger's hair, allowing its softness to appease his nerves. The last weeks had been rough on him, but ever since he'd talked to Arathiel, his near-breakdown state had shifted toward calmer and more productive energy. To Jaeger's great relief. After Branwen's disappearance, Diel had grown forgetful and easily distracted, which meant Jaeger had covered for him, fulfilling both his regular duties and the ones Diel was omitting. As always, Diel could count on his steward. Yet he hated to make him work harder. He already did so much! And Diel knew all too well how Jaeger would toil until his breaking point without a word of complaint.

With Branwen safe with them and a plan in place to rescue High Priest Varden, however, Diel became calmer and more grounded once more. He even allowed himself small pauses during the day in between the writing of urgent letters, meeting with the local merchants still allied with them, and reviewing finance and security with Garith and Kellian. Branwen had unearthed two new potential trade partners, outsiders looking for a contact through which they could sell their wares, and Diel would dine with one tonight.

First, however, was his appointment with Lord Allastam. Yultes had warned him two days ago of the lord's ultimatum, and half-heartedly pleaded Diel to change his mind. They hadn't argued for long, both knowing how pointless it would be, but Yultes had insisted on sacrificing the priest for the sake of the family. Faced with Diel's unyielding refusal to change their course, Yultes had bitterly declared they ought to pray Keroth would be grateful enough to save their asses.

Sitting behind Jaeger now, gathering his dark hair for a braid and a needed pause before his meeting Lord Allastam, Diel found himself agreeing with Yultes. Lord Allastam had crushed many noble houses in the past, destroying their key trades and even directly attacking House Freitz. House Dathirii might be next. With a sigh, Diel brushed his lover's long elven ears, knowing full well how much Jaeger responded to the sensation. The steward shivered with pleasure, then turned halfway around.

"You're making concentrating on these numbers very difficult," he said.

"I am aware." Diel leaned forward, caressing his hair. "You should take a break too. You never do."

"I will once I'm done with this." He tapped the scroll containing Garith's financial forecasts with the new potential partners and smiled. "You have an important meeting in an hour. We both know how enjoyable Lord Allastam plans to be, so focus on being rested and cool."

Diel pinched the bridge of his nose. As always, Jaeger was right. This meeting with Lord Allastam would try every ounce of patience he had. How could he convince him not to take this as a personal offence? Yultes' advice in this regard was sound but difficult to follow. Arathiel had freed the assassin convicted of killing Lady Allastam a decade ago. If they'd found Hasryan, it might be easier to defuse the tension. As matters stood now, however, Arathiel was their best lead. Removing him from prison, even temporarily, implied Diel cared little for tracking down this assassin.

As his mind imagined possible consequences of his decision, Diel's hands started to shake. He picked up Jaeger's hair again and began a complex braid pattern, one he'd often used for Branwen to make her feel like a princess. As a young girl, she'd loved fashion and fairy tales, but she'd had no mother to share these passions with. Diel did his best despite his busy schedule, relying on Aunt Camilla to be there when he couldn't. Almost a century had passed since Branwen's youth, but playing with Jaeger's hair still soothed him.

He was halfway through the braid when the door to his office slammed shut and made the walls shake. Jaeger sprang to his feet, but Diel grabbed his shoulder.

"Leave it to me." Few would dare to enter without knocking, or be bold enough to slam the door. "Whoever this is, they clearly want to talk with me. Plus, you can focus on your numbers while I'm not playing with your head."

Jaeger's warm chuckle infused Diel with more courage than the hair-braiding ever could. He stole a kiss before hurrying out of his bedroom, to the front office. The leftover contentment vanished as he laid eyes on his visitor.

"Hello, Lord Hellion."

The greeting crossed his lips without the slightest warmth. Intra-family conflict always began with Lord Hellion. Diel's distant cousin and Kellian's brother, Hellion was the spiritual heir to Diel's father's politics: he valued titles over decency and reputation over human life. Worse, Hellion's influence among the Dathirii made him impossible to dismiss out of hand. His beliefs spoke to others of an age with Diel or older, who remembered the days under his father's rule, when Dathirii elves thought themselves superior—to the humans because of their elven lineage, and to the commoners because of their titles. When Diel's sister, Tatiel, had married an exiled elf without noble blood, she had created the first dent in that belief. Ever since, Diel fought to bury their supremacist notions as deep as possible.

Lord Hellion kept them well alive.

He stared at Diel with utter contempt, then flicked his head to send his long hair flying back. Unlike Diel, he didn't tie or braid the emblematic Dathirii golden mane, instead letting his locks spill down his back in all their silky glory. "You are out of your mind."

Hellion met Diel's eyes as he made his declaration with complete certainty, his thin lips curling into a sneer. It took only a few seconds for Diel to remember why he preferred dealing with Yultes a thousand times over. For all his melodramatic arrogance, Yultes at least tried to cooperate. If he didn't harbour inexplicable resentment toward Jaeger, they might even manage to get along. Hellion, on the other hand, only showed up to repeat to Diel's face what he usually kept behind closed doors.

"I thank you for this precious information," Diel said. "I'm afraid I have little patience for recriminations I've heard a thousand times before, however."

"Has it not occurred to you that their frequency is directly tied to your urgent need to start taking them into consideration?" Hellion strode across the room, coming to stand just a few feet away from Diel. "You're a fool. It's no secret your father would rather have passed his title to your sister, and I marvel every day at how you convinced him you could ever be in charge of our family's success."

Diel gritted his teeth. Hellion didn't often dare to bring the previous Lord Dathirii into the picture. "Father understood the need for change. He knew it was impossible to progress by staying entrenched in old beliefs. I may not have been everything he hoped for, but I proved times and again different tactics could get us better results."

"Where are your results now? I know it's hard for you, Diel, but don't be silly." Hellion leaned forward with a sneer. "This isn't about keeping up with the other Houses. You've antagonized every human of note in this city. First, you refused to forge a trade alliance with the Myrians, then you practically spat on their leader. Less than a month has passed since you provoked Master Avenazar, yet they've drained our resources down to the last coins. And now?

You should be sucking up to Lord Allastam for our survival, but no! You have to get your latest love out of—"

"Arathiel is not—"

"Then he should be nothing to you." Hellion cut the air with his hand, stepping forward and into Diel's space. A strange anger burned in his eyes, deeper than the typical condescending irritation. Diel reflexively stepped back, then cursed himself for his reaction. He should not give weight to Hellion's words, but the brief stare left him with the uneasy feeling his cousin would gladly push him down a bridge. "The Dathirii are the best this city has to offer, but we won't survive your destructive and childish rule. Let the freak rot in prison."

"No."

He couldn't. They needed Arathiel to save Varden, and Diel refused to go back on his choice for the likes of Hellion. It didn't matter if the other elf was right. They had to try. He couldn't compromise on the torture of good men for their personal gain.

"This matter isn't up for discussion, Lord Hellion." It took every ounce of Diel's willpower to keep his tone neutral. "It might not please you, but I am Lord Dathirii, and my decision is final."

They stared at each other for what seemed like an eternity. Diel held true, stomping down his doubts to hide them from Hellion. After a while, the other lord sneered and shook his head.

"You're unbelievable," he said. "I refuse participate in this. Mark my words, Diel. I won't let you bring ruin to our family."

He spun on his heels, golden hair flying with the movement. Diel inhaled deeply as Hellion strode for the door, his chin high and his shoulders squared. No wonder Yultes always made such theatrical exits: he'd learned from the only other elf even more melodramatic.

As Lord Hellion reached the door, he lifted a hand and threw one last threat over his shoulder. "This isn't over."

Then he was gone, slamming the door and leaving a tired Diel behind. He wished it *were* over, but he still needed to face Lord Allastam's anger. Diel ran a hand through his hair, then hurried back to Jaeger, eager for some comfort before his next confrontation.

DIEL Dathirii stopped at the entrance to Lord Allastam's gardens. He had no intention of walking down the white pathway again, enveloped by blue-leaved trees and eerie light. Lord Allastam enjoyed making others come to him—a mark of superiority in his mind—and the gardens' deadly beauty wouldn't make Diel forget that. He might have obliged last time, when he'd begged for troops to save Branwen from the enclave, but the circumstances had changed. Branwen was safe, and he already had a special team to rescue Varden. Lord Allastam expected Diel to crawl to him and wait for the inevitable ire with his head bent, but Diel refused to be treated like a servant. He let the door close behind him with a resounding bang, announcing his presence.

Hellion's fluid but spiteful voice clung to his mind in the silence that followed. What if he was right? What if Diel was dooming them all for the sake of a stranger? Shouldn't his family come first, now and always? No. He couldn't allow himself to doubt like this. He closed his eyes, recalled the warmth of Branwen hugging him tightly, and decided to get this over with.

"I'm here," he called.

Diel crossed his arms and waited. Patience wasn't his strength, but Lord Allastam fared even worse. Especially when angered, which would be the case today. As predicted, Lord Allastam stomped down the path after only a few minutes, the sound a mix of small stones crunching under boots and the regular stab of his cane into the ground. Diel smiled as the old lord came around a bend and stopped to glare at him.

"This is not my audience chamber."

"It is now," Diel replied. "Say your piece. I have a busy schedule and little time to waste strolling down pretty magical forests."

"Oh, yes. You've been busy all right." Lord Allastam wasn't even trying to hide his bitterness. "It must demand a lot of energy to humiliate my family and free the wretched freak who let my wife's assassin escape. I forget how much you enjoy hooking up with filth."

Diel had expected to be spat on, yet something about the way Lord Allastam said "hooking up" set him even more on edge. The insult wasn't aimed at him. At the very least, he'd just called Arathiel "filth," but he'd also implied this was a recurring event. Diel scowled. He had a unique couple dynamic with Jaeger, with the occasional addition of a third partner. Many of them had been human, however, and aging eventually strained their bond. Unlike

Jaeger, who remained his one steady love, and had been for over a century now—a time span much longer than Allastam's life.

"I do not 'hook up with filth.' They are not filth." Diel stepped forward, glaring at Lord Allastam. His patience for arrogance had vanished with the jab at Jaeger. "I'm not surprised you'd believe so, however. You think people need a title to deserve your respect. A title, and to be constantly licking your boots. Arathiel has more heart than you ever will, and Jaeger is worthier than any noble in this city. If they and those who won't submit to you are filth, then I would much rather be with them than by your side."

Diel kept his tone calm despite the roiling anger in his stomach. With every new word, he expected Lord Allastam to burst into a furious rant and throw him out. Instead, the lord's expression turned into a sneer. The intense smugness doused Diel's indignation and squeezed his insides. What now?

"I'm glad to hear you would rather be by their side. The next Golden Table should make you quite happy, then."

Quite … happy? "It's not for another week." Diel had hoped Arathiel would have returned with Varden safe and sound by then, and a better arrangement for him than the dark cells of Isandor Sapphire Guard's headquarters could be discussed. That matter settled, Diel could focus on fixing the Dathirii's finances—or at least on shoring them up long enough to survive their struggle with the Myrians. A shiver crawled down his spine. Judging from Lord Allastam's tone, his vague plan might never see the light of day.

"I'm afraid it has been moved. I can only imagine how packed your schedule is if you didn't receive the note."

Or the note had never been sent. Diel gritted his teeth. "When?"

"Tomorrow, at noon."

A swear crossed Diel's lips. Tomorrow? How could he hope to be ready in time? That was Lord Allastam's plan, of course. Now Diel knew why he'd given Yultes such an ultimatum, and what those letters Branwen had mentioned were for. He must have spent the last forty-eight hours pushing the other nobles of Isandor to move the Golden Table a week earlier. If they had complied … they might agree with Lord Allastam's motion to throw him out, or were at least willing to consider it.

"Understood." Diel spoke very slowly, giving time for his thoughts to settle as much as possible. "Should I assume this is about the Dathirii's two seats at the Table, and that we will want our most recent wealth status?"

"I hope your young coinmaster has more free time than you do. He will need it tonight."

"Garith is nothing if not efficient. Goodbye, Lord Allastam."

There was nothing else to add. Diel refused to throw a tantrum or let Lord Allastam know how unstable his stomach now felt. He spun on his heels without bowing, strode to the great wooden doors, and pushed them open. A derisive snort followed his steps out of the audience gardens, and Diel forced himself to remain calm.

The Golden Table wrote Isandor's laws. Thirty nobles gathered around it monthly, debating the city's issues and how to fix them. Bickering between rival houses consumed a lot of their time, but every now and then a major event came up, and the attention of Isandor's ruling class could be focused on it. The next order of business should have been the Myrians and their growing economic hold on several Houses, but it seemed Lord Allastam meant to make it about House Dathirii.

At any other time, Diel wouldn't worry about it. Even nobles he often disagreed with liked him, albeit in a patronizing way, and the elven family had been around since Isandor's foundation. True, House Dathirii wasn't the richest, not by a long shot, but they had enough power to consider their two seats at the Table safe. With a few well-placed speeches, Diel even managed to carry more weight than a few of the bigger houses during debates.

His recent stunt with Arathiel would have killed a great deal of his political influence, however. Most lords had been relieved to see Lady Allastam's murderer finally caught. They'd felt safer, like these things wouldn't happen again, or go unpunished. As if this assassination hadn't been ordered by someone more important than this dark elf. This arrest marked the end of the feud between House Freitz and House Allastam, however, and Diel had ruined that. With time they might forget or forgive, but he couldn't count on their support right now.

Which meant the Golden Table would seek to determine if House Dathirii was still worthy of its two seats through the official means: finances. The more money a House had—either handling it through trades or keeping it in coffers—the more seats they were awarded. When two families went to war with one another, they typically destroyed established trade deals or blocked new ones. Smaller Houses often teamed up to secure good business partners before Isandor's three biggest houses—the Lorns, the Allastams, and the Balthazars—nailed them. When the fortunes of several families changed, the Golden Table examined their current relative wealth and reassigned seats accordingly.

Diel hated the system, which gave no voice to tiny businesses, and even less to the poorer folk. It had spurred him to conduct small deals with dozens of local merchants, promising to speak up for them in exchange for a little support. At least once a year, he brought forward a motion to reserve half of the Golden Table's seats for lowborn citizens, but it was inevitably ignored. Some of the families snorted at the word "citizen." His summer reminder was a joke to them.

The way things were going, Diel wasn't sure he'd be there to give it when the warm season returned. The Dathirii had no money left, and barely enough trades for a single seat, even counting the one he meant to conclude tonight. He would ask Garith to make it look as good as he could, but he doubted he could fool the thirty nobles around the Golden Table into thinking House Dathirii still held an economic weight worthy of their two seats. One would be a stretch.

Diel emerged from the Allastam Tower, and a cold blast of wind hit him. He ran a hand through his hair, his stomach lurching left and right. What would he do about the Myrians if they weren't even lords anymore? Avenazar had already thrown Branwen into a wall and tried to capture her. Deprived of their titles, the Dathirii would lose the unspoken protection that came with the standing. They would have only Kellian's men left to shield them from harm.

Diel couldn't help but glance around, wondering if he shouldn't have a bodyguard trail him. Kellian had hounded him about it for decades, and for the first time, Diel was inclined to agree. He looked at the eccentric spires rising all around him, and the crisscross of bridges below his feet. Vines hung down from them, obscuring part of his view. The greenery used to soothe him, but this afternoon it seemed to hide danger and treachery. Isandor had never felt so hostile.

Chapter Sixteen

ARATHIEL set his palm on the Shelter's door and inhaled deeply. Although stepping out of the guards' headquarters had removed a weight from his shoulders, he hadn't felt good until he'd reached Larryn's little haven, nestled in the bowels of the Lower City. Shackles clamped around his wrists still, and they'd assigned him an escort of three to ensure he would behave: a thin, sharp woman in Allastam livery, one of Kellian Dathirii's men, and Sora Sharpe. None of them had uttered a word on the trek down to the Shelter, and tension had built in the prolonged silence. House Allastam might not know *why* Diel wanted Arathiel's help, but they would try their best to figure it out and perhaps stop it.

Arathiel hated the idea of entering the Shelter with noble guards, however. He'd made his way there because Diel had told him to bring any allies he wanted to their meeting the next morning, and he couldn't think of anywhere else to go. He hoped Cal still came, because he wouldn't know where to find the priest's home in the Middle City.

"This is where I require privacy." He infused his voice with as much assurance as possible, squaring his shoulders despite his bound hands and the filth of prison sticking to his clothes and body—as if his demand were justified. He was, after all, a member of House Brasten.

The Allastam guard bristled, but Sora raised a hand to stall any protest. "Everyone but me stays outside. You're here to prevent escape, not spy."

She gestured for Arathiel to open the door, and he spared her a smile before he entered.

When Arathiel stepped inside, silence spread through the Shelter like a wave as patrons turned to stare. Everyone recognized him. Not as the strange man who'd shared the occasional meal and drink in the common room, but as Lord Arathiel Brasten, the unflinching warrior who had saved Hasryan from execution and run on a broken ankle. Arathiel wondered if their silence was filled with gratitude or animosity. Did they approve of his rescue, or feel betrayed by his title? Perhaps both. Arathiel swept his gaze over the crowd, and when he couldn't find Cal or Larryn, he crossed the room to the main corridor, Sora on his heels. Her presence didn't help their wariness, and to his surprise, she advanced with her shoulders hunched and a guilty frown. When they left the heavy silence of the common room behind and slipped into the corridor, she sighed.

"Can you smell it here?" Sora asked, her voice subdued. "The stink, I mean."

Arathiel shook his head. Sweat and refuse permeated the Lower City, but he knew only from memories over a century old. Nothing tickled his nose, unlike his prison cell.

"I can," Sora said. "Colleagues pretend it makes them want to gag and puke. They don't care about what it means for those who live here. The Upper City smells of lilacs and lavender and other delicate flowery scents, and some days I go straight from that to the Lower City on a noble's request, and it makes me want to quit."

Arathiel hadn't expected a confession. Cut off from the stink of the Lower City, his first shock had come from elsewhere. He had been used to large quarters and never-ending food supplies, then to the wide spaces of the open road. There had been the stasis-like time in the Well, but none of these compared. In the two years after his escape from the Well, he'd witnessed people fight over a piece of bread and experienced the misery of sleeping outside and struggling for food, yet even these had been tempered by the distance his numbed senses imposed. Arathiel barely distinguished between hard ground and a soft bed.

The tightness of the quarters here got to him first. People packed themselves in small lodgings or spooned with strangers on the Shelter's floor. They lived elbow-to-elbow, keeping their belongings in tiny bags or chests, unafraid to climb to precarious heights if it afforded them a little privacy. Arathiel's cramped room had soon felt like a luxury. Even if Sora grasped the poverty reflected by the Lower City's stench, she couldn't fully understand life around here. He had barely glimpsed it.

"You should," he said.

"This city needs someone who won't accept a bribe," she said.

"What's the point? Your superiors do, and you obey their orders. You know Hasryan has been framed, but you're still putting all your energy on him. Imagine what else you could've accomplished in that time."

"He committed those crimes." Sora pushed herself off the wall, pulling her fur coat tighter around her shoulders. Her body had stiffened and her tone hardened—an attitude he sensed hid her true thoughts about him. "The point is that most days I conduct the investigations of my choice and go after whomever I want."

"Until they shut you down. All I'm saying is that 'most days' could be 'every day' if you were independent."

"I wouldn't hold any power on my own."

No arguments against that. To have any legal weight, she needed to belong either to Isandor's Sapphire Guards, who applied the laws voted for by the Golden Table, or to one of its noble families. Neither gave her complete freedom. Her skills would still be useful without the law to back them up, and many problems could be solved without needing an arrest, of course, but Arathiel wasn't in a mood to argue about Sora's potential career. The kitchen door swung open before he could answer, and Larryn stepped out. His curious expression turned into a scowl as soon as he spotted Sora.

"When will we be free of you? What do you want this time?"

"Finding Hasryan would be nice," she replied casually.

"Sure can't help you with that," he said.

His gaze shifted toward Arathiel. Sora's eyes followed, and for a long, awkward moment, they both stared at Arathiel. Never had he expected Sora and Larryn to so naturally team up and combine pressure, and he raised his eyebrows. "Hasryan is safe, and I'm not telling either of you where or how. Is Cal here, Larryn? I … I'd like to speak with both of you."

Larryn's cheeks darkened, and Arathiel sensed a storm brewing under the surface. He crossed his arms, fingers digging into his shirt, emotions barely under control. Arathiel had no idea what to expect of him. Would he deal with the angry Larryn who had thrown him out of the Shelter, or the one who had pointed an arrow at Sora and called Arathiel one of his own? Judging from the expressions flitting across the Shelter owner's face, Larryn himself might not know.

"Yeah. Room 7, with Nevian. He still comes every now and then to chat with him."

Arathiel frowned. Every now and then? Cal used to spend entire days at the Shelter, helping Larryn and chatting with patrons. They were inseparable. They had fought during winter solstice, however, and although they had seemed to put the conflict on hold for Hasryan's execution, it clearly hadn't vanished. Tiny weights dropped at the bottom of Arathiel's stomach as he contemplated the dissolution of the tightly-knit group of friends that had welcomed him into Isandor.

"Nevian is the Myrian apprentice, isn't he? Let's go to his room. Sora, I will only be a moment."

"I should come," she said. "I must stay with you."

Arathiel tensed. He couldn't speak freely with Sora over his shoulder. If word of Diel's plans spread, they could never make it into the enclave unnoticed. The enormous risk he'd taken provoking Lord Allastam would amount to nothing. "It depends on who you mean to serve. If you truly believe this knowledge belongs with you—and whoever will demand it of you—then neither Larryn nor I have the institutional power to stop you."

He didn't wait for her reply, instead striding directly for the apprentice's room. Arathiel's eyes trailed for a moment on his old room across the hall before he knocked on Nevian's door. Larryn followed close on his heels, but Sora hadn't moved. Her stillness was choice enough; she must have trusted Lord Dathirii's intentions.

Cal's voice sounded worlds away as it called for them to enter, muffled by the door and his numbed hearing. Arathiel traced the wood's relief for a moment, wishing he felt the rough lines in it. Although he had sent Vellien to heal him, Arathiel knew nothing of the teenager he'd saved with Cal. Nevian had lived in the enclave, however, and their expedition could benefit from his knowledge. Arathiel doubted he'd have a better occasion to learn what had happened to him, why, and how he fared now. He pushed the door and entered with Larryn.

Cal sat on Nevian's bed, a large tome opened in front of him. A pile of coins rested next to him, and he snatched one to mark a page. Meanwhile, Nevian bent over another book at his desk, with his notes to the right. He ran a hand through his blond hair and made an obvious effort not to look Arathiel's way, as if too busy to bother. Cal, however, let out a squeal of joy and leaped down the bed, scattering the book and coins as he rushed to Arathiel. He wrapped his chubby arms around the tall legs, squeezing hard enough to be felt.

"Arathiel!"

Intense warmth coursed through Arathiel at the charming, spontaneous hug, and he ran a hand through Cal's blond hair, holding the chain of his shackles up with the other. He'd missed Cal's exuberance, and how simple everything always seemed with him.

"It's good to see you," he said.

Nevian cleared his throat, staring at them. "Can't you do this elsewhere? I need to study."

Cal stifled a laugh in Arathiel's clothes, then stepped back. Before he could agree to move out and give him some space, however, Arathiel shook his head and signalled for Larryn to shut the door.

"We can't," he said. "This concerns you, too."

Horror flashed through Nevian's expression. He tried hard to appear calm, lips pressed together into a thin line, but Arathiel noticed the tightness in his jaw, the whiteness of his fingers. Cal moved back to Nevian and reached out for him, only to stop just short of touching him.

"It'll be okay," he said instead.

"It's time, Arathiel." Larryn leaned on the door, blocking the exit. A strange light burned in his grey eyes. "Seems like you have a lot of important elven friends in town. First you send us a healer, and now they free you? What else have they been helping with?

Because if they're what you call 'safe' for Hasryan, I have bad news for you. You can't trust them with anyone below their station."

Arathiel gritted his teeth. He hated how close to the truth Larryn landed, and how fear and bitterness laced his accusations. He couldn't reassure them about Hasryan—better for Larryn to be angry at him for staying silent than for asking Lady Camilla's help. "Yet Vellien came here, didn't they? Have they been causing trouble?" Silence met Arathiel's question. Larryn huffed and cast his gaze down. "No one but House Dathirii knew me in the entire city. I trusted them to send a competent healer, and they did. Now they're offering me a way out of prison despite the political cost in exchange for help, and I intend to accept."

"What help?" Nevian asked, a hitch in his voice.

"I was asked to infiltrate the Myrian enclave and free High Priest Varden Daramond. We go tomorrow evening. In exchange, Lord Dathirii will vouch for me, and try to negotiate better conditions for my imprisonment. I doubt he can do much, but it'll be a full day without a cell, and from the sound of it, this priest is being tortured."

Nevian whimpered at the mention of the Myrian enclave. He clutched his chair, staring at the wooden floor, sweat rolling down his forehead. Arathiel couldn't hear him breathe, but his chest heaved in an irregular pattern.

"Nevian?" Cal asked. "Are you okay?"

"I–I knew it. Don't go in there. You can't."

Arathiel strained to perceive Nevian's tight, low voice. He cast a worried glance at Cal and walked closer, kneeling next to Nevian.

Diel had assured him Varden was worth the risk, but what if Larryn was right about the Dathirii, or some of them? Perhaps he had lied. It didn't sound like the idealist elf he'd met over a century ago, but time could change people.

"You know more about this than I do," he told Nevian. "Is there a reason I shouldn't free Varden? I can still back out."

Nevian swallowed hard. "It's not Varden. The High Priest is the only good thing left in that enclave. But there's no point." He flattened his hands against his legs, licked his lips, and lifted his chin to stare at Arathiel. "You can't succeed. They'll catch you, and Avenazar will rip through every inch of your mind. He'll know I'm alive and I'm here. He'll know Cal saved me. He'll know you helped. He'll know Larryn fed and housed me, too. You don't understand how he is. We'll all pay. He'll find everyone involved."

Nevian's voice grew shakier as he spoke, urgent and desperate. He moved one hand from his leg to his forearm, as if it hurt him. Arathiel didn't know what to tell him. Avenazar had inflicted deep scars on Nevian, and his fear went beyond his crash on the bridge. But if his claims were true, saving that poor priest only became more important.

"I can't leave him in there, but I won't be alone." Arathiel straightened up, and looked first at Larryn, then at Cal. "Lord Dathirii said they'd welcome any and all allies I chose."

"Absolutely not," Larryn's immediate response didn't surprise Arathiel. "If you want to go kill yourself for the sake of a high-born fake, that's your loss. I'm not risking my hide on a prissy elf's request. Too many people rely on me. I'm … glad you saved

Hasryan, even if you refuse to tell me where to find my best friend. But don't think I've forgotten you lied to me for a month, or that I don't care about the preferential treatment you're getting because you're a noble. If any of us wore your beautiful shackles, we'd rot in that cell forever, no matter how close to Lord Dathirii we were."

Larryn's anger swirled inside Arathiel, almost as if he'd transmitted his outrage. Arathiel reined it in, wrestling it into a cold fury. Larryn was right. None of them would have escaped that prison, but not for the reasons Larryn wanted to believe. Steel laced Arathiel's voice when he spoke.

"Do you know why they asked me, Larryn? Lord Dathirii didn't care about my title. Of his own admission, he came because I could break my ankle, snap it back into place, and walk on it like nothing happened. Because I don't feel pain, and I barely notice sword stabs. They said I was half-dead, held together by unknown magic." Bitterness crept into his words. "I guess that means there's less of me left to lose! But maybe you're right. Maybe resistance to pain isn't such an invaluable asset on this risky mission, and the hundred years of a strange Well sucking my life force away have nothing to do with this opportunity. It's *all* about my title."

Larryn huffed and crossed his arms, but he didn't apologize. Instead, silence stretched between them, heavy with the bitterness of their respective pasts. Arathiel withheld a sigh, deciding that unravelling the layers of conflict wasn't worth his time or energy, and turned a questioning gaze to Cal. Things were simpler with him, weren't they?

Cal smiled. "Of course I'm coming, Ara. I wouldn't let you

down." He stared meaningfully at Larryn, who flung his hands up.

"I'm not helping a Dathirii! Have fun getting yourselves killed!" Larryn turned on his heels and left, slamming the door behind him.

Arathiel rubbed his temples, then looked at Nevian. The young apprentice swallowed hard and shook his head, terrified. "I'm not asking you to come," Arathiel said, "but if you have any sympathies for Varden, you should tell us what you can about the enclave. Help us out."

Nevian stared at the ground, pale and distraught. He wiped his sweaty hands and forced himself to breathe slowly. "But Avenazar ..." He stopped and fell silent for a long minute, as if considering the argument he'd meant to put forward. Then he closed his eyes. "Okay. I'll tell you what I know. About layout and guards. I-I've been in and out a lot. But you need to do your best. Not just for me! Varden is ... He would have come for me."

Cal grinned and pumped his fist. "You bet we will."

For the first time in days, Arathiel wanted to laugh. Cal's determined expression smothered his sadness. Although Cal might not understand him like Hasryan, he'd always welcomed him without conditions. His presence acted as a constant balm for Arathiel's soul, and he was glad his small friend had agreed to come. Despite Nevian's obvious fears, Arathiel looked forward to their expedition. He relished the last chance to spend time with Cal and accomplish something good with his stretched life.

Chapter Seventeen

BRANWEN had tried to get to sleep early, aiming to be as rested as possible for Varden's rescue, but she couldn't even keep her eyes shut for more than a few minutes. The blankets pressed down on her or became too light; the winter wind howled too loudly, or the room turned too quiet when it died. Her back still hurt, and her heart hammered in her chest. She knew her problem: anxious excitement had taken over, and she wouldn't sleep until she was ready to collapse. How convenient that Garith had no plans to rest tonight, either! Soon enough, she stalked down the corridor, entered his room without knocking, and threw herself on his bed.

Her cousin had dressed for work, his long golden hair pulled into a ponytail and his rectangle optics on the tip of his nose. Countless scrolls spread across the desk, and a pyramidal pile of rolled ones overflowed to the ground. When Branwen stepped inside, Garith had thrown her a glance, waved briefly, then bent back over his work. His fingers trailed columns of numbers on the scrolls, and he seemed to occasionally transfer one to the book in front of him. She waited in silence, knowing better than to disturb him. Garith usually only needed a moment to finish up and listen to her. It wouldn't be long. She started playing with her nails.

One minute passed. Then two, and three. Branwen kept glancing at her cousin. Ten minutes later, all he'd done was mumble to himself, and scribble more sums. She rubbed her thumb on the inside of her skirt, the soft texture settling her growing anxiety.

"Garith?"

"Hm?"

He still didn't look up, or even tilt his head in her direction. Instead he wrote another number, then removed his finger from the scroll he'd been reading and rolled it. What was she supposed to make of his silence? Garith always made time to talk.

"Something wrong?" she asked.

A soft knock interrupted before he could answer. Garith set down his quill with a relieved sigh. "Come in, Vellien."

Their youngest cousin pushed the door open, slipping their head in first, as if to make sure everything was okay before they truly entered. Their expression brightened as they greeted Branwen. Vellien carried a cup of tea so voluminous it might be more accurate to call it a bowl. They made their way to Garith's desk, hugging the walls, and set it down. Branwen wondered if they noticed they always moved this way, along the edges as if to take up as little space as possible.

"I devised it with Camilla," Vellien said. "There's an herb inside that will improve your concentration, but it's very bitter so we infused it with other plants to attenuate the taste. She offered to make more at any point tonight, if you want."

"Thanks. I'm going to need all the help I can get." Garith leaned back, then stretched his arms above his head for several seconds. "If you have time, Vellien, you could entertain Branwen. She seems under the impression I am available for a chat."

He motioned in her direction, and for a moment Branwen was vaguely offended. When was he not, for her? Her gaze went from the huge tea cup to her young cousin, then back to Garith. She'd never seen his desk in such a state, and Garith's usual relaxed demeanour had vanished. He was tense and worried. She frowned and sat cross-legged.

"Okay. Something happened, and no one's told me yet."

Silence stretched as her two cousins looked at one another. Garith leaned over his tea to sniff it while Vellien shifted from one foot to the other. Branwen stared at Vellien, knowing they would give in faster. They cleared their throat.

"It doesn't concern your priest …" Their words trailed off, and they turned to Garith for help.

"And you have your hands full preparing your expedition," Garith continued.

"So we thought we'd let you be?"

Vellien's hesitant tone convinced Branwen they knew she would have wanted to know. She lifted her chin and allowed her skeptical gaze speak for itself. Vellien was a few decades younger than Garith and Branwen, and still a teenager in many regards, but the three of them had grown up together. She didn't need to voice her disappointment. Neither of them volunteered further details, however, and after a few minutes, she tired of their tense silence. "So? What happened and why is Garith planning an all-nighter?"

Garith turned to her fully. She expected him to grin, to laugh and joke and dismiss whatever stressed them, even just for show, but his expression remained grim. It worried Branwen more than their avoidance of the topic.

"Lord Allastam successfully moved the next Golden Table meeting to tomorrow. He told Uncle Diel he intended to challenge our right to the two Dathirii seats around the Table. I'm reviewing all of our recent transactions—what little income there is, and all the expenses—and will spend the night desperately trying to arrange them in a way that makes it look like we have a significant amount of gold passing through our hands."

"That asshole." Branwen found nothing else to add. Lord Allastam's resentment went deeper than she had expected. His wife had died a decade ago, and he had been ready to make amends with Lord Freitz after Hasryan's arrest, but now he sought to shove them out of the table? Could their deal with Arathiel really provoke this much anger, or had he been waiting for his chance to cut House Dathirii out? Both, perhaps—Alton's warning about letters and their timing echoed in her mind. Guilt wracked her stomach, but she dug her fingers in Garith's blankets and pushed it back.

"But you'll show him, right?" she asked.

"How do I put this?" Garith linked his hands without the

slightest smile. "I have been occupying our second seat for years now, and this is without a doubt my last attendance at the Golden Table. No amount of number tricks will cover the gaping void in our finances, even considering the brand new income arranged today. At this point, the miracle would be to save Uncle Diel's seat, and with it our official status as a noble House in Isandor."

With a deep breath, Garith picked up the next scroll. He secured both ends under small weights, then drank slowly from his tea. Branwen and Vellien stared at him, as if the simple movement possessed some fascinating meaning. Garith held the family's fate in his hands tonight. No wonder he had lost his carefree composure. He snatched his quill up again, but didn't start yet. He was eyeballing his book, searching for the courage to dive into the mind-numbing work once more.

"I really hope your rescue mission goes well, Brannie, because there's a chance by the time you come back, no one in this city will give a shit about us, or our well-being. What pretense our title afforded us will have been pulverized." His voice dropped to a whisper, and he added, "Please don't disappear again."

Branwen's throat tightened. Despite everyone relying on him, Garith worried about her. She forced enthusiasm into her tone to reassure him. "Have no fear. We'll be in and out in no time, and we'll have the best and kindest fire wielder in the entire city with us. He'll care, and he'll help us."

She turned to Vellien, hoping they'd add something. Instead, they squeezed Garith's shoulder, then sat on the bed beside her. "Maybe I should come with you, Branwen," they suggested. "That way if someone gets hurt, I'll be there."

"Don't. We'll be fine." She forced certainty into her tone. Vellien could have helped with Varden's state a great deal, but she couldn't bring herself to risk her younger cousin's safety. They would not fare well in an infiltration mission, and if they got hurt, no one would be able to heal Varden once they returned. "With Kellian protecting me, what could even happen? Besides, don't you have a meeting with Nevian?"

Vellien's face broke into a smile, and Branwen arched her eyebrows. Last time they'd mentioned him, Vellien had said Nevian only tolerated the visits because he knew it helped his memory—not the kind of relationship that sparked an eager grin. "Supposed to be the last. Nevian is capable of working on new spells now, and he means to cast one tonight. We meet later, to make sure everything went fine. After that …" Vellien pouted. "I don't think Larryn wants me to linger. He only accepted because I promised to help others. We've reached a truce—I avoid him, he avoids me, and no one gets yelled at again. Overstaying my welcome could break it."

"Sounds like an important meeting with an important someone. Can't miss it." Branwen watched with satisfaction as Vellien's freckled cheeks brightened. "I hope he's grateful. I risked a lot to save him, and you're spending quite a bit of time with him."

Vellien laugh-snorted in their characteristic way. "Don't expect a show of it, even if he is."

Branwen pouted. "Then the least he can do is help Arathiel. He should come with us to repay his debt!"

Vellien tilted their head to the side and frowned. "Why would he? He's terrified of the enclave."

"Who isn't? But Arathiel helped Cal save him! He's the one who asked Camilla to send you down there in the first place."

Faced with Vellien's continued confusion, Branwen decided to give them the full tale. It would keep her busy, and perhaps by the end of it, she would manage to sleep. She and Diel had talked for a long time after he'd announced his plan to save Varden. Once he'd shared what he knew of Arathiel's story with her, she'd added it to what Vellien had heard from the Shelter to get a more complete picture of what had happened on winter solstice.

Garith returned to his huge pile of scrolls and columns of numbers, sometimes pausing to drink from the tea. His mutters and soft swears served as background noise while Branwen related what she knew of the night's events. She'd thrown a dagger at Avenazar, interrupting his abuse long enough for Nevian to roll off the bridge. Cal and Arathiel had found him right after he'd crashed below, and Arathiel had climbed through the city and knocked at Camilla's door. By that time, he'd known their aunt and shared tea with her for a few weeks, which was why he'd turned to her for help.

"That's when she sought you out and came to my quarters," she finished.

She expected Vellien to be amazed at finally receiving a complete picture of that long night. Instead, they frowned, wringing their hands, legs kicking in the empty space. They even turned away, refusing to look at Branwen. What did they worry about? Vellien always found small things to fret over, and perhaps she should try to reassure them.

"You know, everyone wants us to believe this Hasryan is a heartless murderer, and Arathiel is evil for saving him, but the more I hear about them, the less it makes sense. I mean, Arathiel agreed to risk his life for a man he doesn't even know, didn't he? It's not like he'll get a lot in return."

She did wonder why he'd accepted. A day's freedom didn't seem like a great reason. But Arathiel had seen the results of Avenazar's assault on Nevian, and maybe that had sufficed. Perhaps the short glance at the kind of pain Varden might be enduring was enough. She liked to think he was that kind of person, and that Diel had taken all these risks for someone worthy of them.

"I guess," Vellien said without sounding reassured at all. "Cal is very sweet, too. Then there's Larryn. He's not … I'm told he has his reasons, but he really hates nobles. That doesn't make him a bad person. Maybe Hasryan is like that too. Maybe he killed for good reasons?"

"Maybe? I don't know." Branwen yawned, then flopped down on Garith's bed. Exhaustion always crashed hard into her these days, as if all her energy drained at once. "At this point though, I'd cheer him on just to spite Lord Allastam."

Vellien chuckled, yet the tension didn't vanish from their voice. "I hope that's it, but … I don't like the results. People dying. We don't know that they deserved it. Why can't everyone be nicer?"

"You'll like Varden," Branwen said. He hadn't been able to let her burn or capture her, despite the risks to himself. Living in the Myrian Empire might have given Varden a hard edge, yet inside thrived nothing but generosity and kindness, and it escaped his outward shell more often than not. Branwen stretched and rolled over, the soft blankets and cushy mattress calling to her, demanding she stayed in their embrace.

"Hey Garith, since you won't be using your bed, mind if I occupy it for a night? I'm too lazy to move."

"Sure," Garith said. "Your snores can be my company."

Branwen answered with a rude gesture, knowing any denial would be met with more mockery. She turned her attention back to Vellien and, ensconced in Garith's bed, she started telling them about Varden. It was long past midnight by the time they both dozed off, but the scratching of Garith's quill continued deeper into the night.

Chapter Eighteen

BRANWEN stifled another yawn as she dragged her feet toward her quarters. She should have slept more. Varden depended on her and the mission tonight, and it wouldn't do to be jelly-brained from exhaustion. But it made her so anxious! If they failed, they would have called the wrath of House Allastam and lost seats at the Golden Table, if not their titles themselves, all for nothing. When she and Vellien had stirred awake in the morning, they had forced Garith to catch a few hours of sleep, too. He would need his wits to answer the Golden Table's questions about his accounts.

When they'd left, she had accompanied Vellien back to their room, inquiring further about Nevian's state. Varden might occupy her thoughts most of the time, but she hadn't saved that kid to let him rot, forgotten. Even if he was a bit of a grumpy bear from the sound of it. Besides, she enjoyed Vellien's revealing flush. How the lanky, ungrateful teenager had somehow caught her cousin's heart might be beyond her, but Branwen knew a crush when she saw one. Too soon, it became time to return to her quarters, prepare her outfit and equipment, and join Uncle Diel to meet Arathiel.

She was hurrying down the stairs toward her quarters when she came across Kellian, making his way up with a limp. Her eyes found his bloodied leg right away, and her heart dropped.

"Uncle Kellian, what happened?"

She scrambled to him and reached for his elbow, intending to offer support. He waved her away. "I'm fine. Don't worry, just a scuffle."

"Just a scuffle that left you bleeding, yes!" She grabbed his arm and ignored his protest. "Let's go see Vellien."

"I don't need—"

"No one gets on my expedition with a wounded leg." Her voice carried a decisiveness she wasn't used to, and which surprised Kellian too, judging by his wide eyes. He studied her, and Branwen's tone softened. "You're coming to save Varden, aren't you?"

"Of course." They reached the top of the stairs, and Kellian turned to face her. He put a firm hand on her shoulder, and although her uncle was small and wounded, his presence became a solid comfort. Branwen might tease him about his rigidity and protectiveness, but you could always count on Kellian. "I won't let Avenazar or anyone else touch you again."

"Aw, Uncle!" She wrapped him in a big hug and laughed when he grumbled a protest at the display of affection. It didn't stop him from squeezing back. "You can't trail every single Dathirii you like all the time. I hereby release you of your guilt over what happened at the tailor's shop, or Avenazar's attack when I escaped. You're doing your best."

She withdrew, only to find herself facing a deep frown.

"Thank you, but I know I've failed you."

Branwen snorted, rolling her eyes. There would be no convincing Kellian otherwise. He'd have to work through that guilt himself. She stepped back, set her hands on her hips, and threw a pointed look at his wounded leg. "Then you'd better get that healed, and make sure it doesn't happen again."

Kellian answered with a solemn nod. "You're right. I'll need to be in the best of shape." He bowed, drawing an annoyed huff out of Branwen. She prepared to tease him until she saw the mocking gleam in his eyes. He was pulling her strings with exaggerated propriety. "Milady, I leave you now to limp away and find a soul kind enough to tend to my burning leg."

His mask remained steady, but Branwen laughed and landed a peck on his cheek. She'd missed these quick back-and-forths, the push and pull of their differences, and the ease with which they joked about it. She enjoyed bending the rules as much as he did applying and protecting them, and it had caused more than a few sparks over the decades. But she loved her uncle, and she knew without a doubt that he returned it in his own stiff way. As he turned away, Branwen touched his forearm.

"Uncle, one last thing!"

"Yes?"

"The guard who greeted me the night of winter solstice—the one who brought me all the way to Diel's quarters—what's her name?"

"Cordelia, why?"

"I must extend proper thanks to her." Branwen noticed the flicker of approval in his gaze, and she grinned. "Also, she's very pretty. Thank you!"

He groaned. "Don't flirt with the guards, Branwen!"

Her eyebrows shot up, and she pouted. Garith had in the past, although she suspected he had never received Kellian's blessing. She didn't need it either. If she wanted to know more about the beautiful knight who'd been so kind to her, she saw no reason not to. Kellian stared at her for a time, no doubt guessing she'd ignore his words the moment he turned his back. He sighed, but she heard the touch of mirth in it and grinned harder.

"You are incorrigible," he said, and walked away.

Branwen watched him go, his steps slow and his back straight despite the pain. The brief interaction had refreshed her, bringing her back to solid ground. Family did that to her. When her thoughts whirled out of control, she could always rely on her cousins, uncles, and Aunt Camilla to steady her. And while no one but Kellian would follow her into the Myrian Enclave, the others would stay in her heart.

Vellien didn't sleep well after their short conversation with Branwen. They kept rethinking it, worry crawling up their throat. So many little things didn't add up. When they'd arrived at the Shelter that night, Larryn and Cal had been fighting, and Hasryan's name constantly cropped up in their shouts. Vellien had stayed silent about it to avoid bringing trouble to the Shelter, but now that they knew Arathiel was involved … Where had he been? Vellien had remained at the Shelter until dawn, and they'd never seen him. Had Arathiel talked with Camilla that long? And if so, *what about?*

Vellien stared at the ceiling. They knew. They'd come to the conclusion right away, and they had spent the last hours trying to deny it, focusing on Branwen's stories rather than on the certainty settling deep within their bones. Not even Camilla would fill a whole night chatting over tea without an important topic. Arathiel had been with her, and two days later, he'd freed Hasryan in front of the entire city. Now the assassin had vanished. Everyone had thought only Arathiel knew where to, but what if he'd had help? Camilla travelled around the bridges all the time, visiting the elderly. No one would question her movements, and she often carried homemade food in her basket. It would be so easy for her to reach a fugitive! What if Branwen was wrong—what if Hasryan and Arathiel weren't nice people? And what was Vellien supposed to do about it?

The answer knocked at their door early in the morning, shortly after Branwen had left. Vellien's eyes hurt from the lack of sleep, their heart hammered from the stress of this new secret, and they almost tripped themself as they hurried to the door.

Kellian stood on the other side. He held the doorway, leaning against it to keep his weight off his leg. A long gash ran down Kellian's calf, and blood soaked his pants. Vellien's fatigue vanished, and they reached for the older elf, offering support. Kellian put a hand on their shoulder with a crisp smile.

"I had an encounter with young Drake Allastam and his cronies," he said. "They must have believed three thugs could take me down, because they really wanted that fight."

"Are they okay?"

Vellien knew they shouldn't care, but they hated when anyone got hurt. Not to mention wounding Drake Allastam right before the Golden Table wouldn't do Diel any favours. They led Kellian to a chair and forced him to sit down, then crouched next to their uncle's stretched-out leg.

"They'll be fine. Light cuts, large bruises, and one of them might find it hard to walk for a few days." Kellian tilted his head back with a sigh. "They're bullies. Show them you're stronger, and they'll run."

"You should be careful. Branwen is counting on you." Vellien grabbed the bottom of Kellian's pants. A blade had shorn them almost all the way down, so they ripped apart the inch left and peeled them aside. The cut wasn't too deep under all the blood. "Don't move. I'll get bandages and clothes to clean it."

It always surprised Vellien how much their tone changed when they had to heal someone. They hated imposing their will, yet if someone's health was at stake, another side of them surfaced. Nothing else gave them such confidence, except perhaps singing.

Not that they dared to try the latter in front of a crowd. One day, Vellien promised themself. They knew they had talent, but the idea of so many people looking at them always sent them into a cold sweat.

Vellien pushed the thoughts away and returned a few minutes later, equipped with a small bowl of water, a clean cloth, and a long roll of bandages. They wouldn't even need to sew Kellian's wound. Vellien settled down near Kellian's leg, dipped the cloth in water, and started wiping all the blood away.

"Kellian … how dangerous do you think Hasryan is? The assassin, I mean."

At first Kellian didn't answer, gritting his teeth, his breath shuddering from the pain. "Why would he come after us, Vellien? We're safe. We're even helping his buddy."

"I-I know that." Vellien swallowed hard. They didn't fear Hasryan would try to kill them, not really. But what if Hasryan felt trapped and thought his only escape meant hurting Camilla? Or if someone bad found out and blamed the family? No matter how Vellien looked at it, it seemed like aiding Hasryan could lead to danger. They just didn't know how to voice their concerns. "What if … what if we provided help for him?"

Kellian scowled. "We're not."

Vellien pressed their lips together, letting the topic go, and set the now-bloodied cloth to the ground. They put cold fingers on Kellian's calf, around the wound, and closed their eyes. Alluma's divine strength flooded into them. It was patience and kindness, perseverance and humility all at once. Vellien basked in the Elven

Shepherd's presence, allowing the power to gather within their palms. They sensed Kellian's blood flow, and how the wound disrupted the pulsing stream. Vellien redirected their energy there, and suddenly everything felt red and urgent and painful, like they'd stepped inside the gash. Hundreds of little cuts surrounded them, crying for help. Vellien wrapped themself in the inherent serenity of Alluma's presence, shielding themself against the panic, then closed the wound. They could have shoved healing power into it without care, and for a slice like Kellian's it would have sufficed, but the more careful Vellien was, the thinner the scar would be, and the less strain their uncle would feel.

Once they were satisfied with their work, Vellien allowed Alluma's strength to slip out. They opened their eyes, fighting against the emptiness settling in. The sensation would pass, they knew, and they'd closed Kellian's gash so well they wouldn't even need to bandage it. Vellien smiled. Compared to the complexity of the damage to Nevian's mind, healing straightforward physical wounds had become effortless.

"There you go," they said. "Almost as if nothing happened."

Kellian was staring at them intently, dark eyes boring holes into them. Vellien flushed and cleared their throat, ill at ease with their uncle's sudden intensity.

"What did you mean by 'what if we were helping him?' Do you know something, Vellien?"

"No, I mean …" Vellien sighed. Was talking about this even a good idea? They were starting to regret it. "It's only a suspicion. I don't have proof, and I don't know if Aunt Camilla really would."

"Would what?"

Kellian's tone had become pressing, and a little scary. Vellien lowered their head.

"The night Branwen returned, Camilla asked me to go to the Lower City to heal a wounded teenager. Apparently that was a request from Arathiel, but I'm sure Arathiel wasn't at the Shelter at all during that time. I would have recognized him. I think … I think he stayed with Camilla all night." Vellien's insides squeezed. Camilla must have meant for this to remain a secret, and voicing their conclusion felt like a betrayal. "What if Arathiel needed more than help with a healer?"

Kellian's fingers wrapped around his armchair, and he tightened his grip while staring ahead. "Sora told me … Aunt Camilla dropped her purse near the guards on the day of the execution, and Arathiel jumped into the fray while they were trying to help her pick up its contents."

"Oh." Vellien couldn't believe it. They leaned back, their hand on the floor behind them, and stared at Kellian. Their uncle sprang to his feet with a short snarl.

"She did it," he said. "She's hiding him. She hid him from Sora. She even hid him from us!"

Vellien scrambled to their feet as Kellian strode toward the exit. "Wait! What are you doing? Uncle Kellian, wait!"

But Kellian was out of their door without listening, slamming it behind him. Vellien stared at the wood, their throat tight, certain now that they had made a mistake.

HASRYAN spent most of his days helping Camilla with the small tasks involved in her visits to older or disabled people's homes. Although they talked about Esmera every now and then, neither mentioned his breakdown. Hasryan preferred it that way. He allowed himself to grow more comfortable around Camilla, even slinging around the occasional dark joke about his "misadventures," but he didn't want to dwell on the events surrounding his mother, or how they still affected him. He was content to contribute to Camilla's life however he could.

At least he handled himself well with a sewing needle. He was fixing a heavy red curtain when someone banged on the door. Hasryan dropped everything and dashed for Camilla's bedroom while she called that she was coming. He'd barely slipped inside when the visitor entered. Whoever this visitor was, they didn't care to wait.

"Kellian?" Camilla's surprise and irritation shone through her tone. A moment earlier, and he might have spotted Hasryan. "It takes your old aunt five seconds to open the door. What could possibly be this urgent?"

Hasryan crouched next to the bedroom's entrance, eager to hear the conversation. Yesterday, a teenager had come inside to brew a special infusion with Camilla. Apparently, the Dathirii were about to be cast out of the nobility, all because the head of their House, Lord Dathirii, had reached an agreement with Arathiel. Hasryan could tell it made them all nervous. Camilla had become distracted, often falling into long silences or fretting over details. Hasryan wished he had found something to say to comfort her. Instead, they'd spent part of the night talking about Arathiel and Lord Dathirii. Camilla spoke of him fondly, and she clearly loved her nephew. From the sound of it, she didn't extend the same trust to the elf in her doorway. Or perhaps it was just the circumstances. Hasryan closed his eyes and prayed Kellian had come to discuss the Golden Table meeting.

"Why did you never tell anyone Lord Arathiel Brasten had spent the winter solstice with you?" Kellian asked. "He didn't leave with Vellien."

So much for the Golden Table, Hasryan thought.

"No," Camilla said. "He stayed. We had tea."

"In the middle of the night."

Fear stabbed through Hasryan's stomach at the bitter doubt in Kellian's voice. He moved around the door to get a partial view of the room. Camilla stood next to her counter, her gnarled hand on the surface. She seemed relaxed, if a bit concerned. Hasryan wondered if her heart hammered against her chest like his did. He didn't believe this interrogation from Kellian was a coincidence. Hasryan wished he could see the elf in the doorway, but leaning further forward might bring him within Kellian's sight. He knew what to expect, however. Barely over five feet tall, lean muscles with catlike grace, golden hair held back in a half-ponytail: the captain of the Dathirii guards had quite a reputation for his sword and archery skills. A few of the Crescent Moon mercenaries had tried to mess with him once, and had returned with serious wounds.

"Indeed," Camilla said. "Kellian, everyone has a long and stressful day ahead. If you have something to tell me, please don't hesitate to spit it out. I know you don't enjoy lengthy conversations, and for once, I'm not in the mood for it either."

Her tone had turned sharp. Hasryan wished he could see Kellian's face. He'd never experienced such aggressiveness from Camilla, only ever dealing with the sweet and caring old lady. Hasryan had glimpsed a more adventurous past, however, and it wouldn't surprise him if Camilla had a harder edge beneath the layers of kindness.

Kellian cleared his throat. "Where is the assassin hidden?"

Hasryan shut his eyes and clenched his teeth, afraid of any sounds he might make. He had known that sooner or later, someone would have pieced it together. It was over now; the inevitable had happened. Camilla would give him away. Hasryan knew how much she valued her relationship with the rest of the family, and House Dathirii wouldn't agree with her actions. After a slow, steeling breath, Hasryan peered inside the room again. He at least wanted to see her expression when she betrayed him. She'd pressed her lips together and straightened up, her gaze never leaving the visitor at the door.

"Tell me where, and I won't give your name. No one needs to know." Kellian stepped forward and put a hand on Camilla's shoulder, coming into Hasryan's line of sight. A sword hung at his belt, inside a sleek jewelled scabbard. "Camilla, this could save our family. Who will care about Arathiel if we find Hasryan and bring him back? You can't protect a murderer. It's not just Lady Allastam.

Sora can prove he assassinated several others!"

"Oh, get over yourself, Kellian." She brushed his hand away and stepped back. "Hasryan was fifteen years old when Lady Allastam's death happened. He's not a cold-hearted killer. Life forced him down that path. Everybody used him, and you want me to do the same?"

"Camilla, he is—"

"Don't you dare say a dark elf." She lifted her chin and glared at him. "You're better than that. We've been perpetuating myths about their morality for centuries, but they're just that: lies to justify our war against them when they sought to understand nature. As far as we can tell, the dark elves have yet to upset the natural balance between creation and destruction despite centuries of experimentations. We need to stop calling them murderers. Alluma welcomes all Their children, white, brown, or obsidian."

"Tell that to the ones who killed Clara," he said.

Camilla stiffened and paled. When she answered, sadness laced her voice. "A raiding party does not make an entire race, Kellian. I remember that day just as well as you do; I was there. They didn't just kill your wife—they stabbed my son, too. If that's your excuse, we're even guiltier than they are. We've sent military forays into their lands for longer than I have been alive."

Hasryan held his breath, stunned by the intensity of her words. She'd never mentioned a son, although she had given him her grandson's winter coat. Garith's. He hadn't bothered to ask if she had any direct children within the extensive Dathirii family.

Kellian shifted back in the heavy silence. Light-headed, unable to see him anymore, Hasryan leaned against the wall and closed his eyes. He couldn't believe it. Camilla defended him against her own family! It was so absurd his chest threatened to burst. She wouldn't break her promise, not even for another Dathirii.

"He still killed these people," Kellian said in a low voice. "Sora wouldn't make murders up, you know that."

"Miss Sharpe might get a lot more help if she was trying to link these assassinations to Hasryan's employer instead of him. It's unlike her to go for the middle man, especially one without an ounce of cruelty."

Dizziness crept into Hasryan's head, and he couldn't feel the ground underneath him anymore. Did Camilla realize she talked about him as if they knew each other intimately? That she might as well admit complicity? She had to stop. At this rate, they would arrest her, and the best she could do was to stay quiet. He wished he'd provided advice on dealing with guards, should it come to that, but he had never believed she would stand up for him. They'd already put Arathiel in a cell, and he was a noble, too. What would stop them from doing the same to Camilla?

Kellian scoffed. "If you're so convinced he's worthy of help, you should tell Diel. He loves rescuing poor misunderstood souls hated by the entire city, even if it means losing everything we have."

"You're starting to sound like your brother."

Camilla said it as an insult, and judging from Kellian's sharp intake of breath, it was a deep blow. Hasryan almost felt bad for Kellian. Almost.

"I'm not Hellion."

"Then stop mocking Diel for seeing beings worthy of consideration where everyone sees pawns." Her voice lashed out even harder than before, and Hasryan took note never to anger Camilla. Every word sounded like a slap. "He would help him, but I will not force such a meeting upon Hasryan. I promised to keep him hidden, and I will not betray his trust. The rest is up to him."

"This is ridiculous. Don't do this." Kellian's voice hovered between exasperation and despair, almost a plea. "You know I can't let this go."

Hasryan forced himself to peek again. Camilla smiled, though the mirth didn't reach her eyes. She lifted her wrists a little, as if offering them. Kellian had his hands on a pair of handcuffs, and suddenly Hasryan didn't want her to do it either. He tried to imagine Camilla in a dank cell, sitting with her back straight even on the ground, her lilac dress stained with shit and mud. His stomach sank.

"Do it, Kellian. Bring me to prison, if you must. I'm not afraid of what I did."

"You're family." Guilt dripped from his weak protest, and when Camilla said nothing, he gripped her arm firmly. "I'm sorry."

Camilla shut her eyes. "Don't be. Tell me you think this is right, and I won't be disappointed in you."

He didn't. Lord Kellian Dathirii walked his aunt out with a huff. Hasryan watched the door close behind them, his throat raw, his breath shaky. He couldn't believe what he'd just witnessed. She would be accused of aiding in his escape and withholding information, at the very least. Lord Allastam would use this against them and destroy them. Hasryan hoped Sora wouldn't put her in a cell. She was an old lady. Bad things happened in prisons when guards weren't looking. Or even when they were. It wasn't safe for her.

He had to help somehow. This wasn't fair. She hadn't committed any of his crimes. They were his actions, his responsibility. But if he stepped up, they would hang him. Hasryan rubbed his face, trying to fight the rising panic. Trust should go both ways. Nothing had felt worse than his friends abandoning him, and he refused to allow Camilla to bear the brunt of these consequences. She hadn't betrayed him, and he wouldn't let her down.

What would she want him to do? His mind went to Lord Dathirii. How often had she urged Hasryan to talk with him? She had done so just now, in front of Kellian, knowing full well he was listening. She clearly trusted her nephew's heart. If he was already helping Arathiel … Hasryan pushed himself off the wall. He would need to sneak through the Dathirii Tower to the highest level. He hoped she was right about this Diel, otherwise he would ruin all the sacrifices made by Arathiel and Camilla.

He had to try, though. Sooner or later, they would return to search her rooms. Hasryan had to be far away by then, and he needed someone to help Camilla. It was time to make good use of his freedom.

CHAPTER NINETEEN

HASRYAN thanked Larryn's frequent stealing expeditions into the Dathirii Tower for his insider knowledge of the layout. How often had they sat together, two friends with a bottle of strong ale, drinking as Larryn explained how easily he navigated the tree-like tower and snatched precious ornaments from right under the elves' noses? As Hasryan emerged from Camilla's quarters and stalked down a corridor, he realized how many details he'd memorized from Larryn's favourite thieving grounds.

His friend would enter through one of the nobles' private rooms. Someone in Camilla's family always left his window open, even when the nights grew cold. With the numerous handholds provided by the tree bark on the outside walls, Larryn could easily climb up to it, or escape through the same exit. The hardest part was avoiding household staff, but the servants worked in pairs and typically chatted together, giving advance notice of their arrival. Only one posed a problem, Larryn warned: a dark-haired elf who frequently stood by the door on the uppermost floor, perhaps protecting Lord Dathirii's quarters and the family's most valuable possessions. Hasryan suspected that elf to be Jaeger, Diel's steward and lover. Camilla often spoke of him, of his dedication and kindness, and of how he kept unwanted visitors away, especially when Diel already had an audience.

Hasryan's feeble wish he wouldn't find the steward in his way vanished when he reached the top of the last staircase in the Dathirii Tower. He hovered at the edge, staring at the tall elf standing in front of Lord Dathirii's office, his back straight and proud. Climbing this far had demanded every ounce of discretion and good reflexes he had. Servants did roam these halls in too-large quantities, and if it hadn't been for Larryn's advance warning, Hasryan might not have paid enough attention to dodge them all. The chase had slowed his progress to a stressful crawl, however, and by the time Hasryan reached Jaeger, he was exhausted and certain Camilla had already arrived at the Sapphire Guard's headquarters.

At least Jaeger's presence at the door meant Hasryan should find Diel inside. The way Camilla told it, these two never left one another. Work during the day, play during the night. But how to sneak in unnoticed?

No, that was the wrong question. Hasryan chided himself for reasoning like an assassin again. Lord Dathirii wasn't a target to reach unseen, but a potential ally. Did that mean Hasryan could trust the steward? Would Jaeger even let him utter a single word before calling for the guards? He'd have to risk it. His most sensible alternative involved climbing the façade in bright daylight, when anyone could spot him.

Hasryan would rather bet on one elf, especially one tied to Lord Dathirii. He stared at Jaeger, his throat tightening at the enormous leap of faith he needed to make. Hasryan hated to rely on strangers, to trust them with his well-being. If he didn't, however, Camilla would pay the price. With a final, deep, steeling breath, Hasryan stepped out and strode down the corridor.

Jaeger's gaze trailed him as he approached, and heat rushed to Hasryan's cheeks. Every instinct screamed at him to turn around and flee, to choose a different path. Hasryan didn't deal with problems head on. "Head on" always led to majestic failures. But Camilla depended on him. She had wanted him to do this, and he owed it to her. At worst, he told himself, he would have another misadventure to share in their common prison cell.

Hasryan stopped in front of Jaeger, raised his chin and met the dark blue eyes. He quaked under their scrutiny, aware that he'd tied his future to Jaeger's judgment. Hasryan cleared his throat and declared in a self-important tone, "I need to talk with Lord Dathirii. Now."

Jaeger's eyebrows twitched, and he remained unimpressed. At least he didn't panic, but Hasryan had hoped for a bigger impact.

"May I ask what about?"

"Your guard leader, Kellian. He just arrested Camilla. I need to—"

"I'm sorry, what?"

The steward's composure vanished, horror and confusion flashing across his expression. He quickly forced his professional mask back on, but a new tension tightened his shoulders, and Hasryan knew he'd caught his attention now. "He arrested her," he repeated. "Please let me in. We need to help her."

Hasryan's fears seeped into his voice toward the end, and as Jaeger studied him in stoic silence, he tried to read the steward's body language, desperate for a clue. The elf stayed stiff, hands clasped behind his back, eyebrows knitted. Should Hasryan run, or insist again? He couldn't tell. Jaeger's earlier flash of emotion had vanished, and nothing else showed. Hasryan noted never to play cards with him, and the absurdity of his thought alleviated his stress. Until Jaeger's next question.

"May I have the pleasure of your name?"

Hasryan half-stumbled back at the request and almost blurted out "Larryn" again. But surely Jaeger had guessed already. Hasryan had managed to reach the top of the tower unaccompanied, and Isandor counted few of dark elven descent who would need an audience with Lord Dathirii. Why ask, then? Was this a test, a confirmation? It didn't matter. Hasryan couldn't hide, not anymore.

"I'm Hasryan. The assassin. You know that already." A solid lump formed in his throat. Here he stood, in front of Lord Dathirii's office, voicing his name and occupation to a lord who had every reason to send him back to the noose, and relying only on an old lady's word that he wouldn't. How had this happened? When had his elementary prudence vanished? This was how people like him died—trusting the wrong folks, those who couldn't understand. He lowered his head, his voice falling to a whisper. "She said I could trust her nephew. I don't want her to pay for my crimes."

Jaeger touched his shoulder with the tip of his fingers, causing Hasryan to look up again. He was … smiling? Hasryan's heart leaped as the steward reached for the doorknob behind him. "Lord Dathirii is not alone and won't be for several hours. Lady Branwen Dathirii, his niece, is with him."

Hasryan hesitated. Wasn't Branwen their spymaster? At this rate, every member of the elven family would know about him.

"Accept my humble advice, and trust her," Jaeger added. "She will follow Lord Dathirii's decision and keep what secrets he asks. Furthermore, they are waiting for your friends to arrive."

"My …" Hasryan's voice trailed off. In his panic, he'd forgotten that Arathiel left the Sapphire Guard's headquarters today! Excitement swelled Hasryan's heart at the chance to speak with him again, even if he brought bad news concerning Camilla. All he needed was to face two Dathirii elves first—to put his fate in the very hands Larryn hated so much. His friend's countless warnings echoed in Hasryan's mind, but he shoved them away. Larryn's gripe was personal. If Camilla trusted Lord Dathirii, then so would Hasryan. She had never let him down. "Thank you, sir."

Jaeger opened the door. Hasryan's head buzzed as he walked past the steward, his feet light, his stomach churning. On the other side of the room, two elves bent over a map around a desk. Golden hair spilled down Lord Dathirii's shoulders, tied back to keep it from his face. He wore the finest doublet Hasryan had seen in ages, deep green and embroidered with gold, with slashed sleeves that hid the elf's thinness. A fur-lined cloak nearly as warm hung on the chair behind him, and between the two of them, Hasryan suspected Lord Dathirii could have bought the entire Shelter. By contrast, Branwen's practical shirt, trousers, and short-slit skirt made her stand out in the tastefully furnished room. She looked as if she didn't belong, and Hasryan was grateful not to be alone.

"Lord Dathirii," Jaeger's voice announced behind him, a hint of amusement underlying its formal tone. "Sir Hasryan Fel'ethier has urgent news for you. I believe you should hear it."

Diel Dathirii straightened, his intense green eyes flying to the newcomer. Hasryan wished he could melt into the floor and disappear, or find a shadow to hide in once more. Put a wall at his back. Anything not to stand in the middle of the sunlit office. Thoughtful, Lord Dathirii turned to his steward.

"Thank you, Jaeger." His smooth voice betrayed nothing of his intentions, but he smiled before he continued. "Please instruct our guards to have Arathiel and the others wait for you in the lobby. I fear if they climb up here, Miss Sharpe might attempt to walk into the office."

Jaeger agreed, then left and closed the door behind him. Heavy silence followed the soft click, and Hasryan looked everywhere but at Lord Dathirii and his niece. A second desk occupied the room's left wall, with the neatest arrangement Hasryan had ever witnessed: regular stacks of parchments, ink bottle and quill on one side, and half-melted candles on the other. Light flooded it from the opposite direction, where a large window offered an incredible vista of the surrounding city. A handful of spires reached above the Dathirii

Tower, but most of Isandor lay below, its network of bridges falling into shadows toward the bottom. An ivy-like plant covered the rest of the wall, as if crawling out of the window and into the office. Hasryan wondered if it was another one of those magical plants, and if the strings of spherical golden flowers gave a soft light at night.

"So, are you going to spill the beans or just look around in a daze?"

Branwen's question startled Hasryan, and he realized they had both been staring at him, waiting. She leaned on the first desk, her palms flat over a letter opener—ready to pick it up in case of need. The hole in the bottom of Hasryan's stomach spread wide, but he forced himself to look at the two elves. He had to convince them to help.

"I'm here on Camilla's behalf. She was arrested by your captain this morning."

"Kellian?" Branwen scoffed. "That doesn't make any sense. I brought him to Vellien's quarters, and he's supposed to return here."

"Well, he's not around, is he?" Hasryan asked, his voice tightening.

Branwen pinched her lips. "Fair enough. Why would he do such a thing, though? It's unlike him."

Was it? Camilla had seemed disappointed, but not surprised. If anything, she had implied Kellian's behaviour had its roots in their past, and in other dark elves' actions. "You think I'd risk showing up here just to tell lies? Camilla … hid me since the execution. He must have figured it out and—"

"I believe you." Diel set his palms flat on his desk and heaved a sigh. Branwen spun toward him, but any protest died on her lips when she took in his slumped shoulders and the renewed weight on his back. In a low voice, he added, "It just never stops these days."

"She said I could trust you." Hasryan had always hated pleading. He hadn't thought about what he would tell Lord Dathirii, once he got there, and now he had no idea what to add. "She's too nice to pay for me. I couldn't let that happen. Please, anything I can do to help, even if it's …"

He didn't finish. If he returned to the headquarters and surrendered, they would execute him, and the city would cheer again. Considering it nauseated him.

"Turning yourself in won't do any good." Once he'd killed that thought, Lord Dathirii fell silent. He rubbed the bridge of his nose, sometimes letting out small hums or long sighs. Every passing second eroded Hasryan's patience. What was he supposed to do? Wait? He didn't want to stay behind and fret and hide. He'd had enough. Except he didn't have any other solution. He couldn't break Camilla out of prison—not only was he likely to fail, but where would she go after? She was a lady, not a fugitive. He ran a hand through his hair and tugged at his pants, trying to relieve some of his stress.

When he glanced at Branwen, he noticed she was rubbing the fabric of her skirt in a manner not unlike his own fidgeting. He'd heard a lot about the Dathirii's spymaster, but he'd never met her. She was even shorter than he'd imagined, with thick arms and large breasts. Her pale brown hair and eyes had surprised him—he'd started to think every Dathirii was golden-haired with blue or green eyes. It must help her go unnoticed, chat up rivals, and drag precious information out of them. Apart from the ears—and Isandor had its share of non-noble elves—she didn't have the typical Dathirii look. She half-smiled at him when she caught him staring, and Hasryan's throat dried, heralding the kind of desire he knew would get nowhere. He had tried, but it inevitably led to a vulnerability and risk he couldn't afford. Sometimes Hasryan wondered if he shared Cal's aromanticism, but most of the time he brushed the question away—examining would involve more introspection than he cared for.

"This needs to stay quiet until the Golden Table is over," Diel said at last. "Camilla will understand the delay. I'll have to convince Miss Sharpe to do the same and to treat her well."

Hasryan's chest tightened. How long did the Golden Table meetings go on? He didn't like the idea of Camilla in prison, even for a few hours. Then again, neither did Lord Dathirii. Hasryan had promised himself to trust the elf's lead. "Sora's decent. Stubborn, but decent." He smirked. "I'd say hi, but I don't think she'd appreciate the humour."

Both Dathirii did, at least, because his small quip drew a chuckle from the House's leader and a sharp laugh from his niece. Lord Dathirii gave two final taps on the desk, as if steeling his resolve, then captured Hasryan's gaze. "You can do little more for Camilla at the moment, but you have my most sincere thanks for coming to me. I understand the risk involved for you, and it means the world that you would take it. Do you need our help escaping the city?"

Escaping … The thought left a bitter taste on his tongue. He had chosen to stay and trust Camilla, to cling to the shreds of home he still had in Isandor. With Lord Dathirii's aid, he could start over elsewhere, yet the prospect only brought weariness, and no relief. Once again, Hasryan ran a slow hand through his thick white hair. "It's a nice offer, and the safest thing I could do, but …"

"You don't want to."

"No, I don't." His meeting with Esmera had clarified that much, at least. Isandor was his home, and he meant to fight for his place in it. Yet the city rejected him, and so did almost every friend within. Only Arathiel and Camilla had stayed by his side. His presence had brought them nothing but problems. "I should, right? I should leave."

"That depends," Lord Dathirii said. "Regardless, you cannot remain in the Dathirii Tower in the near future. I'll have to allow guards to search it top to bottom, providing proof that we are not sheltering you. They will ask to do so as quickly as possible— tonight, or tomorrow morning. I know what you could do until then, however."

His gaze slid towards Branwen, and she gasped. "You want him to come with us? What about Kellian?"

Anger flashed through Diel's expression, and he answered in a tight and controlled tone. "Kellian obeys direct orders, even when they displease him. He's welcome to voice his thoughts after the mission. Our priority goes to extracting Varden." Branwen grinned at the uncompromising reply, and Diel turned to Hasryan. "Lord Arathiel Brasten should have arrived by now, accompanied by a friend. With their help and Kellian's protection, Branwen will infiltrate the Myrian Enclave and save High Priest Varden Daramond tonight. They could use a professional's skills."

Shock glued Hasryan's tongue to his mouth. First at Diel's confidence that Lord Kellian would accept his presence at all, then at the casual proposition. He had entered the quarters terrified to be flung right back into prison, and yet … "Is that some sort of job offer? You're offering me work?"

Lord Dathirii's clear and melodious laugh tempered Hasryan's agitation. "It's an exchange of services. Help us, and we will help you."

"I'm an assassin. You know that, right? Brune framed me for Lady Allastam's murder, but Sora can show you the rest of the list. She loves to wave that thing around."

"Is that all you are, though?" The elven lord's mirth had vanished, and his question cut right through Hasryan. No. It never had been, despite how often others tried to confine him to that box. Hasryan snorted, and Lord Dathirii continued with a slight smile. "I abhor killing, but you cannot boil down a life's value to its crimes. You sought me in order to save Aunt Camilla, and Arathiel counts you as a friend. This speaks volumes about your character to me. You have unique skills which could spare a good man from horrible torture, and for that I will gladly overlook your past."

"We need someone like you," Branwen added. "Everybody's been so obsessed with the mess around you, they won't see how dangerous Avenazar is, and they refuse to help."

"Hey, I didn't ask for this mess. One night I headbutted an asshole for mocking my friends, the next I was lined up for a hanging!" But of course, they would blame him. Always, he ended up the scapegoat, even when he had no control over events. If Hasryan had to work with Branwen, however, he wouldn't let that dynamic stand. He'd suffered through it often enough. "Your priest isn't the only one who got the short end of the stick. Find your culprits elsewhere. I can even offer names if you want."

Branwen glared. "I didn't mean—"

"Okay, sure. Accidentally implied it, whatever." Hasryan didn't have the patience for long apologetic explanations that lasted forever. What she'd meant didn't change what she'd said. "I'm still coming. How could I not? I owe it to Camilla, and I owe it to Arathiel."

Beyond his gratitude, Hasryan looked forward to a chance to know Arathiel better and deepen their relationship. Arathiel had risked everything to save his life, yet their time together had been limited to card games and that brief, intense first talk. One outsider recognizing another and understanding his struggles. Hasryan couldn't deny he'd grown fond of Arathiel, more so than he'd ever expected. And when everyone else had deserted Hasryan … With a deep breath, he turned to Lord Dathirii.

"I've been cooped up too long. I'm sure I can save lives just as easily as I can snuff them out."

"Glad to hear it." Diel strode around his desk and to Hasryan. For an instant, Hasryan thought Lord Dathirii would squeeze his shoulders, but the elf stopped himself. "Let me get the rest of the team."

The team, Hasryan thought, as a warm feeling spread through him. His rare and disagreeable experiences cooperating with others to reach a target had led him to work alone, yet he knew today would be different. People would trust him. They would listen to his advice and respect his skills. Hasryan still wasn't safe, not even remotely, but tonight he would venture out of Isandor with Arathiel and others, putting years of training to good use and earning Lord Dathirii's gratitude. The world was finally giving him a chance to go forward, rather than start over.

CHAPTER TWENTY

SORA clipped her fur cloak around her neck and pulled thick gloves over her hands. She hadn't needed to wear her winter gear for months, but the weather was growing colder with every passing day, and her mission required an official uniform. She needed the city to understand her short walk through Isandor was sanctioned by her superiors, and that any threat to Lord Arathiel's security would be dealt with accordingly. Clad from head to toe in the emblematic sky blue of Isandor's Sapphire Guard, their symbol stamped on her shirt and the back of her cloak, her message would be clear.

It needed to be, if she meant to escort Lord Arathiel Brasten to the Dathirii Tower without incidents. News of the exceptional meeting of the Golden Table today had spread fast, sliding from the top of the nobles' towers to the bottom of the Lower City. Everyone with a hint of political sense recognized it as Lord

Allastam's counterattack on Lord Dathirii. But how far would it go? And would his revenge include Arathiel? She couldn't imagine Allastam without a plan for her charge.

Until he reached the confines of the Dathirii Tower, Arathiel's safety depended on her. She wished he had decided to wear more than a leather jacket to venture into the freezing weather, but she'd learned not to question such choices. He didn't feel cold, so why bother? Yet she regretted not pressing for a more normal outfit as they trekked through the street. Arathiel's passage provoked glares and the occasional whisper, and Sora's hand often wandered to the pommel of her sword. She was glad to reach the root-like bridges that stretched out of the bottom of the Dathirii Tower.

Arathiel stopped near one, and his gaze slid from his manacles to the city below. He hadn't said a word while they walked, but now that they stood in the shadow of the Dathirii Tower, he allowed his worry to show. "I get the feeling I would be safer behind bars."

"Correct."

"Will Diel be all right?" he asked.

"It depends on your definition of 'all right,' I think." She doubted he would emerge from this unscathed. Not if other noble houses had allowed Lord Allastam to move the Golden Table, thus silently agreeing that Lord Dathirii's actions needed to be discussed urgently. Lord Dathirii had ruffled feathers for as long as she could remember, however—and probably even longer than that—so Sora figured he knew how to navigate trouble. "He'll survive, but I suspect House Dathirii's struggles won't get any easier. And the entire city wonders why you are worth the damage."

Arathiel snapped his attention back to her, as if she'd slapped him. After a moment, he admitted, "It's not me. I'm the means to an end."

"Aren't we all just tools in their games?" Sora couldn't keep the bitterness out of her tone. Arathiel's words from the previous day had haunted her. Could she do more on her own? Would she have any power to change her city if she abandoned the Sapphire Guard? At least she wouldn't have corrupt commanding officers to answer to. Then again, how long before Brune's thugs came knocking at her door and made her pay for daring to work solo? She hated her current position, how her cases were mostly dictated by whoever held the most power. She used to think of it as a necessary part of the job, but now she couldn't help looking for other options.

"No. I chose to accept this, just as I chose to save Hasryan." Arathiel smiled, then shook his wrists. "I have the manacles, yet your hands are more tied than mine. Tool or no, at least I know Lord Dathirii is worthy of my help."

Sora frowned at the implication she couldn't say the same, but she didn't have the strength to contradict him. Truly, who would benefit from Hasryan's execution? Brune had set him up to take the fall, and Hasryan's escape had rallied everyone behind Lord Allastam. She might be doing this for the six families who had lost a loved one, but in the end, she served the Crescent Moon and House Allastam, and it left a bitter taste in her mouth.

"Keep telling yourself that." And she would keep telling herself she enjoyed her current situation and did not feel constrained by the investigations imposed by her superiors. If she could cling to that illusion and to her obstinate desire to bring justice to Hasryan's six other victims, she might forget how much she hoped her target assassin escaped safe and sound from this mess, despite her efforts. Just as she caught herself wishing she could speak with him again without this investigation between them. All thoughts better left buried deep within. "How many allies are you expecting before we enter?"

"Only Cal," Arathiel said.

"No Larryn?" That felt wrong. Weren't these two always together? And what could Lord Dathirii plan that would require the help of Ren's chubby, genial priest?

Arathiel turned back toward her, and she could sense him weighing words, choosing what to say and what to hide. They might deny any involvement in the prison break last week, but Sora knew better. Larryn had come, if not all three of them. "Larryn refused to take part in anything concerning Lord Dathirii, or any potentially dangerous endeavours. He has the Shelter to think of."

"I'm sure." Sora could believe Larryn wouldn't work for Lord Dathirii. He'd always made his distaste for nobles quite clear. No doubt Arathiel had left his other reasons unsaid. "Not going to tell me why Cal is there, are you?"

Arathiel's soft smile hid a layer of amusement. "Cal came because he is a friend."

They both knew that hadn't been Sora's question, but before she could press for more information, the subject of their discussion appeared at the top of a nearby staircase. Unlike Sora's tailored outfit, Cal's threadbare clothes were obvious secondhands. The coat pinched too tight at his waist, the winter hat kept falling over his eye, and the colours clashed horribly. A small mace hung at his belt, which raised more questions than it answered. Did Cal even know how to fight? He sprinted when he spotted them, and arrived with red cheeks but breathing evenly.

"Hello, Miss Sharpe!"

The chirpy greeting caught her off guard. She expected Hasryan's friend to stay wary of her, but neither Arathiel nor Cal showed any animosity. Masking her surprise, Sora smiled to him. "Good morning. Let's go."

She motioned for the entrance, and two guards led them into the vestibule. Sora relaxed as they stepped into the warm room, away from public eyes. Although it slowed her investigation, she wouldn't complain about a day without Arathiel. He had a way of asking the right questions and hearing her unsaid thoughts that set her on edge, and she was honest enough with herself to understand he'd planted a solid seed in her mind. She needed the distance to get her bearings, secure her footing, and dive back into her work without so many doubts needling her.

ARATHIEL'S gaze kept returning to Cal as they waited for Jaeger to arrive. How intense could the colours of his winter clothes be if he could see such richness in them? Either Cal had nothing else—probable, considering the ill-fitting size—or he'd forgotten the stealth component of tonight's mission. Darkness would conceal the worst of it, but still. Perhaps Lord Dathirii would have something better to lend him. Arathiel made a mental note to ask once Sora had left them.

For now, cold silence stretched over them. Even Cal's arrival hadn't sparked the lively conversation it should have. Something in the city's tense mood affected them all, dousing impulses to laugh or chat.

To Arathiel's surprise, Diel himself came down to the entrance hall. Warmth filled his greeting as he smiled at the gathered group, but Arathiel sensed his exhaustion underneath. It became even more obvious when Diel turned to Sora, his shoulders tensed.

"I'm glad you're here, Miss Sharpe. I need an unexpected word with you."

The slight confusion on Sora's expression lasted a second, soon replaced by irritation. "More favours I can't refuse, milord?"

"I can only hope so." This time, Diel's smile never reached his eyes. Arathiel disliked the soft weariness in his tone. It bore bad news. "Lady Camilla Dathirii will be waiting for you in your headquarters, brought there by Kellian. If you could … keep her presence quiet until the end of the Golden Table, I would be in your debt."

Arathiel froze at the mention of Camilla, and only through careful control did he stop his fears from showing. Nothing but Hasryan could lead Kellian to drag his own aunt to the Sapphire Guard's headquarters. Arathiel threw an alarmed glance at Diel, who pointedly did not look in his direction. Sora's expression had hardened, her eyes narrowed.

"I'm afraid you will need to explain very clearly why Camilla is at the headquarters for me to agree to anything."

Diel straightened, meeting Sora's gaze without hesitation. "Lord Kellian has reached the conclusion that Lady Camilla was involved in sheltering Hasryan Fel'ethier following his escape. I know my aunt, and must admit such behaviour falls within the realm of possibility." Diel glanced at Arathiel, as if to apologize, but his tone stayed firm. "I only want this suspicion and the corresponding investigation to remain private for half a day."

"Why would I do this for you? You're asking me to hide her, at great risk to my reputation, for little in return." Sora crossed her arms. "You do realize you've already hindered my progress by claiming Arathiel? I respect the work you do in this city and the fights you choose to lead, but I owe you nothing."

Diel sighed, and in that brief gesture, the immense weight on his heart showed. Arathiel checked his impulse to rush to him, squeeze his forearm, and promise they could fix this. Camilla wouldn't be involved if Arathiel hadn't asked, and between his guilt and his undeniable attraction to Diel, Arathiel needed all his willpower not to intervene. He watched, unmoving, as the elven lord rebuilt his mask.

"Will you take care of her, then? I suspect I will have little power by the end of the day, and I'm worried. Please, at least protect Camilla. I will return after the Golden Table to speak with her, and we will comply with the guards' demands."

Sora softened. "I wouldn't let any harm come to your aunt. I didn't when she stumbled ..." Her voice trailed off, and she turned to Arathiel, a weird sound crossing her lips, halfway between a cry of rage and a laugh. "When she distracted me and the surrounding guards from Arathiel's leap to our bridge. You are quite right. She is involved in this."

"That sounds like her," Diel said, mirth creeping back into his voice. "Miss Sharpe, you have my sincerest thanks. Would you please tell her I'm aware of the situation?"

"I will." She stepped back with a frown. "Expect us to return for a thorough search of the Dathirii Tower by the end of the afternoon."

"Of course."

Sora Sharpe turned away from Diel, striding to Arathiel and unlocking his shackles. He sighed in relief as they left his wrists. The metal might not press against his skin, but it had against his mind, and he breathed more easily in its absence. "Good luck," she said, "with whatever it is you're up to."

She left without waiting for an answer, striding back through the massive entrance doors. As soon as they slammed behind her, Cal tugged hard on Arathiel's arm. "Is it true, Ara? Did she help you? Does she know where Hasryan is?" His questions spilled out like he'd been holding them all along, and his voice grew higher in pitch with every word. Arathiel squeezed Cal's shoulder, but his gaze flicked to Diel. How much could he say now? It might be best not to risk it yet.

"She did help me distract the guards." He left the other questions unanswered.

"She'll be fine," Diel added. "Camilla might give the impression of a delicate lady with her tea and cookies, but she's seen—and caused—her share of trouble. Perhaps we could continue this conversation in my office? My niece, Branwen, is already waiting for us there. She's very eager to meet you, Arathiel, and I'm sure we'll both be pleased to get to know your friend."

"Cal," the halfling volunteered. "I mean, that's not my full name, but everyone calls me Cal. If that's not too unofficial to you. Milord!"

Arathiel put a hand in front of his mouth, hiding his amusement at Cal's sudden self-consciousness. Diel chuckled without bothering to conceal his mirth. "It's perfect, as long as you don't mind Jaeger calling you "Sir Cal." We've been together for more than a century, and he still uses "milord" on me, so there's really nothing to do about it."

"Oh. I think I can handle that! Sir Cal." He repeated it twice, his grin growing bigger each time. "Larryn would shit himself."

A split second later, Cal's eyes widened, and he gasped at what he'd just said in front of Lord Dathirii. He slapped a hand over his mouth and flushed several shades of red deeper. Diel laughed, and Arathiel watched his shoulders relax and the crow's feet appear at the corners of his eyes with satisfaction. Better this than the barely-contained despair from earlier. As they headed up a first flight of stairs, Cal fumbling for an apology and Diel emphatically telling him not to fret, Arathiel's mood escaped the tense worry it had been soaking in all morning.

Chapter Twenty-One

AFTER Lord Dathirii's departure, an awkward silence had settled in the office. Branwen tapped her letter opener on Diel's desk, looking everywhere but at Hasryan. He stared straight at her, wishing she would stop being so damn ill at ease. What was it this time? Did she hate dark elves like Kellian? Or did she disapprove of his assassinations too? No, that made no sense. Branwen had acted suspicious when he'd stepped in, yet confident. Whatever bothered her now had stolen that away. On most days, Hasryan would ignore her attitude, but they had to work together, and he didn't want to walk on eggshells around her.

"Looks like we're alone!" he said, gesturing with his hand toward the empty room. "Now's a great time to get what's bothering you off your chest."

Branwen followed his movement, then stopped tapping the knife on the desk's wooden surface. She pouted. "What's wrong with my chest?"

What? Hasryan struggled with her retort—was she really that literal? Branwen seemed dead serious, almost offended. "That's not—" A grin split her face, and he stopped his spluttering. "Sure. Mock my offer to smooth out whatever has you fidgeting."

"Couldn't help it." She dropped the knife, then heaved herself onto the desk and sat with her legs dangling. "You made it sound so gracious. I don't need invitations to speak my mind."

"You looked like you did."

"I didn't."

He regretted saying anything. Hasryan huffed and crossed his arms. Let her stew next time! Hasryan used to have no patience, but between the long days locked in a cell and those alone in Camilla's quarters, he had practised waiting in silence a lot. Branwen hadn't, it seemed, because she piped up right away.

"I was just wondering how to properly apologize," she said. "I never meant to blame you for Varden's torture. If anything, it's my fault. I should have found a way to save him sooner. I promised him."

"You're going to now." Late wasn't always better than never, but for tortured friends? Definitely. Hasryan cracked a smirk and gestured to himself. "Plus, you're bringing the best of the best with you!"

"Arathiel?" she suggested with a grin. "Yeah, I can't wait to meet him!"

They stared at each other, Hasryan searching for a quick and witty reply. He'd grown rusty over the last weeks. His long conversations with Camilla never ended in verbal sparring matches, and Sora always reverted to business after one dry counterattack.

"You got me there," he said. "I'm really looking forward to it, too."

"What's he like?"

The way she asked sounded like she expected Hasryan to answer "dreamy," then tell her all about him. He chuckled and shook his head. What was Arathiel like? Secretive, but Hasryan doubted that was in his nature. He recognized the habit born out of bad experiences. Arathiel's lasting impression had nothing to do with lies and cover-ups.

"Soft, I'd say." He frowned, unsure how to explain, or how that simple word encompassed Arathiel so well. "He only talks when he needs to, only makes himself known as necessary. But he's always there, smiling. That was how our card games went. He played in almost complete silence, yet not a serious or competitive one. Casual silence, the kind from people who prefer paying attention to others over drawing it to themselves. Then he'd put his cards down and rake in all the damn tokens." Hasryan grinned at the memories. Cal's legendary luck often took a mysterious backseat when new players sat at the table, unless the halfling meant to clean them of their money. Arathiel's calm, unapologetic but nonchalant manner of winning embodied how he went about everything. "Arathiel is a warm blanket: simple, reliable, soft. He's the friend you kind of forget, but when it really matters, he's there. Leaping off bridges to save your neck from the noose, even though you expected nothing of him."

His gaze had wandered the room as he explained, and Hasryan found Branwen staring at him, eyebrows raised. He ran a hand through his hair. She smiled. "He sounds amazing."

Voices drifted down the corridor before Hasryan could agree, chief among them Lord Dathirii's, rising in a loud and clear laugh. After the exhaustion and stress he'd exhibited earlier, the joyful sound was a refreshing surprise. The small voice that answered instead petrified him.

"I didn't mean to say it like that!" Cal exclaimed. "I can behave myself, I swear. I'm the most well-behaved halfling in the city! Or Lower City at least. Or the Shelter's neighbourhood, for sure!"

Hasryan stared at the door, frozen, thrilled and terrified. All of a sudden, he remembered Diel and Jaeger had mentioned Arathiel bringing a friend. He'd never stopped to consider who, had forgotten immediately. Yet here was Cal, in the Dathirii Tower, about to step inside the office. Cal, the friend who hadn't even turned up at the prison headquarters, who hadn't deemed him worthy of that risk.

"For someone so well-behaved, you certainly speak at a needlessly loud volume, sir." Amusement tinted Jaeger's tone. The doorknob shook as Jaeger grabbed it.

"Sir Cal."

The reply drew another laugh from Lord Dathirii, and this time, Arathiel's deeper voice joined in. Hasryan clung to the latter, certain Arathiel would defend him if they fought. The door opened, Diel entered first, and Hasryan gritted his teeth.

Cal stopped short when his gaze fell upon Hasryan. The

following second stretched into a painful eternity, his heart threatening to burst, his hands shaking. Cal cried his name, delight and surprise transforming the sound into a high-pitched squeal. Relief flooded over Hasryan as his friend sprinted past Lord Dathirii and threw himself into his legs. Cal hung there for a short but incredible moment, then stepped back. He had his big grin on, exactly the same as when he won an umpteenth game of cards. Hasryan crouched to return the embrace, his throat raw.

"Hey," he whispered, light-headed, half-convinced this wasn't real.

"Hey yourself! I'm so glad you're safe." Cal squeezed Hasryan's arm. "I didn't know you'd be on this mission with us!"

"I … I didn't either." Hasryan ran a hand through his hair and straightened up. "I thought you were angry at me. Or something."

"What?" Cal set his hands on his thighs and pinched his lips in an expression meant to be serious, but which had always seemed rather amusing to Hasryan. "Why would I be?"

Larryn had implied Cal couldn't even be bothered to show up at the prisons. His unbridled anger at Cal's absence that night had led Hasryan to think their halfling friend had abandoned him. He should have guessed Larryn would be pissed no matter Cal's reasons. "Never mind. I listen to Larryn too much."

This time, all traces of amusement vanished from Cal's round face. Sadness replaced it, only to be washed away by something altogether new to Hasryan: anger. Cal's nose scrunched up, his hands curled into tiny fists, and he stomped once with a strange growl.

"I can't believe it! What did he even say? I wanted to be there!" He stifled a cry of rage and threw his arms up. "That no good … unthinking ball of rage! I can deal with punching me, but telling you I—"

"What? Larryn did what?"

Hasryan's loud exclamation interrupted the low conversation happening between Diel, Branwen, and Arathiel. They turned in Hasryan's and Cal's direction, and a heavy silence followed. Hasryan stepped back, paying closer attention to his friend's appearance this time. Under the usual mismatch of clothes, Cal had lost some weight, and his cheek held the yellowed traces of a bruise. Cal cleared his throat, brushing the old wound.

"It's nothing, really! We already talked it over. Kind of."

From the sound of it, they hadn't gotten anywhere with that talk. Hasryan set his hand on Cal's shoulders. "It's not 'nothing,' Cal. Friends don't hit each other, and Larryn's no exception. He has no excuses."

Why would he even punch Cal over this? Larryn had turned his back on him too, leaving Hasryan in his cell on an impulse. In the end, Arathiel had saved him, not either of them.

"He's very worried about you, too," Cal added. "We all were. We've always been. I would have come, but you wouldn't believe what happened to me!"

Cal's normal enthusiasm crept back into his voice at last, but Hasryan didn't pay close attention. He still reeled at the idea that Larryn also cared, that despite his desertion in the prisons, his best friend didn't hate him. Had they both been frightened for him all this time? His hand went to Cal's shoulder, both for moral and physical support. Hasryan's legs had turned to soft wool, and his chest threatened to burst. Brune had thrown him away, treated him as nothing more than a tool, but his friends never meant to. He smiled, fighting to keep his voice steady as Cal's words finally reached him.

"I'm sure it was something very improbable, Cal."

"I know what!" Branwen's large grin reeked of confidence, and Cal turned to her with raised eyebrows, a strange light shining in his gaze. The low anger from earlier vanished, but Hasryan guessed it had only been buried. For all that Hasryan loved Larryn, he couldn't forget what he'd heard today. No one touched Cal. Not Drake, and not Larryn either. Hasryan might long for nights sharing a drink in silence on the Shelter's rooftop, but he'd have a few, well-deserved harsh words for his friend first. For now, however, Hasryan let his own foul mood slide. Branwen's declaration had brought a well-known mischievous expression to Cal's face, and he didn't want to miss the challenge that would inevitably follow.

"Wanna bet?" Cal asked, like clockwork.

"Oh, don't do that," Hasryan told Branwen.

"Bad idea," Arathiel added, and he met Hasryan's gaze with a smile. Everyone quickly learned not to bet against Cal.

"Sure, I'll take this wager." Branwen set her hands on her hips, straightening up. "And yes, I am aware of Cal's faith."

Curiosity gained on Hasryan. What could she know to muster this kind of confidence? He'd never seen Cal lose a bet, even against horrible odds. His friend had even drunk a man four times his size under the table once, despite his inability to take any alcohol without sleeping.

"Deal." Cal withdrew his holy symbol, a half-melted silver coin that somehow remained perfectly balanced despite the damage done to it, and he extended it to Branwen, palm facing up. She placed her own hand on top of it, covering the burnt black side, and repeated, "Deal." Lord Dathirii muttered a few words about planning a rescue, but his smile belied any seriousness. He wanted to know as much as anyone else in this room.

Branwen stepped back, then recited in a solemn tone, "A Myrian teenager fell nearby, no older than eighteen. He had short blonde hair, was tall and gangly the way only teenagers can be, and his memories had just been wiped out to some extent. He's called Nevian Ollu."

Cal clapped his hands with a happy squeal. "Amazing! He wouldn't even tell me his last name. How did you learn that?"

"Must I reveal all my secrets?" she asked with a wink. "It's my job to know what happens in this city."

"Or you have a well-informed cousin," Arathiel suggested.

Branwen laughed. "They have quite eloquently described the Shelter, its kind halfling, and the teenage grump they happily heal, yes, but I was there when he fell. I flung a dagger in Avenazar's shoulder, and Nevian threw himself off the bridge."

"Does everyone know he's at the Shelter?" Cal asked, his eyes widening a little. "Nevian thinks it's such a secret."

"He's a bit of a fool, then," Branwen said.

"Neither Vellien nor you bothered to tell me," Diel said, and Branwen's smile faltered at the remark. "Don't worry. These last few days were hectic, and I trust you to handle matters well. Now that your bet is settled, however, I suggest you start planning. Kellian should arrive soon enough, but time is flying. I have to prepare for the Golden Table meeting with Garith. Jaeger will be at the door all afternoon, keeping any indiscreet ears away."

They all nodded, and Lord Dathirii's gaze passed over each of them in turn.

"Branwen, be careful with your back. I'm no fool, and I know it hasn't healed completely yet. Sir Cal, it has been a pleasure, and you have my deepest thanks for joining this mission. Arathiel …" He shook his head, then met Arathiel's gaze. It felt like suddenly they'd stepped into another room, just the two of them. "I'm sorry for the circumstances under which we first spoke again. I'll do my utmost to free you, but I fear my influence in this city is waning."

Arathiel smiled. "I created my predicament to save Hasryan. I'll rest easier knowing he can count on you."

Hasryan flushed, fighting not to shrink in on himself as every eye shifted toward him. He stared at Arathiel, words of gratitude stuck in his throat. Lord Dathirii spared him the need, stepping forward to put a hand on his shoulder. "He can." He turned to Hasryan. "You won't have to leave forever, even if it's safer for now. We'll help you escape, and one day we'll go after your old boss, too. Sometimes corruption comes from within, and I've ignored the Crescent Moon for too long."

Good thing he'd done so until now, Hasryan told himself, or

they'd have wound up enemies. Deep inside, Hasryan doubted Lord Dathirii would ever get around to it. Nobles promised a lot but rarely followed through. Larryn's existence proved at least one Dathirii broke them without remorse, yet Camilla hadn't abandoned Hasryan. He wondered on which side Lord Dathirii would fall, but such thoughts ought to stay silent.

"Help Camilla first," he said. "Brune is more dangerous than you realize."

Branwen snorted at his warning. "Stop, you're encouraging him."

Diel's eyebrows arched, but he didn't deny it, instead sharing a knowing look with his niece. "Aunt Camilla first, I promise. We have enough on our plates for now. Stay safe if you can, everyone, and come back with High Priest Varden." Lord Dathirii stepped back and inhaled deeply. Tension returned to his shoulders, and new lines of worry grew around his eyes, as if in a single breath, he'd discarded one topic and continued to the next. "Wish me luck."

Hasryan said nothing as he moved for the door, but Branwen piped up with a small "Good luck, Uncle!"

"Wait!" Cal called, then ran up to the elven lord. He offered his symbol once more, and Diel touched it with a surprised smile. "Stride without fear and trust the future, for within every moment is threaded the fabric of luck, and Ren rewards the kind, the daring, and the ugly." The coin caught the light, holding it briefly as Cal intoned the words in an amused, sing-song voice.

"And which one of these am I?" Diel asked with a laugh.

"Only Xe knows!" Cal winked, and added, "Maybe all three."

"Thank you, Sir Cal," Lord Dathirii said as the light vanished. With a final farewell, he left the office. They heard him exchange a few words with Jaeger—some that sounded like instructions, others like reassurance. Hasryan ran a hand through his hair, uncomfortable in the brief silence that followed.

"Planning," he said. "I imagine we go in as night falls. Do we have a map? Ideas of a route to take?" He turned to Branwen, who pointed at the desk. They all gathered around it without another word about the Golden Table or what might happen in Isandor today. They had a mission to complete, and until they'd brought Varden safely back into the city, nothing else mattered.

Cal and Arathiel shared Nevian's precise description of the guards' routes, down to the minute. It seemed he'd sneaked in and out of the enclave on a regular basis over the two last years and, unlike Cal, the apprentice left nothing to chance. They started tracing likely paths to the prison, Hasryan slipping in the occasional joke about the compromising positions he often surprised people in as he sneaked around. None of it seemed real. He stood at a table, planning a delicate operation, and no one questioned whether he could be trusted, not even Branwen. Kellian would, he knew, and a small voice warned Hasryan to watch for the next betrayal, to stay wary of such good fortune, but he silenced it. Perhaps it wouldn't come—perhaps that part of his life had ended with Brune's treachery. At last.

Chapter Twenty-Two

Lord Diel Dathirii strode into the Golden Table's hall, head high and shoulders squared. Garith trailed a step behind him, clad in the cleanest, most decorated outfit of his wardrobe, all forest green and golden threads. Rectangular optics hid the bags under his eyes, and the fatigue he'd exhibited as they prepared in his rooms had vanished. Garith had the same determined look as his uncle, his usual smirk replaced by a grim line. They both knew they were going into battle—one of words and numbers, perhaps, but battle nonetheless.

The council's chamber was located in the bottom half of the Middle City—a high point in Isandor, in its beginning. Several nobles already filled the room, and despite the hundreds of meetings Diel had attended, he was always surprised by how diminished everyone seemed in the Golden Table's hall. The massive table at the centre, made of dark onyx and flecked with gold, dwarfed the gathered nobles. A thick golden foot supported it, carved in the likeness of Isandor's early spires.

Above the table, the ceiling rose into a great arch, most of it painted with a complex fresco. Diel traced the familiar figures of the first family lords, his youthful father among them. Prollys, patron of trades and money, watched over them as they settled. The first towers emerged under the amused gaze of Kaisa, the Stage Mistress and an embodiment of Alloran culture. She would love the spectacular competition of the ever-higher spires. Isandor's history continued through the ordeal of the Neimen Plague, past their rare military victory over eastern Nal-Gresh, and up to the first luminescent gardens at the top. A little room remained, and Diel wondered if their centuries-old independence would end with the depiction of a foreign enclave settling nearby, overtaking their trades and political institutions.

No chairs surrounded the table, which stood just under four feet tall, stopping on average at people's chests. "Seats" was a metaphor. The founding members of the Golden Table had decided they preferred to stand when yelling at each other.

Diel smiled at the thought and cast his gaze around the gathered nobles as they moved toward their assigned places. How many of them had never travelled farther down in their city than the Golden Table? Lord Allastam wouldn't bother: a large, clean ramp allowed Upper City residents to exit without ever truly entering the dirtiest parts of town. He was speaking in low tones with Lord Lorn, the head of Isandor's most powerful House—another noble who knew little of the city's bottom third. Although perhaps this one did. Tall and thin, Lord Lorn had a pointed chin, piercing eyes, and a much more hands-on approach than Lord Allastam. He negotiated deals and hired mercenaries himself rather than through an intermediary, and he might have needed the Crescent Moon at some point over the last decade.

These two occupied one end of the table along with other members of their respective families and the city's third House in importance: the Balthazars. Unlike many of Isandor's Houses, which had grown through a network of foreign trades, the Balthazars had uncovered and exploited nearby mines and grown their coffers. They now occupied four seats around the Table—just one fewer than either the Allastams or the Lorns, who both held five. These three families together made up almost half the Golden Table. The nineteen remaining spots were distributed among the other Houses with enough influence to deserve them. In the end, fifteen different families held political power in Isandor. Everyone else had to pray they decided right. The state of the Lower City proved that didn't always work out.

Diel stopped next to Lady Carrington, single representative of House Carrington, which had also been among Isandor's founding houses. They had once been a power to reckon with, but a botanical spell gone wrong had infected half of her people with virulent spores, and the string of deaths that followed had left the family in shambles. Lady Carrington had inherited it at the age of fourteen, and although trade allies had deserted the House, she had done a solid job of keeping everything together. Still, House Carrington should no longer have held their seat, but no one had demanded to see the family's wealth status, and as a consequence, their position at the table wasn't questioned.

House Dathirii would get no such favour.

Everyone edged toward their respective places. Diel brushed Garith's back, and his nephew relaxed. He put the account books down on the smooth surface, glanced at his uncle, and smiled. They were as prepared as possible. Diel looked over the gathered nobles one last time. Most avoided his gaze, and the eyes of those who met it without hesitation held little sympathy. His throat tightened, and he wished Jaeger had come, to wait outside as usual. Branwen needed him, however. After a deep breath, Diel finished his look around by staring at Lord Allastam, raised his chin, and set his hands flat on the table.

The Golden Table hushed. Isandor's nobles weren't fools. They knew the confrontation about to unravel, and the moment Diel locked eyes with Lord Allastam, they had drawn a collective breath. In the heavy ensuing silence, Lord William cleared his throat.

Even by the standards of Isandor's nobility, the man was an oddball. Unlike others around the table, he did not belong to a family, and William was his first and only name. His personal fortune sufficed to grant him a place on the council, and he barely participated in local struggles for trade deals, preferring drama plays, balls, and re-enactments of famous battles. A constant string of artists came and went from his house, but since William never interfered with the political strife in Isandor, nobles often called upon him to act as neutral ground in personal conflicts. He had tried and failed to resolve the Allastam–Freitz conflict a dozen times over the last decade. He was well-suited to the role of presiding over the Golden Table and guiding its debates. No doubt today would turn particularly heated.

"We are the Golden Table, the heart of Isandor, the creators of its future."

Lord William's cold voice boomed in the tense silence. Once, this sentence had begun a much longer, almost cult-like declaration that preceded meetings of the Golden Table. Even slashed down to this short version, Diel hated it. The heart of Isandor? The pretentious lie reeked of self-importance, but he had more significant fights ahead of him today and no energy to waste. He let Lord William continue—their president loved his dramatic introductions anyway.

"Although our last meeting was not long ago, many events have unfolded since we bid each other goodbye. Several of them surround House Dathirii, and we have gathered to speak of their actions and status." With a flourish, William turned to Diel. "Milord, if you desire, the honours of first speech are yours."

Diel shook his head. "I see no need." He allowed his voice to carry and was relieved to hear his own resolute tone. The confidence Diel projected didn't reach into his guts. Garith cast him an alarmed glance, but Diel knew his nephew would follow his lead, no matter how terrifying. "I know what I've done and see no wrong in it. I would rather defend myself against clear accusations instead of answering to whispers, rumours, and exaggerations. Let Lord Allastam state his complaint first."

Lord Allastam scoffed, infusing the sound with an amazing

amount of disgust and derision. "We're not here to discuss your disgraceful actions. We're here to examine whether your wretched family even deserves a place around our illustrious Table."

"Ah, yes, of course. This has nothing to do with Lord Arathiel Brasten's presence in my tower this morning." Diel couldn't keep the edge out of his voice. He hadn't expected Lord Allastam's level of aggressiveness. Wretched family? Insults around the Golden Table tended to be implied rather than direct. But if Lord Allastam didn't plan to grant him a hint of respect, then Diel wouldn't waste time on politeness. "I'm sure every lord here believes that."

His comment drew a smattering of snickers, but most of the nobles around the table looked aside. They might not believe it, yet none of them seemed willing to point out the obvious source of Lord Allastam's attack.

"Whatever else happens doesn't change a simple fact, dear Diel: you sank House Dathirii's entire fortune into a pointless war against the Myrian enclave. I would wager your dashing outfit this morning is worth more than what's left in your coffers."

"That would be demonstrably false," Garith replied. "Please do bet. From hearing you, we're in desperate need of the gold you'd lose on such a gamble."

"I'm sure you are, but, unlike certain elves, I don't waste money on lost causes."

"We haven't lost yet," Diel said.

"Oh, come now." Lord Allastam tapped the end on his cane on the ground twice. By his side, his son Drake snickered. "You have nothing to fight them with. Your allies are fleeing you, and your wealth is gone. What will you do? Blow them up? We all know that's not your style. Far too … efficient."

"Just because you can't see a way out doesn't mean there isn't one." Diel straightened and spread his palms on the table. "I do have to wonder why my finances are called into question now, in the very middle of this confrontation with the Myrians. It's unusual. By tradition, we give our own more leniency, allowing for a few months of recovery after a conflict before we reexamine any House's finances." Several eyes turned to Lady Carrington, present by the council's grace. She didn't waver under their stare—decades at the Golden Table had taught her everything she needed about composure. "But perhaps Lord Allastam only extends such courtesy to those who pay lip service to him."

"I pay such courtesy to the Houses worthy of it."

His choice of words cast silence around the Table. Somehow, "unworthy" rang worse than his earlier "wretched." Allastam had often called rivals the latter, yet always considered them deserving of their position. A sneer curled his lips as his gaze rounded the gathered nobles.

"What a magnificent silence. You're a disgrace, Lord Dathirii, and your recent partnership with the freak who saved my wife's murderer exemplifies it. Have you listened to yourself in the last, oh, decade at least? You're so in love with Lower City filth and those emerging from it that you forget who your peers are." He gestured widely at the Table. "They didn't, however. No one here wants to defend you."

The silence grew even heavier. Blood rushed against Lord

Dathirii's temples, and even the tips of his fingers throbbed. He didn't dare to look around the Golden Table and focused instead on staying upright, chin held high. Always before, when he had risen against the city's conservative ways, a handful of other nobles would be nodding along with his arguments, or rolling their eyes at his opponents. Now, they remained stiff, not encouraging Lord Allastam, but certainly not countering him. Diel stood alone against everyone, and although he had suspected this might happen, he struggled to contain his rising panic. Diel exhaled slowly, forcing his breathing into a regular pattern. He didn't need them. If no one around Isandor's Golden Table could see how twisted this was—how secondary Arathiel's one-day freedom should be in comparison to repudiating the Myrians—then perhaps he didn't want to call them peers.

"I'll defend him."

Lady Brasten's deep, young voice shattered the silence. Diel's heart jumped as he spun to face her, a wave of relief coursing through him. She stood halfway between him and Lord Allastam, straight and proud, her dark brown eyes meeting Diel's briefly before they turned to Lord Allastam. Lady Brasten had chosen a silver dress for the occasion, its heavy velvet enhancing her thick rolls of fat and contrasting against her dark skin. Her lips pressed in a thin line, she flicked her myriad of twists and raised her head. All of a sudden, she seemed to fill the entire room.

"House Brasten has, of course, condemned the actions of our most recent, yet oldest, member. But if I recall correctly, so has House Dathirii. I will say this: we are glad one of our own no longer rots in a cell in conditions far from acceptable for one of his status."

"He freed—"

"I'm well aware."

Lady Amake Brasten shrugged, exemplifying a calm and confidence neither Lord Allastam nor Diel had shown so far. Regal and wise, she commanded everyone's attention, and Diel thanked the gods for her presence at his side. He had an ally, someone willing to defend him, who had expressed gratitude for his actions. Someone ready to take Lord Allastam down a peg in one simple and beautiful sweep.

"You may not realize this, Lord Allastam, but your son is known to harass commoners and beat them. He has a horrendous reputation in several respectable taverns, and I daresay only his title keeps their doors open." Everyone knew Drake's reputation, and Diel caught slight nods from other nobles around the table. Tales of his misbehaviour travelled both to the highest and lowest levels of Isandor, whispered about to avoid trouble. Drake himself was fuming, fists curled on the table, glaring at Lady Brasten. She continued as if she hadn't noticed, her hands flitting through the air as she spoke. "Yet no one here questions his worth, or yours for protecting him from legal consequences. Should we? You seem to think of Lord Arathiel's single mistake as an unforgivable act that should inform our opinion of everyone he allies with. *This* is why I'll defend Lord Dathirii and his family. You berate him for forgetting his peers, but willingly omit any consideration for Lord Arathiel's title and position within my House. I question your logic and your coherence, and find your incessant attacks on Lord Dathirii's character quite undignified. Our records show Lord Arathiel to be kind and loyal, prompt to self-sacrifice. I have been given no reason to believe otherwise."

"No." Lord Allastam slammed his cane against the ground. "He is a monster, an abomination of nature held together by magic unknown and unhealthy. I have read the reports. He should not be alive."

"Yet he is, returned to us by the grace of Evzen, who rules over both Death and Rebirth, and I recognize his claim to our house." Lady Brasten laid down the words with finality, closing the matter. She tilted her head to the side then, her expression softening. "Milord, I have lost much of my family to illness and understand your grief. I remember Lady Allastam inviting me to dance as a young girl. Your wife was a beautiful and generous person, and she is still missed by all of us, every day. Isandor has witnessed the depth of your sorrow, but you're misdirecting it. This assassin is your only solid lead to the true culprit. If you see him dead, we'll never uncover who hired him. Don't you want to know?"

At first, it seemed like Lord Allastam listened to her, his stern expression firm but open. Yet as Lady Brasten spoke, his sneer crawled back, and a dangerous light shone in his dark eyes. His knuckles whitened on his cane, and he banged it hard at her question, making several nobles around the table jump.

"How dare you suggest I don't care about Elena's death! I have—"

"I never—"

"Enough, shut up!" He half-snarled the words, and although Lady Brasten obeyed, she met his glare without flinching. "You're implying I should overlook how this dark elf slit my wife's throat to work with him, a distasteful suggestion if I ever heard one. Couch your words in false sympathy all you want, Lady Brasten, but you've yet to experience brutal loss."

"Yet?" For the first time since she'd spoken up, Lady Brasten's countenance slipped. Her voice cracked, and she gripped the table with both hands. Diel wished he could express his sympathy. The very illness that had claimed Arathiel's sister continued to affect the family as a whole, passed down through generations, ripping lives apart.

"That's enough," Lord Dathirii said, and though his voice stayed controlled and soft, it carried through the room. Diel nodded in Lady Brasten's direction, both as thanks for her support and acknowledgment of her pain. "House Brasten deals more closely with loss than any of us. I believe you've made your vendetta against Arathiel and any who would dare stand by him clear. Stop pretending this is about anything but vengeance, and let's get it over with. I have no patience for lords who think so highly of themselves that they destroy other Houses and put the entire city at risk of being overtaken by the Myrians for the sake of their petty feelings."

"You're always so melodramatic, Diel." His sneer firmly in place, he leaned back from the table. Drake snorted besides him, but most of the gathered nobles didn't dare react. "I consider the Myrians economic partners, not conquerors. Don't get angry because I won't side with freaks and murderers like you do."

"They're slavers, but why would that bother you? The step between cheap labour and slavery is small, and you've always advocated for paying pennies to the poor folk forced to drag our buckets of piss to the slides. I refuse to bow to the Myrian Empire, nor will I allow corrupt mercenary leaders to blame their crimes on subordinates and escape justice."

At the room's collective intake of breath, Lord Dathirii knew he'd stumbled. Too much emphasis on the "I." How many in this room had denied him help when he asked for it? How many had congratulated Lord Allastam on the capture of his wife's assassin, perhaps suspecting Brune was shoving responsibility where it didn't fully belong? Diel didn't need to attack them directly. They would know this concerned them too. They would feel assaulted and withdraw. He stared ahead, resisting the urge to examine their reaction more thoroughly. It would be admitting his mistake. With a victorious smirk, Lord Allastam raised his hands in a movement that could only mean 'you see?'

"Such disdain for your peers," he said.

A part of Diel wanted to defend himself, to deny it. Yet his throat tightened, blocking words he knew would be lies. His peers, as Allastam said, always stood by and watched in silence when there was no direct gain for them. Some had excuses—the Carringtons couldn't afford to speak up, and Lady Brasten had despite the risks— but so many of Isandor's nobles had only ambition and misplaced pride to guide them. He did have disdain for them, for their egoism and shortsightedness. Right now, standing under their reproachful gazes, Diel found he had little respect left for any of them. But his job was to mask that, to make allies out of them despite his feelings, and he had failed.

"Garith, please show the Golden Table our wealth reports."

His nephew grew paler, and the bags hidden behind his glasses seemed more obvious to Diel. "Isn't there a vote?" he squeaked.

In normal circumstances, there would be one to decide if it was worth it to open a House's finances and reevaluate its status. The Golden Table had assembled early for that specific purpose, however, and Diel had just messed up. He motioned with one hand for the other nobles to raise theirs if they were in favour, and all but three did. Lady Brasten placed both hands in front of her and offered him a saddened smile. Lord Khaldun also refused—his family had recently climbed to the Golden Table, and not without a fair bit of help from Diel. The third, to Diel's surprise, was Lord William. The Table's president watched him with a smirk, as if the entire process was nothing more than a game. Lord Dathirii hid his irritation over William's careless attitude and thanked each of them with a nod while Garith opened his account book and several scrolls.

"There's a lot of it." The brief vote had sufficed for Garith to regain his countenance, and his tone turned serious, almost solemn. His nephew would know what he had to do now. His seat at the Golden Table would not survive this trial, but Diel's place might also be compromised. Whatever followed, however, would not be Garith's fault. Soft pride warmed Diel as he watched him straighten, meet the other nobles' gazes, and add calmly, "Let me walk you through it." Garith might spend a lot of time playing around and flirting, but he always rose to the task when needed.

The Golden Table spent the next hour arguing over numbers and their meanings. The others battered Garith with questions about his methods, implying more often than not that he was faking these incomes, and Diel's nephew answered each in a calm and serious tone. He had likely tried to disguise the extent of their debts, but Diel had advised him not to go overboard. Counting tricks didn't survive the Golden Table's examination, and they'd tolerate none of them.

By the time the nobles seemed satisfied with their answers, Diel had acquired a solid headache and the desire to dive into the Reonne's waters to refresh himself and block out all sounds. The lords and ladies passed Garith's notes around one last time, and everyone was allowed a final question. When all was said, Lord William gestured to the great gates leading into the Golden Table's hall.

"You'll have to wait outside while we decide, I'm afraid."

Diel nodded and motioned for Garith to go before him. They left without a word, very aware they might never attend another council meeting. Garith glanced around the antechamber, then slumped against a wall.

"What do you think?" He stared ahead, not a trace of hope in his voice. "I lost us both seats, didn't I?"

"You handled yourself perfectly in there. I'm proud of you."

Garith laughed, pushed his glasses back up, and turned toward Diel. "What I hear is that yes, they're gone, but it's not my fault?"

"Precisely." Garith didn't seem to believe him, so Diel walked to him, and put a hand on his shoulder. "You did what you could, and making gold appear is not one of these things. I provoked them. In a good mood, they might have left us a seat, but I shoved their lack of ethics right in their face. My words cost us the second spot, not your maths."

"Uncle … do we even need them? The seats, the titles? Do we want to be with the rest of these people?"

Diel wished he had an easy answer. The prospect of losing the family's nobility status constricted his insides and nauseated him. He shouldn't care—being Lord Dathirii shouldn't matter—but they had been nobles since Isandor's foundation. Perhaps Hellion had been right to call him the downfall of his family. All because he'd followed his heart, and what had seemed like the only moral path.

"We do, Garith. It's not about being with them; it's about having the power to protect ourselves and change things. For Isandor's sake."

Even working against the flow, he had accomplished a lot for the Middle and Lower City through the years, counteracting laws that would further separate nobles from the rest as well as protecting local traders and manufacturers. That was over, at least for now, but his inability to impact legislation didn't worry Diel the most. Their status brought a massive advantage: it was ill-advised to attack a noble in Isandor. The strong solidarity with Lord Allastam after his loss, even ten years later, demonstrated how Isandor's nobility cooperated with and protected each other, especially against an outsider like Hasryan—or like the Myrians. House Dathirii might come into frequent conflict with others, but they remained nobles. Without a title, however, the entire Dathirii household became naked targets.

How long would it take before Master Avenazar used this chance?

The doors opened once more. Diel and Garith scrambled to their feet as Lord William stepped out, a solemn expression etched on his face. It amazed Diel how similar to Jaeger he looked when he dropped the aloof smile. They were of a similar build, both pale with dark hair. Lord William cut his short, however, and his traits were rounder, less sharp. Their postures were worlds apart, too. Jaeger always stood straight, respectful. Lord William slumped back, as if he preferred to be slightly removed and study those around him. Diel stepped forward.

"The debate didn't last."

It could only mean one thing. He met Lord William's dark gaze, and the council's president nodded. "I'm afraid so."

Diel's ears buzzed, as if filled with a thousand bees. The floor under his feet didn't seem solid anymore, and for a moment, he felt far removed from the antechamber. Garith's hand touched his back, exactly as Diel had done to him at the start of the Golden Table meeting. The cool fingers grounded Diel.

"We'll go in and hear it from them," he said.

"Of course. Before you do, however, please know I will always welcome Jaeger, yourself, or any member of your great family in my humble manor."

Lord William's grand mansion had nothing modest about it,

unless compared to the most eccentric spires of Isandor, but Diel kept his comments to himself. This offer fell on attentive ears. With or without a title, Lord Dathirii would need to shore up his finances until his confrontation with the Myrians was over. He hated the thought of borrowing money, yet did he have a choice? There were worse nobles than Lord William to be indebted to.

"Thank you, milord. I believe it's time for me to hear my sentence." Not bothering to hide his bitter irony, he turned toward his nephew. "Ready to dive in again, Garith?"

"Of course! What's a little demotion to us, Uncle?"

Garith grinned, and though the smile didn't reach his eyes, his return to a relaxed confidence reassured Diel. He was right. They were only losing a title. It would make everything more complicated and dangerous, but in the end, it was nothing but prestige and influence. As long as he had his family by his side, Diel Dathirii didn't care for the 'Lord' in front of his name.

Chapter Twenty-Three

THE creak of his prison door woke Varden with a start. His heart jumped into his throat, and he scrambled for the corner of the tiny cell, hands scraping against the uneven stone beneath him. He curled up there, trembling, keeping his eyes away from the newcomer. He didn't want to look there, knew too well who he would find.

Who, though? Terror clawed at his heart as he struggled for a name. He could not allow himself to forget. Avenazar. Master Avenazar of the Myrian Enclave. He had to remember that. Arms tightening around his knees, Varden reached into his mind for his personal litany—his shield against the ravage in his memories. He was High Priest Varden Daramond. He was Isbari, and respected by his community. He loved men. He loved to draw. He had tried to save Branwen and to protect Nevian. And he was proud of these things. As long as he let none of them go—as long as he remembered who he was—he had won. Avenazar would not erase him.

"You grow more pathetic with every day."

The snide voice buzzed in his ears. Varden cocked his head and tried to make himself tinier, to vanish into the wall. He had learned not to retort, to just let Avenazar talk and endure. Anything else launched the wizard into the most horrible flights of destructive magic. The best he could do was wait for the torture to start, then wait for it to go away. Although … they'd brought several minuscule meals since the last visit. Perhaps it had been a while? Varden tried to count, to get a measure of time, but the days blurred into one another. Once, he knew, he had been able to instinctively feel sunset. Iced shackles had blocked that away, stealing Keroth from him.

"I don't understand what Jilssan sees in you." Avenazar's boots scuffed on the floor as he approached. He set his toe against Varden's leg and pushed it. "She thinks it's a shame I'm letting you rot away. Poor girl. It only took a little romance to destroy her pragmatism."

Varden's fingers dug into his shins. Jilssan's admission of interest had disturbed him, but the idea that it had pulverized her cunning manipulative skills held its own kind of ridicule. If she'd implied to Avenazar that she had more than a passing fancy for him, then she must have wanted something. But what? Varden tried to gather his scattered thoughts. Avenazar often mocked him, yet he was clearly aiming for a longer conversation today. What had changed? Did it relate to Jilssan? Hard to say what. Hard to do anything at all. But the wizard's cruel enthusiasm had morphed; of that, Varden was certain. He lifted his hand and risked a glance at the thin face. Avenazar's skin had always been drawn tight against his skull. The cell's dim light gave it an even deadlier appearance.

"She does have a point," Avenazar said. "We could do much better with you."

Varden's throat tightened. What had Jilssan told him to elicit such a response? She'd visited him once after Avenazar had stopped burning the days in his back, to tell him she'd done what she could. She had wanted him to know whom he had to thank for the small break. Apparently, she had kept trying. Varden would rather not hear the result, but as always, he had little choice in the matter.

"Free me?" Varden followed his suggestion with a derisive snort.

Avenazar's ugly cackle filled his ears. It bounced on the stone walls, sending a horrible shiver up Varden's spine. How often had the sound announced sudden pain? His breath quickened, and he recoiled, preparing himself for the discharge of energy. The Myrian wizard bent and patted his tangle of curly hair.

"Fascinating, how your sense of humour lingers. I've always wondered what goes into people's personalities. How much do their memories build them? What remains once you begin to erase these? And how much control could I have over the void left?" Avenazar's casual tone terrified Varden. The wizard's hypotheses typically became pretexts to inflict further pain upon him. Varden prayed this time would be the exception—he already struggled to keep himself together without Avenazar stripping away layers of memories for fun. Avenazar crouched next to Varden, his voice falling to a whisper. "Aren't you curious?" he asked. "Don't you want to know how much of yourself you can save?"

A choked sob escaped Varden's lips. All along, he'd expected this to happen, yet the knowledge crashed into his chest and laid there, an immense weight pressing down. Avenazar could wipe entire memories away, had perfected his technique on Nevian for two years. Why would he stop there? Why wouldn't he transform Varden's mind in a playground and push the limits of his power?

"Please, no."

Another cackle. No use in pleading, not with him. Avenazar grabbed the iced shackles and straightened himself, pulling Varden up in the process. Shards dug into the priest's scorched skin, drawing a pained cry from him as he stood. The cold constricted his wrists and his head spun violently. Varden fell back to his knees, his woolly legs unable to support his weight.

"Varden …" Disappointment dripped into Avenazar's tone. "Don't make me drag you there. You won't like it."

As if he'd enjoy what was bound to happen. He stared at his hands, palms flat on the ground. His arms shook, his stomach shifted around in an unpredictable manner, and his head felt miles away. If only he could close his eyes and return to his miserable sleep. But Avenazar loomed over him, his enthusiasm barely contained at the idea of his future experiments.

"Why now?" Avenazar had left him alone for so long. Something had changed, it must have. Varden lifted his chin, scraping together the energy and courage to look straight at Avenazar. "Can't I at least know what to expect?"

Avenazar grinned at him. "I guess I could tell you … if you stand."

Of course. Trying new spells was only half the fun Avenazar drew from this. Always, he'd played these games of dominance with Varden. Most of the time, he'd sent the priest running after Nevian, revealing only that the apprentice needed healing yet never indicating where to find him. Avenazar needed control, and he needed to remind everyone who was in charge.

With a deep breath, Varden straightened his back, slid one knee underneath his body, and pushed himself up. His delicate balance threatened to collapse at any moment, the world spinning under him. He kept rising, one hand on the wall, until he was standing at full height, wobbly but determined not to stumble. His gaze fell down on Avenazar, and Varden waited for the wizard to bend his neck backward, even a little. Enough that Avenazar would notice.

"Tell me," Varden said, removing his hand from the wall. It sounded like an order—a dangerous gamble, considering who he was addressing. But why would he grovel? Varden squared his shoulders despite his exhaustion. He would hold onto his pride until he could no longer remember why he should love himself. Avenazar's games only fanned his resilience, and he would willingly risk the wizard's anger if it meant resisting servitude. With a barking laugh, Avenazar snapped his fingers under Varden's nose.

"I'll enjoy crushing that out of you."

He started down the corridor, forcing Varden to follow. So much for the promised explanation. As always, defiance brought delays and struggles. Varden gritted his teeth, every step an exercise of willpower. His bare feet scraped against the ground, but he endured, unable to lift them higher. He just had to keep walking despite his nausea, despite his muscles screaming and his paralyzing terror. He could walk. He had to.

"Tell me," Varden repeated.

"We had news from Myria. Great news! You are no longer a High Priest. Your traitorous actions and disreputable activities were deemed unacceptable. Many agreed it was well past time you returned to your rightful place in society." Avenazar reached into his pocket and removed a folded paper. The official wax seal glinted in the torches' dim light, and Varden didn't need to be shown the letter. Every Isbari knew what these were.

"Slave."

"Glad to see you agree!"

"I don't," he whispered.

Varden had always feared this day would come, but nothing could have prepared him for it. He stopped, leaning against the wall. He felt stripped and small and crushed, dismayed and desperate. Yet revolt, anger, and determination simmered under those, threatening to take over. Isbari never stayed free in Myria, not when they raised their voices or tried to make their lives better. Sooner or later, someone would have found a reason to tear his freedom away. And although the smear clung to his heart, Varden reminded himself they'd blamed him for actions he was proud of. A meagre consolation, but one nonetheless.

"You should be glad," Avenazar continued, leading him up the prisons' stairs, and Varden pushed himself to follow. Fresh air reached him, renewing his awareness. His gait gained certainty and his mind cleared as he listened to Avenazar drone on. "Jilssan convinced me to change the nature of our quality time together. Nevian's death created a void in my daily life, one which you could easily fill. Replacing one slave with another is the logical step, especially considering I'll have a new guest tonight."

"Nevian wasn't a slave." Easier to discuss someone else's fate than his own, even someone dead. Avenazar's vivid descriptions of the fate he had inflicted on Nevian sprang to Varden's mind, and he buried them. Nevian had pushed Varden away at every occasion, shattering any chance they'd had to bond over their two years in the enclave together, but Varden had grown fond of the teen's subtle, stubborn defiance. It took a special kind of courage to stand up to Avenazar every day, knowing what he could do.

"Not quite," Avenazar agreed. "I allowed Nevian a measure of freedom, and what did he do with it? Sell our information to the Crescent Moon and betray his homeland!" Avenazar scoffed. "You won't have that opportunity. I have devised an innovative spell. It requires a tremendous amount of power, but if all goes well, you won't remember enough of yourself to even consider rebellion."

Cold horror numbed Varden's mind as Avenazar's earlier jibe echoed in it. How much would he be able to save, if anything? Would his efforts to keep himself together turn out all for nothing? Avenazar meant to erase him exactly as he'd wiped out Nevian's memories. But Varden wouldn't even be granted the mercy of death. He would continue living—moving according to Avenazar's wishes, perhaps unaware of what he'd lost.

"You devised it?"

Varden wasn't certain how the words had made it past his lips. His feet shuffled onward on their own, bringing him closer to his fate with every step, as if Avenazar had already transformed him into a mindless slave.

Avenazar turned to grin at Varden. "Indeed, and you're the perfect test subject. No one will care, and your peculiar connection with Keroth will help me achieve success."

Varden froze, reeling from the possible meanings of Avenazar's implied threat. Keroth would never allow it, his mind countered, yet where had the Firelord been since the Long Night's Watch? Varden prayed to Them whenever he could muster the strength, certain his god would not abandon him, but this inexorable path toward servitude instilled doubt in him. "No one will care," Avenazar had said. He had brutally murdered Varden's few allies in Isandor, leaving him alone and stranded. And now the wizard threatened to use even Keroth against him.

Avenazar grabbed the bridge of ice between Varden's wrists and pulled, and the sharp pain in his forearm grounded him. He couldn't despair now. Varden had little fight left, but he would continue to pray and resist with all of his exhausted willpower.

He was High Priest Varden Daramond. He was Isbari, and respected by his community. He loved men. He loved to draw. He had tried to save Branwen and to protect Nevian.

He was proud of these things, and he would fight to the end for them.

CHAPTER TWENTY-FOUR

L ADY Camilla Dathirii wielded silence the way Kellian used swords: with deadly precision. Most of her silences were pauses in the conversation, space for her interlocutors to consider their words and thoughts. They were benevolent offerings of time, soft and sweet and undemanding. You could either take them for self-reflection, or you could move on.

Her current silence, however, was meant to force introspection on Kellian. She strode out of the Dathirii Tower at a good pace, ignoring Kellian's firm hand on her arm, and when he asked her again why she would hide an assassin, she refused to answer. She shot him a single glance, imposing her silence, and he obeyed.

Never in her lifetime had one Dathirii arrested another. House conflicts remained internal: one did not expose their siblings to outsiders, especially without first talking with Lord Dathirii. If Kellian had foregone any discussion about her arrest, it meant he knew he'd be rebuked. Even if he didn't admit it to himself, he'd understood from the start this was wrong. His arrest might prove that she'd acted on her own and that House Dathirii did not condone her choices—a logical political decision—yet it went against everything their family stood for.

And as they progressed in silence, Camilla watched Kellian's frown deepen. He tried to maintain a neutral expression, but she had learned to read him and other Dathirii decades ago. His jaw stiffened, the corners of his mouth dropped, and his stare forward had unfocused. He was looking inward, and perhaps he didn't enjoy what he saw. Good. Kellian's grief had spanned ninety years and left deep scars, but it did not excuse his knee-jerk reaction to dark elves. She wanted him to think hard on his behaviour, like a child she'd sent to stand in the corner of an empty room. She wished she could say she expected Kellian to change his mind, but that would mean disregarding his natural stubbornness.

They carried on in almost hostile silence, one staircase at a time. The highest parts of the city were almost deserted: many nobles would either be attending the Golden Table, or waiting for news in their respective towers. In many ways, Isandor was holding its breath. Camilla would have preferred to do the same, and her wish redoubled when a deep voice called to them.

"It's not every day you see such tension between two Dathirii."

Kellian's head snapped to the left, and he stepped closer to Camilla as soon as he spotted who had addressed them. She turned much more slowly, schooling herself into a calm expression. Maintaining the mask demanded her entire willpower as she faced

Brune.

Hasryan's old boss strode past two other citizens to close the distance between them. A maroon coat kept her warm, and her dark hair vanished into its hood. Brune had mastered the art of brown—clothes, accessory, skin tone, and make-up, everything on her was one shade of it or another. Although she held no weapons, neither Kellian nor Camilla relaxed. They knew Brune's strength resided in her magic, both divine and arcane, not in swords.

"What a pleasing coincidence to find you both on these bridges. I assumed your family would be too busy to wander around the city." A brief smile lit her squarish features, but she didn't bother to maintain it. The rare potential onlookers hurried on their way, and although Brune's tone remained clear, her voice didn't carry much farther than the two elves. "Are you heading for the Sapphire Guard's Headquarters?"

"We're on business," Kellian retorted. "Our business."

Brune showed no offence. "Of course. Every House must have its secrets, no?" She laughed, but the sound contained no mirth or warmth. "I won't insist. I know enough of House Dathirii to understand this is nothing like an unofficial arrest. I'm simply glad I have this chance to speak with Lady Camilla."

Camilla's throat tightened. She knew. How could she? Camilla wore no handcuffs and strode in front of Kellian, not dragged by him. The tense silence between them could not reveal enough for Brune to infer an arrest, yet Camilla didn't believe this particular phrasing was a stab in the dark. She lifted her chin, hurriedly burying her fear behind a peaceful smile. "What could possibly have earned me this honour?"

"I wanted to thank you for taking such good care of my assassin," she said, her voice dropping even lower. "I do hope he'll remain safe until the end of the day. After his miraculous escape, it'd be a shame if something were to happen."

Dismayed silence met her words, and a grin split Brune's serious expression. She bade them both a wonderful afternoon and strode past them, continuing on her business as if she had expressed the most casual, meaningless thoughts of the year. Kellian's hand tightened on the pommel of his sword as she passed, and Camilla knew he'd jump into battle at the slightest sign of aggression.

Questions bounced around Camilla's mind. How had Brune learned so much? No one knew about the arrest except Hasryan. For a brief instant, Camilla considered the potential meaning of the mercenary leader calling him *hers*, of how this information had spread. What if …? No, she dismissed such thoughts. She trusted Hasryan wholeheartedly. If she began to doubt his loyalty, then Brune had isolated him yet again. Perhaps that's all she wanted, but Camilla couldn't help search for more. The Crescent Moon would never have become a deep-reaching mercenary organization if Brune wasted time amusing herself with personal vendettas. So what did she gain in telling them how much she knew?

Kellian touched her forearm, drawing her out of her thoughts. "I don't like it," he said.

"Bring me home, Kellian." She wanted to speak with Hasryan— to warn him of the threat and pick his brains about Brune's potential game.

"No." With a firm hand on her back, Kellian started toward the headquarters again. "In other circumstances, I might, but I will be absent most of the day. You will be safer with Sora."

"Under arrest." Camilla didn't hide the doubts in her voice. She trusted Sora, but once Isandor learned that she didn't even deny helping Hasryan, her fate would be out of the investigator's hands. "I would rather be at risk with my family than safe and alone."

"You should have thought of that before hiding him." His expression shut down, and Camilla knew any further arguing would be pointless. She lifted her chin, returning to the cold silence they had shared earlier. If Kellian refused to change his mind despite Brune's worrying intrusion, he deserved to spend more time in his corner.

LACK of outside news made Camilla's confinement to Sora's office difficult. She had spent her day replying to Sora's questions and apologizing as she declined to answer. Every time the investigator asked about Hasryan's location, Camilla offered only a pained smile and a polite refusal. She might open up once Diel had come, but until she met with her nephew, Camilla was determined to remain silent. All she'd revealed was that she had used her personal entrance to sneak Hasryan inside and out, and that Lord Dathirii had no knowledge of her plans. Diel had enough problems with the Golden Table without an even more direct connection to this.

Camilla wished for tea to ease her worry and make the wait

more bearable. She leaned against the office's window and stared at the sun, peeking behind towers and sitting low on the horizon. The Golden Table would finish soon, and she wondered how her nephew and grandson had done. Was Garith ready with the accounts? Did they have the fortitude to withstand the long debates? How many seats had been lost, one or both?

Camilla's concerns went beyond the Golden Table to the secret expedition bound out of Isandor tonight. She suspected Kellian would be welcomed by Arathiel and Branwen with a cold shoulder after his actions this morning, but he'd provide the team with essential fighting skills. They ought to be all right. Camilla could only hope. After hearing Branwen's tales, she shuddered to think of what Master Avenazar would do if he caught them.

And then, perhaps most preoccupying of all, there was her brief encounter with Brune. The mercenary leader's words clung to her mind, the implied threats and knowledge staggering her. *Thank you for taking care of my assassin.* How had Brune learned that? And what did she mean by wishing he'd stay safe until the end of the day? Did she intend to attack once more? Had she waited for an occasion to finish what public execution had failed to accomplish? Camilla's throat tightened and her mind flew through possible ways to warn Hasryan.

Any message would have to go through Sora, however, who was staring at Camilla with an annoyed frown. Their gazes met, and her eyebrows shot up. "Glad you're back with us, Lady Camilla."

"I'm terribly sorry," she said. "I never meant to leave. I get horribly distracted when I cannot occupy my hands and stave off worry."

Sora's sober office did not exactly offer many options. She had a single abstract painting behind her desk and a tall snake plant in the corner of the room. The papers on her desk were in neat stacks, her inkwell clean, and Camilla suspected the seven leather folders in a pile contained documentation on Hasryan's assassinations. Sora kept one hand flattened on top. She set down her quill with a sigh.

"Are your chances at the Golden Table so slim? The other guards are betting against Lord Dathirii, but they are pessimistic by nature."

"I hope they're not too attached to those coins, then," Camilla answered. "Even if we lose our seats, Diel will bounce back. We never give up. I'm sure you've noticed we tend toward stubbornness that way."

"'Pigheaded' is the word I'd use." Sora half chuckled and shook her head. "What's on your mind, then?"

"Brune." No point in hiding it. Camilla turned her hat in her hands, fidgeting with its edge. How much could she tell Sora about this? "Kellian and I met her earlier, coming here. She must have sought me out. She implied she knew where to find Hasryan, and that he might be in danger."

She hoped he had left her quarters. Sooner or later, they would search the Dathirii Tower for him, and her rooms for clues to his location. Hasryan would never hunker down there, but where had he gone? Would it be safe, or would they catch him after all? Camilla prayed he'd sought help, yet she doubted it. Hasryan barely trusted her.

"I could protect him." Sora's offer surprised her, and Camilla raised her head. She studied the investigator, taking in the earnestness in Sora's tone, the way she'd leaned forward, and the barely-concealed worry in her eyes. She wanted to. Camilla continued to stare with a soft smile until Sora's cheeks reddened. "From Brune," she added, "not from the justice he deserves."

"You don't want him to hang any more than I do," Camilla said. "You met him, and you know it's pointless. Only one more senseless death."

"I met him, and I know he's insufferable, shameless about his deeds, and …" Her initial clipped tone had grown soft, and Camilla wondered where Sora's mind had gone. Hasryan wouldn't discuss his time in prison or his interactions with her. She tapped on the folders with her knuckles. "These people deserve justice. Allowing Brune to do as she wishes doesn't give them that."

Camilla suspected a deeper attachment, but she let the issue rest. "Your cells wouldn't keep Hasryan safe from anyone."

Before Sora could protest, a soft knock interrupted them. Sora rolled her eyes and called, "Yes?"

"Miss Sora Sharpe?" Vellien's small voice pierced through the door, and Camilla's heart jumped. How many in the family knew Kellian had brought her to the headquarters? "May I speak with Aunt Camilla? Please?"

Sora stared at Camilla, as if asking "what now?" then sighed. "Come in," she said, exhaustion lacing her tone. "And close the door behind you."

Camilla straightened as the office door opened with a creak. Vellien entered with their shoulders hunched, one minuscule step at a time, hugging the wall. They ran a hand through their golden-red hair, refusing to look at her. Although she was glad to see them, their presence confused Camilla. Had they worried about her health? But then why did they act so … guilty? She smoothed the front of her robes.

"Is something wrong, Vellien?"

A slight nod, but they continued to stare at their feet. Camilla frowned, almost convinced they were fighting tears. Something ate at them, drawing out Vellien's natural anxiety and sensitive streak. Although they were more mature than most at their age and calmer than their two exuberant older cousins, Vellien's feelings had their own way of taking over.

"It'll be okay," Camilla reassured them. "Tell me."

"I—" Vellien's voice broke, and they tried to clear their throat. "I wanted to apologize."

"I'm not sure what for," she said. "Come here."

She motioned for Vellien to draw closer, but they shook their head and looked up. Their soft expression hardened. "You wouldn't be here without me. I saw all the connections and understood, and this morning I told Kellian. I was worried about you!" Words spilled out faster and faster as Vellien continued. "I know Branwen thinks they can't be that bad—Arathiel and Hasryan, I mean—and maybe she's right, but what if she'd been wrong? What if you got hurt? I had all these bad scenarios in my head all night, and I couldn't get them out, but I never thought he'd arrest you. I didn't want him to do that! I thought, I don't know, I thought—"

"Vellien, stop."

They drew a long, shaky breath and obeyed. They looked terrified, as if they'd committed a heinous crime and would never be forgiven for it. Camilla rose, skirts flowing behind her as she walked to the youngest Dathirii, the kind and talented child who had come all this way to apologize. She placed one hand on Vellien's shoulder and lifted their chin with the other.

"This isn't your fault," she said.

Vellien shook their head with a faint smile. "Perhaps not all, but I helped. I'm so sorry, Aunt Camilla, I—"

Camilla stroked their cheek, stopping them. "It isn't at all. This rests solely on Kellian's shoulders. You were afraid for my safety, and seeking him is the best thing to do in such cases. You couldn't have predicted his reaction, not without knowing a history that predates your birth." This morning, she had glimpsed a side of Kellian she had thought long buried. The loss of his wife had deeply affected him, and Camilla remembered with dread the choleric, unpredictable elf he'd become. It had taken Kellian over a decade to stop drinking, and he still never touched alcohol. It seemed not all his scars were gone, however. "Your Uncle made a mistake—"

"He obeyed the law," Sora interrupted, "which should not be considered optional."

"I'm afraid his latent racism had more to do with it." Camilla met Sora's gaze, unflinching. "You'll excuse me if I'm pretentious and trust my personal compass over laws voted by the Golden Table."

In the heavy silence that accompanied their stare-down, Vellien shrunk back. Camilla held Sora's attention long enough to drive her point home, but she didn't want to debate the differences between law, ethics, and justice. Not now, with her nephew fighting for House Dathirii's seats, with Hasryan's safety in question, and with young Vellien still riddled with guilt. She turned towards them and smiled. "I'm glad you came to see me. That's very considerate."

Vellien nodded eagerly, and their smile became more genuine. "I have to go to the Shelter tonight, but perhaps I could stay until then? Do you want company?"

Camilla wouldn't mind, but she turned to Sora. A sigh met the unspoken question. "You should be in a cell," Sora said, "but I can't bring myself to that yet. It seems Lord Dathirii got to me after all: I'm in no mood to deal with the storm that would follow official paperwork about your arrest."

Lady Camilla couldn't help but laugh at the strange mix of resentment and fondness in Sora's voice. "Diel has a way of getting into people's minds."

"Then pray it'll save your House today." Sora leaned into her chair. "It'll become difficult to protect you if your family no longer has a shred of influence."

Camilla stiffened at the mention. She hadn't considered the impact of losing her title on her position. Sora's grace wouldn't keep her out of a cell without a noble's privileges. She squeezed Vellien's arm to reassure them, burying her own fears deep inside. "We'll manage. We always have, and we've been in this city since its foundation."

"It's you I'm worried about," Vellien answered.

No doubt they had new scenarios running through their head, spinning and spinning. Camilla smiled at them. "Vellien, dear, I've been around almost as long as the family. Your old aunt spent three decades travelling the world on her own, got involved with an all-girl scamming group, and brushed with death a time or two since her birth. I can handle myself."

Stars lit in their eyes, and they gasped. "You never tell those stories!"

"Garith and Branwen are enough of a handful without giving them ideas," Camilla replied. "You can have them, but on two conditions. First, you're not allowed to repeat them to your cousins. Second, I'd love to hear you sing."

"N-now?" They grew a deep shade of red and threw her a silent, pleading look to withdraw the demand. When Camilla only nodded, Vellien glanced at Sora but agreed. "All right. Consider it a second apology."

Their voice shook, and they didn't start immediately. Camilla smiled gently. "Take your time, Vellien. Start as slow and low as you need."

Their gaze flickered to Camilla. With a thankful nod, Vellien cleared their throat and picked up a soft tune. At first, the singing was barely audible, as if Vellien couldn't bear for anyone but themself to hear, but it picked up strength as the young elf fell into the rhythm of the song. Soon, their light voice carried through the office. Camilla closed her eyes and leaned against the wall, her thoughts swimming between Diel and Hasryan, both so close to her heart yet so different—the golden politician, always at the front of any debate, pushing for changes his city refused, and the dark assassin, hovering in shadows as he struggled to even survive, hiding his wounds behind quips and smirks. Two strong men, each in their own way. She had to believe they would both be all right.

Chapter Twenty-Five

YULTES had stepped into the Allastam Tower this morning desperate for one final chance to alleviate the diplomatic disaster of Diel's last audience with Lord Allastam, only to be turned away by a condescending note from the family's first steward. He should have returned to the Dathirii Tower after that. Should have abandoned everything and continued the well-deserved break Hellion had passionately advocated for. Instead, he lingered on, walking through the familiar halls one last time. Yultes knew with absolute certainty that Diel's decision to ally with Arathiel would lead to the end of their House. He'd witnessed Lord Allastam's bitter resourcefulness too often to hold any illusions.

How strange, to bid the Allastam Tower goodbye after all this time. Yultes had worked as the liaison to this House before they'd even climbed high in the hierarchy. He'd watched Lord Allastam grow from a turbulent child to a passionate adult, had witnessed the switch from an ambitious man to a bitter, grieving widower. In many ways, House Allastam had become a second family. He didn't want to leave, not yet, and he couldn't find anything useful to do. He couldn't attend the Golden Table, he wasn't welcome around Branwen and her expedition, and all his paperwork was up to date. It always was.

Lingering around was his break, then—his well-deserved pause from work. Better to stay here and suffer the occasional hostile stares from household staff than to lock himself in his quarters and wait for the axe to fall. Perhaps it wouldn't—Hellion hadn't expressed an inkling of worry—but Yultes had never been an optimist. To think that after all these years and all his mistakes, he would lose his title because of Diel's unyielding morality.

His feet led him to the inner gardens, high in the Allastam Tower. Fake windows arched above the green space, shedding warm light and allowing for exotic and often alchemical plants to grow. Unlike the blue-leaved trees of Allastam's audience chamber, these gardens' flowers bloomed in pale and soothing colours. Yultes discovered that someone else had found refuge in the tranquil space.

Lady Mia Allastam bent over an iris, one hand on her cane and the other lifting the petals. She had tied her long blond hair into an intricate coiffure and taken pains—literal, in her case—to wear a flowing, open-back dress and a light white scarf across her shoulders. Mia's affliction often kept her in bed or exhausted her too much for long conversations, but she seemed in high spirits today.

Yultes called out to her, hoping his presence wouldn't ruin a good day for her. She lifted her head, and her smiled widened when she spotted him. As always, Mia proved herself the most agreeable company in House Allastam, and he hurried closer. He wondered if she even knew of the wedge between their families—her father and brother tended to keep her in the dark—but they'd barely exchanged pleasantries before she cleared that question away.

"I'm sorry for Father's aggressive attacks," she said before gesturing for him to sit on a nearby bench. "None of this will bring my mother back. Your family will be missed from Isandor's politics."

"We're not gone yet."

Mia's blue eyes settled on him, her silence all the confirmation he needed. She didn't believe Lord Dathirii would come out on top of the Golden Table meeting. Yultes wanted to argue further, both by pointing out it wouldn't stop Diel from fighting, and by repeating Hellion's reassurances that House Dathirii did not depend on his stepbrother. He'd had these debates with himself and others too often, however, and Mia hadn't meant it as a challenge. Yultes would rather turn his mind to less stressful topics. He sat down, shoulders slumped, and she joined him with a sigh of relief, placing the cane beside her.

They spent the afternoon discussing unrelated events. Mia asked about news from the Dathirii family, while Yultes insisted on seeing more of the flowers she crafted as a hobby. It distracted him from everything else. No Myrians, no long rants from Hellion on Diel's inadequacy, no worries concerning the information Brune would next demand from him, and not even any thoughts of Larryn. His son hadn't tried to contact him since his requests about Hasryan.

Too angry, probably. Perhaps it was better that way. Yultes only ever seemed to make their relationship worse.

The artificial light atop the garden eventually began to dim, however, and Yultes took his leave, bidding her farewell. Mia was tiring—slower to answer and more easily distracted—but she nevertheless thanked him for the afternoon. Her graciousness would never cease to amaze him, considering the rest of her family. He offered to help her back to her quarters, at which point she laughed. "I will manage fine, milord, and there are plenty of servants on my way there should I turn out wrong."

In truth, her refusal relieved him. He didn't want to be in the Allastam Tower when the Golden Table truly ended. He'd rather learn the bad news from his family than from a smug Lord Allastam. Yultes tried to cling to the future satisfaction of pointing out to Diel he'd been right about angering Allastam, but his heart wasn't in it. He had fought too hard to prove his worth and validate his acceptance into House Dathirii, and the looming loss of his title left only a bitter taste in his mouth.

Yultes headed toward the closest exit, near the base of the Allastam Tower, where another large courtyard occupied two whole levels. Vines climbed up the flight of stairs spiralling around the area, clinging to the railing and outer walls. They kept clear of the ground, as it often served for training soldiers. Anyone could watch from the steps or one of the several balconies they led to.

A significant group of guards occupied the space today, and Yultes frowned as he grew nearer. The troops stood in formation— two rectangles of forty warriors each—and it didn't look like an exercise. They were at ease, chatting with one another, the murmur of conversations echoing in the large area. A strange unease crept up Yultes' spine. He buttoned his winter coat, hurrying down the steps, questions bouncing through his mind. Why had Lord Allastam gathered soldiers? Had they finally found Hasryan? Perhaps he ought to stay out of it, but Yultes' curiosity pushed him into investigating and he approached.

The moment their captain spotted him, he yelled an order and the entire squad saluted. Yultes' breath caught at the powerful synchronicity of the group. He studied the soldiers' serious expressions, hiding his confusion behind his genuine awe before turning to the captain.

"Good evening, Lord Dathirii!" the Allastam officer called. The title jolted him. He was Lord Yultes Dathirii—the title of Lord Dathirii, without first name, was reserved for the Head of the House, who embodied the rest of the family. An instinct held him back from correcting the officer, a deep-seated wrongness about this situation. Better to let the soldier talk while he found his footing, so to speak. "We're ready for the assault and await your orders."

The assault. What was this even about? Yultes' mind rushed for a plausible explanation. Had the officer mistaken him for Diel? But why would he ever speak of an assault? Surely, his cousin hadn't managed to convince the Golden Table to attack the Myrian enclave! He and Garith had headed to the meeting uncertain if they would even keep their seats of power. And either way, the Golden Table should not be over yet.

"The assault, yes." Yultes felt like his tongue was swollen and clumsy, yet his tone remained surprisingly smooth. He smiled at the Allastam captain, who still obviously awaited orders. From whom, though? Who was this "Lord Dathirii," if not Diel or himself? Yultes hated how confused and lost this left him, but he kept a calm mask. Better to appear in control. House Allastam could no longer be considered an ally despite his pleasant afternoon with Mia, and Yultes preferred to show no weaknesses. "I'm afraid I am not quite ready, however. There is a last thing I must take care of."

What exactly, he had no idea. He'd come up with a lie, given himself time to understand what was going on. After all, he'd managed to hide Larryn's birth from even the closest members of the Dathirii family, and he met with Brune without anyone wising up to it. Duplicity had become second nature as the years passed.

"Very well, milord." The captain pinched his lips. "Please do keep in mind that it would be best to have their tower under our control before the Golden Table is over."

"Of course." Yultes infused a measure of annoyance into his tone, as if he couldn't believe the soldier would question him. His insides, on the other hand, tightened painfully, as if a claw squeezed them hard. Their tower? The Golden Table? Yultes forced a sharp farewell, turned on his heel, and hurried out of the Allastam Tower.

The cold hit him in full force, but it didn't ease his panic. Allastam soldiers were waiting for a Dathirii to lead them into a tower assault. Deep down, Yultes knew there could be only one target: his home. But *why* would this officer so casually tell a Dathirii about an assault on their tower? Why, if not that he had expected Yultes to lead it? He didn't understand how it all tied together, only how violent these men's instructions could be. Lord Allastam wouldn't stop at ripping their titles away. He meant to wipe them out from Isandor's scene once and for all. Yultes broke into a run, desperate to reach the Dathirii Tower in time, yet uncertain he could do anything to stop the onslaught.

Chapter Twenty-Six

THEY waited for Kellian all afternoon. At first, Hasryan didn't notice the time passing. Hard to count the minutes with Arathiel and Cal by his side and an infiltration plan to build. Hard to count, in short, when you finally felt a measure of peacefulness, when for a precious moment of your life, trust and good friends pushed away a constant fear of betrayal. The light in the office shifted to gold as the sun lowered in the sky, but the captain still hadn't shown up. Hasryan didn't complain—the less time they spent together, the better—yet as Branwen checked in with Jaeger for news increasingly often, he started to worry too. The light outside grew dim, and she huffed once more before striding to the entrance. She swung the door open, giving Jaeger no chance to stop her if someone was in sight. The steward turned, startled.

"We'll leave without him, Jaeger," she declared. "Please let my uncle know I did not expect him to forget his promise in less than a day.”

Jaeger frowned. “Branwen, this is unlike him. I do not think …” He didn’t finish. Branwen cast her gaze to the ground, and their joint fear didn’t escape Hasryan. “I’ll pass your message along.”

“Thank you. We’ll be on our way, then. Varden’s waited long enough.”

“Kellian will be fine,” Arathiel said, providing a reassurance she obviously needed. “He was an excellent fighter a century ago, and I suspect he only became better with time.”

“Can’t blame him if he’s too busy shoving Camilla behind bars to discover I’m still in his precious tower.”

Hasryan smirked, and the glare he expected from Branwen never came.

Instead, she snorted and put determined hands on her hips. “Too bad for him. He’ll miss out on our epic team. You have anything warm to wear, Mister Assassin, or are you pulling a leather jacket duo with Arathiel? Because I have a huge wardrobe if you need it.”

Hasryan stuttered for an instant, then remembered the winter coat Camilla had found for him when they’d visited Esmera. A bad colour for sneaking, wine red, but Hasryan worried about what might lie in Branwen’s closet, so he mentioned it as fast as he could. Her eyes widened in recognition. “That’s Garith’s! Wonderful, I bet it looks stellar on you.”

It did, and as the group prepared to leave, Branwen didn’t allow him to forget. Hasryan hurriedly threw a cloak over it, both to conceal the glaring colour and stem the flow of compliments. They picked their way down the bridges and stairs, Hasryan often splitting from the others to scout ahead or avoid passing by citizens. Isandor's residents deserted the city on cold days like this one, yet Hasryan needed to backtrack in a hurry more than once to remain unseen.

Their collective mood relaxed as they reached the lower outskirts of Isandor. The enclave's wall rose in the distance, a good half-hour away. Hasryan merged once more with the group, and Branwen greeted him with a cheerful, "Handsome Red is back in tow!" He protested, flustered and ill at ease. In any other circumstances, insults followed his arrivals, not compliments. Yet Branwen wouldn't let go, and neither Arathiel nor Cal seemed of a mind to help. They laughed along with her, poking fun at how they'd never expected to see Hasryan in a dandy's clothes. Hasryan chuckled along, but their good mood grated on his nerves. He couldn't quite explain why, yet he needed everyone to stop and find something else to talk about—to fade into the background once more.

"Isn't Cal the one we normally pick on?" he asked, his tone sharper than intended. "Please give your local assassin a break."

Cal replied with a mock shove, his usual grin unshaken. "We missed you, and who knows how long this will last? I thought … I really thought I'd lost you. That you'd either get caught or vanish, you know? So I want to enjoy this as much as I can!"

Hasryan managed a brief smile. "It's a precious, unexpected chance, I agree. I just … Let's find a better way to spend it? I have too much on my mind to stay a good sport about friendly mockery."

This time, Cal looked up and answered with a quiet "oh." He reached for Hasryan's arm and squeezed it in apology. A surge of guilt climbed into Hasryan's throat, and he almost told him not to feel bad, that it was okay, and maybe they should go on after all. What if Cal became angry at him? What if he didn't want a friend who couldn't take a joke? Hasryan stopped himself and stuffed his desire to apologize deep down. If Cal hadn't dumped him over assassinations, a little rebuttal wouldn't break their relationship. He had to quit worrying and trust his friends not to vanish. Easier said than done, though.

At the lull in the conversation, Branwen spun around to face them. "For the record, I wasn't mocking. You look great. Way better than Garith."

Hasryan choked, instantly glad his ebony-black skin hid his flush. Cal brought a hand over to his mouth to cover his laughter, and a strange mix of irritation, shame, and pleasure filled Hasryan. He met Branwen's gaze, expecting playfulness, but she seemed dead serious. He swallowed hard and ran fingers through his thick hair, at a loss for words.

"The lady's right, you know," Arathiel said. "The sooner you accept it, the faster we'll move on."

"All right, all right!" He lifted his head in surrender. "As long as we do move on. Thanks. I guess."

"Thanks indeed," Branwen agreed. "I have the best fashion sense in all of Isandor. When I pay someone a compliment, I mean it."

"Now that sounds like a self-awarded title—or are there cute design contests between noble houses in which you crush all your poor human opponents?"

"I wish!" Branwen glanced back at the city with dreamy eyes, oblivious to his mocking tone. What a waste of gold that would be! Even worse than the eccentric alchemical gardens decorating the high towers in a pointless show of power. But Branwen had clearly never heard one of Larryn's rants on Isandor's ill-spent wealth because she continued in a wistful tone, "It's a shame that my classiest creations stay almost unused. Isandor never gathers for balls except at Lord William's annual reception. It's all trade with them! They should take a lesson or two from the kingdom of Mehr. It'd be more fun, and it'd make spying easier!"

Hasryan had witnessed the lavish evening Lord William set out every year once, hidden in the shadows of a balcony. The food and riches had dazzled him, and as the night passed and alcohol flowed between the guests, his anger and envy had vanished. It wasn't fair, this bountifulness, this careless waste. Brune had sent him to witness, to burn into his mind that no matter the influence gained by the Crescent Moon, they could never become a part of this, nor should they desire it. The lesson stayed with him as he listened to Branwen ramble.

He wanted to interrupt, to pop her bubble and point out what her extravagance meant to those kept out of wealth, but Cal jumped into the conversation. He asked her about the kind of modifications she made to her outfits, what she loved, how much time she put in it … How did he even come up with all these questions? Branwen adored them, and she answered everything with unbridled enthusiasm. She reminded him of how Larryn sounded when he created a new recipe and was anticipating his patrons' reactions.

Intent on Branwen's detailed discussion of her craft, Hasryan barely noticed when they fully left the cover of Isandor's spires. At one point he looked up, and there were no more bridges above his head, no towers or vegetation obscuring even the corners of his sight. The sun had set, and stars dotted the night sky, impossibly cold and distant. He scolded himself for being so distracted—staying focused with so many allies around was proving more difficult than expected. He had always worked alone before, and after days in a cell or isolated with Camilla, he longed for more conversation. Hasryan stopped and turned around, letting the rest of the group continue. He'd only left the vicinity of the spires once since first arriving in Isandor, a decade ago. Only a few bio-luminescent plants had lit the Upper City at the time, and now they strengthened the contrast between the glowing rich area and the almost-complete darkness surrounding Larryn's home.

"I think I prefer the city at night," Arathiel said, and Hasryan jumped despite the softness of his tone. He hadn't noticed that his friend hadn't continued toward the enclave with Branwen and Cal. How typical of Arathiel to notice Hasryan had stopped—always attentive and silent until he found reason to speak up.

Hasryan agreed with the sentiment. At night, he could hide and stalk through the city without wondering when next someone would spot him, and whether it would mean a glare, an insult, or pointed refusal to acknowledge his existence. Perhaps that applied to Arathiel to some extent, too, but Hasryan felt there was more behind this. "Why?"

"It looks a lot more like what I remember," Arathiel said. "Shadows eat the colours away, and the shades of grey seem normal. In daylight, I know I'm left with a washed-out version of the city."

"So you can't see colours either."

"I can, to some extent. I'm not sure how to explain it. Everything is less intense, toned down. Like watercolour diluted too much and a splash of grey on top." Arathiel shrugged in dismissal, yet longing laced his voice. "I'm used to it now, but my arrival here was brutal."

They turned away from the city and started down the path. Hasryan walked alongside Arathiel, unsure how to help. He'd never thought of a single place as home, although the Shelter had always come close. It was a safe space, one filled with friends, lively music, and the permission to be himself. His reluctance to leave Isandor stemmed from that hard-gained comfort more than from any love of the towers looming above Larryn's unsteady shack. He tried to imagine how it would feel to return there, only to find all of it changed and everyone he had trusted dead, but he couldn't. Hasryan cleared his throat and kicked a small rock.

"Well, hey, at least I was here to welcome you."

His jest drew a laugh out of Arathiel, but he immediately reverted to seriousness. "You were. Somehow, at the bottom of Isandor, I found a tiny haven with someone who understood me. Not all changes are for the worse. Don't make it sound like your presence didn't matter."

Hasryan's throat tightened, and his fingers slid through his thick hair once more, the familiar gesture grounding him. "Do I understand you?" he asked. "I don't know … I never expected you to free me. Outsiders don't stick their necks out for each other. They skulk back into the shadows, glad they're not the target for once. Why did you save me? We just played cards, no? Why would you risk so much?"

"'So much?'" Arathiel scoffed and fell silent. Hasryan waited, hoping Arathiel would elaborate. He needed to know, and they might never get another chance to talk. "You deserved someone to do the right thing for you, and I had access to means beyond Larryn's and Cal's reach. Besides, what is there to risk?" He gestured to himself and continued with a calm so absolute it froze Hasryan's blood. "I'm a body held together by magic, and I should have died more than a century ago. Who knows how long it will hold? This new life … it's borrowed time. I'd rather give it to someone else— do something important while it lasts."

"Is that why you agreed to this?" Hasryan pointed towards the enclave with a sharp gesture. The road provided little cover between its walls and the city, and as a result it stood out against the night sky. "Does it even matter who you're saving, or are we just a list of worthwhile feats to accomplish before something kills you?"

It was wrong. Wrong for Hasryan, wrong for Arathiel, wrong for everyone involved. Hasryan hated the thought.

Arathiel stopped in his tracks, shifting away, his calm composure vanishing. His mouth opened and closed a few times as he struggled for an answer. Hasryan crossed his arms. He could wait forever if he had to, but he refused to let this slide.

"It's not that simple," Arathiel said at length—admitting in the same breath that this was a part of it. "I felt like a ghost. I floated above everyone, watching this future-yet-present Isandor evolve, never interacting with it in a meaningful way. The card games and the tea with Camilla grounded me, but I needed more. I couldn't stay on the sidelines forever. Whenever I catch myself thinking I shouldn't exist, I try to remember that I do, in my own way, and that's enough—that I matter by virtue of existing. You … you turned my mental reminders into a concrete feeling. You understood without questioning or pushing my boundaries. I could just be, no explanations required. You're not anyone, Hasryan. No one in the Shelter wanted you to die, and neither did I."

"And Varden?"

Hasryan stammered the words to keep Arathiel talking while he recovered from his answer. The implicit trust troubled him more than he cared to admit, yet he understood what Arathiel meant. They had always had a silent contract not to make the other feel out of place, to accept one another without demanding explanations. They could share anything, but nothing would be asked. How long had Hasryan wished for a relationship like this? With Larryn, they joked about trading secrets; with Arathiel they waited for them to emerge.

"If Diel says he's worth the risk, I believe it. And you're right, it does feel good to help others. The Well disrupted how I perceive the world and interact with it. I always thought of it as a curse, but perhaps I can turn it around. The impact on my life doesn't have to stay negative."

"Just don't get killed. This Well or whatever, it gave the borrowed time to you, not others. You deserve it more than most, and you're not alive just to pass it on. What's the point of saving me if you can't enjoy it?" His awkward jest fell flat. Arathiel stared ahead, his gaze distant. Hasryan regretted prattling on—as if he had any right to give lessons. He should thank Arathiel instead. His friend had to think he was both insolent and selfish. "Sorry. It's none of my business what you do with your life. I'll shut up and worry about my own first."

"Please don't." Arathiel's hand landed on his shoulder, a little too heavily, and he squeezed hard. His soft voice held no derision. Hasryan turned around only to find Arathiel grinning at him. "You really should speak up more often. I wasn't aware you filled the wise one's role in your infamous Halfies Trio."

Hasryan laughed, and his unease vanished. "There's no 'wise one' in the Halfies Trio. That's why we're always in trouble." He cast a glance at Cal, far ahead, then added, "You know, since you're technically half-alive, you should consider joining."

"Ah." Envy and regret filled Arathiel's voice. "I don't think Larryn would approve."

Hasryan made a show of rolling his eyes. Cal's half-healed bruise stood fresh in his mind, and he couldn't give Larryn's opinion a lot of weight. "Larryn needs a solid encounter or ten with my miraculous wisdom. Don't worry about him."

"Then I would love to!" Arathiel clapped his hands, the warmth in his smile going straight to Hasryan's heart. No more Halfies Trio. Larryn would have to swallow his pride and deal with his issues because from now on, they would be a Halfies Quartet. One more way to ground Arathiel solidly into this new present.

Cal's bright laughter travelled down the path, and they both turned at the sound of it. Arathiel's smile widened even more. "We ought to catch up with the rest of tonight's team. They're both becoming so excited, their voices will warn the Myrians of our approach."

Hasryan snickered, then sped up. Arathiel had a very good point. It was high time they got off the road and started treating this rescue mission with the professionalism it deserved.

Chapter Twenty-Seven

JAEGER hadn't been alone in a long time. He didn't count standing at the door—you never knew who could walk up, or when Diel would push it open and insist Jaeger shouldn't waste precious hours watching the entrance. As if he would truly lose a single minute! Even when he couldn't write official letters, sift through numbers with Diel, or plan their next political move, Jaeger worked. He reviewed events in his mind and unravelled webs of intrigue, using the silence as an opportunity to ground himself once more in Isandor's ever-shifting alliances.

Today he had spent a lot of time—entirely too much of it, in truth—pondering the possible outcomes and consequences of the Golden Table. When Branwen left with her team, the grim future and his constant vigilance had wearied him to the bone. For once, he had acted as a guard dog, watching over the office's door and the secret within. One he had chosen to allow after nothing but a short exchange with Hasryan.

The decision weighed heavily on him. Jaeger made frequent snap verdicts in his life, judging people and their intentions in a few seconds, either reaching behind himself to open the door or firmly but politely refusing entrance to the petitioner. Yet despite the serious consequences linked to supporting Hasryan, this decision had been one of the easiest to take. Camilla trusted Hasryan, who obviously reciprocated that trust enough to risk his fragile freedom for her sake. Diel's aunt was the first Dathirii Jaeger had been formally introduced to, and he had grown to love her and rely on her judgment. He didn't regret his decision, even though it worried him.

With everyone gone, Jaeger abandoned his post at the door. He stretched his legs and back, heaving a sigh of relief, then considered his options. Finding a secure escape route for Hasryan would become one of their most pressing concerns. They might manage to dodge one inspection from the Sapphire Guard, but how long could House Dathirii hide him when they stood at the centre of the city's attention? Jaeger couldn't predict the outcome of the Golden Table, and he'd done everything he could for Branwen's rescue mission. It seemed a good idea to turn his thoughts toward devising secret pathways for Hasryan to take, at least until more urgent news arrived. For a moment, he considered retreating to his quarters, where others were less likely to disturb him, but messengers would inevitably wind up in Diel's office in case of an emergency, so he opted for his desk there.

Jaeger had barely settled into his chair when the doors burst open and Yultes hurried through, panting, cheeks red from exertion. The elf hadn't removed his winter coat, and heavy bullets of sweat ran down his temples. Before Jaeger could comment on the intrusion, their eyes met, and the fear he read in Yultes' gaze pushed him to let it slide.

"What's going on?" Jaeger asked instead.

Yultes raised a hand to hold Jaeger off. He needed several long seconds to catch his breath, and even then, he seemed uncertain what to say. Yultes was insufferable, arrogant, and manipulative, but rarely at a loss for words. What could this mean?

"Fetch Kellian immediately, then exit the Tower. Disappear."

"Lord Kellian left for the Sapphire Guard's headquarters this morning and has not returned since." His tone turned dry and sharp. Why had he ever expected Yultes to explain himself? "I do not take orders from you, Lord Yultes."

Yultes' violent swear caught Jaeger by surprise. When had he ever used such coarse language? "This is bad. They must have stopped him," Yultes said, then he grabbed Jaeger's arm. "We don't have time for bickering. Are there any guards here?"

"A few. Most are scattered across the city, defending our merchant allies."

Yultes rubbed his forehead with two fingers, and long minutes of silence trickled by, his lips moving without words. Jaeger stared at the mute panic, unsettled. Yultes often raised his voice, but always in pretentious indignation, never fear. Yet the unnerving sight only worsened when the other elf's shoulders slumped in defeat.

"We're doomed. I can't think of a solution."

With as much patience as he could muster while addressing Yultes, who despite his breakdown made a point of keeping him in the dark, Jaeger replied, "I might, if you deigned to tell me what is going on."

His remark snapped Yultes back to their situation, and he ran a hand through straw-coloured hair. "Eighty soldiers are waiting at the Allastam Tower, ready for an assault, and upon spotting me they saluted and asked for my orders. Jaeger, they called me Lord Dathirii. They wanted control of a tower before the Golden Table ended, and I've no doubts that they are coming here."

Jaeger's foot slid backward as if Yultes had shoved him. Isandor's noble Houses didn't attack each other in such a direct fashion. They conducted fights through trade deals and "expendable" mercenaries, otherwise they would have killed each other long ago. But had Lord Allastam ever played by the rules? He'd pushed several members of House Freitz to their deaths and instigated the first bloody feud in over a century. Not to mention that if House Dathirii lost its titles at the council, they would become fair game.

"We can't allow it," Jaeger said. "This is our home."

"Can you stop it?"

Jaeger's mind scrambled for a solution. Anything. He couldn't let the tower fall! The Dathirii had lived here for as long as Isandor had existed. They'd been nobles before Jaeger was even born, and their name and deeds shone throughout the city's history. There had to be a way out of it, even without Kellian—and where was their guard captain? For once, Yultes was right. Jaeger hated to admit it, both to himself and to Yultes, but he couldn't do anything against so many soldiers. He looked around, at the beautiful wall of golden flowers and vines, and his heart shrivelled as he shook his head.

"Who's in the tower?" Yultes asked. "Garith is at the council and Kellian has disappeared, but who else among those from whom Diel takes advice?"

"Only me." Jaeger straightened. Yultes hadn't meant him, only the actual Dathirii elves—Diel's blood relations, not the lowborn steward. "The Dathirii present in the tower are friends of Hellion or liaisons to other Houses, which leaves me. But I assume you referred to his noble close guard."

"I didn't." Yultes smirked, drawing obvious satisfaction at contradicting him despite the situation. "You were my first concern, and I ran to the office hoping I'd find you." Jaeger stared at him, more stunned by the concept Yultes cared for his safety than by news of the imminent assault. His surprise must have shown, because Yultes scoffed. "Just because I could do your job better doesn't mean I want you to die. Diel loves every inch of you, but you have no titles to use as a shield, and never did. Which means that to whoever is coming? You're a prime target. You matter—to Diel, to them, to all of us. Let's run."

Yultes grabbed Jaeger's forearm, pulling him along, and they reached the first staircase before the steward shook off his daze. He smiled a little despite the situation. "You matter." Jaeger didn't need Yultes to tell him that, nor did he care that so many nobles thought otherwise. The day would come when Yultes would again imply Jaeger was a superfluous distraction to Diel, however, and then

Jaeger would have a glorious reminder for him.

As heartwarming as the prospect of future gloating was, Jaeger didn't need to be pulled along like a child. He withdrew his arm, and although Yultes' current behaviour confused Jaeger, he rolled with it, flying down one staircase after another in Yultes' wake. Dread crawled up his spine as they neared the exit, with second doubts close on its heels. He didn't want to flee. How would he warn Diel about this? What could they do if they ran and hid? But Yultes had a point: he was a target—leverage, even—and Diel would want him safe.

The echoes of surprised screams and metal armour reached them as they neared the front doors. The smattering of house guards present shouted orders, and weapons screeched as they met. Yultes and Jaeger skidded to a stop. The steward's stomach twisted. The sounds of battle crushed his silent, secret hope that Yultes had overreacted. Jaeger spun on his heels without waiting. There were other exits and they needed to get out.

"We'll use the servants' way."

Yultes stiffened, then followed without a word. Jaeger pushed open a narrow door resembling a cupboard and led them to a long flight of stairs at the centre of the tree-like tower. The household staff used it to move from one floor to another without getting in the nobles' way, but Jaeger avoided it when he wasn't in a hurry.

A single pair of footsteps echoed, heading up as they hurried down, and Jaeger slowed, tense. Had soldiers found the passage already? Surely they couldn't know the tower that well. Then a young ginger-haired boy came around the corner, hands clasped around a tray, huffing. Jaeger recognized the kitchen boy right away, and relief turned his knees into cotton. He pressed one palm against the wall for support.

"Fernandillion, stop." A vague irritation passed on his face. He preferred to be called "Fern," but such a level of familiarity unsettled Jaeger. "Whoever this meal is for will have to wait. Hostile soldiers have entered the tower. Warn everyone you can find to stand down and make themselves invisible. Hide in the stairs or leave the building if you must, but stay as safe as possible. We're heading for the kitchens. I'll tell them the same."

Horror passed over Fernandillion's visage, then resolve. He nodded, and with a simple "yes, sir," he was off, dumping the tray on a step and tearing up the stairs. Yultes had to flatten himself against the wall to give him room, and once the boy had disappeared around the next bend, he turned to Jaeger.

"I can't go to the kitchens," he said.

Jaeger huffed. Did Yultes think they had time for his self-importance? "I don't care what kind of misplaced pride and reluctance to mix with commoners you have, Lord Yultes. That's our way out."

Yultes followed him as he started down the stairs, arguing from a few steps behind. "You misunderstand. It's the kitchens. They won't take kindly to my presence."

"And I'm certain their hatred is deserved. It's our best exit route, and we are not changing plans because you mistreated House Dathirii's staff in the past." They reached the right level, and Jaeger pushed open the door and checked around the corridors. He could neither see nor hear soldiers. Good. "I'll protect you from their righteous fury, as a courtesy for your admittance of my worth."

Jaeger pressed on, unashamed of his sarcasm and glad for the choked sound Yultes emitted. Whatever happened next, he would treasure this moment. His long strides led him to the kitchens, and he entered through the revolving door without hesitation. Yultes followed with a resigned sigh. A myriad of smells assaulted them, along with the clanking of pots and pans and orders yelled by cooks to their helpers. Dinner wasn't far away, making the area even noisier than the soldiers at the gate.

"Nicole!"

Jaeger called the kitchen's head, scanning the bustling room for her. Yultes retracted against him, his shoulders hunched, thin lips pressed into a wistful line. What a strange expression from someone who thought the kitchens would lead to his death. Not a mystery for which Jaeger had time, nor one he really cared to solve. He focused on the organized chaos around, calling Nicole again. Servants started to notice them, and all activity slowed down. They whispered to one another, pointing, until Nicole's deep voice boomed across the kitchen.

"What do you mean, Lord Yultes dared to step in here?"

"I warned you," Yultes said from behind Jaeger.

Jaeger gritted his teeth. "I wish I could stand by and watch."

Nicole emerged from two rows of counters, wooden ladle in hand. Long blond hair fell upon her full bust, and she set thick hands on her wide hips. Nicole was large in every sense of the term, and she was one of the most beautiful women Jaeger had met.

Anger flushed her skin and stole her usual welcoming smile, however. Jaeger stepped forward and spread his arms before she attacked Yultes.

"Nicole, there are soldiers coming. We need to escape."

"Let them take him." She pointed the ladle at Yultes, who cringed and made himself as small as he could—not a sight Jaeger had ever thought he'd witness. "He knew better than to step in here."

What was going on? When Yultes had spoken of the staff "not taking kindly" to his presence, Jaeger hadn't expected anything special. Most of their employees disliked Hellion, Yultes, and others enough to glare if they entered spaces usually meant for staff. Nicole's anger spoke of something a lot deeper, however, and Yultes' uncharacteristic terror exposed both his guilt and regrets. Whatever it was would wait. They needed to escape, find Diel, and warn him. Household politics were meaningless in comparison.

"I forced him." They stared at each other. Jaeger had never needed to impose his will on Nicole before. They got along well, and he allowed her full control of the kitchens, offering advice only when she asked. Yultes shouldn't be worth this breach in their dynamic, but they lacked the time for subtlety. Jaeger grabbed Yultes' wrist and started around Nicole, dragging the stiff noble behind him. "If soldiers enter, stand down. Don't fight, don't disobey. They're taking over, Nicole."

She glared one last time at Yultes, silently warning him his turn would come. When she refocused her attention on Jaeger, however, the anger drained away. She inhaled deeply and squeezed Jaeger's shoulder. "Understood. Stay safe, Jaeger. We'll be waiting for your return."

He smiled. Plenty of other Houses would gladly offer these people jobs should they desert House Dathirii, but Jaeger doubted many would leave. Diel paid better wages, punished any abuse, and had asked Jaeger to accommodate their employees as much as possible. House Dathirii's staff knew they wouldn't find better elsewhere, and most would risk staying for a time. He hated leaving his peers behind. They would be fine, though, and he might not.

Jaeger thanked her, and Nicole repeated her orders as he pulled Yultes between the large fires in the wall and the cutting board counters, towards the exit. Several servants nodded at Jaeger, and the small acknowledgments of his passage twisted his heart. He would miss them, and the tower. Despite the urge to escape before soldiers found them, Jaeger almost stopped in his tracks. He couldn't believe he was abandoning the Dathirii Tower like this.

The two elves arrived at the door as the cooks slowly started working again. Nicole's commands turned into adjustments to the dinner plans instead of safety advice—something about diminishing quantities in light of the Dathirii nobles who wouldn't return to eat. At least many of them were already out of reach. Jaeger grabbed the doorknob, eager to leave.

Burning heat seared his palm, and the door's handle burst into hot pieces. Jaeger snatched his hand back with a pained cry, stumbling away. Yultes caught him before he fell, and as smoke and soldiers rushed into the kitchen, they drew closer. Booted steps at the other end of the room warned him of the futility of turning back. Yultes and Jaeger froze, their breath short and their faces pale. They were trapped, and they both knew it.

Jaeger cleared his throat. His hand throbbed and fear spun his mind in wide circles. "Yultes?"

"Yes?"

"Thanks for trying."

Soldiers grabbed their arms and wrists, pulling them apart and searching for weapons. House Allastam's crest shone on their outfits, and Jaeger fought to quell his rising panic. The kitchens had gone silent, and Jaeger closed his eyes, steadying himself for the hardships to come. Yultes might not be the best companion, but at least he wasn't alone.

Chapter Twenty-Eight

ROPES chafed at Yultes' wrists, a painful reminder of the surreal situation they'd landed in. He was sitting on Jaeger's bed, captured in their own tower and waiting on guards to lead them to this new Lord Dathirii. Yultes dreaded the encounter, and every passing minute frayed his nerves further.

At first, he'd basked in the surprising mess of Jaeger's quarters, and the amusement overrode some of his worries. Jaeger did *everything* in a clean and orderly fashion. His desk in Diel's office stayed in perfect condition, piled neatly with papers and devoid of the slightest stain of ink. The same went for Jaeger's notes and letters—written in precise and fluid script, with complete headers. Nothing like the clothes strewn on the ground here or thrown across a chair, or the collapsed pile of tomes on the floor near the bookshelf, as if vomited by it. Every object seemed flung on the closest surface available with one single exception: Jaeger's wardrobe. It was a haven of order in an otherwise chaotic room. Jaeger had classified every outfit within by colour, and Yultes spied tags on the rare green and red ones. A quick glance revealed he preferred tones of grey, dark blue, beige, and black—shades he'd have no problems distinguishing. Yultes had thrown the steward a long look as they sat on his bed littered with scrolls and clothes, but Jaeger only shrugged. Too worried for shame.

Neither of them had uttered a word since their botched escape, and in truth, Yultes didn't know what to say. He'd reviewed the events leading to this and failed to convince himself House Allastam had forged an alliance with the Myrian enclave. How could that explain the arrival of a new Lord Dathirii? Someone *inside* had done this, seeking to replace Diel. Someone relentless in his criticism, yet who had assured Yultes he shouldn't worry about House Dathirii's future.

Hellion.

Yultes juggled with his contradictory feelings as guards retrieved them from Jaeger's quarters and escorted them to Lord Dathirii's quarters. Why had Hellion never told him about this? How long ago had he contacted Lord Allastam behind his back? And why would he risk this now, when House Dathirii had so much on its plate? But he must have a plan. These soldiers had executed the takeover with terrifying efficiency, and Hellion always built precise strategies. Yet even knowing House Dathirii would fare better under his mantle, the assault left a bitter taste in his mouth. His heart hammered with the memory of his wild sprint with Jaeger, of fear and urgency coursing through his veins. When he laid eyes on

Hellion, sitting on Diel's desk with legs crossed and a victorious smile, Yultes' teeth clenched in anger.

Jaeger stiffened next to Yultes, choking down a sound of protest. He raised his chin in defiance and met Hellion's gaze without hesitation. Yultes wanted to grab his sleeve and tell him not to be a fool, to do like he'd advised the other servants: bow his head, stay discreet, and weather the storm. Yet Yultes knew it was pointless. Whatever Hellion's plans, Jaeger wouldn't remain safe. A soft hatred irradiated from Jaeger's tight jaw and burning glare, and he was stubborn and daring enough to unleash it on Hellion.

"Why did you do this?" Yultes asked.

He spoke first, hoping it might stop Jaeger, hoping the answer would squash down his conflicting feelings. Hellion had been his best friend for over a century. He had supported Yultes when his brother had left, or when Jaeger had stolen his place as Diel's main adviser. Hellion had taught him to trust his instincts and believe in his worth when everyone else shunned him. He had taught him the art of negotiation, making Yultes quick-witted and good with numbers. He had helped him prove he deserved his Dathirii title, even if he'd gained it through his brother's marriage. But this … Yultes wished it had never happened.

"Surely you've pieced it together by now, Yultes." Hellion linked his fingers and levelled a judgmental stare at him. "I must say, what a disappointment to find you fleeing with the likes of Jaeger! I expected better. Perhaps you can prove I wasn't wrong about you. Why *did* I do this? You already know the answer to your own questions. What did I teach you about leaders?"

Despite his anger, Yultes' mind scurried for the right answer. They'd discussed these things so often! Hellion enjoyed testing him, bouncing ideologies off him and correcting Yultes when he slipped and uttered nonsense. The proper words spilled out of his mouth as if he'd said them a hundred times before. "A great leader knows when to compromise, when to lie, and when sacrifices are needed. He knows which allies matter and which must be discarded. Willingness to manipulate isn't a weakness, it's a strength."

Jaeger's clear scoff made Yultes flinch. The steward's mouth twitched in disgust before he schooled his expression back into the mask he always greeted Yultes with. Jaeger usually concealed his dislike out of professionalism and respect for Diel. Did he keep the charade up by reflex or to hide the rest of his feelings? A cold fear had to simmer under there, locked away from Hellion's sight. Yultes turned back to his old friend, who ran a nonchalant hand through his vibrant hair.

"Has Diel ever compromised over his precious morality? Has he ever accepted a sacrifice or discarded a dangerous ally?"

Yultes closed his eyes, nauseated. Why did he have to answer these? "No, but …"

"There is no but," Hellion interrupted. He slid down the desk and approached. "Not if you're with me."

Rough hands grabbed Yultes' wrists and a soldier cut through the ropes tying him. He stumbled forward in his surprise but quickly caught himself. Hellion smiled, and with a firm grip on Yultes' shoulder, he pulled him toward Jaeger's desk. Yultes' throat dried, and he complied, lightheaded.

"I'm in a forgiving mood, and we've been partners for so long … I can overlook this escape attempt." Hellion set his palm on the steward's desk. A light smile danced on his lips—the kind he had whenever he reached the pinnacle of a well-crafted argument—and Yultes knew exactly what would follow. How often had he dreamed of it? Always, he'd wanted the offer to come from Diel, but Hellion's words were still music to his ears. "I *need* a good steward, Yultes. Someone I can trust. You've waited more than a century for this opportunity. Take it! Help me become the Lord Dathirii this family deserves."

Yultes stared at the desk. He ran a shaky hand over it, thinking of how much he could do, how great he would be in this role. Hellion was right. He'd always wanted this, only to have it stolen by Jaeger. Yultes' gaze settled on the perfect stacks of scrolls and on a note with Jaeger's clean handwriting. From there, it moved to the steward, flanked by two buff guards, his dark blue eyes digging holes in him. Less than an hour ago, they'd tried to escape together. "You matter," Yultes had told him, and he believed it. Where would Diel be without his steward? His stepbrother made a horrendous leader, and Yultes resented him for choosing another right-hand, but he also liked Diel. And although he would never admit it out loud, especially in front of Hellion, Yultes loved Diel's doomed ideology. He wished life worked that way instead of the dark reality they faced every day.

"What of Jaeger?" he asked, fingers still trailing the desk's smooth wood.

"His safety rests entirely upon his personal conduct and Diel's compliance once he returns."

Which meant they would hurt him as often as necessary until both elves stopped resisting. Blood drained from Yultes' face, and he croaked his answer. "Release him, and I'll take his place."

A flash of anger passed through Hellion's gaze. "Release him? Are you negotiating your position?"

The dangerous inflection he put on "negotiating" sent a shudder down Yultes' spine. He'd learned long ago to detect the warnings in Hellion's otherwise pleasant tone, and he wanted nothing more than to retreat and apologize a thousand times over. "I *am*," he said, confidence creeping into his voice. "You need a competent steward, don't you? No one else in this family has what it takes. I'll do it, but only if you let Jaeger leave. He is superfluous now."

"Oh, Yultes. Your sentimentality will destroy you one day." Hellion patted his left cheek, and both burned from the humiliating touch. "Strong leaders know when to make sacrifices, remember? It's like you know the words but forget their meaning! Perhaps that proves such concepts cannot truly be understood by commoners."

Yultes recoiled from the implication, mortified. He'd pushed too far and failed the test, and Hellion had brushed away decades of hard work with a single reminder: Yultes should never have received his title, nor should he presume to demand more from Hellion. He should be grateful to even be offered this position. What had gotten into him? But before he could apologize, Jaeger's calm voice broke the silence.

"If anything, Hellion, you're proof a title is meaningless, and that ornaments often hide the ugliest beings."

Hellion spun around, his smile sweet and sick. He motioned at the guards behind Jaeger, and they kicked the backs of his knees, sending him sprawling headfirst to the ground. Jaeger stifled a grunt and struggled to his knees. Hellion reached him in two long strides, then crouched and grabbed his chin. Bile crawled up Yultes' throat, but he remained frozen, unable to look away.

"I'm afraid you're going nowhere, and your lifelong love isn't here to protect you anymore. We have a welcome party waiting for my dear cousin." Hellion's voice was a whisper, just loud enough for both Jaeger's and Yultes' ears. "I believe in discipline for disobedient servants. Since you have a knack for proper etiquette, however, I'll give you this one chance. Call me by the right title, and I'll let you off without the beating you deserve."

Their gazes locked, and Yultes' stomach sank. The three elves in this room had known each other long enough to predict the outcome of such a challenge. Jaeger did not beg, and he did not lie. He either said nothing or unleashed his stubborn tongue. From the slight smile at the corner of his lips, he had chosen the latter.

"I am not your servant. I am the real Lord Dathirii's steward, and your dangerous game won't change that. Claiming to be Head of the House with borrowed soldiers will not make it so." Jaeger scoffed, making Yultes flinch. "Go ahead. I'll take your beating, then I'll sit back and enjoy watching your pathetic plan unravel around you. House Dathirii will never be yours. It has too much heart to sink so low."

Hellion hit him first, the slap echoing in an otherwise silent room. The rings on his fingers split Jaeger's lip. The steward licked the blood, unable to clean it with his hands tied. When Hellion motioned for the two guards to continue, Yultes squeezed his eyes shut and turned away, wishing he could block all sounds too. He should be grateful for his new position, he told himself, and he should accept the necessity of this. Diel's leadership had led them nowhere except into failure. This change would benefit House Dathirii, in the long run. Yet every hit, every groan from Jaeger, every thump of fists and feet gripped Yultes' insides, squeezing until nausea dizzied him.

He hated Hellion for creating the situation, but he hated himself even more for letting it happen.

CHAPTER TWENTY-NINE

SINCE the Long Night's Watch and Varden's capture, Branwen had conceived countless daring rescues after the winter solstice, but she'd never imagined today's strange team. Kellian's absence weighed on her mind, worry and betrayal unsettling her. Branwen dreaded learning what had kept him away and struggled to stop her conjectures and focus on the mission at hand. Arathiel's swordsmanship and unusual skills reassured her, and with Hasryan among them, they might not need to fight. These two weren't the cruel criminals Lord Allastam painted them to be. Even Hasryan's roughness had been offset by how awkward he'd become when she'd teased him about Garith's coat. Hard to see the cold assassin between his stuttering scramble for safer ground and the way he always ran a hand through his hair, hiding discomfort behind a smirk. He was guarded but cute, which had flared Branwen's curiosity. She needed to investigate.

The strangest member of their "elite" team had to be Cal, however. It made sense to bring Hasryan and Arathiel, but the over-excited halfling who'd shown incredible interest in her sewing skills? She hadn't known what to think. Having Ren's favour on their side might save their skins, though, and she feared Varden would need a solid dose of healing. Every little helped, Branwen told herself, but she only discovered how useful Cal could be when they reached the enclave's wall.

They'd chosen to climb here because according to Varden's map, a large tree on the other side would ease their way down. They could see the tips of its branches against the night sky, confirming the information, and although the climb from this side might pose a problem, they only needed one person to reach the top and throw a rope to the others. Branwen turned to Hasryan. "Think you can manage it?"

"I know I can." He scoffed at the wall as if the very question amused him, then looked at his short friend. "Cal, care to make sure our initial plan isn't fraught with unforeseen dangers?"

"Yes, sir!" Cal straightened like a soldier taking orders from his captain and set one hand on the wall. "Okay, Ren, here we are. You infiltrated the Conqueror's fortress and emptied his pantries, sneaking in and out on your own several times. Surely you can help us with our nice little enclave?"

Branwen frowned. Who addressed demigods this way? Cal's prayer sounded like a chat with old friends, not a formal petition to a being of luck so incredible Xe had become revered throughout the world. Vellien never spoke of the Elven Shepherd without some level of fascination, and Varden mentioned Keroth with a mix of gratitude and prudence. Perhaps it was because Ren had no organized church. Xir priests just seemed to appear here and there, each with their own interpretation of what their faith meant. Maybe Cal considered he had a friend in his deity, not a patron to serve.

A flicker of light crawled above his hand, and he frowned. Without a word, Cal clucked his tongue and walked away, fingers trailing the stone. Every now and then, he mumbled something or tapped the wall with a small 'here?' Then he moved on again. Hasryan followed without hesitation. Branwen glanced toward Arathiel, and his obvious doubts relieved her. At least she wasn't alone in questioning this! Yet after a short pause, Arathiel fell behind Hasryan. Branwen cast a longing look at their chosen climb spot and started after them too.

The group stayed close to the wall and its shadows as they travelled around, sometimes halting their progress as a soldier passed above, his torchlight almost reaching them. Each time, they held their breath, and each time, Branwen would have sworn they were about to be caught. Yet the guards always moved on, unaware of the intruders at their feet. When Cal finally stopped and turned to the group with a grin, Branwen's stomach unwound with relief.

"Here?" she asked.

The wall had no special structure, nothing that justified this spot over the one by the tree. In fact, they would enter the enclave farther away from the prisons. No obvious reasons explained Cal's choice—nothing but Ren's counsel must have guided him.

"Yep," he said. "This is where we should climb."

Hasryan thanked him, withdrew the rope from his bag, and heaved himself up without questions. He scaled the wall fast at first, but his progress slowed as handholds became rarer. On the far left, the bobbing glow of a guard's torch approached.

"Why here?" Branwen asked.

Hasryan stopped to look down the few feet he'd climbed, and the dim moon shed light on his wide smirk. "What's wrong? You win one wager, and now you're a non-believer?"

"Luck requires faith," Cal said. "Trust me. Trust Ren."

None of their words helped the fear needling at her heart, but Branwen held her peace. She watched Hasryan's muscled limbs move from one handhold to another, Garith's coat tight against his body whenever he stretched his arms. Every now and then, his foot scraped against the wall, but he otherwise produced no sounds—no grunts, no huffs. She brushed the stones, trying to judge the difficulty of the climb, and her breath caught as she discovered how smooth the surface was. How could he move so fast with so little to hang onto? Practice, no doubt—a city of towers and bridges offered plenty of training opportunities. How often had he hiked sheer façades, sneaking through windows and balconies to assassinate someone?

"Cal, the guard's getting nearer," Arathiel whispered.

Hasryan had almost reached the top and would hang there in plain sight for the soldier to spot. He stopped and glanced down, waiting for instructions. It wasn't too high a drop if he needed to let go—not enough to wound him unless he fell wrong. Cal frowned, then shook his head.

"Keep going. You'll be fine."

"What?" Branwen mouthed the word more than she said it. There was no way he'd be fine. Torchlight would wash over him, they would ring the alarm, and then they'd have an entire enclave to fight to get to Varden.

"Just watch," Cal whispered back, his tone as urgent as her exclamation.

Branwen obeyed. She watched every second of the guard's advance, her fingers pinching and rubbing the fabric of her sleeves, her heart hammering against her chest. This was dangerous nonsense, and she shouldn't have agreed to it. Why would they risk their mission on a lucky strike? They needed to succeed. She wouldn't be able to live with herself if she had to leave Varden behind. Hasryan's hands reached for the top of the wall. The light's radius almost touched him. Branwen closed her eyes, unable to stare any longer.

"Hey, Martin!" A woman's voice rang through the night from far away, off to their left. "Did I show you my boy's new carving? They sent it all the way from Myria to keep me company."

The man near Hasryan—Martin—stopped. They could hear him grumble something under his breath, but he turned around. "Coming! But you better not make me late on my schedule with more of your family stories."

"Look who's talking! You'll be blabbering about that little girl you left at home before you even get here. What's one or two minutes anyway?"

"Don't let that kind of talk reach Master Avenazar," Martin

warned. "I heard the last time a guard displeased him, he reassigned them to the deepest hole in the Myrian Empire and told them they were lucky to leave with all their limbs intact."

"Gotta wonder what's even more isolated than this shitshow of a city. I swear, the mountain range between Myria and Isandor makes it feel like two continents away."

They continued chatting, their voices booming in the otherwise silent night. Branwen exhaled and wiped her sweaty forehead as Hasryan pulled himself over the edge and tied the rope. Cal grinned at her, the proud little jerk, and she couldn't help but smile back. Hard to hold it against him if this turned out to be their best option. Soon enough, the hemp rope dropped at their feet, and Hasryan leaned over the wall.

"Cal, you genius, there's an actual cart of hay on the other side. Let Branwen up first. She can jump down and extinguish the torch next to it."

Branwen stretched, pulled her winter gloves on firmly, and grabbed the rope. She climbed as fast as she could, but even with help, she felt like a slug compared to Hasryan. Cal started up before she reached the top to avoid wasting time. Martin the guard might return at any moment, and everyone needed to be down in the courtyard by then. Hasryan held his hand out as she arrived and pulled her up onto the parapet. Below them was a wooden cart filled with hay.

"Might hit a bit rough on your ass, but you should manage."

"My ass has seen worse, I can promise you that." She flashed a grin at him, and he choked down his laugh. Branwen leaned over the side to gauge the distance and prepare herself for the shock. "I jump, then I scramble out and snuff the torch."

"Exactly."

He removed his hand from her arm, and only then did she realize how long it had stayed. Well, only seconds, but warm and pleasing seconds. Branwen hoped this mission wouldn't mark the last she saw of Hasryan because she had no time to deal with her quickly-building attraction. She sprang down to the hay cart, gritting her teeth as pain shot through her back, and hurried to the torch while the rest of the group climbed up. How strange to stand inside the Myrian enclave once more. Nothing seemed to have changed except for the silence from the temple. Their chant during the Long Night's Watch had followed her long past the walls, which made the silent night feel even more threatening. The ceremony had caused Varden so much anxiety. She hated the thought of Avenazar ruining it for him—that, and everything else.

Branwen fumed as the rest of her rescue team dropped from the wall, joining her in the obscurity. Hasryan jumped last, somehow landing without much noise. He slunk out, rubbed both hands through his thick hair to get the straws out, then glanced around the compound. His gaze darted from one shadowy area to another as if tracing a route in his mind.

"Branwen, you tell me if I head in the wrong direction," he said, "and Cal, you warn me if Ren sets off your alarms. Arathiel, think you can keep an eye out on our backs?"

"I can try, but I doubt I'm the best lookout."

"Oh, right." Hasryan puzzled over this for a moment, then

shrugged. "It's okay. Do your best. Knock out anyone coming too close, if you can."

Then he was off, slinking through the compound and signalling for them to reduce the noise level. Every little bit carried in the chill air. The man embarrassed at a few compliments had given way to a professional infiltrator, and Branwen's confidence built up. She would have to thank Aunt Camilla for helping him and Diel for offering him this mission. Hasryan, too, obviously. Branwen's expertise lay with disguises and bluffs more than snooping around, and, while she could've handled herself, she was glad he was there. Varden deserved the best he could get, and as she watched Hasryan advance, she knew they had found it.

THEY had quite a few close calls on their way to the prison, and Branwen's heart was hammering against her chest long before they made their way down the stairs leading to the Myrian cells. More than once, Hasryan had backtracked in a hurry to avoid being spotted, and at one time, Cal had sprinted ahead to grab his coat and pull him to the ground, holding a finger to his lips. Seconds later, the window right above their heads had opened with a resounding creak. Voices drifted out, haughty and sneering. They had been joking about "House Dathirii's pathetic floundering," which had made everyone turn to Branwen. The relative darkness might have hidden her blush, but they all saw her rude gesture toward the window.

They would show them. It had taken ten horrible days, but Uncle Diel hadn't let her down about Varden. He would find a way to ruin the Myrian enclave.

She put these concerns out of her mind as they crawled away from the window. Her role tonight was to save Varden from his private torture sessions. She could worry about the rest later, once he was safe. Her stomach tightened whenever she thought of his pain, and she couldn't wait to see him, to see the smile on his tired face as they unlocked his cell and freed him. She'd be there to nurse him back to health, to tour him around their tower, to introduce him to Garith's ridiculous humour and Camilla's delightful tea. All Branwen wanted was to show him the world outside of Myria's oppressive yoke, and as they grew nearer to the prisons, she took the stairs two by two, ignoring Hasryan's hurried whisper to be careful.

No guards waited for them at the bottom, and Branwen ran down the small corridor, her boots echoing against the stone floor. She checked each cell one by one, ignoring the rising level of noise. They were here, finally, just a few steps away! She noticed a door ahead, half-open, and she sprinted to it. Hasryan followed close on her heels, and Arathiel stayed at the bottom of the stairs while Cal kept watch above.

An horrible stench wafted out of the cell as she approached it. Branwen let out a disgusted exclamation and brought her scarf over her mouth, scrunching her nose. The mix of sweat, piss, and dampness made her retch, and she froze while she fought the nausea.

"That'll be his, all right," Hasryan said, walking past her and into the cell like the place smelled of fresh daisies. "There's no mistaking the sweet scent of occupied prisons. Empty, though."

"No!" Branwen flung the door wide open, throwing her bitter rage into it. She stared at the empty room, her body blocking most of the torchlight, and searched every corner visible in the flickering light. As if Hasryan could be wrong. "He has to be here! Where else?"

Maybe in another cell. The Myrians could have more than one prisoner! Wouldn't Varden have heard her, though? He could be unconscious, she told herself. Knocked out by the torture. They ought to check all of them. She whirled around, but before she could step out, Hasryan grabbed her wrist and shushed her. The faint torchlight made his red eyes seem to glow.

"Branwen, you know he was here as well as I do. Don't panic." His voice stayed low and calm.

She shook off his grip and struggled to whisper back. "We can't be sure. Once we've examined all of them, we can think of something else. But he's not … he's not gone. He can't be."

"I'm not saying they killed him," Hasryan said. "Did he mark down where they torture people? We should check there unless it's close enough that we'd hear him scream."

Her stomach clenched at the thought, but she fought through her nausea and reviewed what they knew of the enclave's layout. "Nothing specific—Avenazar uses magic, anyway. Didn't Nevian say he enjoyed irony? He might—"

Clatter from the stairs interrupted her, and Branwen cringed at the loud noise. Arathiel had tried to sprint up, almost stumbling in his hurry. Branwen and Hasryan exchanged an alarmed glance before dashing after him. The prison's corridor was an isolated dead-end, but they could be heard upstairs. Cal's voice echoed down to them as they reached the bottom, but he was speaking to someone else.

"Hey, Isra, hey!"

"Cal, what are you—"

"It's okay, Ara. She's a friend of Nevian's."

Isra? A friend? Branwen swore under her breath and scrambled up. Varden had shared enough tales about the snobby teenager for Branwen to know she cared about little but herself. How had Cal gotten another version in his head?

"What are you doing here?" Panic laced Isra's voice. When Branwen emerged from the stairs, her eyes widened in recognition, and she stepped back. "You're the Dathirii he—what's going on?"

Torches lit the deserted corridor, casting an orange glow on Isra's blonde head. Arathiel shifted toward the exit, blocking Isra's way out, fingers wrapped around his sword's hilt. Good reflex, even if he seemed reluctant to use it. Branwen circled around the other end, boxing Isra in. Cal looked at their group nervously.

"Why is everyone on edge?" he asked. "Isra can help us stay clear of the guards with her eagle form!"

He turned to her, and her perfect pink lips parted in a stunned 'o.' Branwen snorted. "She won't. You can't rely on this racist little princess to get Varden out. She probably thinks he deserves it."

"No!" Isra withdrew until her back touched the wall. "I didn't mean it. When I told Avenazar, I never thought—"

"Oh, because it's your fault?" Anger rose, a hot tide climbing from her stomach and into her throat, threatening to turn into tears. Ten days. Varden had stayed in Avenazar's clutches for ten days, enduring relentless torture, and this pretentious brat had triggered it? She strode forward with clenched fists, ready to unleash her worry, anger and bitter helplessness.

Black fingers clamped on her arm and squeezed it. "We don't have time for this, and we're making too much noise." Hasryan's soft voice held no reproach, only a firm demand to calm down. "Varden isn't below, but she might know where to find him. No doubt she'll tell us, if she's so full of regrets, and then she'll understand our only safe option is to leave her unconscious and gagged in a cell."

"What?" Isra asked.

"No!" Cal hurried to Isra's side, raising a protective arm high. "You can't do that. Isra won't alert anyone."

Hasryan ran a hand through his hair, his shoulders slumping. "Cal, you're the most trusting person I know, but that's not always a good thing. Just because Isra is Nevian's friend doesn't mean she's Varden's. It doesn't mean she's ours at all. We can't take any chances."

They stared at each other, a contest of silent pleading. Branwen expected Cal to look elsewhere at any time, but he held on, chin raised in defiance. Seconds passed—long, painful seconds during which another Myrian could walk in on them—and Branwen struggled not to step past the halfling and knock Isra out herself.

Every moment lost was one in which Varden suffered more.

Arathiel cleared his throat before either gave up. "As dangerous as she can be, I don't have it in me to hit a teenager."

"I do," Hasryan said. "Age doesn't mean shit. I was eight when I killed the first time."

Eight? How could that happen? Branwen wanted both to hug him and to step back, so instead, she stayed rooted to her spot. Isra grew paler, and the group's collective surprise must not have reassured her. Even Cal's eyes widened, but he renewed his determination and strode forward.

"Please … We have to try."

"I'll help!" Isra exclaimed, her voice a squeak. "We don't—I mean, no Isbari deserves this. I don't enjoy this, but what was I supposed to do?" Her question received only a glare from Branwen, and she swallowed hard. "Master Avenazar is planning an awful spell. He wants to create the ideal slave, someone without enough personality to resist. And today he asked acolytes to keep the brazier in Keroth's temple higher than ever. I think he means to try it there, and I doubt the results will be reversible."

"That's where, then," Branwen concluded. Nevian had been spot on with his comment about cruel irony. "He's not in his cell because Avenazar is doing this … this thing to him."

A mindless slave. The worst thing one could do to Varden. He'd fought so hard against this, for himself and for his people. She wanted to rush out without any care for silence, guards, or danger— to just burst into the temple and demand that Avenazar put an end to this. He would mock her.

"Let's move," she said, stalking off without waiting for their approval. They needed to get there fast. "Isra can trail. I don't care."

Avenazar could laugh all he wanted, but she refused to leave the enclave without Varden, even if it meant facing the powerful wizard. Her determination smothered the smallest inkling of fear in her, and as she left the prisons' building, Hasryan grabbed her arm and stopped her from striding through lit paths with a quick scolding. She forced herself to slow down. They couldn't afford to be spotted, and she had been careless. Most Myrians might stay inside to avoid the cold, but what if one looked out a window? Heard her angry stomping? One step at a time, she reminded herself.

Then, with her mismatched elite rescue team—now including Isra—behind her, Branwen headed toward Keroth's temple to put an end to Varden's torture.

CHAPTER THIRTY

LARRYN set his three-foot-tall mirror on the floor and sat next to it, across from Nevian. The young wizard had required something to stare into for his spells, and since there was no way Larryn would waste money on a looking glass, he'd slipped inside a rich-ass house and grabbed the first one he could find. He could sell it after. The intricate floral motif carved into its frame would fetch him a good price, and he could put that gold into a welcome back feast for Hasryan. One with tons of cheese for Cal. The Shelter's atmosphere had changed without them—even the lively music had slowed, as if the players knew part of the place's soul had disappeared. He had done this, lashing out at those around him—at Cal more than anyone else—and pushing away those who had helped him. Larryn promised himself he would fix this mess. The first step was to find Hasryan, the second to apologize properly to Cal.

Nevian fidgeted with his notes, rereading the words to his spell over and over. His fingers kept folding the corner of the page, and his foot tapped against the ground. He didn't look ready, despite his earlier assurance.

"Can you do this or not?" he asked.

"I can, I can!" Nevian's firm tone would have had more credibility if he hadn't been wringing his hands.

"You can take another day," Larryn offered. He hadn't expected Nevian to figure his spell out so fast, but the surprise had delighted him. He should have known better.

"No." Nevian met Larryn's gaze and stopped his restless movements. "I'm ready. Working on this spell brought back memories. I used to sneak out of the Myrian enclave to meet with Isandor's most powerful wizard. I traded information for lessons, and she's a master in divinations. I can do this."

"Maybe I should have asked her."

"You can't afford her."

Larryn rolled his eyes. Of course not. He knew that better than Nevian ever could, but jokes tended to fly straight over this kid's head. "Then let's hope your spell is worth more than what I paid you."

Nevian snorted, but the hint of a smile curled the corner of his lips. "We'll see." He scanned his notes one last time, inhaled deeply, and set the papers aside. "Put your hands on the edges of the mirror and think about your friend. Imagine him as clearly as you can, but try not to latch onto a past event. Just him, with as little else around as you can. Focus on his name and his person."

Larryn frowned. Nevian sounded like a fortuneteller. Then again, these spells were their specialty, weren't they? They just made a spectacle out of it, in true Allorian fashion. Besides, Nevian had none of that over-dramatic flair. He had no show to give and instructed Larryn with the tone he'd use to recite a grocery list, then stared at him, as if daring him to comment. With a sigh, Larryn closed his eyes.

"Don't do that," Nevian said. "How are you going to see what comes up in the mirror?"

A dozen sharp replies warred at the tip of Larryn's tongue, and he swallowed all of them. Not the time, and he was trying to be nicer to people who deserved it. In little steps. Nevian might be infuriating, but he was young and wanted to help. And he was right, too.

"Okay. I'll stare at the mirror."

"Wise choice," he declared, and launched into his spell. Nevian's voice deepened as he pronounced arcane words, enunciating each of them in a deliberate process. Like a beginner. Which he was, now that Larryn thought about it. Larryn buried his rising doubts again. If Nevian couldn't do it, who else? This had to work.

Larryn focused on Hasryan, conjuring up the image of the ever-smirking dark elf, then supplying details: the way Hasryan's thick white hair swept backward because he was always running a hand through it, the smaller elven ears and broader shoulders that marked his human blood, the squint in his eyes when he laughed. It had been too long since he'd heard that sound—not since they'd mocked Drake at the *Skyward Tavern*. What a glorious evening—

topped by that majestic head–butt Hasryan had given Drake! The mirror's surface clouded before Larryn's eyes, then cleared to show the Middle City tavern where his friend had been arrested.

"I said no events," Nevian's voice broke in. "Don't make this harder."

Larryn grumbled something but refocused his attention on Hasryan himself. His thoughts strayed immediately, so instead of maintaining a single image, he tried to vary how he imagined his friend. Sure, the smirking Hasryan who'd just delivered a quip came to mind first, but Larryn had witnessed many different moods. He'd seen him sulk after a rough encounter with some bigoted fool, he'd seen him drunk and sprawled over a table, he'd seen him hurt and keeping it all inside. The only facet Larryn had never seen was the cold–blooded killer. *That* remained hard to imagine.

Nevian's arcane words became more forceful, and smoke swirled in the mirror again. When the apprentice let out a groan, Larryn risked a quick glance at him. Sweat rolled down his forehead.

"Focus!" Nevian snapped. "Something's … wrong."

Larryn buried his urge to retort and poured his offended energy into remembering Hasryan. After another small grunt from Nevian, the picture cleared again.

Hasryan stood inside a room so dark the details around him blurred. His friend didn't look too horribly off—no wounds, no scars, no unnatural thinness. Heck, he wore a winter coat worth more than the combined value of every shirt Larryn had ever owned! The tension in his shoulders betrayed his peaceful appearance, however, and he seemed to be arguing in low tones.

The image shifted, drew back. Larryn caught sight of a prison cell door and swore. It was open, but between the exit and Hasryan stood an elf.

Not just any elf, either.

Larryn had long ago learned to identify the Dathirii guard captain and their spymaster. Yultes' protection kept city guards away, but if either of them discovered he'd stolen from their towers for years, they could make him vanish without a word of protest from his so-called father. It would have been reckless not to know Kellian and Branwen Dathirii on sight. Their presence at the Shelter could spell doom for him.

Now one of them was watching Hasryan. In a cell.

Nevian drew a sharp breath, choking on an exclamation. He reiterated his arcane words in a forceful tone, but the image clouded once more, then turned pitch black. His voice trailed off, and the mirror lost all traces of magic.

"I don't understand," he said. "None of this happened as it should have."

Nevian rambled on about the shifts in his spell—something about a wall at first, easy sailing, and then a force pushing him out. Larryn didn't pay attention. His fingers clenched hard on his knees as he inhaled deeply, wrestling with the anger coiling inside. Of course the Dathirii had Hasryan. Who else? They'd played so nice with Arathiel, helping him after he saved Hasryan, getting him on their good side until they'd snatched the assassin out of sight. Was that their plan to regain the Allastams' favour? Spare one noble, and sell them Hasryan in secret; retain the gloss of their benevolent reputation and solidify an important alliance. And they'd sent Arathiel and Cal to retrieve yet another ally. Larryn sprang to his feet, his head spinning and hot.

"Nevian," he said, cutting him off. "Vellien is coming tonight, aren't they?"

"Yes."

"Soon?"

Nevian frowned. "Why?"

"I need to have a chat with them."

Larryn had kept a close watch on Vellien's coming and going. As promised, they'd brought a cloak every time, and stayed after healing Nevian to care for the patrons' ailments. Larryn avoided them when he could, glaring from a distance, yet Vellien had never shown anything but patience with his people, and as time passed, Larryn had started thinking of the young priest less as a Dathirii, and more as a kind teenager.

Not anymore.

"I'll grab us something to eat, and we'll wait together."

Alarm flashed through Nevian's expression. "They're not involved in this. I need them. Whatever you're—"

"I won't rip their throat out, if that's what you're thinking." He didn't even manage to sound dismissive, and Larryn hated the casualness of his tone. Vellien was a *teenager*, and Dathirii or not, they *were* not involved in this mess. Larryn could believe that. He couldn't hit them—couldn't let his anger take over as he had on winter solstice—but he needed to help Hasryan. Larryn clenched and unclenched his fist, trying to get the whirling rage under control. Nevian spotted the movement and paled.

"Eliminating one option amongst many does not ease my fears. Leave them alone."

"I can't." Larryn knew one thing with absolute certainty: noble families protected their own, no matter what. Vellien's safety would be priceless to them, no matter Larryn's actual intent—well worth Hasryan's release. "I won't hurt them, but there's too much at stake. Don't argue."

Nevian did anyway. Larryn cast one last glare at the darkened mirror and stalked out of the room, ignoring him, blood still beating against his temples. He would save Hasryan, no matter the risk.

CHAPTER THIRTY-ONE

VARDEN collapsed to his knees in front of his temple's great brazier, palms flat on the ground. Not his temple anymore, not really. Myrian authorities had stripped him of his High Priest title, as if that alone could destroy his connection to Keroth. The intense warmth radiating from the flames seeped into him, soothing his nerves, piercing through the iced shackles. Water slid along his wrists and to the ground, and Varden closed his eyes. His bonds melted with every passing second, and Keroth's proximity grew stronger, more comforting.

To think Avenazar had chosen this one last refuge as the source of his doom. At least Varden would disappear with his god nearby. He stared at the growing pool under the curve of his palm while Avenazar traced patterns on the ground around him—runes to call upon magic and harness the power imbued in their surroundings. Not that the wizard could draw on the biggest source. Keroth chose to whom They answered.

For a moment Varden considered flight, but what would be the point? He'd manage three steps at best, and while those could take him to the flames, he'd never have the strength to fire-stride out of the temple. Vanishing into the fire plane demanded incredible energy, and leaving it even more so. He doubted he could protect himself from burns at the moment, so he lumbered to his feet and stood as straight as he could manage in the centre of the large rune.

His gaze sought the dancing flames, and he lost himself in the eternal movement. The thousand needles prickling his heart vanished as he forced deep breaths into his lungs. It was over. He should panic, perhaps, but he couldn't. Somewhere in the last ten days, he had accepted it would end soon. He'd fought it, clinging to parts of himself as a litany, yet he had never foreseen an escape. He hoped Avenazar's spell worked well enough for him not to remember how much he'd lost. It would be easier that way. Varden didn't have it in him to fight anymore. He focused on the fire, on his urge to find charcoal and draw one last time, on all the peaceful moments he'd spent within the flames.

A weak chant escaped through his cracked lips, a final prayer to Keroth. He had done all he could. He wished it had been more, so much more—for Nevian and Branwen, for Miles back in Myria, for all the Isbari who had looked up to him. Varden shut his eyes once more to focus on the heat. He could feel the inferno burning close, so close—warmth brushing him, flames leaning toward him, calling out to him. His strength returned, leaking in, and he raised a hand, a smile touching his lips as the brazier responded to his movement, bending in his direction.

A thin lash snapped against his back, sending a shock wave of pain up his spine. Varden cried out, stumbling back down.

"Don't you even think about it," Avenazar said. "Not until ordered to."

Varden's slow breathing was gone, replaced by sharp gasps. He struggled against the flaring pain in his mind, his brief serenity destroyed. Avenazar grabbed the back of his ragged shirt and yanked him up.

"Stay on your feet."

He almost let himself fall just to spite Avenazar. Something held him back—the remnants of his pride, perhaps. He gritted his teeth.

"Just get on with it."

Avenazar cackled, then walked back in front of Varden, between him and the brazier, letting the green whip in his hand disappear.

"Your enthusiasm is heartwarming," he declared before slamming his palm on Varden's chest and knocking his breath out. He stumbled back, but tendrils of magic erupted from Avenazar's hand and held him tight. When Varden tried to inhale, his lungs refused to respond. A tiny wheeze escaped his lips as his limbs stiffened, the wizard's cold magic crawling through his body like a thousand ice spikes, growing out of each other and reaching ever further. He choked, sought the brazier's warmth once more. It had been so close a moment ago! Avenazar stepped back, a thick fire-gold thread of magic linking his palm to Varden's chest. The cold continued to spread, stealing his energy and leaking it to Avenazar. It climbed into Varden's throat, around his jaw and nose, encasing his head until his ears rang and the world turned black.

All but the golden link. It moved, floating to the left, thickening with every second. The contour of a hand appeared on the other end briefly, a pale shadow. Its fingers clamped on the magical connection.

Avenazar's massive mental presence shot through the thread and crashed into Varden's. The crushing pressure had become familiar by now, and the priest's mind gave way without a fight. Varden knew the routine. Easier to hide and wait. Why struggle when he could emerge later and rebuild himself?

No, no!

Varden tried to get a hold on himself. There wouldn't be a next time. He needed to fight now. His consciousness stirred, attempting to see past the invasive cold and Avenazar's bloated presence. The movement triggered a wild laughter from his attacker, and the pressure intensified. Pain blossomed in Varden's mind, and icy fingers shot down from his head into every nerve in his body. He moaned, his grip slipping as the agony spread. He could feel Avenazar's mind coursing through the energy, mixing with Varden's, eroding it. Becoming him. Varden struggled against it, desperate to retain control.

His eyes opened. Varden took a jerky step forward—one he hadn't meant to. Panic started to replace the priest's determination. Avenazar might not be tearing his mind to shreds, but he was pushing Varden so far he couldn't even dictate his own movements.

Be patient. Mockery laced Avenazar's voice. *We just need a little more magical energy, then you'll be gone for good. Thank Keroth I had a source of power built in your honour.*

Another stride forward brought Varden closer to the great brazier, to the flames that had called to him, soothed him, been a part of his life and his very self for so long. Intense nausea washed over Varden, and the world spun under him. He recoiled at the thought of using the fire to fuel this spell. Avenazar had to stop moving his body. He shot quick pain through Varden's mind—the mental equivalent of a solid jab—then they were walking again at a good pace, until he stood on the dais in front of the blazing fire. Varden's hands rose, and flames jumped at them, wrapping around his arm in a minuscule tornado of heat.

Keroth's power surged through him, and Varden was distantly aware of Avenazar's triumphant laugh. He ignored it and basked in the familiar sensation, allowing it to wash over him, envelop him. Why would he want anything else? Let the fire take him. At least there he could be happy. He didn't need to *exist*. Or … That last thought jarred him. Something about it was wrong—more aggressive, violent. Varden recognized neither his exhaustion nor the Firelord's serenity in it. It wasn't him; he didn't reason like that. Were any of these thoughts his own anymore? He tried to spread his consciousness. To find his mind, find his body through the flames. A massive presence blocked him, and its terrifying familiarity snapped Varden back into reality. Avenazar was manipulating him into giving up, using Keroth's power and the peace it brought Varden against him.

Except Varden had spent a lifetime connected to his god, and refused to abandon Them now. The temple had vanished from his perception, leaving nothing in his mind but darkness, fire, and the blazing link to Avenazar. Strength filled him—Keroth's strength, *his* strength. He wrestled control over the energy, wrapping himself in it like a cocoon. Avenazar slammed against it, and Varden hardened the protection, layering it, one wall of mental fire after another.

He wouldn't let Avenazar infiltrate him again. He couldn't. He *did* need to exist, even if his spirit felt ragged and battered, even if it led to more suffering. Varden gathered the smatterings of his willpower and directed his focus against the crushing presence of Avenazar's mind.

He would resist until the bitter end and make the wizard fight for every sliver of control.

Chapter Thirty-Two

THE Dathirii Tower's great tree blocked the setting sun as Diel approached it. The closer he got, the more he dragged his feet, and the heavier his heart turned. A long debate had followed the Golden Table's stripping of their title about who should inherit the seats. Diel's last input as a member of the council, and he'd had to fight for every single word they'd allowed him to say. The constant silencing had infuriated him and exhausted what remained of his energy, but at least Diel had helped convince the Table to give one of his two seats to House Brasten. Amake Brasten's jab at Lord Allastam and their subsequent fight repaired his dwindling hope. Perhaps she'd carry his legacy at the Golden Table while he rebuilt the family's fortune.

The biting wind whipped his face, stealing what warmth he had left. Garith trailed behind him, shoulders hunched and nose hidden in a golden scarf. When Diel caught his gaze, the young elf forced a smile. "At least it'll be warm inside."

True. Diel looked forward to sitting in front of a roaring fireplace, his arms wrapped around Jaeger, waiting for news of Arathiel and Branwen. Devising what plans he could for Hasryan's escape. Later, though. First, he needed to find his aunt. At least he'd tell her himself about their fall. Diel didn't know what her answer would be—something wise and comforting. After, he could enjoy the combined warmth of fire and Jaeger. Gods, this day had stretched on for too long already.

"Plans for tonight?" Diel asked Garith as he pushed open their main door.

"I have an excellent bottle of old wine hidden in my quarters, and it's the only plan I need."

A soft chuckle escaped Diel as he moved inside. Belatedly, he realized no guards had greeted him. Had Kellian pulled them away? Then he registered the nine soldiers in House Allastam's livery, standing in the main antechamber, blocking all exits. Their leader advanced as the door slammed behind Garith, and Diel's blood drained from his face. The walls closed in on him for a brief moment, but he pushed the shock away and stepped forward with a scowl. "Who allowed you to enter our home?"

An awkward silence followed. Garith moved closer, gloved index finger tapping a stressed melody on the top of his leather account book. Diel exercised great willpower not to fidget at the foreboding presence of Allastam guards in his tower. He didn't believe in coincidences.

"The current Lord Dathirii did, sir."

"There's no 'Lord Dathirii' anymore," Diel snapped, his gaze flying to the ceiling, past the delicate fresco of the Elven Shepherd and toward his office. The title might no longer exist, but the family still needed a leader. It seemed someone had decided to replace him. "I assume you're here to take me to him."

"I am."

Diel tried to wrap his mind around this mysterious Lord Dathirii. Over the last days, he'd felt increasingly threatened while striding through Isandor's streets, but never here, at home. He'd thought to sit for a few minutes, eat a brief dinner while he discussed with Jaeger, then leave for the Sapphire Guard's headquarters. Instead, his tower wasn't his anymore, and hostile soldiers waited for him.

"Uncle, there's blood everywhere," Garith whispered.

Diel shifted his attention to the ground, and his throat tightened. "Everywhere" was an exaggeration, but several considerable splashes of blood stained the walls and floor. The paintings hung wrong, and several seats had been shoved to the side. One was even slashed through. Kellian's guards had fought and lost. Diel hoped his cousin was safe. If blood had been spilled … Diel pulled his mind away from the dark paths it wanted to follow—away from the crushing fear regarding what orders Allastam soldiers would have about Jaeger. *Stay calm*, he ordered himself.

"Indeed. Garith, I believe we stand before the first military takeover in Isandor's recent history. Most rivals stop after they've busted their opponent's finances and stripped them of their titles, but Lord Allastam once again defies even my most awful expectations." He set a hand on Garith's shoulder to reassure him and turned to the guard. "Take us, then."

Despite his solid tone, his heart jumped when the soldiers fell into lines around them, weapons drawn, their professional scowls leaving no place for any emotions. Diel swallowed hard and followed them to the nearest staircase. His stunned calm eroded as they climbed. His mind browsed through the multitudes of terrible outcomes this attack could have led to. Had Branwen already left when the soldiers had arrived? What did Lord Allastam know, and how long had he been planning this? He'd organized this, obviously, but which Dathirii had he enrolled in his treasonous plot? Diel prayed it wasn't Yultes. His stepbrother spent a lot of time in House Allastam, and Diel knew he valued them as family, but this coup … it couldn't be him. Diel refused to believe that. Even if their relationship had worsened over the last month, Yultes wouldn't go that far.

But despite his best efforts to focus, one question looped ceaselessly to the front of his mind, squeezing his chest so hard it made breathing painful.

Was Jaeger safe? Had they hurt him?

Diel pressed his lips together as they arrived at his office door. He struggled with the idea that a family member had betrayed him, and that he hadn't foreseen it. But whenever Diel thought about someone striking Jaeger, a thick layer of rage added itself to the guilt. A hostile takeover, he could deal with. Jaeger wounded—hurting—though … not that. Some lines should never be crossed.

He shoved the door open, slamming it against the wall and

drawing surprised exclamations from the guards flanking him. They scrambled after him as he strode into his office, Garith slipping behind them. Diel ignored them all, his chin high, his outrage burning strong.

When his eyes fell upon Lord Hellion Dathirii sitting on top of his desk, he stopped. A wave of relief briefly buried his spike of hatred. Diel had been so terrified to find someone he'd thought of as an ally, someone close to him, that his response flew on its own.

"Oh. It's only you."

Of course it was Hellion. Who else would even consider superseding all of Isandor's customs and betraying the implicit trust between family members to organize a coup with their enemies? Who else would dare to call himself Lord Dathirii mere hours after striking against his peers, as if the mantle had always belonged to him? Diel ran a hand through his hair as the guards once more surrounded him, and exhaustion pressed down on his shoulders.

"Desist now, Hellion, and I might be lenient."

Hellion scowled, anger and incredulity struggling for supremacy in his expression. "Lenient? What do you think is going on here, Diel? You don't have the power for magnanimity anymore." He motioned at the soldiers, and they grabbed both Diel and Garith. "I'm in charge now."

"For how long? House Dathirii won't let you control it."

Guards shoved Garith against a wall before Diel continued, and his nephew's pained moan extinguished his desire to mock Hellion. Every little squirm from Garith dropped a stone in his stomach, a reminder that if he wasn't careful, others could get hurt in Hellion's game.

"What foolish deal did you strike, Hellion?" he asked. "You're Lord of Nothing—we're no longer nobles, and you'll be lucky if half the family recognizes you as a leader."

"They won't have any choice." Hellion slid down the desk and strolled to Diel, his smile sweet and confident. "You surrounded yourself with weak sentimentalists, Diel. What do you think they'll do if they know you'll pay for their disobedience? What will you do, knowing Jaeger will pay for yours?"

Diel lunged for Hellion, but strong hands squeezed his shoulders and held him back. Blood rushed against his temples, and all of a sudden, the ground seemed distant under his feet. He forced a whistling breath inside and glared at Hellion.

"Where is he?"

Hellion clacked his tongue, and he lowered his gaze to the floor, raising his eyebrows meaningfully. "Recovering."

Diel glanced down, and a cold horror crept up his spine as he noticed the blood patterns. He repressed a cry of anger first, then one of anguish. They'd already touched him. He'd been here, waiting for Diel, and they'd attacked him. Hellion moved closer, amusement dancing in his eyes.

"You see, Diel, all I really need is to know which levers to pull and to be willing to do it." He sidestepped and motioned at the desk that had been Diel's for over a century. "Perhaps you should use it one last time and write a letter of resignation. If you refuse ..."

Diel squared his shoulders and glared at Hellion. He wanted to see Jaeger, to hold him into his arms and apologize for everything.

"Do you truly believe a piece of paper will give you the power you need? Sure, a handful of friends will call you Lord Dathirii, but it takes more than that to lead. It takes courage and heart, and you seem to have misplaced yours."

Hellion laughed and wrapped an arm around Diel's shoulder, as one would an old friend. "This is why you lost, dear cousin. Heart is a hindrance. It takes cunning to rule, and the ruthlessness to see your plans through. Now … I've already punished Jaeger once for his stubbornness. You wouldn't want me to punish him for yours, would you?"

Diel closed his eyes, struggling to cool his rising panic and think through his options. His heart urged him to yield now and spare Jaeger another beating—to give in to Hellion's demand and resign. Who cared about the title if it meant sacrificing his beloved? Except … why would Hellion abandon his leverage over Diel, even after becoming the official Head of the House? Resigning gave him a free pass to do whatever he pleased and no obligations to free Jaeger. He would continue to use him against Diel to keep him in check. Giving up never solved anything. Jaeger had already known that—what other stubbornness would Hellion have punished him for? Stepping down offered no protection to Jaeger, only guilt at being used. Diel had to believe that because his heart shrivelled as he met Hellion's gaze.

"Your terms aren't good enough," he whispered.

Hellion's eyes widened, and his mouth formed a small "what?" Diel gritted his teeth, and apologized to Jaeger in his mind before clearing his throat and squaring his shoulders. In a single breath, all the prestige and countenance acquired over years as Lord Dathirii—Head of an old and noble house, proud representative of his family—all of it flowed into him as he declared loudly and firmly, "Your terms aren't good enough."

Before either of them could add anything, a third voice joined the conversation—snide and self-satisfied, the same that had led the charge against him today, and from which Diel had hoped to be freed for a time.

"His terms are too generous." Lord Allastam strode into the office and sniffed with disdain as he examined his surroundings. "Thankfully, Diel's fate has already been decided."

"Milord?"

Hellion obviously didn't know what that meant, and his confusion alarmed Diel. He threw his cousin an annoyed glare. Didn't he plan any protection against Lord Allastam? Anything to ensure he'd retain control over the Dathirii Tower despite the soldiers now overrunning it? Diel pinched the bridge of his nose, a terrible headache ensnaring his mind. This situation could only worsen, and he had little say in anything.

"Out with it, will you?" he said. "I'm here, I'm defenceless, and I have absolutely no patience for games and charades. Assuming you also double-crossed Hellion—"

"He didn't—"

Lord Allastam's bark-like laugh cut off Hellion's protest. "Of course I did. Partially. Nothing you need to worry about, my friend," he added for Hellion's sake. "Focus on pulling your finances upright, and you'll have my support. A seat on the Golden Table should be well within your reach." He waved his hand midair as if to dismiss the topic. "Was the Brasten freak here, Hellion?"

"I'm afraid not. He must have left the tower."

"You bet your ass he did," Garith said, his voice muffled as the soldiers pressed his face against the wall. He fought to look over his shoulder and glare at Hellion, and Lord Allastam motioned for them to ease up. Garith turned around, rubbing his jaw. "Too bad neither of you two despicable worms know where to."

A thin smile reached Diel's lips. Garith had always struggled with staying silent, and while insults wouldn't help, they soothed him. It would take more than being shoved against a wall to crush his family's fighting spirit. The answer amused Lord Allastam, who pushed the tip of his cane against Garith's chest.

"We will soon enough," he said. "Thankfully, I'm sending your uncle to a master of information extraction. He was quite adamant to have that as a clause in our brand new deal."

A new deal? Diel scowled, but his expression turned to a horrified grimace as Branwen's long and detailed rants about what Master Avenazar could do—how he'd dug through Varden's mind to discover she'd been in the enclave—flooded back. Information extraction. A tame way to put it. What had Lord Allastam said, when Diel had first come to him for soldiers? That he regretted not forging an alliance with the Myrians, and that neutrality was the best Lord Dathirii could expect of him. His legs weakened, and for an instant, Diel believed they would give underneath him.

"No … You're …" He couldn't say it, could barely form the thought.

"Oh, but yes."

"You're sending me to my death."

Diel's voice broke. Not just any death, either. His mind blanked, words failing him, and he turned towards Garith. Pale and shaky, his nephew leaned on the nearest guard for support.

Hellion stepped forward, flustered, no longer smiling. "Lord Allastam, that was never part of the deal!"

His meagre protest was brushed aside with a dismissive wave. "You did not specify anything. Care to stop me, Lord Hellion? Think you can?" Silence followed—an admission of defeat from Hellion. "Don't forget to whom you owe your new position, or I might leave with the guards. Your brother would love that."

If Diel needed one more piece of proof Hellion had unwittingly sold House Dathirii to the Allastams, that was it. They had trapped him, and he was about to be shipped like vulgar cargo in a trade. How had they fallen so low? Diel closed his eyes, fighting his rising nausea and tears. He could cry when they dumped him alone in a cell. For now, he must stay strong. Garith was watching him, and his nephew would need courage in the coming days. Besides, he had one important thing to do before they sent him away.

"Please let me see Jaeger." Diel clenched his fist then unfurled it slowly, forcing calm and control back into his voice. "One last time."

Lord Allastam allowed several seconds to trickle by before he answered, each of them an eternity to Diel.

"Granted," the noble said, "but let's get this over with. Your escort is waiting."

PAIN lanced through Jaeger's body, supplied by dozens of bruises and cuts. He sat on his bed, pressing a bloodied rag to his nose, staring ahead. He had too many wounds to count, and yet none hurt as much as the cold numbness in his mind. He couldn't think, couldn't formulate a plan to warn the other Dathirii or a way to be useful. His brain had shut down, obliterated by the acute pain at the base of his skull, as if someone had run a nail through it. Anything except staying awake, seated, and silent was now beyond his ability.

How long had they stayed alone in this room? A few minutes? Hours? Hard to tell when pain stretched seconds into an eternity, or when his mind blanked and extensive lapses of time passed in a blink. Yultes had remained with him, fussing over his wounds, switching between apologies and justifications. His excuses had petered out after a blank stare from Jaeger, but despite the burning sense of betrayal swirling at the bottom of his stomach, the silent company helped the steward's mood. When little remained to be done, Jaeger looked out the window. The sun was gone now. Winter nights came so early. Yultes must have caught his glance outside because he squeezed his shoulder.

"He'll be fine."

Yultes' tone held no conviction—he was too pessimist by nature for that. Jaeger was preparing to repeat the words with more certainty when the door to his quarters opened.

And there was Diel, small and pale, his smile forced and unconvincing. It vanished the instant he noticed the swollen eye, split lips, and countless bruises. Jaeger cast his gaze down, unable to quell his shame.

"Yultes, if we could have a moment?" Diel asked.

Yultes jumped to his feet, hurrying across the room, toward Diel and the door. He slowed down as he passed him and cleared his throat. "Diel, I … I didn't plan this with him, I swear, and I tried to stop …"

Diel tore his eyes from Jaeger, turning to Yultes. His shoulders tightened, and Jaeger thought he saw anger and hope flash through his expression. Hard to tell, which was perhaps the most surprising part of this. When had Diel ever been so controlled?

"The second desk is yours, isn't it?"

A pause. Yultes looked away. "Yes."

"Make good use of it. Hellion may give orders, but you execute them. Think about how much power is in your hands now and what you want to do with it." He waited until Yultes raised his head and met his gaze. Did Diel trust him to differentiate between right and wrong? Jaeger doubted Yultes even trusted himself—he'd always referred to Hellion's dangerous advice when faced with problems. "I know you can be a great architect, Yultes. It's up to you to decide what you build."

Yultes stared at his stepbrother, shaken and uncertain. "I–I'll leave you alone."

He hurried out as Diel thanked him. Something in his love's tone pushed Jaeger's exhaustion away, clearing his mind of the cobwebs of pain. Tears. He could hear the tears Diel refused to shed in the thickness of his voice. They flowed the moment Yultes closed the door behind him, a heavy and rapid flood. So much for composure—Diel had barely held it together, forcing a fake and fragile strength to the surface for Yultes' sake. There was no need for that between the two of them. Jaeger tried to stand, but pain shot through his back and glued him to the bed.

"Don't move!" Diel hurried his side, climbed on the mattress, and knelt next to Jaeger. He wiped his eyes with the back of his hand, then ran his thumb over Jaeger's split lip, his expression hardening. "Hellion did this to you."

Jaeger picked up Diel's hand and squeezed it, ignoring the jolts of pain through his body. He smiled at his own earlier defiance. "He wanted me to call him Lord Dathirii."

Diel responded with the expected chuckle. A weak, bitter one, but a chuckle nonetheless. It didn't last. "I don't have long, Jaeger. Please, look at me."

Jaeger forced himself to meet Diel's eyes. He knew the green he perceived differed from everyone else's, but Jaeger loved to think Diel's eyes were unique to him. No one saw them like he did, and no one ever would. If only they weren't filled with fear and sadness.

"I'm okay, Diel. I'm okay."

"Liar." Diel gathered his courage with a deep breath. The spectre of terrible news hovered between them, and Jaeger willed time to stop, to keep the inevitable blow away. "Lord Allastam pulled strings behind Hellion's back. As part of a new deal with the Myrian enclave, he is sending me to Avenazar." Jaeger's heart squeezed, and he started to say something, but Diel put a finger on his lips. "Let me finish. Please, I need you to hear this."

His voice cracked. Jaeger leaned closer, enduring the stinging pain every movement caused. He resisted the urge to pull Diel into his arms—they ought to do this face to face. It … it sounded like goodbyes. A confused laugh escaped Diel, and he pinched the bridge of his nose.

"I'm such a mess, I don't know where to start," he said. "I want to thank you. Thank you for the hundred forty years together, for being there and being you. I don't understand how I ever deserved you. I hope … if I never make it back, I hope there will be someone else for you. Just stay safe, okay? You need to make it through this." Diel paused to wipe his tears again. Jaeger squeezed his hand. He wanted to protest even considering Diel might not return, but denying it wouldn't make the danger vanish. He wouldn't waste their time with such words. Diel had to know he was thinking them. "I would ask one last favour, too. Hellion isn't forever. This family … it has always been yours, too, and Garith and Branwen will need your help. I meant for them to lead. I groomed Garith to handle diplomatic meetings and numbers, and Branwen to discover and love the city beyond its politics. She's the decisive one, and I trust her to understand the right thing to do. This won't be easy for them—not for anyone—but if I know you're there …"

"I will be. Of course I will be." They'd become his only family fifty years ago when his parents had moved away from Isandor and farther south. Jaeger had no idea where else he'd go.

Diel closed his eyes, and his shoulders slumped. "I don't want to leave."

Jaeger stared at Diel in silence, trying to think of something to say, of words that could encompass the growing void inside of him. His strength was slipping out of this new hole, vanishing as his mind slowly accepted the idea he might lose Diel. So much had seemed unreal today, from Yultes' help to Hellion's betrayal and the brutal attack that had followed, but through it all, he'd always known he at least had Diel. Not anymore, not for long.

"Diel, I …"

Jaeger gave up on words. When had speeches been his strength anyway? Stubborn pride and pushing his limits for Diel—that, he could do. He hooked trembling fingers in Diel's outfit and pulled him closer, ignoring his screaming muscles to press their lips together. Jaeger had wanted to tell him it wasn't about deserving someone—that he'd loved every moment by his side, every laugh and caress, every crisis and every new flutter of Diel's heart. He had loved watching their dynamics change and evolve as a third joined their romantic lives, to see Diel happy and be the frequent source of it, to grow with him. His time with Diel and his family had brought him more than he could put into words, and Jaeger knew better than to try. He held onto Diel, clinging to his clothes and to the warmth of his kiss, until he found himself crying too. Jaeger didn't want him to go either. He needed some hope to hang onto. He drew back, his mind reaching for the first sliver of it he could imagine.

"Maybe Branwen—"

"Shh, yes," Diel said, leaning his forehead against Jaeger's. "I'll be praying to every deity and demigod I can think of, but we can't assume …"

"They'll go back for you."

"I hope."

They stayed like this for a long time, silent. Jaeger breathed in Diel's scent, recording all of his voice and presence nearby, as if any memory would ever compare to the real elf. When three loud knocks echoed on the door, they both jumped. Diel withdrew and slid down from the bed.

"Jaeger …"

"I know." *I love you too*, he added mentally. "Keep it for when you return."

Diel turned around and looked at him, with a hint of a smile. He'd forced it, but it lit up his expression and smoothed the lines of worry. Jaeger could almost superimpose his memory of Diel's full grin above it. He promised himself that was the version he'd remember most.

"All right. I will."

Their gazes locked for a moment, a final goodbye, then Diel turned away and left.

Chapter Thirty-Three

SOME days should never exist. Sora stared at the young teen who had barged into her quarters, carrying more terrifying news. Ne had dyed nir kinky hair a bright red since their last meeting, in addition to painting nir nails and lips in a similar colour. Sora distrusted most official Sapphire Guard spies and informants, but Lai was her protégé and never interacted with other investigators unless Sora asked. Astute, discreet, and efficient, ne had become an essential part of her work. And when ne explored new facets of nir gender identity and how they related to being intersex, Lai knew ne could count on Sora's respect. Though vastly different, their experiences still overlapped, and Sora loved to support Lai however she could.

Today, she'd asked Lai to watch the Dathirii Tower and report on anyone leaving through Lady Camilla's entrance. No doubt ne had pieced the rest of the story together, but Sora knew the word wouldn't spread. Only, Lai hadn't returned with clues about Hasryan's location. Ne had shoved the office door open, striding in as if ne owned the place, slowing only as ne caught sight of Camilla staring out of the window on nir right. Sora motioned for nir to come closer, and Lai leaned over the desk to whisper.

"Eighty Allastam soldiers entered the Dathirii Tower. Most never left, and I doubt the elves hold control anymore."

Sora stiffened, her gaze flying to Camilla. The elf stared right back, questioning eyebrows raised, but she stayed silent. Sora focused on Lai, trying to ignore the incredulous buzz between her own ears. She didn't bother to keep her voice down. "Do we know the Golden Table's conclusion?"

Lai grinned, straightening with pride at nir foresight. "Checked it before I came. They're out. No seats left to their names. Rumours say that was pretty unanimous too, but I'm not sure I trust that bit."

"What about Diel? Garith?" Camilla's controlled tone didn't hide her fear. "Lord Dathirii and his bookkeeper."

"Hard to know," Lai said. "People saw them heading home though. Don't think anyone warned them it wasn't theirs anymore."

Camilla closed her eyes but only answered with a brief gesture to carry on. Lai turned back toward Sora. "Remember my zucchini? He still works inside that tower. Once he leaves, I'll know more." Ne hesitated, and for a moment, nir confident stance fell. "He'll be safe, right? He's got nothing to do with these politics."

Sora wished she could promise that. Lai had met this boy months ago when Sora had asked nir to snoop around the Dathirii household and discover if any of them helped that thief who had snuck inside and stolen from them for years. They'd grown close, creating a special dynamic Lai described as neither friendship nor romance, but deep and thrilling—soulmates without love, voices singing in perfect harmony. Since Fern's shortened name was a plant and he worked in the kitchens, ne had taken to referring to him as nir zucchini. Nir attachment to Fern reminded Sora of the profound connection Arathiel had often expressed having with Hasryan. Lai should have the truth.

"I don't know. Politics rarely spill the blood of those who deserve it." Thoughts of Hasryan hovered at the edge of her mind, and she shoved them away. He had killed people for money! "Thank you for the information, Lai. Come back as soon as you have more."

"I will." Nir worry hadn't vanished from nir tone, but ne carried on with nir usual confidence. "No one in town will know more than you, boss!"

Ne saluted with a smirk, and Sora groaned. She hated the formality, and ever since she'd voiced her irritation at it, Lai had teased her accordingly.

"Off you go!" Sora called, and Lai scampered away, laughing. The joyous sound echoed down the corridor, contrasting with the office's heavy mood. Sora waited for it to vanish before she turned to Camilla. The elf sat with her back straight, hands clinging to each other, lips tight with worry. If Lord Allastam learned why she'd come to the Sapphire Guard's headquarters, Sora might not be able to keep her safe. "Milady, do you have anywhere safe to stay?"

"There are soldiers in my home." Her sharp tone surprised Sora, but Camilla pinched the bridge of her nose. "I'm sorry, Miss Sharpe. I did not mean to snap."

"Don't worry," she said, "but surely if you headed to wherever Hasryan is …"

Sora couldn't believe the proposition had crossed her lips. What was she thinking? She'd been badgering Lady Camilla with questions a few hours ago to learn where that might be, and now she was suggesting the elven lady should slip out of the headquarters and hide there, too? Lord Allastam's attack on the Dathirii Tower unsettled her. How far would he go? What would he do if he discovered a Dathirii had hidden Hasryan? He owned their tower and might keep other elves trapped in it.

Lady Camilla tore her gaze from the window slowly, as if she'd miss crucial news if she relented for even a single second. Deep worry filled her eyes, but she managed a sad smile. "As I said, there are soldiers in my home."

For a brief instant, Sora considered clarifying her suggestion— then Camilla's layered meaning sank in, snatching her breath away. *In the Dathirii Tower.* She couldn't believe Camilla had kept him right under everyone's noses. And now … Lai hadn't spotted anyone leaving while ne staked the door. If Hasryan hadn't escaped in time, Lord Allastam would have him. "For his sake, I hope he vanished this afternoon."

"I never thought …" She sighed. "Lord Allastam has a history of bloody vengeance. He attacked everyone tied to House Freitz that he could touch without incurring the city's wrath. Hasryan has no protection, and what little remains of ours will disappear if they find him in my quarters. We have to do something."

"I can't demand to search the tower without revealing I believe he's in there. I'm afraid Hasryan is on his own." With how things had evolved this afternoon, Sora hoped he would remain out of sight. Her meagre desire to catch him had vanished. She wished he could make amends for his crimes instead of paying for them, but between Brune and Lord Allastam, he would never get the chance. "The best I can do is locate the missing members of your family and keep them out of immediate danger."

"Thank you, Miss Sharpe. We will remember."

Sora quirked an eyebrow. "Are you promising not to hide my targets again?" Camilla laughed at the question—answer enough for Sora, who hadn't expected anything else. She reached into her pocket and withdrew the solid iron key to her home. "I'll get you settled at my place. It's not luxurious, but the tea collection ought to interest you. Relatives from the Tuen Peninsula sometimes send me the most unique leaves, or so they say. It's kind of wasted on me."

The invitation breathed new life into Camilla. Her gaze snapped to Sora, her arms and shoulders relaxed, and she rose to her feet with surprising speed and fluidity for a lady her age. "I—You are most gracious, Miss Sharpe, and I find myself at a loss for proper words."

"Then don't say any." Sora didn't need thanks. They'd only embarrass her and drive home the contradiction between her duty to Isandor's laws and her current actions. Her job demanded she warn Lord Allastam about Hasryan's most recent location. She should rush to the Dathirii Tower in case she could find him still hiding in Lady Camilla's quarters, and she should accuse the elven lady of complicity. Yet as she gathered her belongings and slipped her winter fur on, Sora's heart lifted. She would do none of those things, and for the first time since she'd led Hasryan to the noose, she didn't need to justify her actions to herself. She just *knew* this was right, legalities be damned. Arathiel had convinced her. She didn't work for Lord Allastam, or for Brune, and she refused to stay their pawn, not when she could help so much more elsewhere. House Dathirii deserved protection, not attacks. Sora's smile widened, and she offered her arm to Lady Camilla.

"Let's get you to safety," she said, "and we'll see if I have more luck finding a handful of golden elves than a single dark one."

Lady Camilla studied her, sharp blue eyes piercing Sora with unsettling intensity. Sora felt evaluated, and she flushed with anticipation. It shouldn't matter, yet when Lady Camilla smiled and accepted her arm, relief flooded through her.

"Hasryan thinks you make a poor cook," Lady Camilla said. "Perhaps I can help with that to compensate for my stay?"

Memories of quips in bad taste about the kitchens and her initial clash with Hasryan returned. He'd apologized for the sexist comments, which was more than any of her colleagues had ever done, but she wouldn't forget so soon. To think he still taunted her now, through Camilla! "Don't believe him. He's jealous, I bet."

"Well, I'll admit he lacks experience himself."

Sora snorted, then laughed. They left her office in good spirits, and with every new step, Sora felt better about her decision. Perhaps Camilla would even have a tale or two about Hasryan to share. Sora yearned to know more about the dark elf, but the murder accusations had limited their interaction heavily. She couldn't deny her curiosity. Hasryan used to make her blood boil, but he'd revealed a completely different side of himself after Brune's betrayal—one she'd worked hard to ignore. Now, she had this slim chance to both explore it and help nobles she respected, and Sora intended to seize it. Some days should never exist, but even in those, one could find a sliver of good news.

A STRONG hand slapped over Vellien's mouth when they stepped into Nevian's bedroom, muffling their yelp of surprise. Larryn pulled them back against his wiry body, slamming the door behind them. A knife glinted in the candlelight in front of their chest—not in a position to strike, but terrifying nonetheless. Vellien trembled uncontrollably, their panicked gaze sweeping across the room. Nevian sat on the bed, staring at his hands and refusing to look their way. In the middle, a chair with ropes waited. Vellien whimpered, and Larryn released his hold enough for them to speak.

"I–I don't understand. I didn't break any rules!"

To think they'd come to the Shelter hoping for a distraction from the family's problems and their guilt. At least with Nevian, they contributed to something. They helped—his memories, his gruff moods, even his unshakable fear of Avenazar. Calling upon Alluma always soothed Vellien, but listening to Nevian list both his most recent progress with magic and Efua's growing reading skills had another kind of rewarding effect. They'd been eager to reach the Shelter and settle into that comfortable routine, and now Larryn threatened them, weapon at the ready.

"*You* didn't," Larryn confirmed. "Our little truce still holds." Larryn dragged them to the chair, shoving them down and snatching the ropes. "You did well, kid—my favourite Dathirii, not that you had a lot of competition. Blame your rotten family for this."

Favourite or not, Larryn grabbed their hands to tie them. Vellien knew they should fight, do something, try to run, but they couldn't. Fear froze their muscles, and they let Larryn bind their wrists and ankles to the chair, their only resistance a constant shake. Vellien wanted to piece together Larryn's motivation, to force some logic into his attack, but their mind drew a blank. They'd get hurt, Vellien knew they'd get hurt, and the certainty blocked all rational thoughts. Their tongue stuck to their palate, and even speaking became a battle.

"Why?"

"It's a trade," Nevian volunteered, his voice empty and distant. "His assassin friend for you."

"What?"

Larryn walked back in front of Vellien, calm and grim. Vellien wished he'd yell. They'd witnessed and received Larryn's anger before, and it would almost make the situation normal. Instead, the rage stayed contained, burning in the cook's grey eyes, controlled. Larryn leaned forward, hands on his knees. This close, Vellien noticed the lines of exhaustion behind Larryn's mask. "Your family holds Hasryan. Don't try to deny it."

A pit opened at the bottom of Vellien's stomach. How did

Larryn know anything like that? It wasn't even true! They didn't *hold* him, Hasryan stayed willingly! But why would Larryn listen? Panic crawled into their throat. Larryn had punched Cal over this, no? What would he do if Uncle Diel couldn't make Hasryan magically appear? He'd brought a knife—a knife! Tears welled up in Vellien's eyes, blurring their sight. They tried to convince themself that Camilla would explain everything, that their family would find a way to save them, but the ropes digging into their wrists cut through their hopes and any chance of calming down. Suddenly, Vellien's words poured out, pushed on by desperation.

"We don't. We're not keeping him trapped! Please, it was just Aunt Camilla. She helped him." The tears rolled down their cheeks, and they tried to wipe their face, but the bonds held them. They squirmed, choking on a sob. "She's in prison now. In prison for aiding him, and she won't tell anyone where he is, so Uncle Diel can't make that trade. He doesn't know where to find your friend."

Vellien blinked hard, trying to push out the last tears and control themself. They hated this undignified position and their panic and endless crying, but Larryn terrified them. One day ago, Vellien would have sworn Larryn acted tougher than he was, but now … now they didn't know how far the Shelter's young owner would go—if that knife was for show, or if he meant to use it. And when faced with uncertainty, Vellien's mind always focused on the worst. They would get hurt, or die, and no one could do anything about it.

"They're crying, Larryn. Crying," Nevian said, unease and reproach lacing his tone. "Stop it. Untie them."

Larryn cleared his throat and looked away, the muscles of his jaw working. Had regret flickered through his expression, or had Vellien imagined it? But then Larryn slammed the knife on Nevian's desk and scoffed. "They're lying, too. We saw Hasryan with your spy girl—Branwen. In a cell, and she blocked the exit."

Vellien hadn't believed the night could grow more confusing, yet Larryn's bitter words threw their mind off again. "That can't be. Branwen's with Arathiel. They're … Maybe your friend is at the enclave!"

"Or maybe they don't tell you everything." Larryn's tone softened. He leaned on the desk, crossing his arms. "Your family has an amazing track record for shitty secrets. Just because you can swallow your pride and follow the rules doesn't mean they're all angels."

Vellien's head snapped up, and they met Larryn's grey eyes, forcing themself not to flinch. "They wouldn't hurt him." Their voice didn't shake now, and Vellien took comfort from their surface confidence. "I know them—Uncle Diel and Branwen and Aunt Camilla—they would never harm him. He's safe with them. Just look at all they risked for Arathiel! We might not even be nobles anymore because we angered Lord Allastam."

"What a *terrible* loss. You're giving me reasons to celebrate." Larryn rolled his eyes and a brief smile passed over his features before he crouched in front of Vellien. "Listen, I know two things for sure: this city wants my best friend dead, and your family has been hiding him. If he's safe, then so are you. I don't mean to hurt you—you're just a naive kid."

"I'm decades older than you are."

Larryn laughed, the sound bitter and strained. "Yet you'd never been in a kitchen. Age doesn't mean anything—not when it comes to understanding the level of shit this world can throw your way. You've been lucky. And that's good, really. Good for you. The other side of that coin stinks. But it teaches you a lot." Larryn's shoulders slumped, and he ran a hand over his face. He picked up a folded parchment. "I'm going to send out this missive and come back with something for all of us to eat. If your Lord Dathirii is as nice a person as you think, this will be over in no time."

Behind Vellien, Nevian emitted a low grunt of disapproval. Larryn raised his head. "I wish I had another messenger I could trust. No one will look twice at the delivery girl. And unless you can handle a trip to the Upper City to knock at the door of Avenazar's biggest rival, Efua has to be the one."

Nevian didn't respond. Vellien had only met Efua once, but they knew Nevian had grown fond of her. He hid it behind gruff comments about her progress, as if they didn't all know she was learning faster than he'd anticipated. Nevian's fear of Avenazar obliterated everything else, however, and Vellien doubted he would leave. Cal had convinced him to do so once, and since running into Isra, he had stayed in his bedroom. Somehow, Nevian's obvious discomfort and terror allowed Vellien to stomp down their own, if only briefly.

"She'll be fine," they said. "If anything, Diel would reward her for delivering the message."

Larryn rolled his eyes and left the room without comment. Silence stretched onward, and Vellien's panic morphed to confused shock as seconds trickled by. *Kidnapping.* Larryn had tied them to a chair and proposed a trade for his assassin friend. Without the memory of a hand over their mouth and the ropes binding them, Vellien wouldn't believe it. How had it gone so wrong so fast? They closed their eyes, trying to calm the tears still flowing and their panting breath. Nevian shifted on the bed again and again, unable to hide his discomfort. After a while, he muttered, "I'm sorry."

Vellien turned to him. "It's not your fault," they said.

"I know. I told him not to. It's a bad plan. A wrong one. But he wouldn't listen, and he threatened to make me sleep in the common room if I got in the way. I can't do that, Vellien, it's full of people and—"

"It's okay, Nevian. Please just stay." They didn't want to be alone with Larryn when he returned, not with that knife so close. "It's less scary with you around."

Nevian's face brightened at their words. "This is my room, and my healer is here," he said. "I don't see why I'd leave. I … Larryn says he doesn't intend to hurt you, but I … I'd get in the way. I would."

A mirthless chuckle escaped Vellien. "Thank you. I'm sorry your last check-up will have to wait."

Vellien prayed to the Elven Shepherd they would have the chance to heal Nevian—or anyone else, for that matter—again. They clung to Larryn's promise that they'd be safe if Hasryan was and hoped their uncle would eventually find a way to prove they had never hurt the assassin. Vellien sunk deeper into their chair, knowing they couldn't expect a rescue anytime soon.

Chapter Thirty-Four

An Allastam soldier glared at Yultes, silently intimating that he should go and hide, as he waited in front of Lord Dathirii's office. Yultes didn't budge, nor would he unless the guard decided to forcefully remove him. He needed to speak with Hellion and would stay however long it took. His brief exchange with Diel had shaken him to the core, and he knew he sought reassurance—that, like a coward, he hoped Hellion would convince him no one else would get hurt, including and perhaps even especially Diel. Yultes didn't want to fight; he'd rather trust his old friend, and he was ready to believe that remained possible.

Hellion's high-pitched voice from the office gave him hope. "That was never part of the deal! I needed Diel here for everyone to fall in line. You can't sell my family like that!"

What did he mean by sell? Yultes caught a hint of fear under Hellion's indignant anger, and his stomach squeezed. His friend should have been in control, not scrambling to protest against a Lord Allastam who only laughed.

"You're right, dear Hellion, Diel didn't figure in our deal, which means you failed to protect your assets, not that I betrayed my promise. Master Avenazar was quite clear on his conditions, however." Cold horror drenched Yultes, and Diel's parting words resurfaced with more weight than before. How could Allastam do this? Yultes imagined him leaning on his cane with a stiff smirk. Despite the smooth tone, Allastam didn't sound amused. Perhaps he disliked that it had come to this, but if such was the case, he'd buried any regrets far away. "Stop wailing about it. You won't redeem this family by clinging to the elements poisoning it. Diel's presence would have given his crew a core to gather around and fight for. They might be more docile now, and if they're not? If you can't get that smart-mouthed accountant and his cousin in line? Then you need to cut them loose, too."

A resounding silence followed Lord Allastam's instruction. Hellion didn't protest—not against the idea of cutting anyone loose nor against its necessity. Yultes ground his teeth together, staring past the guard and at the door behind him. Could the human soldier hear this as clearly as he did? If it bothered him, it didn't show in the least. Yultes tried to stomp down his horror and control the shake of his hands. Hellion didn't say a word because he knew it would be pointless, not because he intended to follow the suggestions. He cared for House Dathirii, and that meant caring for those inside, too, even through frequent disagreements.

"If that is all, Lord Allastam, I'm afraid I have a lot of work ahead of me." Hellion's glacial tone reassured Yultes. "I'm sure we'll have ample opportunity to discuss the merits of your ruthlessness over the next months."

Lord Allastam only laughed again and headed for the door. Yultes listened to the cadence of his steps and cane, straightening as it grew closer. He retreated, half-hoping the lord would continue on his way without a word to Yultes. The burning shame left by their last encounter still haunted him, and he had no desire to spar with Allastam's cutting mockeries right before he spoke with Hellion. When the door opened, however, Lord Allastam's gaze snapped to him, freezing him.

"Lord Yultes!" he exclaimed. "Congratulations on your promotion. You're a bigger, better lapdog now."

Acid dropped at the bottom of his stomach, but he forced a smile to his lips. "Your kind hospitality will be greatly missed, but alas, one must move on with their life. I'm sure you'll find a suitable replacement."

Allastam's appropriately bark-like exclamation startled Yultes—he must have been in a good mood to think that funny. "None as entertaining as you, I'm afraid, but we'll meet again."

He tapped Yultes' forearm with his cane, then left, still smiling. Anger burned in Yultes' cheeks, but he swallowed his urge to reply. Better to let him go and retain what little dignity remained. Instead, he hurried into Diel's—no, Hellion's now—office. He glanced at the spot of blood from Jaeger on the floor, fought his rising nausea, and focused on their new leader. Hellion glared back.

"Close the door," he snapped.

Yultes waited for the guard to act, but the Allastam soldier stared back, impassive. He did not mean to obey. With a huff, Yultes strode to the door, slammed it shut, and sighed. "I saw Diel." He did not bother to mask the accusation in his voice.

"Did he say where he hides the wine? I'm in terrible need of a glass." Hellion closed his eyes and leaned on the desk, his shoulders slumping. "I'm glad you're here with me. This is not how everything should have unfolded."

In one simple admission, Hellion melted away Yultes' resentment. He couldn't blame Hellion for what happened to Diel. "Allastam would have found a way. Nothing stops him when he sets his mind on revenge."

"And we have to make sure we never become a target again. Yes, you're right." Hellion squared his shoulders, his smile returning, a new light in his eyes. Pride swelled in Yultes at cheering Hellion with a few choice words. "Lord Allastam is an ally, and we must put this quarrel behind us. He'll help us rebuild our name."

Quarrel. The euphemism threw cold water on Yultes' bliss, and stark images of the past hours rushed to his mind. Fleeing down the stairs with Jaeger. The steward's muffled cries when they beat him. The haunted look in Diel's eyes, and his last words to Yultes. *I know you can be a great architect, Yultes. It's up to you to decide what you build.*

"He won't. He'll lord his contribution to your success tonight over you as proof of his help, then use you whenever he needs it. As long as he has troops in here, you're not an ally, you're a subordinate—someone to order around."

"Don't be—"

"I'm not being ridiculous," Yultes interrupted. "I've watched Allastam grow since he was a baby. I know how he thinks and works."

"The soldiers are for our protection, not to force us into submission."

"Then disobey," Yultes said. "What do you have to worry about? Disregard his advice and refuse to cut loose more of the family. Don't downplay the fact he sold Diel out to torture. We're not assets. He didn't deserve—"

"Enough." Hellion used the same sharp tone he'd wielded against Allastam earlier. Yultes' stomach plummeted, and his words dried out. Hellion only directed his anger toward him when he fumbled—if he forgot important trade relationships, if he parroted Diel's political opinions, if he allowed anyone to address him without a proper title—and each time, Yultes had both earned the retaliation and sorely regretted his actions. They had been lessons—hard-learned from difficult experiences, but important nonetheless. Hellion had shaped him into the ruthless negotiator and planner this family needed. Every time Yultes had ignored his advice, the results had been catastrophic. Yultes often doubted he'd achieve anything without Hellion's help. "That matter is closed. Over. We can't do anything about it. We have to look forward, to our future and how we can build a greater House. I promised I wouldn't let Diel be our downfall. This is a necessary step. Don't you want to regain the honour that was ours?"

How could he say no? Of course he wished to restore House Dathirii to its former glory and to play a fundamental part in the process, but at what price? How many would Hellion cut loose on the way? What would the family even look like in the end? Yultes already didn't belong—he had no noble blood, only ties through his now-gone brother. Efficiency, professionalism, and the systematic, costly burial of his biggest mistake had allowed him to stay a Dathirii, but what would Hellion do if Lord Allastam declared Yultes superfluous? Hard to believe his old friend would throw him out, but Yultes would never have guessed he would go around his back to strike a violent deal with Lord Allastam either.

In truth, he didn't know what to think anymore. When Hellion spoke, Yultes' world fell back into its comfortable, rightful order. Yet nothing could make him forget Diel's disappearance or the bruises covering Jaeger. *Think about how much power is in your hands now, and what you want to do with it.* Yultes closed his eyes, letting Diel's words sink into him.

"You're right." Tension slid off his shoulders, and his voice calmed. Yultes didn't know what he wanted to do with his new position, not yet, but he had one certainty: Hellion's future was not it. He would have to fight. "Tell me what you need. I'm your man."

Hellion smiled, regaining the assured countenance so natural to him. He swept across the office to Yultes' side, wrapping an arm around his shoulders. "I'm glad to hear it, my good friend."

The warmth in his voice almost melted Yultes' resolve. How could he plan to undermine him? Hellion had supported him for decades and taught him to be an experienced and astute negotiator.

Yultes owed him everything—his skills, his acceptance in Hellion's Dathirii circle, and now his dream job. Yet the first time the roles flipped and Hellion needed help, Yultes prepared to betray him.

He could deal with that. He had done so much worse before. Yultes had let down the only love he'd had, throwing her out into the street. He had let down their son, only appearing eighteen years later—too late to have any say in Larryn's life. He had let down House Dathirii, albeit secretly, selling information to Brune. And now he would let down his best friend, crashing Hellion's dreams one ill-executed order at a time until Diel's heirs could once more claim the heart of House Dathirii.

Yultes had known the right path when he'd tried to rush Jaeger to safety. Hellion might never have wanted things to get this far, but he had still assaulted the steward, and he had no plans to counteract Lord Allastam's grip on their family. He meant to roll with it and obey. This couldn't stand. Yultes couldn't accept it. And somehow, for reasons that were beyond him, Diel believed he could stop it—he believed in him.

For so long, Yultes had sought to prove he belonged to the family and was worthy of the Dathirii name. Now, he could either rebuild their former glory, following Hellion's lead, or trust in Diel's idealistic and dangerous vision of their future. Always before, Yultes had listened to his best friend's smooth and reasonable voice, even when his heart called for a different path. Not this time. Yultes had made too many mistakes, and Diel relied on him to avoid one more.

This time, Yultes wouldn't let him down.

Chapter Thirty-Five

IT started as a twist at the bottom of his stomach. Arathiel ignored it—no one else seemed affected, and they struggled to keep the group together. Branwen strode through the compound like she no longer cared how many guards she'd have to kill to get to Varden, Hasryan trailed behind with constant and irritated admonitions to slow down, and Isra had the terrified wide eyes of someone heading straight to her death. Cal's expression varied depending on whether he tried to reassure her or to keep up with his longer-legged friends. Arathiel followed last, watching their backs, calling to Branwen and Hasryan in angry whispers. The handful of minutes they would gain by rushing wouldn't save Varden, but being separated might get them all killed.

Something was happening, however. As they grew closer to the temple, Arathiel's slight discomfort turned into a strong nausea. And when the doors came into view, Arathiel would have sworn he saw the magic seeping out of them like waves of heat on a summer day. When they spotted the two soldiers guarding the front door, they slid behind a nearby building and stopped. Arathiel leaned against the wall, trying to fight his spinning world.

"I can show you a way around them," Isra whispered.

"Let's," Hasryan said. "Dead soldiers at the front would give us away."

A powerful burst of energy shot from the temple before they moved, punching Arathiel in the gut. He choked, grabbed Hasryan's shoulder for support, then shook his head to clear out an extra layer of blur in his sight. Light had flared behind the glass windows, but no one was looking at the building now. They'd all turned to Arathiel. Hasryan put a hand on his arm and held him up, making sure he didn't fall.

"You all right?" he asked.

Arathiel's mind buzzed under the constant assault of magic. "I'm … Can't you feel it?" Everyone shook their heads, even Isra and Cal, both more attuned to their respective types of spells. Why him? Hadn't Sora's healer suggested that nothing but magic held him together? Did that make him more sensitive? Arathiel squeezed Hasryan's shoulder, then swallowed hard and straightened.

"There was a huge surge of power. It's still growing. We might not have time to go around."

He didn't say anything about his nausea, but Hasryan caught his gaze for a second, as if looking for the information he knew Arathiel silenced. Then he nodded and let go.

"Okay. Take a minute to recover. I'll get the guards."

He walked off before any of them could protest, into the shadows stretching from their current hiding place to the temple. Arathiel's gaze trailed him as he advanced in short and silent sprints, crossing open spaces and crouching behind what cover he could manage. If Arathiel hadn't known where to find him, he'd never have spotted Hasryan, despite the cloak not completely hiding his wine-red coat. His friend didn't even make a sound. Then again, perhaps he wasn't half as good as he seemed to Arathiel's dulled senses.

Beside him, Branwen huffed and readied a dagger. "He better not mess this up."

If either guard had time to raise an alert, their team would be in trouble. Arathiel wanted to prepare to jump in too, but if he tried to sprint with his current nausea, he'd trip and fall. Instead, he inhaled deeply to clear his head. He needed to be in a state to fight, and soon. Diel hadn't pulled him out of prison for magic to sicken him in the middle of the Myrian enclave. As he exhaled a second time, Hasryan crept about five feet away from one of the two guards, who'd made the mistake of standing in half-shadows. Arathiel caught the glint of moonlight against a blade. The four of them stared, silent, entranced by the inexorable death they'd sent after two soldiers.

It was one thing to think of a friend as an assassin, and another to watch him execute someone with perfect professionalism.

Hasryan surged from the darkness, one hand covering the guard's mouth as he plunged a dagger through his neck. The second man started to turn around, but Hasryan reached for another weapon, leaving the first embedded in the soldier's throat. He threw the new dagger with incredible precision. His victim collapsed, and Hasryan caught him before he crashed to the ground, laying him down. All Arathiel had heard was a little clanking from the first guard. Two men were dead.

"Whoa," Cal whispered.

Judging by the dazed silence, everyone agreed with the sentiment. Hasryan retrieved his daggers, then turned to the group, wiping the blood off with his cloak. When none of them moved, he gestured with impatience. Branwen swore under her breath and started off. Cal followed, grabbing Isra and pulling her along. Arathiel struggled against his nausea, glanced back to ensure no one had spotted them, and joined the rest of the group.

"For someone who couldn't stop rushing, you sure took your sweet time coming here," Hasryan told Branwen.

She glared at him but didn't counter with anything, instead turning to the others. "Cal, can you stay here with the girl? Make sure she's not trouble."

"Can't I just leave?" Isra asked.

"And risk finding every guard in the enclave waiting for us when we leave the temple?" Branwen replied. "No thanks."

Hasryan looked at Isra, and she paled. What they had just witnessed must have extinguished her desire to provoke him. "Stay, shut up, and stop arguing," he said. "That's all we ask."

"We'll go right inside," Cal said. "I want to see what's happening in case you need healing, and outside we risk getting spotted. I can fight a bit, you know. If it comes to that."

"You … can?"

"Yeah. I hate it, but I can." Cal wrapped his fingers around the butt end of his little mace. "I learned as a teenager from my big brother. We were fleeing religious zealots, and I figured my luck might run out one day."

Cal's hushed tone and white knuckles unsettled Arathiel. Why had he never mentioned a family before? Did he have other siblings? Where were they now? Hasryan reached out, bending forward to put a reassuring hand on Cal's shoulder. Neither said anything, yet Arathiel had the distinct impression of an entire conversation passing, an understanding between them, not unlike his first connection to Hasryan. These two might jest and laugh a lot every day, but in that instant, Arathiel glimpsed how much more they kept silent.

Arathiel's hand slid over his sword hilt, and he gritted his teeth. Waves of magic washed over him, leaving him dazed and worried. His curiosity about Cal and Hasryan would have to wait. "We should go. It's getting worse … Building up."

Branwen grabbed the double doors' large handles and pushed them open, slow and steady. The plaintive creak sent a shudder up Arathiel's spine, and magic drummed through his head, beating down on him. He tightened his grip until the sword felt solid under his palm, grounding himself. He was ready to follow Branwen inside.

❦

A HEAT wave greeted Branwen as she opened the doors to Keroth's temple, swooshing around her to rush into the cooler outside. She peeked in to get a sense of what awaited them, her heart beating in a frenzy, bracing against what would follow. The sight stopped her dead, horror crawling up her throat.

Avenazar stood a few steps behind Varden, to the priest's left. A golden-red link of throbbing magic led from his outstretched palm to Varden, digging into his chest and extending around her friend. It slithered across torn clothes and skin, sliding into his hair and ears. Varden himself leaned slightly back, as if only the power held him, and pain twisted his round visage. Branwen choked down a scream—of rage and disgust, of terror at what Avenazar was doing to Varden's mind, of guilt at not arriving sooner—and lifted her slim sword.

Someone's hand pushed her forward, and she realized she'd been blocking everyone. Whatever. They could enter as she stalked to that monstrous wizard and cut him into tiny pieces. She started off, straight for Avenazar. He wouldn't notice anyway! Magic enthralled him as much as Varden, but his expression hovered closer to exaltation than pain. He loved this, the sick bastard.

"Branwen!" Hasryan whispered. She ignored him. "Come back. You can't just rush in!"

She waved him off, a sharp 'just watch me' at the tip of her tongue. She couldn't endure the wait, no matter how ridiculous the risk. Varden stood *right there*, with Avenazar trampling down his mind. Swears followed her, but she didn't pay attention until Isra's shrill warning.

"Stop, no, he'll have a shield!"

She spun on her heels, hesitating. Could Branwen trust the girl? Isra had always hated Varden, and she could just be pulling Branwen's leg. Then Varden moaned, a noise both weak and raw, as if he didn't even have energy left for a proper sound. Her stomach twisted, and she turned back toward him.

Avenazar stared at her.

Fuck.

"You're not the Dathirii I expected," he said.

"What?"

Avenazar smiled. While his left hand maintained the link to Varden, he summoned a green rope with his right one and shot it toward her. Branwen stumbled back, shocked. *What Dathirii?* She lifted her sword, instincts screaming at her to defend herself, but her brain wouldn't let go. She took a clumsy swipe at the green whip and missed. The rope lashed at her forearm, wrapping around her wrist and pulling her off-balance. Before Branwen fell, Arathiel rushed to her side, slashing the rope clean through.

"Get your friend," he said.

Arathiel's voice sounded rough, broken. How much was the magic affecting him? She wanted to help him, but Varden was her priority. Arathiel could handle himself, and she would welcome the opportunity to stab Avenazar. She dashed for the thick golden thread, trusting Arathiel to cover her. Green ropes danced at the corner of her vision, snapping through the air, and Arathiel always intercepted those directed at her in time. Branwen stopped next to the wide ribbon of magic—the disgusting, slimy, throbbing link holding her friend prisoner—gripped her slim sword with two hands, and spread her feet.

"All right. Keroth and Ren and every other deity out there watching, I need your help."

She slashed down, putting all her might and hope behind the strike. Her blade hit the thread and stopped, the shock reverberating into her muscles. It didn't slice through, not even a fraction of an inch. Branwen's stomach sank, and at the contact point, energy sizzled, gathered, and exploded. The force shattered her sword and flung her across the room, into a wall. Pain blossomed anew in her still-sensitive back. What was it with Avenazar and stone walls? Branwen shook her head, desperate to clear her daze away and muster the strength to stand and try again.

The link taunted her, complete and pulsing, as if she'd never even touched it.

Arathiel dealt with several ropes now. His blade flashed with amazing speed, catching the flickering light of the fire as it kept the green lashes at bay. He was losing ground, however, his feet sliding backward. Something in his movement felt off to Branwen, unlike Kellian's easy and efficient grace. Perhaps the nausea affected him, or one of the several particularities of his body. Either way, Avenazar's attacks got closer to latching onto him with every strike. Arathiel needed help, and Hasryan had disappeared.

She struggled to her feet. Her spine groaned, making her feel like the oldest lady on earth. She only had a thin dagger, exactly like the one she'd thrown at Avenazar that night on the bridges of Isandor. Better a small dagger than nothing at all, she told herself as she dashed forward.

A line of bright fire cut off her path. The flames flew past her with a *whoosh*, and she stopped just in time to avoid being burned to a crisp. They'd come from her right, from the great brazier—and Varden. Branwen turned to him. He was standing by the flames, eyes empty, his mouth a grim line. More fire curled between his palms, and he stared at her. A predator focusing on his target. Her heart sank. It couldn't be. They had come for him—they were right there, right now! She refused to believe they were too late.

"Varden!"

The priest hesitated and lowered his hands an inch, his frown easing. His link to Avenazar pulsed faster, and its shade slid toward golden instead of red. Branwen's heart pounded against her chest. Varden was still in there. "You have to fight him. I came back! We'll get you out."

The fire between Varden's hands intensified, and his scowl returned. How could Avenazar maintain such a hold on him while battling Arathiel? They had circled each other, Arathiel staying away from the golden thread to avoid Branwen's fate, the pair moving closer to the fire and the twin stairs that wrapped around it like two huge arms. It gave her a nice, clear shot at the wizard.

One dagger had saved Nevian, and another would save Varden. She smirked and let go.

The weapon flew straight into Avenazar's shoulder again, and he stumbled with a surprised cry. Arathiel pressed his sudden advantage, dodging one rope and lunging. When his sword came close, a force field deflected it and pushed him back. What should have been a few steps to balance turned into a full-blown fall, and Arathiel landed heavily on his back. Branwen sprinted toward him, only to be cut off by fire again. She let out a frustrated cry. That golden thread pulsated bright red now, giving her an intense headache. They needed Varden to snap out of it.

Panting, Avenazar clutched at his link to Varden, glaring at Branwen. Only one rope remained, and he wrapped it around Arathiel's ankle as her companion struggled to stand. Arathiel didn't even feel it until the wizard yanked him up. His eyes widened, and he dropped his sword with a yelp. Branwen swore and renewed her attempt to get closer, but Varden's flames inevitably forced her back.

"Someone needs to pay a visit to Keroth's great brazier," Avenazar said, shaking the upside-down Arathiel. "Then I can chat with Miss Dathirii here."

With a flick of his wrist, Avenazar flung Arathiel high up in an arc that would land him in the middle of the large fire. Branwen's stomach sank into her heels, and suddenly Arathiel wasn't the only one with intense nausea. She stared at his flight, horrified and entranced, until she noticed a shadow leaping down the stairs behind Avenazar.

Hasryan landed on his back and wrapped his legs around Avenazar, crashing both of them to the ground. He grabbed the hand controlling the fire-gold thread as they fell, and when they smacked against the stone, he flattened Avenazar's palm on the floor. His dagger flashed, and in a fluid, perfectly balanced strike, Hasryan stabbed it through Avenazar's wrist.

A high-pitched keening buried the wizard's shrill scream as his shield flared to life. It shone a bright light, only to crack into a hundred crystal shards and explode outward. Several sank themselves into Hasryan's chest and side with a horrible *thud*, and he stumbled back. Branwen dashed to help, and no wall of flames blocked her path.

The pulsing link had broken, retracting upon itself in a thick, throbbing ball of energy. It shed more light than the nearby fire, bathing Varden in a red glow as he gasped and collapsed to his knees.

Behind him, Arathiel fell into the brazier, a dark shape in the shifting shadows.

The flames ripped a surprised and terrified scream of pain from him, and Varden's head snapped in his direction. Fire tendrils burst from the inferno in an instant, enveloping Varden and dragging him into the flames. Branwen prayed the sudden interruption of Arathiel's cry meant good news. She heard nothing but Hasryan's ragged breathing, the humming ball of energy, the crackling fire, and her own heart, beating and beating. No screams, no calls.

Branwen shifted her focus back to Avenazar, who had struggled to his feet. He held Hasryan's bloodied dagger but ignored both the dying assassin and Branwen, staring at the unstable remnants of his spell. Terrifying greed shone in his eyes as the immense power contained in the link gathered in the centre, so intense Branwen could feel its buzzing pressure. If Avenazar reached for it ... Branwen didn't know the horrors he could cast, nor did she want to find out. She dug panicked hands into her pockets, looking for something—anything to stop him. When her fingers clamped around her room's iron key, she didn't hesitate: she flung it at the ball and prayed it wouldn't kill them all.

It disappeared within, and for an eternal second, nothing happened. Then the magic stretched out, growing a sick dark green as it reached from one pillar to the next. It had turned almost black when it snapped back into a ball, unleashing a surge of power that shoved her backward. Avenazar folded over from the shock, murder in his eyes.

"You little elven—"

"Genius?" Branwen cut off.

Avenazar snarled, holding his wounded wrist close. Blood streamed down his forearm, soaking his robes. How did he even stay conscious? He lifted his other palm toward the freed energy, enunciating each arcane word with a surprising amount of spite. A shudder coursed through the ball, and it shot to him. Avenazar flung himself to the side, cursing, and the bolt grazed his leg. Branwen stared at the smoke where the pure magical power had hit the stone, the frenzied beating of her heart covering the energy's constant crackling. What had she done?

"Good job getting yourselves killed," Avenazar said.

He snapped a word, his voice deepening with the power it contained, and vanished. Another black jolt of energy crashed where Avenazar had stood a split second ago, as if called by his magic, and shards of stone flew in every direction. Branwen cursed, but with Avenazar gone, her mind zipped back to Hasryan.

He leaned against the railing, bleeding from a dozen cuts, his legs shaking. She rushed to his side and slid under his armpit, wrapping one arm around his waist. Hasryan clung to her, and for a moment, they stared at the sizzling magical energy without a word. Whips lashed out of it, snapping back and forth with increasing intensity, distorting the air as they passed. Hasryan gripped her shoulder tightly and tore his gaze away, sweeping the room with it.

"Did Arathiel …"

Stones piled at the bottom of her stomach. The fire burned lower, tamer. "I don't know."

Before she could elaborate, Cal came running toward them, Isra in tow. He flailed, pale despite the short sprint, pointing at the wild magic. Branwen's meagre satisfaction at chasing Avenazar away vanished. Judging from their expressions, she might have unleashed an even greater danger.

ISRA refused to look at the battle. The quick glimpse of Varden linked to Avenazar had sickened her, and she couldn't bear to watch him destroy the rest of Nevian's friends. She listened to the ropes whipping through the air, Arathiel's swords swishing and his occasional grunts, and Branwen calling out to Varden, her stomach crawling up her throat with each passing moment. Her palms had turned sweaty, and her heart had threatened to burst through her chest. They would lose, and she would be next on Avenazar's list. She would never convince him she had wanted no part in this. Not with Cal just a few steps away, absorbed by his friends' fight, too busy narrating it through small exclamations and curses. He didn't even look her way. She could have knocked him out at any point. She should have, but she didn't want to.

Jilssan would scold her for ignoring the pragmatic route—her one chance at a lie. It didn't matter. She had never meant to hurt Nevian, and Varden didn't deserve this magical enslavement. Hadn't Jilssan talked Avenazar out of torture? Surely she'd understand why Isra needed to help, or at least stay out of the way. Even if it led to Avenazar trampling through her mind and unravelling the lies she'd crafted about herself. She glanced at Cal, at his small hands clutching his mace and how he leaned forward, desperate to dash out. He confused her. Why did he defend her earlier? His intense level of care and absolute niceness stood in stark contrast to anything she had ever experienced in Myria. Perhaps she didn't have to hide so much.

"Ren's gracious luck," Cal exclaimed, "they did it! He just vanished."

"What?" A rush of hope spun her head, and she scrambled to see for herself. A throbbing ball of energy floated in the hall, and Hasryan and Branwen stared at it. Varden, Arathiel, and Avenazar had disappeared—a wise decision, considering the spectacle before her eyes. Unhinged magic never stayed concentrated in a single spot for long. "How did they—We have to flee. This thing's not safe at all!"

The horror in her tone wiped Cal's victorious grin away. He grabbed her wrist and ran straight toward the uncontrolled power, giving a brand new meaning to the word "flee." Cal flailed as they approached, and Branwen turned to him. Isra wrenched out of his grasp and cut him off to warn Branwen and Hasryan.

"Don't stand there! Magic shouldn't stay concentrated like that! It'll shift and distort and snap, accumulating everything it can until it's too much. And then—" Magical energy lashed out and smashed into a pillar on the opposite side, splitting it in two. Large stones crashed to the ground, raising a cloud of dust and making Isra's point for her.

"We can't leave," Branwen said. "Varden and Arathiel are in the fire!"

Isra glanced at the diminishing brazier. What could they even do about that? "So we wait to get crushed alongside them? Come on, we need to take cover."

"But—"

"Isra is right," Hasryan said, and each word cost him.

"Hide behind another pillar." Isra grabbed Cal's wrist, and this time she pulled him along. Branwen half-carried Hasryan to the spot, supporting his weight, and she didn't bother to conceal her doubts. The last pillar hadn't lasted long, after all, but Isra had no intention of leaving the stone untouched. She knew the spell they needed, had practised it in several boring exercises with Jilssan. And she had always struggled to cast it.

As they reached the pillar, the light behind them intensified and lashed out again, wrecking the archway near the front doors. Isra shoved Cal and his two friends, then slapped her hand on the circular stone structure. She pushed her doubts far inside, raising her voice in a quick chant. The magic swirled around her, wilder and more slippery than ever. She grasped at the currents as the power dashed away from her, or curved in unpredictable ways around her amulet. She needed to succeed, and fast. Magic was always drawn to magic, and it was only a matter of time before the wild power at the centre of the temple lashed out at her. Isra grabbed her talisman, fighting against the tears rising, focusing on the task at hand. She knew better materials than stone. She could protect them, if only she managed this spell before the ball of power reacted to it and destroyed the temple.

As the thought crossed her mind, the flailing whips of magic retracted to the centre. A dragon inhaling before breathing fire.

"Isra, stop!"

She ignored Branwen's warning. Her words flowed more easily, and Isra traced the single rune for Body midair, sealing her intention. She pulled at the pillar's stones, fusing them and transforming them into a translucent bubble of impenetrable material. Isra struggled to maintain control, but she grinned with pride as the protection rose around them. It was working. She had cast a complete and complex spell!

A bolt of pure energy surged from the centre before she sealed the hole. Isra's eyes widened, and she flung herself to the side, releasing her spell, knowing it would close on its own. The jolt of magic didn't flash over her head, however. It bent as it neared, drawn to another source of concentrated power: her amulet, and her father's spell.

Searing pain tore through Isra's hand as the bolt smashed into her talisman, then spread to her body, wracking her muscles. The amber cracked as the unnatural force blasted her away, sending her sliding across the temple floor. Her bubble closed without her inside, and her arm snapped as she hit a shard of rock. The second explosion of pain tore through her mind, leaving her dazed and panting.

The temple collapsed around Isra, but she didn't register the chaos. Her burned hand still clutched the broken amulet as its magic slipped out of her body, immediately sucked in by the unstable power. Her blonde hair turned into a wavy brown crown and her skin darkened. Isra's consciousness dimmed as she shifted back to her original form, leaving her with a single, clear thought: she wouldn't even recognize herself without the amulet.

Chapter Thirty-Six

HASRYAN flinched when Isra's bubble closed above them. Debris crashed into the protection, hammering on it without leaving a scratch. *Trapped*, his mind yelled, and he struggled to shut down his screaming instincts. Cal rushed after Isra, blocked by the wall before he could follow her. He pounded on the translucent material, stopping only to peer out through the swirls of dust and zapping magic, but his little fists were just as inefficient as the rocks. Isra's weird transparent stone was impervious—from the outside, and from the inside.

"I hate this. Shields are no good if they keep us locked down for guards to find," Hasryan said.

Cal spun about, his mouth a flat angry line. "At least they won't discover a mess of crushed and burned flesh! She just saved our lives, and now she might …" He trailed off, stomped his foot, then returned to his examination of the demolition outside.

A lash of magic smashed into the wall not ten feet away from them, and nearby windows burst into pieces. Hasryan watched the flying shards and shifting colours with fascination, caught in a daze by the beautiful destruction: slow, brutal, inexorable. He reached for the cuts in his midriff and felt the sharp pain inflicted by Avenazar's shield. Two fragments had stayed embedded, one of which sent lances of agony down his left leg with every step. Hasryan leaned against a pillar, keeping the weight off it, knowing he'd lost too much blood already. Why else would he marvel at the death around him instead of searching for a solution? He closed his eyes, trying to gather his thoughts. "I'm sorry, Cal, you might be right. I'm not used to believing the best in others. But … you can't help her. I-I need healing."

"Oh!" Cal's eyes widened, and with one last glance in Isra's general direction, he came running back. He retrieved his holy coin, fumbling. "I'm so sorry. I panicked and forgot and you must be in so much pain!"

Hasryan leaned against the pillar and lowered himself with a brief smile. His entire body throbbed, and every movement worsened it, but he shook his head. "I'm dandy."

Branwen's eyebrows shot up at the suggestion, but she continued surveying the outside chaos. The explosions rumbled the ground under them, destroying more and more of the temple. Hasryan fought against his mounting dread. Even if Arathiel had survived the fire, how could he avoid getting crushed? They had come to save Varden, and they would lose both of them. Cal's healing helped soothe that growing void, as if his spirit and magic reached more than Hasryan's physical wounds. Had he developed a new technique? Hasryan didn't remember this level of skill from him.

"Hasryan ..." Cal touched the fragment, and the sharp pain jerked Hasryan's leg. It went numb right after, and Hasryan's eyes flew open. They met Cal's worried gaze. "I don't know if I can fix that."

His throat dried. Blood soaked his shirt around the wound, and the stain extended to his pants. "Hurts my leg. I'm losing sensation, Cal. Going numb. Bad sign. You have to ... please."

"What if I make it worse? What if—"

"You'll do great," Branwen interrupted. "I can hold Hasryan down. Focus on your healing and have faith in yourself. Ren showed you the way into this enclave; Xe will guide you now, too."

Cal's grip tightened on his holy symbol, his lips hardening into a determined line. "Right. Luck requires faith, but not just in others. I-I can do this." His gaze met Hasryan's, and guilt flickered through his face. "I won't let you down twice. You can count on me."

For a brief instant, Cal's unwavering love overwhelmed the pain. Hasryan fought against tears and dragged a smirk to his lips. He had smiled through betrayals and hardships. Surely he wouldn't cry over Cal's words. "I have the best friends," he whispered. "Let's do it."

Branwen crouched next to him, one knee pinning down his leg while her hands gripped his shoulder. Cal's tiny fingers dug around the biggest fragment, gripping the shard. His holy symbol shone brighter, and he took a long, deep breath, holding Hasryan's gaze. Then he pulled.

Pain blossomed in Hasryan's midriff, then shot through his body. He cried out, his vision darkening, aware only of Branwen's strong hands and the searing agony in his leg. The collapsing temple vanished, the world closing in on Hasryan at a terrifying speed until he forgot even his friends. Everything turned black, empty, vast.

Warmth reappeared near his knee, growing hotter and hotter. Hasryan opened his eyes, trying to get his bearings, and the universe spun around him. Cal and Branwen stared at him, neither bothering to hide their worry. His gaze slid down to his leg, and he folded it slowly. Pain twinged through it, but it moved without effort, and a wave of relief washed over him. Hasryan smirked at Cal. "See? You're amazing."

Cal flung himself on Hasryan, hugging him tightly and reviving a dozen smaller flares of pain. Hasryan squeezed back with a laugh, then detached his friend and struggled to his feet. The ground shifted dangerously under him, and he set a hand on Cal's head for balance. The chaos outside their bubble had settled. The wild magic had dispersed, leaving demolished walls and broken pillars behind. The main entrance had collapsed along with most of the temple on the opposite side of the aisle from them. Moonlight shone through the dust. The stairs wrapping around the brazier had been smashed, but most of them held. A wall of debris blocked the view to the dais, the fire, and their friends.

"Do we know—"

"It'll be fine," Branwen answered, her voice laced with doubt.

Hasryan's grip tightened on Cal's shoulder. This bubble kept them trapped, unable to run out and check on them. What if

Varden and Arathiel needed healing too? Arathiel couldn't die here, not after admitting he willingly disregarded risks to his own life if it meant saving another's. He deserved to live fully—to enjoy himself, the changed city, and his new friends. Hard not to wonder if the fight could have unfolded differently. Hasryan had slipped into the shadows around the pillars, studying the wizard while Branwen and Arathiel rushed in. Surprise played a crucial role in his line of work, and he would have only one opportunity. Stalking and waiting had given Avenazar the time to fling Arathiel into the fire, though. What if Hasryan could have prevented it? Saved his friend, just as Arathiel had rescued him? He pushed the idea away, aware of how little 'what ifs' mattered in the end. He only needed to know Arathiel had survived.

"So, do you think we can escape before or after the guards all get here?" he asked.

Isra's bubble must have been sentient, because it popped the moment Hasryan finished his question. Rocks leaning upon it tumbled in, and they scrambled out of the way, Hasryan almost falling in the sudden movement.

Cal smirked at him. "I think Isra doesn't appreciate your sass."

"That's her loss. Let's get everyone and leave before we have to fight for every inch."

Branwen and Cal didn't need his signal. They rushed out, Branwen running for the brazier while Cal scrambled over a pile of fallen stones in the direction Isra had gone flying. Hasryan hesitated. Cal could never move the rocks by himself if she was buried under them. But he thought of Arathiel shooting past him, of how he'd intervened just a tad too late, and his brief indecision vanished. He caught up with Branwen as she reached the obstructing pile of debris, and before either could go around, they heard a deep, wracking cough from inside. Hasryan's heart jumped, and he sprinted past the stones, ignoring the pain still shooting up his leg.

Relief washed over him as he found Arathiel on all fours, coughing out a mix of dust and spit. His arms shook, and dirt covered his white hair, but he was alive, and for a moment, nothing else mattered. The fire had gone out, and even the burned logs under them seemed cool. Hasryan called his name and hurried to his friend's side, ignoring the dull throb in his leg. He crouched down, squeezing Arathiel's shoulder hard, words stumbling out in a mess.

"You're—how did you …"

Arathiel met his gaze with a shaky smile and nodded toward Varden, now unconscious. Grease weighed down the priest's curly hair, he was thin and underfed, burns had made holes in his ragged clothes in several places, and the stench of his cell still clung to him. None of these things stopped Branwen from kneeling next to him and feeling for his heartbeat. For a moment, they all held their breath; then she choked and started crying. Hasryan's stomach squeezed, but she smiled through the tears.

"Is he okay?"

"Yeah. I mean, no, but he's alive."

Good enough for Hasryan. Arathiel sat back on his haunches and wiped his mouth. He was frowning as if … as if in pain? That wouldn't make sense. Questions pressed through Hasryan's mind, but his curiosity could wait. "We all are, somehow. Let's get out before guards arrive and change that. We need somewhere safe to recover." He turned to Arathiel. "Can you stand? Walk?"

Arathiel stared at a point above his shoulder. Had he even heard? Worry gnawed at Hasryan, and he shifted into Arathiel's line of sight. Brief relief flooded through him as his friend's attention snapped back, but the fear in Arathiel's gaze washed it away. "The fire," he said, tone hushed and frantic, "it burned me. It burned me, Hasryan."

"I saw. I'm sorry I didn't leap in sooner, I really am."

"No, you don't understand. It *hurt*." His voice cracked, unsettling Hasryan more than he cared to admit. Arathiel had always carried a grounding tranquility, as if nothing could break his calm. Even his laugh was soft, downplayed and reassuring. Not anymore. Panic and confusion had shattered it. "It still hurts! It only lasted a second, but when I touched that fire, it felt like someone had ripped the skin off my back." Arathiel swallowed hard, his breathing shaky. "I don't understand. I still can't smell, I still can't sense the ground under me, or see colours right, or truly feel your hand on my shoulder! I didn't notice the burn of too-hot tea, but fire, yes? Why? Where's the logic?"

"I don't know, I really don't." What was he supposed to say? The collapse of Arathiel's calm terrified Hasryan, but he lacked reassuring words. He refused to lie—he'd lived through enough horrible stuff not to travel that path. "We'll try to figure it out, but not here. Maybe Varden will have answers when he wakes up. He's a fire priest, isn't he? But we need to go."

"Right." Arathiel's features hardened, returning to the more determined expression he had worn through the mission. He struggled to his feet. "At least I'm not nauseated anymore."

Hasryan straightened with him. "Think you can carry Varden? I'm … my leg complains at my own weight, and I'd rather spare it. If you two can handle him, I'll go check on Cal and Isra."

He hoped Cal had found her. They didn't have time to linger, not after the massive explosions and Avenazar's escape. The entire enclave would be bearing down on them soon.

"We'll manage," Branwen said. "Climbing the oak tree to get over the wall is out of the question, though. We'll have to risk a gate."

"Nevian recommended the southern one," Arathiel replied. "Smaller and less guarded."

"Let's try that." The temple stood in the northern half of the enclave grounds, but the distance might become an advantage. The Myrians would block the closest exits in a hurry and rush to the collapsed building. If the group managed to sneak undetected past the first wave of soldiers …

Their plan made, Hasryan nodded to Arathiel and Branwen, then left to find Cal. Every step sent a tiny wave of pain up his leg, but Hasryan had endured worse in the past. He could deal with that until they were safe. Cal worked on a pile of rubble, removing rocks and throwing them away. He had cleared an arm—one a shade darker than Varden's skin. He frowned, hurrying to Cal's side. This didn't look like the pale blonde girl who had shielded them.

"What happened? That can't be her."

"Who else?" Cal snapped back before sniffling and flinging a rock away. "Sorry, I'm just … I don't get it either, but it has to be her, and I don't want to find her head crushed and there's this big rock and I can't lift it and—"

Hasryan put a hand on his shoulder, stopping the flow of words. Cal didn't need to say more. "I'm on it. It's okay. Arathiel and Varden are both alive. We'll get her out, find somewhere safe, and lick our wounds."

Cal raised his chin, wiped his tears, and nodded. "Right. It's fine. I shouldn't panic—this isn't me." Cal forced a smile. "Lift the boulder and I'll pull her out?"

They set to work immediately, clearing out a few extra stones before Hasryan grabbed the larger one which pinned the girl down. She'd have a horrible bruise on her arm, if it wasn't broken. He counted to three, grounding his feet for balance, then pushed to lift the heavy rock. Or tried to. His muscles strained and his left leg burned with pain, but the monstrous boulder proved well beyond his strength and didn't even shift. Hasryan let go and stepped back, panting.

"Cal, I don't think—"

"It has to. She saved us!"

Hasryan turned to the girl. They'd freed enough to reveal she was no more a prissy white girl than Hasryan. Her thin blonde hair had become massive brown waves, the small nose had grown bigger, and her eyebrows had both darkened and thickened. Her arm and ribs would be broken, crushed like this under the rock, but Hasryan had no solution.

"I'm sorry, Cal. I can't free her. Arathiel is shaken and weak, and

Branwen's not any stronger than you are. Even together, we couldn't move this boulder. We can't stay here. Guards are on their way."

Cal stared at the floor, his hands curling into small fists. "She saved us …"

"I know." He crouched, to be at his friend's eye level. "Heal her as much as you can. She's one of them. They'll spare her."

A blatant lie. Would the Myrians take kindly to her change in appearance? What if they discovered she had helped them? But what would be the point in staying back and proving her complicity? They would all die for her sake, and Hasryan had learned long ago to cut his losses while he could. Hasryan didn't have the heart to say that to Cal, however, no matter how much he hated fake reassurances.

Cal answered with a determined nod and knelt next to the girl. His hands shook, and he conjured only a pale light. Hasryan shifted his weight away from his left leg, suddenly self-conscious of his friend's exhaustion. He watched the healing process, wondering when he had become the group's reassuring presence. First Arathiel, now Cal? The latter had always been their source of pep talks and comfort before. Whenever something went wrong, Larryn ranted, Hasryan joked, and Cal promised a better future. Hopefully, they'd fall back into their old dynamic once everything calmed down, and Arathiel could provide helpful solutions. After the last month, Hasryan looked forward to a modicum of normalcy.

"Okay," Cal said. "I guess that should be enough."

His voice startled Hasryan. He tried to shake his daze away, but the long day and constant pain took their toll. How late was it now? The sun set too early in winter, and nights stretched on forever. At least Diel must have returned from the Golden Table and spoken with Camilla. He hoped they'd managed an agreement with Sora, and that his family hadn't lost all their titles. Hasryan glanced at Branwen, providing what support she could to Arathiel as he carried Varden, and joined up with them, Cal by his side. Blood and grime covered every single one of them, and although they'd accomplished what they'd come for, no one shared a victorious grin. Branwen set her hands on her hips.

"Let's get out of this hellhole and bring Varden to his new home."

Chapter Thirty-Seven

JILSSAN watched the carriage containing Lord Dathirii roll through the east gate without a word. Allastam soldiers greeted her, and she answered with a nod but avoided striking up a conversation with them. Her thoughts drifted elsewhere, to Keroth's temple and Avenazar's terrible intent. She had hoped Lord Dathirii's arrival would spare Varden some of the hurt, delaying Avenazar's plan until he could, perhaps, be convinced to abandon it entirely. Instead, he had hurried it along, forcing Jilssan to deal with their new Allastam allies and the package to seal their relationship while he worked on his spell. Avenazar had designed several parts from scratch, and his eagerness to test them dismayed her. He didn't care if the magic went awry and destroyed Varden, not with a new toy arriving.

Jilssan focused on Lord Dathirii as guards pulled him out of the carriage. His shoulders sagged, and his gaze stayed fixed on a random space somewhere behind her knees. Her rare memories of him depicted an energetic man always ready to back his naive convictions with a passionate speech. His drive had been sapped away, and the discomforting sight before her pulled uneasily at her stomach.

"Sorry you provoked him," she said. "You're lucky he's too busy to welcome you."

Lord Dathirii twitched—a slight shake of his head—and answered in a rough whisper, "He was torturing a teenager. In front of everyone."

Nevian. Somehow, Jilssan doubted the apprentice had asked for help, or appreciated it. Avenazar had made him pay for the interruption tenfold afterward. Not that it mattered much anymore. "A lot of good that did him, or any of you. Nevian's dead, Varden is being turned into a mindless slave, and you're here waiting for torture. Some fights cannot be won and are best left alone."

Lord Dathirii straightened up and squared his shoulders, fixing his gaze on Jilssan. Something changed in him. An intense light burned in his eyes, and she found herself sliding back, caught off-guard by the shift. The defeated elf had vanished, replaced by the combative spirit she remembered. As if he had forgotten the hopeless situation he had landed in.

"It's not so simple," he said. "You can't always choose your fights. Some battles need to be fought whether you want to or not—whether they can be won or not."

"Except now, you won't be there to fight the next one."

He smiled. Jilssan's unease grew as she watched his expression lighten with certainty. "Someone else will be. I'm not alone, even now. There is always someone ready to risk everything and do what needs to be done."

What needs to be done. Her secret mantra—words she had abided by all her life. Yet from Lord Dathirii, they implied selfless sacrifice, not pragmatism, and this shift in meaning bothered her more than she cared to admit.

Before Jilssan could answer, a deep rumble shook the enclave, followed by a loud crash. She spun on her heels, her heart racing in her throat as she saw the thick cloud of dust rising around Keroth's temple. Another explosion boomed across the grounds, then flashes of light of varying colours. She glanced back at their prisoner. He had grown pale, and his mirth had vanished, but he didn't seem quite as shocked as he should have. "What's going on?" she asked him.

"You tell me," he answered. "This is your kingdom, ruled by your laws, and it's your boss transforming a man into—how did you say?—a mindless slave."

With untested, unrevised magic. She cursed and turned to the guards. "Hold him here until I learn more."

Perhaps she should have had Lord Dathirii sent to a cell, but she'd rather know exactly where he was. Something about his calm and this explosion bothered her, and Jilssan trusted her instincts. She left as the three guards closed in on Lord Dathirii, her attention fixed on the flashing lights ahead.

Had Varden resisted the spell and caused it to go wrong? Perhaps Avenazar's plan to use Keroth's power through the priest had turned against him. Jilssan hoped so. She would never say it out loud, but if this night ended with Avenazar blown to smithereens while Varden survived, she would celebrate. Even losing Varden wouldn't be that great a price for getting rid of Avenazar. He might have won this trade war, but his brief clash with Lord Dathirii had shattered the delicate balance of power at the enclave. With Nevian gone and Varden at his disposal, Avenazar's behaviour had become more erratic and violent with every passing day. Would she manage to stall him the next time he attacked Isra? How long before he turned on them? The slightest hint of treason would set him off, and this far from Myria, no one would stop him.

The flashing lights and rumbling from the castle finally subsided, and Jilssan wondered in what state she'd find the temple. She couldn't see its top above the roofs any longer and suspected at least part of the front had collapsed. Well, she'd soon know, she thought, approaching the last corner.

Yet just before she turned, she noticed four shapes disappearing between two buildings, hurrying into the darkness. None of them were familiar, and one carried something heavy. Heavy and human-like. She snapped a word of power, draining her reserves to grant herself supernatural speed, and sprinted after them. Their little headway melted as Jilssan moved between buildings, careful to stay out of sight of both the intruders and other Myrians.

She shouldn't avoid her people. What was she thinking? Four of them against her, alone? Even if she added magical endurance to her speed, she might not be able to take them on. Anyone who had messed up one of Avenazar's spells and lived to tell the tale ought to be a formidable opponent. She couldn't stop them alone and should get reinforcements.

Except she had no intention of stopping them, she realized.

There is always someone ready to risk everything and do what needs to be done, Lord Dathirii had said. Four of them, it seemed, and they were leaving without him.

Jilssan dashed down the street, cutting them off some thirty feet ahead. "Wait!"

She got her first good look at the group, and surprise stole her words away. These were Lord Dathirii's great fighters? She recognized Branwen Dathirii easily enough, but not the halfling by her side. She pegged him more as the kind of person who insisted on providing meals than a warrior. At least she knew why Lord Dathirii had freed Arathiel Brasten, however. He stood two steps behind, arms wrapped around Varden's unconscious body, both of them covered in soot and dust. After all she'd heard of his exploits, he would worry Jilssan if his hands weren't full. Which left—wait, where had the dark elf vanished to?

"Out of the way."

Branwen stepped forward, her tone hard, and a dagger gleamed in her hand. Her halfling friend crouched and set his palms on the ground, bringing forth a soft light. Jilssan slid back, wary. They had saved Varden from Avenazar. She had to be careful.

Her heel hit a perfectly round rock, which had somehow found its way under her foot. She strangled a cry as her balance shifted and she stumbled, right under a torch. The bright light blinded her, but she heard the halfling's satisfied exclamation and Branwen's strides as she rushed forward. Jilssan cursed, slammed her hand on the wall, and scrambled through her spell. The magical speed helped her pull out a stone staff in a record time.

And in the moment she connected with the stone around her, sending part of her consciousness into the material to shift and change it, she felt the light footsteps of their missing dark elf, a slight limp to his cadence, right behind her. Within striking range. Jilssan spun about as he slashed upward, slapping her weapon against his blade and parrying it. She jumped aside before Branwen could reach her, retreating toward the other end of the street. Her heart hammered—she had almost died. "Stop, I don't want to fight!"

Branwen scoffed, and Jilssan gritted her teeth. She held her staff at the ready, watching Branwen and her dark elf teammate. Wait. This man had melted into the shadows the moment she had appeared, to sneak up on her with deadly precision. She glanced at Arathiel, then back at him.

"Did … did you kill Avenazar?"

She directed the question at Hasryan—who else could it be? Isandor had a limited supply of dark elves with great stealth—and pleaded silently. If anyone could do it … When he shook his head, Jilssan almost cursed. It would have been too perfect.

"Come on," the halfling said. "She's not stopping us, and we can't linger here. Let's go."

"We can't." Hasryan twirled his dagger. "She knows who I am, has seen me with you. One word from her, and the entire city will want to hang Lord Dathirii beside me."

"A bit too late for that." Jilssan smirked despite her instincts not to provoke them. They had no idea what had been going on elsewhere in Isandor, poor things. "He ruined his reputation without my help, I'm afraid."

They tensed. Jilssan crouched, ready for any of them to jump on her. Branwen glared her way, and when Jilssan caught the elf's gaze, her desire to fool around died. Her eyes contained a storm, anger and sorrow and fear all roiling together, pushing to escape. Beautiful and terrifying all at once. Jilssan did not want to trigger the outflow.

"He's here," she said. "That's why I intercepted you. I thought you should know and … leave by the east door, where soldiers hold him. If Avenazar isn't dead, he can't stay in this enclave. Neither he nor Varden would survive it."

"Here," Branwen whispered, and Jilssan wondered if she'd broken after all. "Is this some kind of trap?"

"He's guarded by three men." Unless Avenazar had gone straight to him. Jilssan hoped not. "I suspect they won't pose a problem for you."

A long silence followed. Jilssan leaned on the wall, keeping an eye on the assassin. With her magic, she could move faster than him, but she didn't trust that to be enough. If he really meant to kill her, he would vanish again, and she might not elude him.

"Why would you tell us?" Branwen asked. "What do you have to gain from this?"

The excellent question left Jilssan at a loss for words. What did she have to gain? Avenazar would be enraged once he learned Diel had escaped, and deflecting that anger would be a difficult and dangerous task. But the alternative meant he'd win, and Jilssan found that her fear of the Myrian wizard ran deeper than she had believed. If Avenazar crushed his enemies and kept his alliances with the two biggest Houses in Isandor, he would know nothing could stop him anymore. She couldn't bear the thought of letting him loose, not if she could help it.

"Avenazar has no real friends within these walls, and no one he considers beyond attacking. I prefer my life and that of my apprentice to remain in relative safety."

If doubts lingered in Branwen's expression, they vanished immediately from the halfling's. He stepped forward, his smile tainted by fear. "You're Isra's master! She needs your help."

The ground tilted under Jilssan's feet. She flattened her hand against the wall behind her and tried to ignore her dizziness and the ache in her shoulder. "What? Tell me."

"She's stuck under boulders, in the temple." His voice shook with barely-contained tears, and the depth of his panic caught Jilssan off-guard. Who was this halfling who so obviously cared for Isra? When had they met? Tonight? He wrestled himself under control and continued, "I healed her as much as I could."

Jilssan swallowed through the lump in her throat. What had Isra done? How wounded was she, even?

"She'll live," Hasryan said. "Tell anyone you saw me, and I'll retaliate in kind."

Jilssan stiffened at the threat but understood its necessity. The ramifications of speaking of their brief encounter tonight would destroy both Jilssan and Hasryan's allies. "No one needs to know, not even Isra."

"Good. Then you'll want to get to her first."

"I will." She started off, her initial shock subsiding. They meant Isra no harm. In fact, the halfling seemed eager to protect her. If anything, she owed them. "Thank you. You should hurry, too. Don't keep Lord Dathirii waiting."

Jilssan didn't linger—Isra needed her. Magical speed still flowing through her muscles, she dashed across the enclave's grounds, fighting to ignore the throbbing in her shoulder. After what she'd done, the light graze was the least of her problems.

DIEL waited, flanked by three Myrian guards, shivering in the winter night. The cold of the ground seeped through his boots, and he could feel the shackles' freezing metal through his sleeves. The enclave's wall rose behind him, blocking Isandor from sight. How long before Jilssan returned to deal with him?

Explosions in the temple had interrupted their argument, but their brief encounter left him full of hope and questions. Jilssan had sounded displeased by how little he had accomplished, as if she was simultaneously rubbing his failures in his face and telling him she'd expected better. And she had seemed almost relieved to escape him and investigate the temple.

Diel's throat tightened as he considered the possible causes of the explosion. Who else besides Branwen could have created it? He hoped it meant good news, but the force of the rumbling worried him. Nothing worked as it should today. Why would his luck get any better? Branwen might have reached Varden, but if Jilssan was to be believed, they'd have to fight Avenazar to save him. Diel prayed to every deity he revered—Alluma, the Elven Shepherd, Ren with Xir amazing chance, Seldare of Light and Goodness—and waited for the outcome, helpless to influence it.

Eternal minutes trickled by. The flashing lights vanished; the rumbling stopped. The ongoing destruction was over, and still, no one came. Shivers wracked his body at random intervals, breaking all his attempts at standing still and regal. He kept his eyes peeled for a clue—something, *anything*—to tell him what had happened. The guards beside him shifted uneasily.

The first soldier fell without a noise, a dagger through his throat. Diel jumped as he caught the glint of the blade and paled as he realized what it meant for the poor man. His head buzzed and nausea spun his world as the two remaining guards shouted in alert. One grabbed his forearm, perhaps intent on pulling him close, but a second later, a dark hand clamped over the man's mouth.

"Let go," Hasryan whispered, and as his voice pierced the night, so did rapid footsteps—two pairs, swooping on the last Myrian soldier.

Branwen and Arathiel strode into the light, well-timed and confident, weapons brandished. The guards glanced at each other, and Hasryan's target let go of Diel while the other threw his sword to the ground. Diel fell down when released, manacles clinking, too stunned to hold himself standing. The cool dirt grounded him, and he focused on the coldness under his fingers as his thoughts spun.

"Three of them," Arathiel said. "We're good."

"I'll get Cal." Hasryan's tone was casual, yet Diel didn't doubt for a second he'd landed the initial dagger throw and killed that man. "Knock yours out."

Without batting an eye, he pulled his soldier into a chokehold, muffling his protest with a hand as he snuffed consciousness out of him. Routine, Diel thought. Branwen and Arathiel didn't have his ease. They hit the last one hard and caught him before he fell. Hasryan had vanished already.

Diel drew a long and shaky breath. Waves of relief crashed into him as his situation sank in. They had come for him—saved him from the horrible fate Avenazar had in mind. Tears blurred his sight, and he stifled a sob. This nightmare had ended. Branwen was with him, his wonderful niece, his own miracle worker. She put a steady hand on his shoulder, and he lifted his head, smiling despite the hollow in his heart where Jaeger and House Dathirii stood. They were lost, but not forever. Together, they would see to that.

"We're here, Uncle. You'll be fine."

Diel wiped his tears and struggled to his feet. He loved Branwen's voice at that moment, confident and warm, reliable in an almost regal way. Diel wrapped her into a tight hug, squeezing with all the strength of his tired arms. "I … so much has happened since I left this morning."

"Is everyone all right?" she asked. "Kellian never joined with us, or tried to. We had to go without him."

A new knot of worry appeared in Diel's stomach. Kellian was too dutiful not to show up unless physically stopped. Had he stayed at the Sapphire Guard's headquarters? Or had Allastam's men intercepted him?

"I don't know. I'm sorry. I didn't see him before …" The weight of the day crashed into him. His shoulders sagged, and he heaved a sigh. They needed to fight, but where would he find the endurance to do so? How could he stand strong against Avenazar again, knowing his family would pay the price? Arathiel slipped closer to the conversation.

"We'll figure it out, Diel," he said. "One step at a time, we'll unravel this mess and set things right."

"Yeah, listen to Arathiel!" Branwen pulled back and bumped Diel's shoulder in a forced, playful movement. "We saved Varden from under Avenazar's nose. If we can do that, we can do anything."

Diel straightened and looked at each of them in turn. Their confidence bolstered his, and he managed a real smile. "Good. There's a lot to accomplish."

"Starting with those handcuffs," she replied. "That's not a sight I want to endure."

Branwen reached into her sleeve and flicked a sturdy lock pick out. He gaped as she began to work on the shackles, surprised at this particular level of resourcefulness. Then again, he had never asked her how she got most of her information. As it turned out, while she could pick a lock, she needed several minutes and swears to do so, and by the time she was done, Hasryan had returned with Cal and Varden, limping and carrying the latter with great difficulty.

Diel struggled to his feet and dusted himself off. He shouldn't have sat down, not with the packed earth so cold.

"You'll have to tell me about your evening as we return," he told his niece, before waving at the approaching men. "Sir Cal, it's a pleasure to see you again, albeit in these difficult circumstances."

Cal waved him off with an amused snort. "Please, no need to be so formal. Friends never use my title."

Diel laughed, his despair abating. Alone, he never knew how to keep his emotions under control and deal with his thoughts. He needed others to ground himself. He turned to Varden, already calmer than a minute ago.

"How was he?" Diel asked. His hollowed cheeks and ragged outfit provided an answer, but he hoped they would know more.

"Not good, but he won't die," Cal answered.

"We got there just in time," Arathiel added, "but I think the last ten days caught up to him."

"He's almost safe, and he can rest as much as he wants. Once we're in the city, we can find Vellien to help him out." Diel pinched the bridge of his nose. Had Vellien returned to the Dathirii Tower? They might be out of reach now. "Let's head back."

They freed the carriage horses, and Cal insisted that Hasryan mount one of them to rest his wounded leg, only to be told Hasryan "refused to approach any of these beasts." It earned the dark elf relentless teasing from the other three, and the back-and-forth warmed Diel's heart. In the end, Arathiel climbed atop the horse with Varden, holding him steady. Branwen held the reins—perhaps both to guide the animal and stay close to Varden. They headed out of the eastern gate.

Their good mood was surreal, and they had left the enclave far behind by the time Diel dared to interrupt. He hadn't wanted to ruin this tiny bubble of determination and confidence, but Branwen needed to know what had transpired that evening. When he cleared his throat to speak, everyone fell silent.

He first explained the Golden Table, even though the Council now seemed like it had occurred a week ago. He couldn't believe Lord Allastam had stood at the table with him, acting like he didn't know what was happening at the Dathirii Tower or what awaited Diel right after. It took a special level of hatred and coldness to do something like that.

Branwen managed to stay silent during most of the tale, grunting in place of the angry swears that burned her lips. When he first mentioned being accosted by Allastam inside their tower, however, she paled. Her mouth worked through silent rage, then intense worry, and when finally she managed words, she asked about Garith. Diel tried to reassure her—as far as he knew, no real harm had come to Garith, and he doubted it would change. Diel mentioned Hellion in his reply, however, and Branwen's tongue loosened immediately.

"That no-good pile of bones and spite! I should have spied on his arrogant ass. Who does he think he is? Even Isandor's shitslides aren't as slimy as he is. I'd rather shower in their contents than spend another minute by his side! I swear, if I see his face again, I'll break his nose into thousands of tiny pieces."

"I ... think I'd like to witness that." Diel didn't like how tired he sounded. He reached for Branwen's hand and squeezed it. "He didn't send me here, though. Lord Allastam swept in, and with his guards all over the tower, he grabbed control. I'm afraid they're now allies of the Myrian Enclave."

"I can't believe it. Won't the Golden Table slam him for that attack? This is unheard of!"

Diel recalled the tangible hostility in the council room and how quickly they had rallied against him. "We're not nobles anymore, and they'll only care if they believe they could be next. But I intend to try. I have at least one ally."

"This happened because you freed me, didn't it?" Arathiel asked.

"To save Varden, yes." He had heard the guilt in Arathiel's tone and would have none of it. "I don't regret my choice. Lord Allastam was already looking for an excuse to grab more power. He's testing them—pushing at our customs to see how far he can stretch them. We'll fight him. I just … need a break first."

Hasryan laughed, the sound heavy and mirthless, his earlier joy gone. "What wouldn't I give for Camilla's tea right now? The room will feel empty without her."

"I'm glad Miss Sharpe was with her. If she hadn't spread word about Camilla's arrest by the time Allastam attacked our home, I doubt she will." Diel had never managed to speak with her after all.

"Is everyone safe, Diel?" Arathiel asked. "Did you see Jaeger?"

Diel closed his eyes. Thoughtful as always, of course. Arathiel had met the family before he had left for the Well, and he knew who mattered most. "I did. I demanded to. I had to say …" He trailed off to fight the tears in his voice. They had saved him, and he would see Jaeger again. "They beat him up. Guards died, too. No one else got hurt that I'm aware of, but a lot could have happened since they sent me away. Once we find somewhere safe, I can share the details, and I would love to hear your side. But where?"

At first, no suggestions came, and the group halted. Hasryan and Arathiel looked at each other, then both shrugged apologetically. Branwen grumbled about the Dathirii Tower always being her safe place, and not knowing anywhere else, and soon enough, they were all staring at Cal. If he didn't have a solution …

"Well, we can't go to the Shelter because Larryn would get super angry, but there's always my place! It's small and a bit of a mess, and I only have one bed, but I keep a lot of pillows, so we can figure something out. It's no palace, but no one knew I was going with Arathiel tonight except Larryn, Nevian, and Miss Sora, and I don't think they'll repeat it to the wrong people. We should be fine."

Diel's smile returned. "Sir Cal, you are most gracious."

"It's an honour!" Cal exclaimed, and Diel laughed at how he sputtered. "No, it really is. I hate watching from the sidelines while the others do dangerous things."

"Cal, I'd be dead without you," Hasryan said.

"And Nevian, too," Arathiel added.

"We might never have reached Varden," Branwen finished. "I'm glad you came along. This team needs more than fighters!"

Cal's cheeks turned a bright red, visible even in the dim moonlight. He stammered through thanks before staring at the ground. Hasryan prodded him with the tip of his boot, then ran a hand through Cal's dust-covered hair, messing it up. "Don't let anyone say you're useless."

Cal lifted his head, meeting Hasryan's gaze with renewed determination. His fingers hovered near his cheek and an older bruise. "Only assholes would utter such a thing. I know better. I'm Sir Cal, Lord Dathirii's illustrious host, and the luckiest halfling in the city!"

"You may very well be the most generous, too," Diel said. "I won't forget it."

He wouldn't forget any of tonight's events—not the people who'd betrayed him, and even less those who stood by his side. Weariness weighed on Diel's mind as they set in motion again, bending his back and slowing his strides, so he drew strength from the strange companions around him. Cal talked almost ceaselessly, recounting card games he had played with Arathiel and Hasryan. His two friends sometimes corrected the gross exaggerations, but mostly they laughed alongside the story. Branwen interrupted with the occasional question, and Diel preferred to stay silent and enjoy. Eventually, they moved to the night's events, and while it dampened the mood, their earlier laughter had soothed his nerves and reaffirmed his decision. Neither Arathiel nor Hasryan belonged in a cell or a noose. He'd fight for them—with them—until both could once more safely claim Isandor as their home.

Chapter Thirty-Eight

JILSSAN arrived at the remnants of Keroth's temple at full speed, and stones dropped to the bottom of her stomach as she discovered the true range of the devastation. Half the ceiling had collapsed, taking down part of the main alley and entrance with it, leaving a skeleton of arches behind. They reached up like bony fingers, witnesses to a once-proud structure, and a warning about the depths of Avenazar's power. She eyed the lingering cloud of dust with suspicion. Already, air whistled through her damaged bronchia. The quick run had made breathing a struggle, and she feared entering would worsen her state.

Somewhere in there, however, under the debris and heavy stones, was her apprentice.

Jilssan angled for the collapsed wall and leaped from one large boulder to another, climbing the rubble with unnatural speed. Guards already milled around inside, moving in pairs as they inspected the damage. Keroth's acolytes huddled near an unbroken pillar, staring at their destroyed temple. A few had cuts and bruises, and Jilssan wondered if any were now missing, stuck under the collapsed ceiling of their room. Doubtful, since most of the quarters had survived, and not her problem.

Hers was probably the reason four soldiers and two acolytes were arguing in low voices, gesturing at broken stones and the pillar they came from. Jilssan strode toward them, and their conversation died as soon as they spotted her. They watched her approach with obvious apprehension, deepening Jilssan's own fears, and parted ways for her.

A young girl lay behind them, partly buried under rubble, with a boulder crushing her arm and a section of her chest. She was the right age, but could this be her apprentice? Jilssan studied the thick eyebrows, broad nose, and full lips, trying to convince herself of what she saw. No one could deny that the short skirt and Myrian blouse belonged to Isra, though. A large mass of wavy brown hair had replaced the straight blonde cut, and the darker colour of her skin had nothing to do with the substantial layer of dust on it. It had to be her. She could feel it in her guts.

"Why are you all standing there instead of helping her?" she demanded, but she knew why—they all knew why. They had no qualms letting an Isbari girl suffocate. Jilssan glared at them, then snapped her second word of power, calling upon her magic to strengthen her muscles. They murmured as she stepped forward, grabbed the largest boulder, lifted it with care, and flung it away. The cacophony of its landing didn't quite cover Isra's moan at her release, and the quiet sound twisted her stomach. Jilssan thanked the halfling for the healing he had provided, even though the girl obviously required more. Jilssan spun to the others, stifling a cough. Displacing the boulder had thrown a cloud of dust into the air, and she could barely breathe, as if every speck clung to the inside of her airways. "Send a healer to her quarters, then someone find me Master Avenazar."

No one moved at her command. They exchanged hesitant glances. "Madam, she's—"

"It's *Master* Jilssan," she snapped. Never had the guards questioned her authority before. Did Isra's Isbari descent weigh heavier in the balance, or could they hear the whistle of her breathing? "Until we know more, you answer to me. Break this rule and Master Avenazar will hear about it, is that clear? Now go."

They scampered off, and Jilssan waited until they'd left the temple grounds to release her wracking cough. The edges of her vision had started to darken, and she couldn't wait to escape this place. She needed to know what had happened, though. How much had Avenazar seen? What had led to the temple's collapse? She needed information to parse which lies to tell and which to avoid. If anyone ever suspected she had come across Branwen and her team and let them go, she could kiss her freedom and life goodbye. The same was true for Isra. Protecting her had become exponentially more difficult.

Jilssan cast her gaze down as she walked off, the apprentice light in her empowered arms. The girl's unbroken arm clutched her lucky amulet, a gift from her father. Shattered, now. What would

Master Enezi say when he discovered what had happened here? He'd be furious, but what could Jilssan have done about this? He hadn't even warned her! Unless … she slowed down, staring at the girl in her arms, whom she had loved and protected for three years now. What if she wasn't the real Isra? What if this Isbari girl had sought to escape Myria and impersonated Enezi's daughter? Cold numbness climbed through Jilssan's spine at the possibility. She would need to ask Enezi. If Isra, the daughter of one of Myria's most powerful mage, wasn't Isbari at all … would anywhere remain safe for the daring, cunning girl she'd trained? She hoped it was the same girl, that the amulet had indeed been devised by Master Enezi. The alternative terrified her. Jilssan tightened her hold, her stomach cramping, and hurried to Isra's room.

ISRA stared at the ceiling above her head and the intricate motifs painted on it. Every morning for two years, she'd woken to the depiction of the Myrian army marching through the dried Bielal Sea to conquer Isbar, and every morning, she had smiled, certain of which side she belonged to despite the heritage hidden under a spell. It had been a lie, to herself and others, but as long as no one pointed it out, she could continue living it.

Not anymore. Her amulet had broken, taking away her protection, and she would be cast out of prestigious Myrian circles. No more shopping in upper-class boutiques with Alanna and her friends, no more beautiful balls with the Empire's best mages and their daughters in gorgeous dresses, and no chance at becoming a wizard herself.

The fresco blurred behind her tears, and she choked down a sob. Beside her bed, Jilssan woke with a start, as if she had waited for nothing but that small sound, that undeniable sign Isra had regained consciousness. Isra wished she had stayed silent. She couldn't bear to look at her master or weather her inevitable anger. Helping Cal and the others had been a terrible, irrational, and ultimately disastrous decision. She shouldn't have—she knew this much deep down—yet she surprisingly didn't regret it.

"I'm here," Jilssan said, as if Isra hadn't realized. "How are you?"

The calm in her voice reassured Isra, but she didn't risk a glance. No words would make it past the lump in her throat either, so she closed her eyes and waited for the storm.

A firm hand touched her healthy arm. "You need more rest. The healer refused to give me something to numb your pain—they say Avenazar demanded every last drop of it. I believe that."

Isra wished they had denied him instead, but who here would ever risk such a thing? Between Varden's torture and the ruinous spell at the temple, they'd had ample occasions to witness the consequences.

"Isra …" Jilssan sighed and squeezed her arm. "I don't know if you're safe here anymore, but we'll get through this. I'll find a way."

This time, Isra's eyes flew open. *She wanted to help.* "You're not leaving me? I thought …" Her words ran out, and she met Jilssan's gaze. Isra's vision swam, but she held onto the smile on her master's face.

"Are you or are you not my apprentice?" Jilssan asked. "I once promised your father I would protect you. Today, I promise you directly. I'll do whatever needs to be done."

"O-okay." Her head buzzed, but the weight pressing down on Isra lightened. She had always believed her world would end if her secret was revealed, yet Jilssan now held all of them, and she meant to fight for her nonetheless. Isra lifted a hand to stare at her fingers, so different from what she was used to. Perhaps it wouldn't turn out so bad, to be seen as she was. She wasn't in Myria, and people had come to save Varden. The world worked differently here. She returned her attention to the ceiling. Her voice dropped to a whisper. "I'm sorry I didn't tell about the amulet and my mom that night, when we talked about … the other stuff. I didn't think I could."

"There's no need to apologize. I said you *could* tell me your secrets, not that you had to. You choose when and how."

Isra pouted. "I didn't choose this time…" She wondered what the future would hold. Would they send her back to Myria? What would Avenazar do, once he learned? "Please tell me how it ended. At the temple."

For all she knew, everyone had died, and she had risked her life for nothing. She hoped they had escaped—that her bubble had held long enough. It should have. Isra had struggled through the spell, nearly failing to grasp the magical energy and warp it into a protective shield, but she'd succeeded. She had cast a complex spell under stress, despite all her previous difficulties, and for a moment, the pride smothered her other worries. Isra listened to Jilssan explain what they'd found—or, more importantly, hadn't found—at the temple, glad to know she had played a pivotal role in Varden's escape. A good thing. The first, but hopefully not the last, and Jilssan had promised to help however she could. Isra propped herself up while, and soon she was explaining her own accomplishments in hushed and excited tones. This wasn't the end, but the beginning of something new, of which she could be proud.

Chapter Thirty-Nine

ARATHIEL didn't say much on the long walk to Isandor, allowing his more talkative partners to explain their expedition at the enclave. His attention kept drifting, to the stinging line on his back. It hurt. The foreign sensation had panicked him at first, but now excitement pierced through. What did this mean? Could specific events trigger his other senses? What if he could recover some of them permanently? He shouldn't get his hopes up—with the exception of the burn, he couldn't feel anything else. No pain from the rough landing, no cold at the winter's night, and no idea of the textures of either Varden's hair or clothes. He wished he could ask him if Keroth's fire could have caused this, or if they could test it.

They abandoned the horse when they reached Isandor's first stairs. The chatter had died, and everyone walked with their heads low. Diel had tucked his golden hair into a hood, Hasryan sulked in the shadows out of sight, and Branwen scouted each bridge and set of stairs before they took them. They climbed through the Lower City until Cal pointed to a yellow door so bright it seemed to shine in the moonlight. Arathiel grinned. How flashy could it be if even he could see its intensity? Cal had been watching him, and he laughed at his reaction.

"You'll love my place, Ara."

And Arathiel did.

Cal's front door lead to a spacious and round living room, furnished with three large sofas—one red, one blue, one green—colours strong enough for him to perceive in all of their glory. Shelves lined the walls, half-buried under trinkets and statuettes of deities. Most were dedicated to Ren's many physical representations, but other divinities were present. Perhaps because of the priest in his arms, Arathiel sought Keroth's statues. An ivory one depicted the pale and masculine fire wielder the Myrians referred to as the Firelord, while the dark wood carving next to Them showed the black woman hailed as the Mother of Flames in most southern regions—both very popular aspects of Keroth. The six core deities had as many representations as there were cultures, while demigods like Ren tended to resemble their appearances before ascension—or what common lore said of them, anyway. Xe had rich brown skin, curly hair, a pear-shaped figure, and Xir eternal mischievous smile.

"Your place hurts my eyes, Cal," Hasryan said.

"Oh, good. I'm not alone!" Branwen spun around, her wide eyes taking in the surroundings. "You need my help with this living room. What's that in the ceiling?"

Cal laughed, clearly enjoying their pain. "The pillows. There's a ladder to get them."

Arathiel shifted his attention from the statuettes to the ceiling. An enormous net hung from it with a myriad of rainbow pillows waiting within. Arathiel squinted from all the colours, grinning. Cal was right. He loved it in all its ugliness.

"It's so lively. I could stay here forever." Arathiel turned to Cal. "If you have no objections, I think we should grant Varden an actual bed. I suspect it's been a long time for him."

"Please do! My room's right there." He pointed at one of the doors leading out. "Meanwhile, we'll get some sort of community resting area going."

Arathiel headed in, and the walls' deep blue disappointed him. They were enveloping and comforting but not as energetic as the sofas. Perhaps that was for the best—Varden might prefer to wake somewhere cozy rather than in a rainbow fest. Arathiel set him down on the mattress, thanking the gods for Cal's human-sized bed. A small moan escaped Varden as Arathiel put a pillow under his head, and he touched the priest's forehead only to remember with a sinking feeling that he couldn't tell if it was burning hot. He'd have to ask Cal to look again. His friend had, in his words, 'shoved some emergency healing' into Varden, but after helping Hasryan and Isra, he'd had little left. Between ten days of torture and Varden's actions in the brazier, the priest's body might just be giving in.

At first, Arathiel hadn't understood what had happened in the temple. The powerful flash of pain had fried his mind, yet it had ended before Arathiel even hit the burning logs. One moment,

Arathiel thought he would die, devoured by agonizing flames; the next, Varden had wrapped an arm around him, curls whipping about in the hot air, and the fire had formed a dome over them without coming close.

"Are you okay?" he'd asked, his voice cracking.

Arathiel had clung to him, panicked at the sizzling pain across his back, repeating "I hurt" again and again.

Varden had squeezed him tight. A smile had brightened his face, erasing several lines of worry. The light had danced across his skin, and in the swirling chaos of flames and agony, Varden had turned into a beautiful, solid anchor. "It's fine," he'd said. "The fire is safe."

Keeping it that way had taxed him. The strain had become more apparent as the temple crumbled around them, stones crashing into the brazier. Varden had scowled, his fingers digging into Arathiel, his breathing raw and shallow. The shield of flames had held. Varden had only dismissed it when silence had returned. Flames had rushed into his body, heat had drained from the coals under them, and he'd collapsed into Arathiel's arms.

How strange to have saved someone he had never met, only to be immediately saved in return.

Arathiel smiled and pulled the covers over Varden, promising himself he'd watch over the priest. He couldn't leave Cal's place anyway. Being forced to hide alongside Hasryan, Diel, and Varden pleased him. With so many of them stuck in Cal's tiny home, Arathiel doubted they'd have a moment of boredom.

HASRYAN'S peace of mind had vanished the moment their group entered Isandor once more. Now he was watching Lord Dathirii with reflexive wariness out of a habit entrenched for years. He couldn't forget his current situation. This lord—a stranger, really— had lost everything tonight, and he could retrieve it in a single exchange: Hasryan for his home, his reputation, his family. Could Hasryan trust Diel's promise of help, made before his world had unravelled? Larryn would mock him for even considering this noble an option, and yet … Worry etched on his face, Lord Dathirii shifted pillows around unhelpfully, unable to focus. Hard to imagine a cold and calculating traitor in the listless man thinking of his trapped love. Hasryan didn't blame him—if any of his friends were in the Allastams' hands, he'd find it difficult to concentrate too. Except that was precisely why he feared Lord Dathirii. Good but desperate people quickly abandoned morals to achieve their goals.

"Is Uncle that attractive, or are you just staring for fun?"

Hasryan dropped his pillow, startled by Branwen's voice. She grinned at him, and he'd teased enough folks to know she thought he would fumble into an apology. He met her gaze and smirked. "Staring is amusing. I wanted to make you jealous, and it seems like it worked."

"What? Of course not!" She huffed, her cheeks burning. Hasryan laughed.

"Hurried denial and immediate blush? Very credible." If she had noted his focus on her uncle, she must have been staring too. Hasryan's stomach tightened. He hated being watched, studied, judged. Too often, those who noticed him meant harm. At least

Branwen didn't feel threatening. Her curiosity and teasing set him on edge, but Hasryan appreciated the change of pace from hostile onlookers. He reminded himself that Cal's place would always stay safe for him as long as his friend had a say in it.

Hasryan's gaze sought Cal out. He'd fallen into step with the halfling during their return, away from the others, and they'd had their first private conversation since his fateful headbutt in the Skyward Tavern. At first, Hasryan floundered when he tried to voice his thoughts, so he thanked Cal for healing his leg, tried to explain why horses terrified him, and eventually shifted the topic toward the Shelter.

"I considered fleeing Isandor while I was hiding with Camilla but … I couldn't leave everything behind. Even thinking neither you nor Larryn wanted to speak with me again. It's my home now. I'm glad I stayed to fight for it, and for Arathiel."

"He's great, isn't he?" Cal asked.

"Inviting him to play cards was our wisest decision this year," Hasryan agreed. "I declared him an official part of our Halfies Trio. Apparently Sora's cleric described him as half-alive."

"That's gross." Cal had glanced back and frowned. "He's as alive as they come. I wonder how they healed him. I tried, and it felt like a cold vortex sucking me in. My fingers became numb."

They had stared at Cal's small hand for a moment before shrugging it off. Just another layer to Arathiel's mystery they had no intention of prying into. "Listen, Cal, I think you should know … I'm glad you stopped to save that apprentice. Nevian?"

Cal's breath had caught and he had paled. "You–you are?"

"Don't get me wrong. It hurt to believe you didn't care about me. But you did the right thing, and I bet you're full of guilt about it." He had smirked when Cal bit his lower lip—of course he had been beating himself up over this. "Please clear your conscience."

"Larryn—"

"Is wrong on so many levels, I wouldn't know where to start."

Cal had laughed, then hugged his legs. When he had whispered "thank you," tears had filled his voice, and Hasryan had been glad he had discussed it. He owed the halfling so much, and he hated the idea of guilt weighing his friend down. Cal deserved nothing less than happiness and endless crates of cheese. Perhaps Lord Dathirii would see to the latter once they had taken back his tower.

Urgent knocks interrupted his thoughts, and Hasryan slid away from the entrance, his heart hammering. How had they found them so fast? But no, guards would have smashed the door without pause. He continued to draw back, ready to disappear into the kitchen, when a young voice called through the thick wood.

"Cal! Cal, please!"

Hasryan recognized Efua's voice, and he hesitated. She sounded terrified, but should they let her see everyone? He had played and chatted with her a few times, but Hasryan preferred to avoid children in general, and he doubted they could trust her with the huge secret this living room had become. Cal must not have shared his worries because he ran and flung the door open. She threw herself into his arms, crouching to compensate for the height difference, and squeezed tight.

"Whoa, Efua, what's wrong?"

She sniffed and pulled back. "It's Larryn, he—" Efua stopped, her gaze settling on the numerous strangers in the room. She clamped shut and straightened. "Nothing. I'm okay."

"We can't help him if you don't tell us," Hasryan said. A low dread built in his mind. Larryn had a knack for getting into trouble and paying tenfold for his mistakes. "You can speak freely here."

Efua furrowed her eyebrows and studied the group. Her eyes lingered on Lord Dathirii, then she dug into her pocket and retrieved a folded parchment. Cal accepted it with a frown, prying it open under everyone's watch. No one said a word, and only Efua moved, pulling at her curly hair: a nervous habit. With every line, Cal grew paler, until he reached the end and groaned.

"Ren's gracious luck, he'll get himself killed one day." He rubbed his face with one hand, concern and anger warring in his expression. "Who did he want to receive this message, Efua?"

"Lord Dathirii." She stared at her feet, doing her best not to look at Diel. Even if she didn't know exactly who he was, Isandor had a limited supply of upper-class golden-haired elves. She must have suspected. "I went to the tower, but the guards weren't Dathirii, and they told me there wasn't a Lord Dathirii anymore, and then they asked me if I wanted to give it to the elf in charge. I asked them if he was *the* Lord Dathirii, and they laughed and shooed me away."

"I'm right here," Diel said. "Since this missive is destined to me, might I perhaps have it, Sir Cal?"

Although Diel continued their little knightly humour, the strange edge in his voice made it clear he'd just ordered Cal. Efua gasped, and for a moment, Cal stayed put, uncertain. His hesitation dug claws of worry through Hasryan's stomach. Just what had Larryn done this time? When Cal finally brought Diel the message, Hasryan was already cringing.

"Please don't get mad at him," Cal said. "I'm sure they're totally okay!"

"They …"

Diel's voice trailed off as he dropped his sentence to read. Hasryan waved Cal over, hoping for some insight into the contents of this letter.

"Are you certain it's real? Larryn can't write." He whispered, but in the heavy silence, everyone must have heard him.

"Oh, it's him all right," Cal said. "Reeks of him. I think he made Nevian write it. You won't like what it says."

A tired laugh escaped Hasryan. He suspected this involved him, and he doubted Larryn's words toward the Dathirii would be kind. Resigned to deal with whatever Larryn had cooked up this time, he waited for Diel to finish the message. And indeed, when the elven lord reached the end, he looked straight at Hasryan.

"The good news is, I know exactly where Vellien is, and we'll have a professional healer for Varden soon." With a heavy sigh, he gave the letter a slight shake. "The bad news is, this Larryn wants to exchange their safety for yours. He seems to be under the impression I'm holding you against your will, Hasryan."

"That does sound an awful lot like Larryn." How had he learned Hasryan had stayed in the Dathirii Tower? Had he guessed it because of Arathiel's friendship and temporary freedom? Except he couldn't prove that, which meant he'd kidnapped a noble and threatened them with nothing but his bitter opinions to support his conclusion. How exactly did he think that would work out? Any House had the resources to track him down, drag him to a cell or a noose, and close the Shelter forever. "I'm touched by his dedication, but this is ridiculous."

"So, you all know him, don't you?" Diel crumpled the parchment, steel in his voice. "I'll admit I have little patience for those who would attack my family tonight. I have lived through enough of it."

"Please don't hurt him!" Cal stepped forward, spreading his arms as if Larryn stood behind him. "He's a good person who puts all his time and energy and money into a shelter where he feeds and houses homeless folk. He's just … misguided, and angry, and since Hasryan's arrest, he's grown more and more erratic. Please understand. His best friend almost got hanged in front of everyone, and he is convinced no one else can keep Hasryan safe. You can't blame him! This city always treated both of them as shit. Dirt under your boots."

The passion with which Cal defended Larryn surprised Hasryan. After the punch, no one would have faulted him for staying silent. "Don't unleash the resentment you've built against Lord Allastam on him," Hasryan added. "He's an easier and unprotected target who made a shit decision, but he doesn't deserve it. I can fix this."

Diel straightened in his seat, fingers playing with the corner of a pillow. "Then please do. I don't care about punishing this Larryn in any shape or form, but I cannot let him hurt Vellien."

"They've been helping at his Shelter for days!" Branwen added.

"Your friend needs to work on his thank-you skills."

"That, and so much more," Hasryan said. "I'll go. It's risky, but we should talk, and I can bring Vellien safely here after."

Lord Dathirii's shoulders slumped, and he nodded. "Thank you, Hasryan. That's all I want, really."

"Happy to serve, milord." Hasryan grinned, then found a cloak to throw over his too-bright coat. "If I can, I'll even return with dinner for all of us. I don't know about anyone else, but I'm dying of hunger, and you haven't really enjoyed food until you've tasted Larryn's cooking."

His comment drew a smile from Diel and a joyful exclamation from Cal and Efua. Hasryan motioned for her to lead the way. "Let's head out together."

She had been standing in silence, always staying close to Cal, and Hasryan's suggestion surprised her. "I thought you couldn't be free anymore. Are you okay now?"

"I am, but I still have to be careful not to be seen by guards." He pulled his hood up and opened the door. "Come on, I'll explain what I can on the way."

She skipped ahead, hair bouncing as she left Cal's place. Hasryan wondered how much he could tell her, but she needed to know she couldn't talk about who she'd seen at Cal's, or even that she had delivered a letter there. Efua had always been a quick thinker, and he believed she could handle the secret if no one asked. He hoped she'd never be in a position where people pressured her for such information.

As they travelled to the Lower City and Larryn's Shelter,

Hasryan's stomach began to knot. Seeing his friend again after their fight in the prison made him anxious—no, more than that. Every step wound his nerves tighter and brought new catastrophic scenarios to his mind. Larryn would hate what Hasryan had to say, even if he needed to hear it. No one else could reach through his wall of anger, though. Larryn trapped himself in it like the city of Nal-Gresh in its stone egg. Those not welcomed never entered. Except Hasryan didn't want to fight for him to listen. Hasryan considered the Shelter his home, and its owner had carved a place for him there. They shared specific hardships and a criminal bent that made their friendship unique. Not to mention Larryn's loyalty had obviously never died, not even in the Sapphire Guard's prisons. Only Larryn would kidnap a Dathirii elf for his sake. Hasryan smiled at the thought despite the short-sightedness of it all. Or because of it, perhaps. It was time to get a few hard truths out of the way and drag the last member of the Halfies Trio—or, well, Quartet now—back into his circle of friends.

CHAPTER FORTY

LARRYN was pacing around and around in Nevian's room, unable to stop. Every time he sat down, he started tapping his foot, earning himself a glare from the young wizard. Then he jumped back to his feet and circled once more. Music drifted in from the common area, but even the lively violins and spoon rhythms sounded discordant and distraught. Patron conversations should bury them, but his people had started talking in low and tense voices. Rumours of attacks had reached them, confusing and alarming, and no one knew the details. Larryn pushed it out of his mind. Only Hasryan and the Dathirii mattered tonight.

What was taking them so long anyway? Were they preparing an assault on his home? Had Efua run into problems? The scary stories dripping down the bridges and stairs conjured terrifying possibilities. Larryn wouldn't admit it to anyone, but he regretted this entire affair. When would he learn to think these plans through? He groaned and collapsed into the chair again, his growing fear threatening to overtake his anger.

Larryn had returned half an hour ago with Hasryan's enchanted dagger, stolen from the Sapphire Guard's headquarters when he had tried to free Hasryan, and dinner for three. He untied Vellien, worried at first that the teenager would try something—use their connection to the Elven Shepherd to invoke Their wrath, or blind Larryn with light and escape. Something—anything—to ruin Larryn's plan. Vellien instead rubbed their shoulders, thanked him for the freedom and the meal, and started eating. Their delighted squeal of surprise at the first bite calmed Larryn, as did the speed with which Vellien finished their plate. They hadn't changed from the kind teenager who had healed so many patrons and respected all his rules; they'd only turned into a ball of anxiety. The food helped appease them, too, and they clearly struggled not to gush about how delicious the meal was. Nevian suggested Vellien could finish healing him since they were untied, and they both stared at Larryn for permission. His stomach squeezed. It wasn't right to have scared Vellien so much, Dathirii or not. They were just a naive kid, in so many ways.

So he let them and watched from his chair, arms crossed, the way an angry parent would. Nevian and Vellien were almost of an age with him, no more than two or three years younger, yet Larryn couldn't think of them as full adults. Perhaps he shouldn't think of himself as one either, but he had run this Shelter for two years now and fed himself for a decade. He had never been a teenager in the proper sense of the term. Larryn listened to Vellien's professional tone as they went through routine questions, their smooth rebuttal of Nevian's gruff responses, and the ease with which they conjured white light and delved into the apprentice's damaged mind. Nevian almost leaned into the touch, and Larryn belatedly realized he'd never seen him comfortable so close to anyone. Physical proximity and contact stressed Nevian, and except for healing, he rarely let others within this boundary. Even now, Vellien restricted their touch to fingers on his forehead, the rest of their body staying clear of their patient's. Guilt wracked Larryn's stomach. He shouldn't think of these two as sheltered kids. Could elven youth ever be called proper teenagers? Decades of experience had changed Vellien's approach to life and granted them the wisdom and humility to submit to Larryn's rules. And while Nevian hadn't carried hundreds of buckets of piss to the shitslides, he had endured his share of disgraceful tasks and abuse. Yet Nevian's stubborn protests against this plan had crystallized their dynamic in Larryn's mind: they were the young ones, and he was the adult—the irresponsible man who'd kidnapped one of them to trade for his friend. Larryn groaned at himself again, but it was too late for regrets. He couldn't back out.

The door handle rattled, and Larryn jumped to his feet. Too late indeed. He stalked to the entrance, his palms sweaty, his chest hurting from stress. "Who's there?" he growled, hoping to make his high-pitched voice more intimidating.

"Larryn, for the love of every god out there watching and laughing at us, let me in before someone comes by."

Hasryan's voice sent a jolt of relief through his body, and he scrambled for the door, a little dizzy. He hadn't expected Hasryan to just appear in the Shelter. He'd thought he would have a threatening message, or guards, or Kellian Dathirii. Behind him, Nevian and Vellien had fallen silent. Larryn flung the door open, unable to keep the grin off his face.

Hasryan stood in the corridor, hood pulled over his head, hands inside his sleeves to hide them. His lips stretched into the usual smirk, and amusement shone in his red eyes. "Wow, you're bad at this stuff," he said. "Good thing no one had coerced me into talking through the door, hm?"

"I ..."

He was right. Any guards with Hasryan would have had a clear shot. Larryn flushed a red deeper than the winter coat on Hasryan's back—the same he'd seen in the mirror. His friend laughed and swept in, closing the door behind himself, and the beautiful sound washed Larryn's mortification away. Hasryan had returned, safe and in good spirits. Everything could change now. Larryn would apologize to Cal, and they could fix their shattered relationship and rebuild what they had before.

Except Hasryan threw a glance toward Vellien, and his smile vanished. "Don't pull this kind of shit again." His tone cut through Larryn's hopes. "What were you thinking? You'll get yourself killed."

Larryn staggered back, stunned. One moment, his heart had been soaring, happy to have his friend beside him; the next, it crashed on the ground, smashing into pieces. Shouldn't Hasryan thank him? Larryn had risked everything to save him! Larryn had expected them to laugh at this ordeal and smooth over the terrible mistakes he'd made, but not ... not *this*. Anger trickled back, nestling in his stomach, familiar and reassuring.

"Wow, you sure have that gratitude thing pinned down," he snapped. "If your Dathirii prison was so comfortable, you can go right back to it."

Hasryan met his gaze, and something in it—exhaustion, coldness, a plea to stop—broke the rising tide of his fury. Larryn's mouth dried. Hasryan had changed since his arrest. Larryn didn't understand the details of *how*, but he felt it in his bones. Whatever they'd had before had shattered. They would need to rebuild a different relationship—a better one. But how? Larryn struggled to reach out to this Hasryan, calmer and more serious, with rarer smiles and a new hard edge.

"I was worried," he said, desperate to explain himself. "What if they hurt you? I couldn't function—could barely cook! Everything else mattered less."

"Yeah, I've been hearing a lot of stories about that."

The acid reproach in his tone startled Larryn. "What's that supposed to mean?"

"It means I know you hit Cal." Hasryan strode forward, his voice almost a growl. "I don't care how angry or terrified you were! How could you? He's your *friend*. How often did Cal save your ass? Where would you even be without him? None of this was his fault, and I hope you're horrified at yourself."

"He never came to the headquarters!" Larryn's mind reeled from

Hasryan's attack. He shook, nauseated, torn between the instinct to defend himself and the desire to apologize a thousand times. His friend was so close—menacingly close, even, and never before had proximity with Hasryan felt threatening. "I don't know how. I didn't—it … it just happened! I didn't mean to, and I was so angry. We needed him, and he'd disappeared, and—"

"You vanished too," Hasryan interrupted. "You left me there. How is that better? But that's just the thing, Larryn. You might not want to hurt others, but you still do. You get angry and lash out and blame those around you. You yelled at me in that prison, for actions *you* undertook to free me, like I had inflicted that pain on you! And it hurt—shit did it hurt to watch you leave—even if you hadn't meant to attack me like that."

"I know! I know …" Larryn stared at the unstable ground beneath his feet. Had Hasryan come only to scold him? Did they all hate him now? They would dump him alone in this trash world, and—no. Larryn squeezed his eyes shut, fighting against his spiralling thoughts and urges to lash right back. He had failed them, and he deserved Hasryan's anger. He needed to listen. "I'm sorry. I freaked out and ruined everything." He forced himself to meet Hasryan's gaze. "None of this would have happened if I had stayed with you."

"It's not just that night, Larryn. You always do that, and it needs to stop. Our shit lives can explain a lot, but at the end of the day, we take these actions. They're our decisions. And if I can resolve to move past assassinations and make up for them, then you sure as heck can deal with your anger."

Heat rushed into Larryn's cheeks, and he struggled for an answer. How often had he thought similar things in the past days? But it wasn't the same as having it laid down by Hasryan so thoroughly—so undeniably. Larryn wished he could disappear into the ground rather than confront the truth. He felt sick and confused and overwhelmed, and he instinctively clung to the one thing he knew he'd done right.

"At-at least I freed you. You're here now, thanks to this."

He gestured toward Vellien, whose eyes widened. They and Nevian had remained deathly silent, making themselves as forgettable as possible. A good reflex because Larryn knew he'd snap if either dared to say a single word. Hasryan's assaults already taxed his control—and the reverse was true, too, judging by the stiffness in his friend's shoulders.

"So what happened, exactly?" Hasryan asked. "When did your brain decide the Dathirii were to blame for this one? Were they too good to Arathiel? Or did you just pick your favourite target?"

Now that was unfair. "You think I'd kidnap a kid on a whim? Nevian used a divination spell, and I saw you in a cell with their spy. I didn't jump to that conclusion! You were there, in a prison, and a Dathirii blocked your way out." When had Hasryan grown so attached to them anyway? He didn't trust these elves, right? He knew where that had landed Larryn's mom. "Listen to yourself. It's … it's like you want to side with them."

"Side with them." Disappointment laced Hasryan's tone, and it struck Larryn worse than anger. "I am indeed going to 'side with them' if by 'side with them,' you mean that I will accept their help.

Because when you look at it, I kind of owe my freedom to a bunch of dangerous nobles right now. Arathiel leaped into that crowd to save my ass, Camilla hid me when the entire city wanted me dead, and Diel promised to keep me safe and clear my name. I walked straight into the Myrian enclave with Branwen by my side to save a man I had never seen before because they needed my help, and I needed theirs."

Larryn listened with a desperate, sinking feeling. He was losing a friend—his best friend. This was a mistake, a horrible mistake, worse than them holding him prisoner. The panic crawled into Larryn's mind, coating his answer with despair. "You can't trust them, Hasryan. You can't." It wouldn't end well. You couldn't believe a Dathirii, not unless you had a title yourself, not unless you had dirt on them to keep you safe. Hasryan had to see that. He knew better. He had to. "They're liars. They'll use you, and—"

"Stop, Larryn! Listen to me. Whichever of them is your dad can rot in hell, but I swear that's not the whole family."

Larryn stepped back, the air knocked out of his lungs, and grabbed Nevian's chair for support. Vellien slapped a hand over their mouth, muffling a gasp, but Larryn ignored them for now. His skull buzzed, and his thoughts spun wildly. It didn't matter how Hasryan knew. This was his secret, sealed shut behind bitter walls, and he had never shared it willingly, not even to his closest friend. Hasryan had no right to throw it into his face like that—and in front of a Dathirii! Anger and betrayal choked Larryn. Unable to look at Hasryan, he whirled on Vellien and focused his pain into sharp rage. The young elf stared at him, recognition and horror dawning clear in their eyes. They knew who—Larryn shared too much of Yultes' appearance for Vellien not to understand.

"Rule number five," Larryn said, his voice strangely flat. "If you utter one word of this to anyone, ever, I will find the most secret, bloodiest rituals to invoke Seiman, Master of Revenge, and we will curse you. Is that clear?"

Vellien paled and swallowed hard. Their hand snatched Nevian's, startling him, but he squeezed back. Vellien nodded.

"Good," Larryn said. "You've never broken a rule before. I'll trust you to continue." What else could he do, anyway? He had hurt Vellien enough already. "This is my secret to share, on my terms if I decide I should. No one else's."

"I–I understand!" Vellien squeaked.

The words hadn't been meant for them. Slowly, gathering his wounded pride and dismay, Larryn faced Hasryan. His friend's shoulders hunched with obvious regret.

"Everyone suspected, Larryn."

"Everyone can go fuck themselves. It's none of their business. But you …"

"I shouldn't have said it." Hasryan ran a hand through his hair, uneasy, but met Larryn's gaze with renewed determination. "It's just … you have to understand. When you left, I hit rock-bottom. The noose seemed a fitting conclusion to the life that had come before. Camilla helped me out of that. She was unconditionally sweet and present, and this very morning, she chose prison over selling me out to her nephew. You don't have to like the Dathirii, but they're not the monsters you imagine."

"I know," he whispered, and his anger flushed out, leaving him empty and exhausted. Larryn glanced at Vellien and shook his head. "I can't trust their family, Hasryan. I don't have that in me, and they don't deserve the chance. Not from me."

"I'll take it. I'll take that chance." Hasryan ran his fingers through his hair again. "But you're still my best friend, you know? It's not you against them. I … I want both in my life."

Larryn tilted his head to the side, considering the words. Hard to conceive of his world as anything except a fight against nobles. They stole everything they could from others, forcing the Lower City to struggle for homes, food, or a minimum of hygiene. Those who helped sought to appease their guilt, and they often disappeared too quickly to have lasting effects. But perhaps Larryn could create a new category in his mind for the rare nobles who didn't actively ruin everything. It would make it easier to deal with Vellien and Arathiel.

He didn't answer beyond a grunt, and after a long and uncomfortable silence, Hasryan leaned against the wall behind him with a heavy sigh. "I don't know how you manage to be angry all the time. I'm exhausted. Can we, like … not fight ever again?"

Larryn laughed. He wanted to fall apart and cry, to grieve over their old relationship and his shattered secrets, but he laughed instead. Maybe something had finally broken inside him after all these years of fighting against everything—constant hunger, stinging cold, relentless guards, harassing nobles, and his ever-present anger. But Hasryan's little joke struck a chord, and he crumbled back into a chair.

"Yeah. Let's not. It's starting to wear me out, I think. All of this …" He gestured vaguely around, not even certain himself what 'this' meant, then rubbed his face, his hands shaky. Larryn wished Vellien and Nevian had left the room. Others shouldn't see him in this state. His voice dropped to a whisper, and he hoped only Hasryan would catch it. "You're right, you know. About the anger. But it's so hard to let go and move on … I'm glad you're back." He wouldn't make it without Hasryan. "I had something for you, too."

With a weak smile, he reached for Hasryan's weapons, still on the desk next to him, and his friend's eyes widened when he recognized the sheath. Larryn pushed himself to standing again. Hasryan hesitated, then stepped forward and clasped his fingers around Brune's poisoned gift, used to frame him for Lady Allastam's murder. Larryn didn't let go yet.

"That's not all." He forced himself to meet Hasryan's gaze despite the shame and fatigue and remaining anger. He had once promised to reveal his age if he learned Hasryan's secret job. It had been a jest, but Larryn needed the reminder of their past dynamic. Those peaceful nights drinking in silence or teasing each other had meant the world to him, and although they might never return in that exact form, Larryn refused to break a promise made during one of them, no matter how silly. "I'm twenty."

"Twenty." A wide grin split Hasryan's face, washing away the exhaustion. "Look at you! This big grown-up man finally reached a fifth of a century!"

Hasryan pinched his cheek, and Larryn flushed, the heat climbing all the way to the tips of his pointed ears. "Yeah, okay, enough! Don't go telling the entire Shelter! No one would take me seriously."

Hasryan snorted and pulled Larryn into a tight hug, the dagger between them. It lasted only a second, but it lifted a huge weight off his shoulders. Things would turn out okay somehow. When Hasryan drew back, Larryn let his weapons go.

"You hungry?" he asked.

"Terribly, but I should bring Vellien back."

Vellien scrambled to their feet and emphatically shook their head. "Please eat. It's too good for you to refuse. I can wait—I can even finish healing Nevian! We could find another room …"

"Your uncle might die of stress before we return," Hasryan said, but he smirked. "I'll take it, Larryn. I'd love to indulge in your meals once more. Camilla can't compare, even though she's a great cook."

Larryn jumped to his feet. Nothing pleased him more than feeding others, especially friends, and he wanted to force the food down Hasryan's throat. As if an amazing meal could vaporize the last half hour and smooth everything over. "I'll be back!"

He hurried toward the door, but as he passed near Hasryan, his friend caught his forearm, holding him back. "Larryn … if a bunch of people are thrown out of their home because of a political coup, could they rely on the Shelter for their first meal?"

Larryn froze. Between the rumours of attacks that had reached the Shelter and Vellien's mention of losing their titles, he could guess Hasryan meant Dathirii elves. Who else would he ask for? He gritted his teeth, struggling with the very idea of feeding nobles. But the request was from *Hasryan*, and after tonight, he couldn't refuse. "They can pay me back later. How many?"

"Round it up to ten. Add cheese for Cal."

Larryn snorted, grinning. He would bring them food—just this once—as a thank you for helping Hasryan. And perhaps as an apology for Vellien, too. After that, they'd have to figure out another solution—sell their silks, plead to their richer friends, whatever. His patrons needed the free meals more than the Dathirii did—every meal they didn't have to prepare freed up time to ply their trades, and every penny they saved could go to other needs. Larryn left Nevian's room, eager to reach his kitchens. The time alone with his pots would allow him to sort through the mess of emotions whirling inside, find his footing, and properly celebrate Hasryan's safety.

NEVIAN escaped into the corridor, Vellien trailing behind him, and finally breathed again. He hated tonight. From the unusual way his divination spell had acted to Larryn's horrible kidnapping plan, including being forced to watch the excruciatingly intimate confrontation with Hasryan. If he could have melted into the bed and vanished, he would have. They slipped into the first empty room they could find—number 7, right across from his—and Nevian collapsed onto the bed.

"That was horrible."

Vellien had stayed near the entrance. "It's over, isn't it? I don't think I can take any more."

Nevian frowned. Did he hear tears in Vellien's voice? What would he do if they started to cry? He propped himself up on his elbows, terrified at the prospect of having to offer comfort. "It is. Come here." Maybe Vellien would appreciate a distraction. "Finish healing me."

Vellien's eyes widened, then they smiled and laughed—a disgraceful snort-chuckle that had come to reassure Nevian. "It was an excuse. You don't need my help anymore."

"I … don't?" Intense disappointment rushed through Nevian. He should celebrate that they had pieced together everything they could, but Nevian understood this meant Vellien would leave for good. Why would they return to a place where they had been kidnapped and threatened? But Nevian couldn't leave the Shelter. Even crossing to another room dizzied him since his run-in with Isra.

He wished their last healing session hadn't involved Larryn staring at them. He always threw everyone out before they worked on repairing his mind. It hadn't felt right for a third person to watch as Vellien had slipped into his head. Nevian had forced his initial panic to recede even though the usual crawling throb had climbed up his arm, a ghostly reminder of Avenazar's actions. It had only been ten days, but Nevian had taught himself to box that particular pain, pushing away the fear and imagined agony as long as Vellien needed him to.

The exercise always left both of them exhausted. Nevian struggled with having anyone in his mind, even though the experience with Vellien bordered on communion. They worked as a team: Nevian guided his companion as they navigated his memories, and Vellien assembled the demolished fragments together. That's how they had described it: knitting loose threads together until they formed a pattern Nevian recognized and remembered. Vellien never did anything Nevian didn't sense beforehand—and more than once, Vellien had sensed his hesitation and slowed or stopped. Nevian remained in control—of himself, of his mind, of who was allowed in it and what they could do. At first, he had held the reins tight, terrified of slipping, of letting anything escape his grasp. How could he trust anyone after all the damage already done? And yet … Nevian did trust Vellien. It had taken three meetings—very little time, all things considered—but he trusted the elf's light touch, the gentleness and patience of their care. Vellien didn't intrude; they were invited. Welcomed, even. And because he didn't need to fight, Nevian could participate in the piecing of his mind together, sharing the thrill of recovered memories with Vellien. The work was tiring but exciting, and he would miss it.

He would miss Vellien too, and the calm smile and reassuring voice. They stared at him now, more shaken than Nevian had ever seen them, and he recalled their sudden gripping of his hand. The touch had sent a surge of panic through Nevian, but he'd endured and squeezed back. Vellien had so often served as his anchor that Nevian had meant to help in return, even if just this once.

"That's what we had said, no?" Vellien replied. "Our progress is stable and won't unwind, I'm sure of it, and although it can speed recovery, you don't need me anymore."

Nevian had limited the number of sessions because he had preferred to stay alone. Yet over the last days, Cal had diminished his time in the Shelter, Efua had respected his wishes for a safe distance, and Nevian had found his room increasingly empty. In the enclave, company had meant problems. Here, however, people wanted to help. They provided incredible food, threaded his mind back together, or looked up to him. None of them—not even ever-angry Larryn—treated him with hostility.

"We should renegotiate." The words stumbled out of Nevian's mouth, and he scolded himself. What right did he have to ask Vellien to keep returning here?

"I would love to see you again, Nevian. I think … you're very strong." Vellien's cheeks turned a deep shade of red, and their freckles stood out more than ever. "What I mean to say is that I *like* you, but I don't know if I have a home anymore. I can't negotiate in such a position, but you will definitely receive word from me when I can."

Nevian's head buzzed, discomfort mixing with pleasant surprise. Most people found him annoying—too stubborn and disinterested in their problems to be worth their time—and Nevian enjoyed the tranquility this granted him. He thought most of them bothersome either way. Not Vellien, however. Never Vellien, and the joy that simple 'I like you' had brought Nevian troubled him. Did *he* like them? He knew he would gladly set aside studying for them, and perhaps he ought to consider that a sign. He trusted Vellien with his mind and memories. Had any other part of him ever mattered more? Nevian didn't want the complicated expectations that came with a relationship, however. He enjoyed Vellien's company because they had explored his head and didn't demand anything of him but himself. Nevian hoped that would never change.

"Thank you," he said. Disappointment flashed through Vellien's expression, and Nevian swallowed hard. "We can negotiate, erm, the meetings and everything else then. Is that … is that sufficient?"

Vellien's little amused snort sent a wave of relief through Nevian. "Of course." And then, more softly, as if they had followed Nevian's thoughts despite not residing in them at the moment, they added, "You will always be more than sufficient, Nevian."

SNEAKING out of Larryn's Shelter unseen while carrying the large pot containing everyone's meal proved even harder than entering the Myrian enclave. Hasryan and Vellien avoided the common room to slip out, instead using the usually condemned door at the back of the Shelter that led into the tower proper. Hasryan wondered if Larryn would one day buy the second floor of this building, to create his children-safe area within the Shelter. It seemed like forever since they had last discussed his friend's long-term plans.

Not a minute of their walk passed in which the young Dathirii didn't stare back at Hasryan, lips pinched, guilt and curiosity warring in their face. Hasryan didn't comment. Most likely, Vellien would build up the courage to voice whatever went through their mind before long—and indeed, no sooner had they climbed out of the worst of the Lower City than they spoke up.

"Um … Mister Hasryan, sir? I-I wanted to apologize."

Hasryan tilted his head to the side. "What for? Don't take the blame for Larryn's misbehaviour."

"No, no! I like Larryn. I mean …" Their small laugh betrayed their unease. "He scares me now, but before tonight, we had managed a truce, and the Shelter is wonderful. I hope I can return and help more one day. I like what he does there."

"It's incredible—the only place I ever called home," Hasryan agreed. "You may have to give Larryn time before you can return. I roughed him up, but he needed to hear it. But what are you sorry for, if not tonight?"

"For Camilla." Vellien stopped at the bottom of a staircase. "I'm the one who put it all together and understood she protected you, and I panicked because I had no idea what you meant to each other, so I told Kellian all about it, and it landed her in prison. I shouldn't have."

Shouldn't Vellien apologize to Camilla instead? What was he supposed to answer to that? No one ever said sorry to him, and niceties remained an unknown territory. "It's fine, kid," he said, embarrassed. "I wish she was with us tonight. I never got to thank her."

"I saw her earlier!" Vellien climbed the first steps, clearly eager to make it up to Hasryan. The assassin hurried after them, Larryn's heavy pot unwieldy in his arms. He shouldn't go so fast and risk losing his balance on these bridges—no railing would stop his fall— but neither did he want to linger. "I felt terrible, so I sought her out."

"How is she?"

"Fearful," Vellien said, "but not even for herself. She worried about whether you could escape, or how the Golden Table would go. She acted calm, but she asked me to sing. I know she finds the sound soothing—she thinks Alluma slips into my voice. A-anyway … I'm sure she would be thrilled to learn you sought Uncle Diel."

Hasryan laughed. "No doubt."

How often had Camilla strongly hinted he could trust her nephew? The idea hadn't entered his head on its own. She had aimed for this since the start, and he owed a lot of his current situation to her. Without Camilla's subtle pushing, Hasryan would have tried to vanish as soon as Kellian left with her. It wouldn't have crossed his mind to give Lord Dathirii early warning of her arrest, or to agree to work with him. He would have escaped Isandor to start from scratch elsewhere, alone and depressed. Instead, he had found new allies, extended his circle of trust, and tied himself down further. When he had chosen to trust Esmera with the secret of his presence with Camilla, he had chosen to stay and fight for his place here, no matter the cost. Camilla had offered him friends to stand by his side and, albeit unknowingly, the opportunity to reach both Cal and Larryn. It had been a long day, and his leg would hurt for a while, but as Hasryan led Vellien back toward Cal's home, he decided it had been a good one. Productive and heartwarming. For once, his life had turned around in the right direction. Then Vellien interrupted his thoughts.

"Sir, can I ask you another question?" they said. "The coup you mentioned in front of Larryn …"

Knots reappeared in Hasryan's stomach. He might come out of this mess with new allies, but the Dathirii no longer had a home, and who knew what had happened to several of them? "We're not going to the Dathirii Tower," he said. "Lord Dathirii can tell you more, but here's what I learned …"

Hasryan explained Lord Allastam's brutal maneuver earlier that day, and with every spoken word, he grew more convinced he had stayed to fight not only for his place in Isandor, but also for his friends'—which, starting tonight, would include House Dathirii.

Chapter Forty-One

BRANWEN snoozed against her uncle, clinging to a sliver of wakefulness only through her worried anticipation of Hasryan's return. Diel had an arm around her shoulders, and she suspected he was slipping in and out of sleep too. Neither of them had uttered a word for the last quarter-hour. Nothing else needed to be said.

She had first settled against him and nestled in his pillow bed to ask about Garith's performance at the Golden Table, and Uncle Diel had indulged her with surprising tales of bravery. He might have embellished them a tad, but Branwen didn't mind. Every time she thought of her favourite cousin being shoved into a wall by brutish Allastam soldiers, stones dropped to the bottom of her stomach. She preferred to imagine him standing up to a hostile council of nobles and slinging witty retorts at Hellion. It eased her fidgeting, and perhaps she wouldn't leave clear marks where she rubbed her fingers into her dress this time.

But then Diel had fanned the flames of her stress anew, albeit in a very different manner.

"I always thought the day I would lose this family, it would be to you and Garith—that I'd grow old and out of touch and would have the wisdom to pass it to the two of you."

She had laughed, unable to take him seriously. Why would he want her to lead? She pranced around town in disguises, chatted people up, and brought back gossip and funny tales. Garith made a better choice: he had a head for numbers, had sat at the Golden Table, and looked like the glorious golden elf a Head of the Dathirii House should. But Diel had squeezed her shoulder.

"Don't downplay your skills, Branwen. People trust you—not only nobles, but other citizens too. When they gossip to you like you're one of theirs, whether you're pretending or under your own name, they open a window into their lives. It's important to listen. Camilla taught me a lot about Isandor through her charges, and you through your rumours. What we do here"—he gestured at Cal's painfully colourful room—"it matters. Always, those living in bridges below can tell you what this city needs. The hardest is to make your peers listen, too. I never had the patience."

Branwen snorted. "And you think I have more? Don't talk like you're dead or gone, Uncle. We came close enough tonight, but I'm not letting you disappear."

"Good. I don't want to leave."

She leaned into him, still stunned by his words. She had no desire to lead House Dathirii, but his vote of confidence warmed her heart. She would always remember that her uncle—her worker of miracles, the uncle who'd braided her hair as a young girl and comforted her when she cried, the one who had been there when her parents vanished—believed in her. Maybe she ought to do the same.

Diel had fallen silent, leaving her to sort through her pride and exhaustion, and they had both almost gone to sleep when the front door creaked open. Vellien stepped in first, shoulders hunched, as if worried they were intruding—no doubt they hated not knocking before entering. Branwen jumped to her feet, and by the time Hasryan had slipped inside, she had wrapped her younger cousin in a tight hug. Her stomach unwound, and she only realized then how afraid she had been. Branwen compensated by pinching their cheek with a laugh. "Tell me all about your terrible kidnapping. We got something new in common!"

Vellien batted her hand away, their bright smile washing off the earlier worry. "I'm fine. I spent the evening in a room with Nevian." Their voice shook, and they avoided her gaze. Branwen knew they had omitted a lot.

"Tsk. No being whisked through intense flames? No simulating hot sex in the middle of the day to scare unwanted visitors away? You must have worthy news to share."

Hasryan's eyebrows shot up while Vellien turned redder than Cal's bright pillows. "I don't—no, no sex with Nevian! He's asexual and struggles with touch. Why would I ever do that?"

Branwen grinned. "Look at you, not even denying the interest! No wonder you were always so eager to go down there and help."

"They gripped his hand through the scarier parts," Hasryan added, his tone gentle and teasing.

Cal gasped, then squealed, then pressed a fist to his mouth to keep the rest of his emotions inside. It didn't last. "That is so adorable. I didn't even notice! But he's so grumpy and rude, and you're calm and sweet and patient and—"

"We brought food," Hasryan interrupted. "We'll need plates, Cal. Maybe think about the hundred ways you love this in your head while you get them?"

"Yes, okay, plates! Of course!" Cal climbed down from his large chair and hurried to the kitchen, still grinning.

Vellien looked like they wanted to melt into the floor. They stared at their shoes, and Hasryan rolled their eyes. "Sorry about that. Forgot how much Cal loves the faintest hint of romance that doesn't apply to him. He did that to Larryn and me early on, and stopping him required an intervention." Hasryan moved past Vellien to set the large pot in the centre of the room, and Branwen's stomach grumbled at the strong scent of rosemary. "Don't be afraid to tell him if it gets too much. He loves playing the local aromantic matchmaker, but he won't push boundaries."

A weak smile crossed Vellien's face, and they shook their head. Before they could answer, Branwen threw an arm around their shoulders and ruffled their hair. "Don't you think I'll forget, or that I won't tell Garith the moment we see him again!"

And then they would tease Vellien to death and enjoy themselves more than they ever had since this whole trade war started. Branwen grinned at her cousin. Their calm and lack of denial betrayed them even more than their flushed cheeks, and now she wanted to meet this mysterious apprentice she had saved ten days ago. If anything serious came out of this crush, she would tell Vellien they owed her for the new boyfriend! Branwen stepped back, the terrible night forgotten for a moment, and she realized Diel waited right behind her for his turn. When she released her cousin, he moved forward and embraced them.

"I'm glad you're safe," he said. "How are you feeling? Do you need to rest?"

"Eventually. Hasryan told me about the Tower. Do we … how is everyone? Did they hurt Kellian and Jaeger?"

"Yes, for Jaeger. Kellian …" Diel frowned. "We don't know. He never joined Branwen for the expedition, but your uncle can defend himself. We'll find out what happened."

Cal returned with plates, forks, and spoons, all balanced precariously in his short arms. Branwen and Arathiel hurried to help, and before long, they'd cleared a circle around the pot, with pillows as seats and a meal for everyone. Vellien passed their turn because they had already eaten, and after the first bite, Branwen was glad there would be more for the rest of them. The skipped dinner had left her ravenous, and instead of the consistent but dull food she'd expected, she discovered a perfectly-flavoured stew, with fresh carrots and the occasional beet to sweeten the deal. Her delighted exclamations brought laughter from everyone except Uncle Diel, who had engulfed half his plate already.

To her surprise, Diel didn't start planning a counterattack as they ate. He sat between Arathiel and Vellien, his gaze distant, his thoughts far away. Then his attention snapped back to the present, and his face lit with a smile. "Did I ever tell you about the time Aunt Camilla slapped my first boyfriend with her purse?"

Branwen and Vellien groaned—of course he had, a hundred times over—but it was already too late. Hasryan's startled laugh encouraged him, and Diel launched into the full tale of the jealous and abusive scum Camilla had chased away with her terrifying weapon. One anecdote led to another until Branwen and Vellien added to the family retellings. More than once, Arathiel slipped into the nearby bedroom to check on Varden, but he sat down and joined when they talked about her love of tea. Soon, even Hasryan had a story to share. He spoke slowly, as if uncertain he had any right to contribute, but his red eyes shone brightly, and the worry vanished from his expression. The change in his presence entranced Branwen, and she stared well past the end of the story. Only Cal didn't talk, and he seemed more than happy for the opportunity to refill his plate, even though he often glanced at it and the huge pile of cheese with more than a hint of nostalgia. Branwen couldn't blame him—she didn't remember when she had last tasted something so delicious. She wished Varden could have tried it, and the thought doused her mood.

"Vellien, do you still have the strength to call upon Alluma?" Her question interrupted the meal. "It's Varden. He's in the other room. Stable, but ..."

Vellien's eyes widened, and they scrambled to their feet. "Of course! How did I forget? I mean, I knew that was tonight's goal, and everyone is here, so—"

"You were kidnapped. Don't stress it," Branwen said, well aware Vellien would anyway. "Whenever you can, though, he'll need it. Avenazar dug deep enough to control him, and I worry about the damage done."

"He was himself enough to save me from the fire," Arathiel said, "but she's right. He's bony and feverish. A healer of your calibre could make a huge difference."

"I'm off, then! I'll do what I can."

They stood straight, almost saluting, and Cal snickered. "Watch it, my romantic friend. Nevian's already affecting you."

Vellien started, spluttered, then turned red once more and scampered away and into the bedroom. Branwen and Hasryan laughed at their hurry. She shouldn't poke so much fun at Vellien, but she knew they would be a good sport about it. And while her younger cousin had established that they were pansexual and their taste in people bypassed gender perception altogether, they had never brought anyone home, or even mentioned a potential crush. She teased Garith mercilessly, so why not Vellien? Family members learned to resist her constant assaults.

By the time the door closed behind Vellien, Diel was wiping the gravy with his fingers. Cal gaped at him, as if he couldn't handle a noble in his house, licking his plates, but her uncle acted like he didn't notice. "So your friend Larryn cooked this? I've never tasted something so delicious. He should apply his skills there instead of in kidnapping teenagers."

"He knows," Hasryan replied, "but Larryn forgets easily in the heat of things."

"He's not a bad person." Cal's cheerful tone had vanished, replaced by a fighting spirit—ready to defend his friend. "He makes mistakes—huge ones, bigger than the city's tallest towers!—but he dedicated his entire life to the Shelter. That's all he does, all the time! That great cuisine? On any other day, it's for the taste buds of those who can't afford a meal or a roof over their head. Once Larryn decides you're part of his people, there's no limit to what he'll do to protect you."

"I noticed." Bitterness still laced Diel's tone, but he raised a hand before Cal or Hasryan could protest. "Calm down, I won't hold it against him. Does his Shelter need funding?"

Arathiel, Hasryan, and Cal snorted all at once, then exchanged long and amused looks. Why did they think the suggestion ridiculous? House Dathirii might not have the money anymore— nor Diel the control to give it—but they would find their footing soon enough.

"Forget it," Hasryan said. "He'd never accept your gold, or even another noble's. He'll manage on his own. He always has."

"A shame."

"It might be, but some lines should not be crossed."

"You mean lines like kidnapping?" Branwen asked. In the finality of Hasryan's tone, she heard a story to unearth and a challenge. If she had the time, she would go digging into Larryn's past to find out why he would refuse help from nobles, but with Lord Allastam and Avenazar still alive, she filed it for later. Perhaps Vellien would know.

"Trust Larryn to cross the lines he shouldn't," Arathiel said, "but they're right. The best approach is to leave him alone. Why provoke him when he accomplishes so much on his own?"

Branwen huffed. "As long as he doesn't kidnap my precious cousin again."

She picked up the empty plates, then rose and brought them to the kitchen. Cal kept a tiny step in front of the water pump to help himself, and two more were gathering dust in a corner. Perhaps those were meant to save him the trouble of moving the steps around all the time, but if so… he obviously didn't use his counters much. Did he always eat out? She left the dishes there, slipping from the kitchens to Cal's bedroom.

Varden rested on the bed, and Vellien had pulled the thick blankets back. They had set one hand on his forearm and the other on his head, and they cast a pale light against the dark blue walls. A line barred Vellien's forehead, and the glow of their palms wavered in intensity as they muttered to themself. Hard work. She knew Varden would need it, but worry constricted her insides.

Branwen scanned the room for a chair. When she found none, she dragged a pillow closer and sat on the floor with her back against the bed. She closed her eyes, figuring she'd rest them while Vellien continued their work. Just a moment. She wanted to be awake when Varden came to.

THE cracks in Keroth's mind shield widened under Avenazar's assault. Varden fought back, struggling against the weighty presence ripping his last defences apart. It wouldn't hold. Branwen had arrived. She sounded distant, as did her companions, but Varden knew they'd come to rescue him. He was no longer alone. They wouldn't reach him in time, though. Already, Avenazar trampled through the shreds of his protection, tightening his grip around Varden's mind and squeezing out the last of his strength. Bright flames appeared in his hands, and he panicked as his body prepared to strike. So close. Varden tried to stop himself, but he couldn't handle the pressure on his mind—Avenazar's spell was crushing his skull, flattening his willpower into nothingness, and creating new holds for the wizard's use. His senses were dimming, his surroundings growing farther away as fire lashed out of his hands and cut a line to Branwen.

Her scream woke him with a start. Powerful nausea leaped to his throat and head, and the world spun around him. He squeezed his eyes shut. He hadn't hit her, he knew he hadn't, but the vivid dream clung to his mind and sickened him. Varden struggled to slow his ragged breath when a firm hand touched his forearm through the blankets.

"It's okay. You're safe, sir. I'm sorry I triggered that memory."

The calm voice belonged to a teenage elf, sitting by his side with an apologetic smile. Freckles lined their cheeks and nose, making their round face appear even more youthful. They wore clean clothes with a sharp but simple cut. Varden blinked several times, struggling to gather his thoughts. He was in a bed—on a comfortable mattress—with a wealthy elf by his side. No longer in the enclave. Branwen had come for him.

"You're a Dathirii."

He croaked the words, then tried to clear his parched throat with a painful cough. The elf reached backward and handed him a waterskin before helping Varden to sit up to drink. The few vertical inches increased the tilt of the world underneath him, so Varden gulped water in a hurry before lying down once more. His companion smiled.

"I'm Branwen's youngest cousin, Vellien, and I will be your healer. Please use they pronouns when referring to me." Their official tone turned shy, and Varden nodded to indicate he had heard. "You're lucky, in a way. I have developed a certain … expertise in countering Avenazar's brand of mental destruction, so you're in good hands."

How had Vellien even practised that? Varden's hazy mind couldn't find an answer, but he thanked Keroth for the care. The very thought of healing himself drained him—the thought of doing anything at all seemed exhausting, in truth. At least he could rest now. His nightmare was over.

"How bad is it?" he asked.

"Surprisingly good, if I daresay. I believe you have all your memories, which is more than I could say of Nevian at first, and—"

"Did you say Nevian?" Varden's pulse quickened, and his breath caught. Avenazar had described Nevian's death in vivid detail, imprinting the scene in Varden's mind as surely as if he had witnessed it. But he had lied so often and falsified so many thoughts and memories over the last ten days … Varden didn't know what to trust anymore. "Nevian is alive?"

"He is. Alive, and growing more stubborn and healthy with every passing day." Vellien grinned, and their cheeks flushed.

Varden stared at them, surprised by how attached the young elf seemed. Never in two years at the enclave had anyone cared for Nevian like that. A shadow flitted through Vellien's expression, however, and Varden braced for the awful news. "Avenazar had left him in a horrible state. The first time, I didn't even know where to start. So many of his mental connections were destroyed … I jogged his memory, then followed in his mind as it tried to rebuild itself, helping him along. It's a complex process, and he did most of the work, no matter how exhausting."

Relief surged through Varden and he forced a smile to his lips, fighting back the tears. "That does sound like him."

"You're in a much better condition," Vellien said. "All the important parts are there, safeguarded."

"Oh. I …" A solid lump rolled up Varden's throat, blocking any other words. He had done it. Somehow, through the daily assaults and final, crushing spell, he had kept himself intact. Tears welled in his eyes, and he blinked them back. He had done it. He was in a bed, safe, and he had salvaged everything that mattered. He was still a priest of Keroth, still an Isbari who loved to draw. He still loved men, and he remembered saving Branwen and protecting Nevian. He had won. Even if nightmares plagued him for years, even if he needed weeks in a bed to recover, he had won.

"That's … thank you," he whispered.

"Sir, I'm not the one who deserves this gratitude. I solidified your memories and lessened the headache, but you held yourself together long before I arrived."

A stifled laugh escaped Varden. Vellien was right. He hadn't had any help in that cell, couldn't even sense Keroth through his iced shackles. His only support had come from Jilssan's willingness to treat his burns and push Avenazar to stop torturing him. It hadn't prevented Avenazar from attempting his final spell. Yet he'd held on. She had been wrong about his pride—it had saved him in the end. Varden allowed the thought to comfort him like a fire dancing in a small hearth. Despite Vellien's efforts, his back throbbed along the burn marks, and his head pounded.

"I can wake up Branwen if you want," Vellien suggested before motioning toward the ground at the bottom of his bed. "I think she meant to wait for you, but we've all had a long and difficult day."

Varden stretched his neck enough to see the top of Branwen's head. Pale light filtered through the window, reflecting copper on her brown hair. Not a single one of them looked singed, and Varden tried to dismiss his earlier nightmare. "Please."

Vellien grinned, then prodded Branwen's side with their booted foot. She groaned and pushed it back, but they insisted until she glared and mumbled, "What do you want?" so low Varden barely distinguished the words. Her cousin laughed.

"Your friend is awake, sleepyhead."

"Morning," Varden greeted her.

Branwen's head jolted, and she scrambled to her feet with such speed she grabbed Vellien's arm for balance. A wide smile lit her features, and its warmth spread to Varden. Vellien wished them a good night—what remained of it—and left them.

"How are you?" Branwen asked.

"My body feels like it's been caught in a rock slide and my mind like it drowned." And yet he couldn't remember being so relaxed. When had he last been surrounded by friends and felt safe? Short meditation spells in Keroth's great brazier couldn't wash away the constant anxiety of life in Isandor's Myrian enclave. Two years waiting for the axe to fall, and now he had survived even that. Varden wished he could clear all the cobwebs in his head, but he suspected Vellien would have if it had been possible. Varden smiled at his impatience—how often had he scolded Nevian for trying to substitute divine healing for rest? "Yet … I feel like myself, and that's nothing short of a miracle."

Branwen sat into the recently-vacated chair, leaned forward, and mussed up his hair with a chuckle. "You look terrible. Pretty sure we can arrange a hot bath for you, unless the whole fire-cleansing thing is literal and you only need wood to burn."

"Water's good." Branwen's forced cheer didn't escape Varden, and he examined her, a sense of unease creeping into him. She grinned, yet the mirth never reached her eyes, and her shoulders stayed slumped. "I missed a lot while I was in there, didn't I? I can tell you're smiling for my sake."

She sighed, and the mask slipped off. "I'm sorry. I'm not faking it, I promise. I couldn't think of anything but reaching you over the past ten days. Meanwhile, my family lost its titles and home, and Lord Allastam even sent Uncle Diel to the Myrian enclave."

Varden's ears buzzed, and he struggled for a reassuring answer. No one knew better than he how awful that place could be. The edges of his vision blurred, and his head lightened, as if he'd faint soon. "Is he … is he still there?"

"No, no! Oh gosh, you're so pale, I'm sorry." She reached for his forehead. "We brought him back, same time as you. Avenazar never had a chance to lay a finger on him."

"Oh. Good." Relief washed over him, yet Branwen's words sparked one dreadful question in his mind. "Avenazar isn't dead, is he?"

"No." She pulled her legs up onto the chair and wrapped her arms around them. "He disappeared when things got bad. Half your temple collapsed on us. Without Isra's bubble, we wouldn't have survived."

"Isra's … bubble?"

How did Isra fit into all of this? He thought of her visit in the prison and the remorse she'd shown. Perhaps she had been more sincere than he had believed. Always hard to tell with her: one day, she was chirpy and nice, and the next, she treated him like dirt.

"She helped. Led us to you, although not without pressure," Branwen said, and that sounded more like her. "We had to leave her there. Jilssan should protect her—she's a callous asshole, but she obviously cared about that girl."

"Isra is the only person outside herself she cares about, yes." He struggled with every hint that Branwen had received inside help from the enclave—and not only Isra, but perhaps Jilssan too? If Avenazar learned … Varden didn't even like them, yet his stomach clenched at what would follow. No one deserved this. He stirred, his urge to leave growing. Avenazar had no limits, no sense of priorities beyond what revenge and wounded pride dictated. They would need help, and they would need it fast. Except he was stuck in his bed and couldn't do anything, not yet. He had to pace himself, heal his frayed mind and body. He ran a hand through his greasy curls and groaned.

"Are you okay?" Branwen asked.

"I'm so … tired." Varden closed his eyes, his breathing unsteady. He wanted to cry—to just let it all out—but the tears wouldn't come. All the exhaustion and relief stayed bottled inside. "I spent all my life imagining the moment Myrians would get me, and when they did, it was every bit as awful as I had predicted, if not worse."

She didn't answer, only reached out and squeezed his forearm. What could she say, anyway? She had dragged him out of this nightmare before it was too late, and nothing else mattered. He was safe now. Safe, but exhausted. "I need to rest. Could you … talk? About anything—unimportant things, funny things, whatever you want."

In the silence with his eyes closed, he might forget Branwen's presence by his side. Varden feared the nightmares would return, that he would sink into a fitful sleep, expecting a cell door to open with a creak and Avenazar to step in. Perhaps a friend's voice could keep the memories at bay. At first, she didn't answer, as if no inconsequential topic came to her mind, and Varden wondered how much had happened to staunch the flow of anecdotes.

"We spent dinner retelling stories about my aunt. Well, great aunt." She grinned and leaned forward. "You'll get to meet her soon, I'm sure, so let me tell you everything!"

Then she was off, repeating the tales they'd apparently shared a few hours ago. Varden enjoyed what he heard, along with the promise of discovering more of Branwen's wonderful family. Talking about them had helped her manage the stress of the enclave, and today, her words wrapped around him like a second blanket, warm and comforting. Varden drifted back to sleep, secure in his friend's presence.

Chapter Forty-Two

"I THINK we'll have to switch quarters."

Yultes stood at the entrance of Jaeger's room, the door closed behind him. His hesitant voice had shattered the silence and drawn the steward out of his daze. Jaeger had been staring at his hands again, his attention focused on the new scuffs and scars, half-stunned from a too-short night. How long had he slept? Not enough, of that he was certain. He had flopped down on the blankets after Diel's departure, filled with little beyond the throbbing pain of his wounds. He used to cherish the few hours by himself, stretching out over the mattress, knowing Diel was but a few doors away. Over the last two weeks, however, Jaeger had chosen to share Diel's bed and bring what comfort he could. He had looked forward to the sanctuary of his single bed when everything calmed down. Nothing had, and despite his bone-deep exhaustion, it had taken a long time for Jaeger to fall asleep.

Now the sun had returned, and all he knew for certain about Diel was that he'd reached the Myrian enclave. Nausea mixed with his anxiety until Jaeger grew convinced his heart would fail. Yultes' unwelcome intrusion didn't help.

"Eager to live next to Our Great Saviour Hellion? Is he moving into Diel's quarters too, or will he wait until he's dead for sure?"

"He won't wait." Intense bitterness laced Yultes' tone, and Jaeger looked up. Large bags hung under his eyes, and his mouth twisted into an angry line. Shouldn't he gloat at their success? But Yultes hadn't planned this, Jaeger reminded himself. He'd attempted to flee with Jaeger. At the end of the day, however, he had accepted the desk. "You shouldn't stay so close to Hellion," Yultes said, "but that's not the main reason to move."

"What is, then?" Jaeger didn't trust this. Yes, Yultes had tried to escape with him, and yes, Diel's fate unsettled him, but he had mocked Jaeger for decades. Even on his best days—rare occurrences—Yultes had listened to Hellion's advice, followed his arrogant lead, and expressed clear disdain for any household staff, Jaeger chief among them. This sudden change of heart didn't fit the pattern, creating more fear than hope.

"I'll need your help," Yultes said.

Jaeger scoffed. A single day in his position and Yultes already pleaded for support. Did he think keeping the chaos of Diel's life under control was an easy task? If he knew every tiny detail Jaeger oversaw while Lord Dathirii met with merchants and nobles, he would give up right away. "Enlighten me, Yultes, because I don't follow your logic." With each word Jaeger hammered out, the frustration of the last day surfaced, piercing through his control, leaking into his voice. "You'll dislodge me from quarters I've inhabited for over a century 'for my safety,' hoping my overflowing gratitude will allow me to forget who you're working with and what he did to Diel, the one elf I've loved from the moment I laid eyes on him—loved to the very core of my being. You, after decades of snide insults. You, who didn't even refuse my position when offered. You—" He laughed, his control fraying, tears choking his voice. "You think I want to help you any more than I want to help Hellion?"

The question hung in the space between them, unanswered. Jaeger ran a shaky hand through his dishevelled hair, grounding himself with the sharp pain every movement brought. He was losing his self-control—the last stable element of his life. Jaeger only desired arms around his waist, squeezing, reassuring, but that embrace and the warm, loving voice that accompanied it were gone, ripped away. Jaeger curled up on himself, ignoring the strain in his muscles, and he stared ahead. He couldn't crack, not in front of Yultes.

"Beat me up again if you want to, but I will never help either of you."

"Jaeger ... You chose the location of my quarters. Do you remember?"

A map of the tower surged to the forefront of his mind, each room falling into its place along the tree-like structure. No one knew the Dathirii Tower better than him, especially since they had reshaped it and relocated everyone forty years ago. He didn't have the patience to recall Yultes' quarters and guess at this charade. "Spare me your games and get to the point."

"I'm above Garith—nice large rooms, but rowdy, especially at night." Yultes smirked, and Jaeger blinked at him. Long seconds passed while Jaeger struggled with the meaning of this, until his exhausted mind remembered the sex noises often drifting out of Garith's always-open window. A brief smile flitted to his lips. Placing Yultes above him was a petty but satisfying revenge. "The point," Yultes continued, "is that you would be close to him. Able to talk, plan, scheme. I think you misunderstood, Jaeger. I …" His voice faltered, and he leaned against the wall. "I need your help to counter Hellion, not to smooth his way into leadership."

Did Yultes mean to fight? How bizarre. A part of Jaeger wanted to laugh, the other to snap at Yultes. He did neither. Every passing minute, the situation became more surreal. Soon, he might assume he had never woken up, that the pain in his muscles and heart could still vanish. He stared ahead, willing that to happen, knowing it wouldn't. He didn't answer Yultes—what was the point? They could turn Hellion's life into a nightmare and it wouldn't bring Diel back. Jaeger hated staying in this tower, left behind, unable to save him in any way. He prayed Branwen would come through, but morning had dawned, and no one had heard anything about them. What if they had not returned? What if they had all died?

"Jaeger?"

Worry pierced Yultes' voice and grounded Jaeger. Whether or not anyone survived the enclave didn't change a simple fact: he had promised Diel not to abandon their family, to help Garith and

Branwen through this ordeal. They deserved better than Hellion. Jaeger closed his eyes, directing his mental energy to the layers of hurt, physical and otherwise, visualizing them as a massive cobweb. Slowly, he gathered the threads in his hands, creating a large ball, heavy and sticky and disgusting. Jaeger imagined a shitslide under it, plunging into the city to dump its contents into the Reonne. With a deep breath, he let go, releasing the grief and exhaustion and despair.

They would come back, they always did, the spider in his mind spinning until he couldn't ignore it any longer, but for now, it was enough. Every inch of his body still throbbed with pain, but he had found his focus.

"Help me gather my clothes. Don't disrupt the order." He pushed himself to his feet, and the world spun around him. Jaeger waited for the nausea to pass, then turned to the mess of his desk. The paperwork that mattered would have been in Diel's quarters or office, but he assembled the handful of personal trinkets he'd amassed over the years—almost all from his decade travelling with Diel—and stacked his most precious books. By the time he'd gathered the strict minimum, his heart was as heavy as the pile in his arms.

YULTES' quarters surprised Jaeger. He had arrived at his door exhausted, feverish from the difficult trek down the stairs, barely able to stand. When he turned his head too fast, his vision darkened at the edges, threatening to wink out entirely. Jaeger needed to lie down, and he had expected to do so in drab and hostile quarters, undecorated or filled with markers of pride—elven sculptures, paintings, or other objects in the Dathirii colours. Instead, he found plants. Plants on every shelf, plants hanging from above, plants climbing over the bed and across the ceiling. His nose registered them as fast as his eyes—the sweet roses, the poignant rosemary, the fresh mint. Sunlight streamed through them, casting shadows in a myriad of shapes, granting the quarters a warm and lively atmosphere. Jaeger leaned against the assault, dizzy from so many scents at once. Herbs, he realized, and as his gaze swept across the room, he noticed most of the greenery was comestible. Chrysanthemums, daisies, impatiens, sorrel, and even dandelions. Jaeger's stomach squeezed as centuries-old memories resurfaced. He had snatched several of these from the city's gardens as a teenager, trying to assuage the hunger gnawing at him or complement the meagre meals he shared with his parents. He shut his eyes and focused instead on the homemade teas Camilla prepared with these. Better times.

"Do you cook with them?" Jaeger hadn't expected to find this specific array of plants in Yultes' quarters, and he caught the flash of surprise on the other elf's expression at the question.

"No. I only taste," he answered, wistful. "I once met someone who experimented with them. I loved ..."

Yultes reached for the nearby mint and closed his eyes. Jaeger recognized his own behaviour from mere seconds ago—his fight against memories buried deep. What in the world was happening?

Diel had been convinced Yultes hid something from them, a secret Jaeger deemed better left unearthed. Yet now that he stood in these private quarters—a literal secret garden, obviously reserved for a trusted few—Jaeger couldn't let go of the opportunity to dig.

"… them?" he said, hoping to finish Yultes' sentence.

Yultes heaved a sigh. "I did, and I handled it wrong. Diel falls in love all the time, but I … I'm the opposite. I thought I never would. I'm not sure I will again."

Jaeger regretted asking. Why did he ever imagine he wanted to know about Yultes' problems? Between Nicole's righteous fury at him and this admission of "handling it wrong," the outline of a revolting tale appeared. He had no desire to discover more. Not now, with his head spinning, his heart shrivelling, and no power to act on the obvious injustice that had happened here. If Yultes needed someone to confide in, he had chosen the wrong person at the wrong time.

"Your plants will have better light in my quarters," he said, ignoring Yultes' heartspill. "There's no higher tower to block it through my window."

Yultes stared at him, aware of the abrupt topic change. The wistfulness vanished from his expression and voice as he moved on. "Lovely," he said, and he strode through the plants, pushing away the thick leaves of a hanging specimen to open the wardrobe. He placed each of Jaeger's shirts and outfits one by one, careful not to break the sequence of colours.

Jaeger sought a desk but only found a small surface buried under paper and cacti, so he decided to put his stack down on the ground.

His wobbly arms almost dropped the heavy books, and he set a hand on top of them for a moment to regain balance. An hour—two at most—awake, and his strength had already vanished. How could he help fight Hellion when he struggled to stay standing and align two coherent thoughts? Jaeger pinched the bridge of his nose—Diel's mannerism, one he'd picked up with time. With a pang of sadness, he dropped his hand.

"Any chance Vellien returned to the tower recently?" he asked.

"Afraid not. I inquired overnight, and most of the family has vanished." Yultes slid the wardrobe closed and moved to the bed, clearing it of a nightshirt. For the first time, Jaeger noticed the signs of Yultes' own exhaustion. His pale hair fell into his face, his shoulders slumped under a rumpled shirt, and his voice had lost the haughty tone he had exhibited when he sought an audience. Perhaps this went beyond tiredness, though. Ever since Yultes had come running into Diel's office to incite Jaeger to flee, he'd acted like a different person—like he couldn't be bothered to maintain a façade he'd spent decades perfecting. "We have no news from Branwen in the enclave, and still no explanation of Kellian's whereabouts. Rumours have Camilla and Vellien at the Sapphire Guard's headquarters late yesterday afternoon, but I've yet to confirm if they stayed. Word of this takeover must have spread, and they steered clear. I'm sorry. It's just us and Garith."

No news of either Branwen or Kellian. Jaeger gritted his teeth. It only meant they hid, nothing worse. "Then get Garith, and tell him I'll need the strongest bottle in his cache."

"Please, Jaeger. I promise working with me isn't that difficult."

"It's for the *pain*, Yultes!" Jaeger's annoyance peaked, then fell as quickly as it had risen when he noticed the other elf's smirk. What had the world come to if Yultes joked with him? "Just go."

A soft laugh escaped Yultes, but he didn't move. They lapsed into silence while he rocked on his heels and slid two fingers through his silky hair. His mouth opened, closed again, then he gestured at the bed without a word. Jaeger would welcome rest if he didn't fear he would only wake up a week later.

"Business first," he said, "but thank you."

Yultes did not leave right away. He turned to the plants, looking at each of them one at a time, giving Jaeger the distinct impression he mentally addressed them one by one. Watching felt like intruding, so Jaeger focused on the growing daylight through the window. He couldn't reconcile this current shyness with the snide arrogance Yultes had displayed for a century. The clash baffled him and set him on edge. What should he expect now? Disparaging comments or a clumsy willingness to help? Yultes hadn't done enough to offset decades of insults and deserve a second chance, yet Jaeger saw no way around it. They needed to work together. It left a bad taste in his mouth, but he reminded himself Diel had reached out to Yultes, too. If co-operation staved off Hellion's ambition, then Jaeger could swallow whatever strange mood Yultes had found himself in—as long as no one expected him to do so silently. They would act as equals, or Yultes would soon discover Jaeger could do far worse than quarters filled with the melody of Garith's lively sex life.

GARITH slammed the door shut again as soon as he spotted Yultes. Although he had expected to meet hostility when he had knocked, this morning continued to surprise Yultes. He hadn't even uttered a word yet.

"Get lost," Garith called. "You're wasting your time."

"Don't be childish, Garith. Open the door. We need to talk."

"Forget it! Hellion can shove his columns of numbers deep up his ass while you lick them for all I care. I'm not working for either of you!"

What a lovely image. Garith didn't make a habit of vulgarities—he usually let Branwen handle those. This conversation promised a difficult and exhausting struggle, with wonderful results. "Jaeger—"

The door opened, cutting Yultes off. Garith's hair fell down his shoulders, and he leaned against the door jamb. "Are you threatening him? Is that your pretty little plan? Diel isn't here to blackmail us anymore, so you'll just use Jaeger instead! He's *family*." Garith clutched the doorway, his knuckles turning white. Yultes caught a whiff of strong alcohol on his breath. "If you had a sliver of decency, you wouldn't dare touch him. But I bet you cheered when they hit him, you piece of shit. This is all you ever wanted, isn't it? Now you can lord your power over us without Diel's interruption because he's gone. Shipped out for torture—dead! So don't you dare 'Jaeger' me. Uncle Diel wouldn't give in to your pathetic threats, and neither will I."

Garith could have continued for another five minutes without surprising Yultes, unlike Jaeger's previous outburst—the steward had never yelled or lost control in front of Yultes before, and the flipped perspective had only driven his decision home. Yultes bided his time, even if none of this was new. He deserved their hasty conclusions and subsequent rants, but he would rather discuss future plans than listen to Garith empty his heart.

"Is it my turn now?" Yultes asked.

"No."

Garith slammed the door once more, and the noise echoed down the corridor. Yultes gritted his teeth, his frustration building. "Garith, come on. This is ridiculous!" Silence met his exclamation, so he hammered on the wood until, *finally*, Garith opened it again. Yultes massaged his irritated knuckles. "Jaeger had a favour to ask."

"And you're the messenger?"

"What great deductive skills." Yultes couldn't contain his sarcasm, but this time when Garith grabbed the door to close it, he was ready. He shoved his foot in the way, blocking it, and he dropped his voice. "I'm serious. He'll move into my quarters, above yours, and for the moment, he has requested your hidden cache of strong alcohol to accompany any … traitorous discussion we might have. Grab a bottle and your account books, and make your way to my rooms. Try not to insult the Allastam soldiers still roaming. They wouldn't appreciate your offers to lick elven rear ends."

Garith snorted, but no smile reached his lips. He stared at Yultes, searching for duplicity, a hint of hope behind the wariness. As Yultes withstood the examination, he was struck by how much Garith resembled his uncle—from the green of his eyes to their body shape, these two had come out of the same Dathirii mold. The accountant didn't have Diel's natural stateliness, though. No one could replace his stepbrother, not truly, and the similarities only twisted at Yultes' stomach. Garith clacked his tongue, then let go of the door.

"I'm afraid the bottle is about to run dry," Garith said, "but I have others hidden. Stay here."

Garith slipped back into his quarters, and Yultes listened to the sounds of him rummaging around. A few minutes later, he reappeared, two bottles stuck under his arms, several account books piled in his arms, and a newfound smile on his lips.

"Which one of Hellion's awful plans are we stopping today?"

Yultes laughed, then checked both ends of the corridor to make sure no one had heard Garith's quip. He would have to be wary of spending too much time with these two and blowing his cover. "Household staff cuts. We must slash through our wages and pare down the cost to a minimum. He recommended throwing as many in the streets as needed, but ..." He had done that once—the biggest mistake and most heinous act of his life. Never again. "We'll find another way, won't we?"

Garith's mouth twisted in a grimace. "There's always one," he said, "but if I learned one thing yesterday, it's to ask, 'at what cost?' before I dive."

Yultes hadn't expected anything so pessimistic from Garith, and his gaze slid to the half-empty bottle. A rough night for everyone involved. "If I learned one thing from your uncle, Garith, it's that we have to dive anyway."

He didn't believe it, yet as he watched Garith straighten with determination, Yultes found he wanted to. Diel's parting words had shaken him, confronting him with a single truth: the expectations of others did not force his actions. He chose them—chose to abide by them or defy them. From now on, his decisions would ripple and impact dozens of people. If he didn't dive, they would drown. They needed help, and Diel believed he could do it. He should. For too long, Yultes had pretended he didn't see those sinking below him, convincing himself he wasn't supposed to. Not anymore. He would accomplish what little he could, however late it was, even at the risk of drowning himself.

Character Guide

THE following is a list of characters featured in *City of Betrayal* with short descriptions to help readers navigate the story. The "titles" assigned to each character are meant to poke fun at them—don't take them too seriously.

House Dathirii

Diel Dathirii (Lord Dathirii), Eternal Idealist, he/him
Head of the Dathirii House, loves political fights and people, but none more than Jaeger.

Jaeger, Stalwart Steward, he/him
Diel's personal steward, the logistics behind the passion, a stickler for titles even for his long-time love.

Branwen Dathirii, Master of Disguises, she/her
Dathirii spymaster, her heart is as big as her multi-gender wardrobe.

Garith Dathirii, Number One Flirt, he/him
Dathirii coinmaster. Has ladies over at irregular hours, beware.
Vellien Dathirii, Anxious Healer, they/them

Dathirii priest of Alluma, youngest cousin. Would sing more if it didn't focus everyone's attention on them.

Camilla Dathirii, Tea of Kindness, she/her
Diel's aunt, has retired from wilder years to grant tea, cookies, and wisdom to those in need.

Kellian Dathirii, Stiff Guard, he/him
Captain of the Dathirii Guards, spends many hours wishing people would stop taking huge risks.

Yultes Dathirii, Professional Impostor, he/him
Main Dathirii liaison to House Allastam. Diel's step-brother and Larryn's father. Is great at lying to himself and others.

Hellion Dathirii, 'Cunning' Shitlord, he/him
Yultes's best friend. Still thinks elves and nobles are superior. Doesn't get along with Diel.

House Allastam

Lord Allastam, Bitter Crusader, he/him
Head of House Allastam. Would watch the world burn to get his way and avenge his murdered wife.

Drake Allastam, High on Privilege, he/him
Lord Allastam's son, heir to the house leadership, typically responds to 'no' and 'fuck you' with violence. Long history of harassing

Larryn.

Mia Allastam, the Discreet Daughter. she/her
Lord Allastam's daughter, often kept away by chronic pain and the family's overbearing protectiveness. The only person Drake listens to.

House Brasten

Amake Brasten (Lady Brasten), Slicing Politician, she/her
Head of House Brasten, ready to own the Golden Table on her own if needed.

Arathiel Brasten, Drifter from the Past, he/him
Stayed trapped for a hundred and thirty years in a mysterious Well that drained his senses. Returned to Isandor recently and stayed at the Shelter.

Lindi Brasten, Afflicted Dancer, she/her
Arathiel's sister, sick when he left for the Well. Dead.

The Shelter

Larryn, Anger Stew, he/him
Owner of and cook at the Shelter. Rages against the machine (and everyone else, really). Member of the Halfies Trio.

Hasryan, Assassin Seeks Friends, he/him

Once Brune's favourite assassin. His sass is as deadly as his blades. Member of the Halfies Trio.

Cal, Luck's Generous Hand, he/him

Priest of Ren, the luck deity. Lover of cheese, quick to develop friend crushes and act on them. Member of the Halfies Trio.

Nevian, Stubborn Pupil, he/him

Avenazar's old apprentice, now hiding at the Shelter. Still determined to learn magic.

Efua, Genius Letter Girl, she/her

Orphan living at the Shelter. Larryn's unofficial little sister. Works as a letter delivery girl.

Jim, Hard-Working Father, he/him

First owner of the shelter. Adoptive father for Larryn and Efua. Dead.

The Myrian Enclave

Master Avenazar, Destructive Ego, he/him

Head of the Myrian enclave. Ruthless and powerful mage who avenges every slight.

Varden Daramond, Gentle Flames, he/him

High Priest of Keroth, imprisoned for treason. Talented artist, loving soul, powerful fire-wielder.

Master Jilssan, Ambitious Pragmatic, she/her
Transmutation specialist and Isra's master. Always ready to do what it takes to survive.

Isra, Conflicted Princess, she/her
Jilssan's apprentice. Hides self-doubts and secrets behind layers of racism and overconfidence.

Other Figures of Note

Lord William, Single Noble, he/him
Presides the Golden Table but has no House. Loves drama in many shapes.

Sora Sharpe, Unapologetic Law Enforcer, she/her
Investigator for Isandor's Sapphire Guards in charge of finding Hasryan. Hates political games.

Lai, Confident Informant, ne/ner
An informant for Sora Sharpe. In a queerplatonic relationship with one of House Dathirii's kitchen boys.

Brune, Ruthless Mercenary Leader, she/her
Leader of the Crescent Moon mercenary, powerful mage, Hasryan's old boss. Has hands in every pockets. Loves the colour brown.

Nicole, Iron-Grip Cook, she/her

In charge of the Dathirii's kitchens. Don't mention Yultes to her.

<u>Alton, Considerate Spy, he/him</u>
Part of Branwen's network of spies and friends. They disagree on fashion, though.

Noble Families of Isandor

<u>House Lorn</u>
Founding family, and currently the biggest family in Isandor. Holds more seats on the Golden Table than any other House.

<u>House Allastam</u>
Second biggest family in Isandor. Its rise to power can be attributed almost entirely to the current Lord Allastam.

<u>House Balthazar</u>
A rising star in Isandor politics. Its wealth increase is recent but, speculation says, unlikely to last. Third biggest house.

<u>House Dathirii</u>
Founding family and the only elven noble house.

<u>House Brasten</u>
House of medium importance. Has managed to retain a seat on the Golden Table despite the family's often deadly hereditary illness.
<u>House Carrington</u>

Founding family that fell from power after a botanical spell gone wrong infected and killed half their family. Still sits at the Golden Table.

House Serringer

Small house that has a fur monopoly. One seat at the Golden Table.

House Almanza

Minor Isandor house. One seat at the Golden Table.

About the Author

Claudie Arseneault is an asexual and aromantic-spectrum writer hailing from the very-French Quebec City. Her long studies in biochemistry and immunology often sneak back into her science-fiction, and her love for sprawling casts invariably turns her novels into multi-storylined wonders. Claudie is a founding member of The Kraken Collective and is well-known for her involvement in solarpunk, her database of aro and ace characters in speculative fiction, and her unending love of squids.

You can also always find all of her books at
claudiearseneault.com

Want More?

At The Kraken Collective, we know how frustrating it can be to reach the end of a book and want more. Within the following pages, you'll find books with a similar feel to help you scratch that reading itch and why we're recommending them.

We hope our suggestions will help you find your next favourite read!

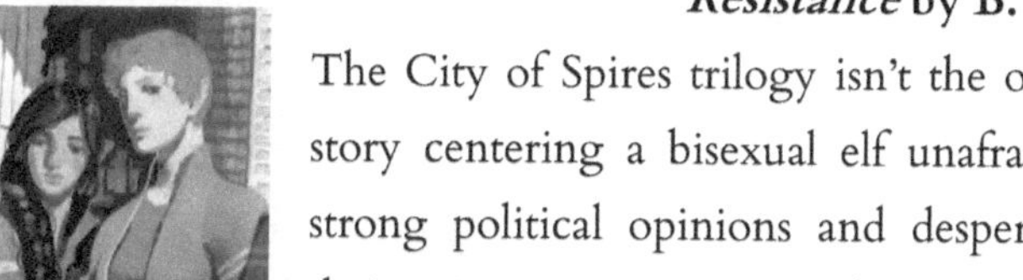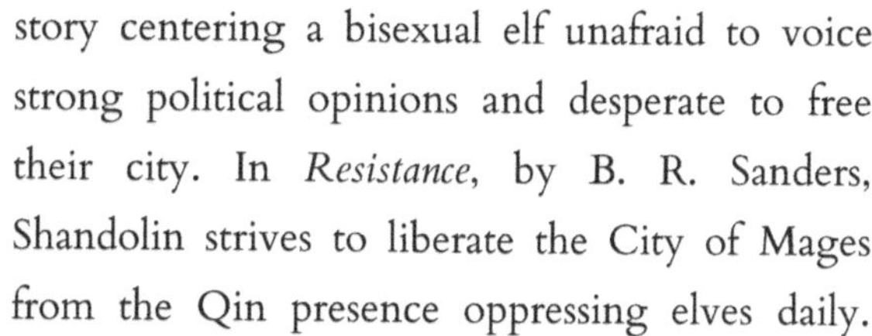

Resistance **by B. R. Sanders**

The City of Spires trilogy isn't the only Kraken story centering a bisexual elf unafraid to voice strong political opinions and desperate to free their city. In *Resistance*, by B. R. Sanders, Shandolin strives to liberate the City of Mages from the Qin presence oppressing elves daily. But in order to do so, she must rally friends, lovers, and all elves of the city to her cause. *Resistance* is a fast-paced tale of trust through rocky relationships and political genius, all set in the intricate and fascinating world of Aerdh.

A Promise Broken by Lynn E. O'Connacht

If you're looking for more political back and forth as well as aromantic and asexual representation, but underpinned by deeply personal stories, check out *A Promise Broken*, by Lynn E. O'Connacht. When four-year-old Eiryn seemingly summons rain at her mother's funeral, the city council fears  she's upset the balance of the world. As her new guardian, her uncle Arèn must learn the ropes of parenting while trying to protect her from harm. Yet all Eiryn wants is to make everyone happy even as grief and fear tear at them. *A Promise Broken* is a beautiful tale of kindness and grief that will slip into your heart quietly and stay with you.

Learn more about these and other titles at
www.krakencollectivebooks.com!

ACKNOWLEDGEMENTS
REMERCIEMENTS

I TALKED quite a lot about the origins of Isandor in *City of Strife*'s acknowledgements, and while those who helped me start this universe will always remain close to my heart, it takes more than a spark to write such a massive project. My eternal thanks to Marianne, who devours everything I write as I write it, to Audrey for the hours of roleplay, to Jonathan who has shared so many hours of plotting, and to Katie and Brenda, whose early enthusiasm let me believe I had a worthwhile story. You were with me long before I even published *City of Strife.*

So many new voices have fuelled my creative energies since publication. There are not enough heartfelt thanks in this world for the readers, reviewers, and fellow writers who have fallen in love with these characters and their story. Your fan art and excited messages brightened my days this year. A very special thank you to the aromantic and asexual communities—little is more motivating and heartwarming than your warm welcome of this representation and the many heartfelt thanks I received. So many of you embraced this story and these characters, especially in the aromantic community, and I want you all to know you will always be the heart of my stories; the people I write for.

Finally, to my patrons, whether you joined in April when I opened the Patreon, or recently: I am so very grateful for every dollar you choose to give, every comment and like and vote. I'm glad we share a tiny space. Thank you so much.

Et au risque de me répéter, je tiens à remercier ma famille pour son soutien, ma jumelle pour les extraordinaires couvertures, mon copain pour le soutien à la maison et toute ma petite communauté d'écriture de Québec (vous savez qui vous êtes—vous faites NaNo avec moi à chaque année!).

Merci à tous, et on se revoit au tome 3!